Praise for the novels of Allison Brennan

TELL NO LIES

"Allison Brennan is always good but her latest and most ambitious work ever...is downright spectacular.... A riveting page turner as prescient as it is purposeful."
—*Providence Journal*

"Bestseller Brennan's intriguing sequel to...
The Third to Die....[has] fast-paced action....[and a] well-constructed mystery plot."
—*Publishers Weekly*

"Engaging from the beginning.... Those who enjoy thrillers and detective novels with lots of action will appreciate the multiple possibilities that Brennan presents before sharing who the bad guys really are."
—*Bookreporter*

THE THIRD TO DIE

"A lean thriller starring a strong and damaged protagonist who's as compelling as Lisbeth Salander."
—*Kirkus Reviews*

"Brennan's broadest and most expansive novel yet, as much Catherine Coulter as David Baldacci, with just enough of Thomas Harris thrown in for good measure. A stellar and stunning success."
—*Providence Journal*

"Leave all the lights on...you'll be turning the pages fast as you can. *The Third to Die* is the first in Brennan's amazing new thriller series. Dive in and enjoy this nail-biter."

—Catherine Coulter,
New York Times bestselling author of *Labyrinth*

Also by Allison Brennan

The Third To Die
The Sorority Murder

Look for Allison Brennan's next novel

The Wrong Victim

available soon from MIRA.

ALLISON BRENNAN

TELL NO LIES

mira

ISBN-13: 978-0-7783-1171-3

Tell No Lies

First published in 2021. This edition published in 2022.

Copyright © 2021 by Allison Brennan

For questions and comments about the quality of this book, please contact us
at CustomerService@Harlequin.com.

Mira
22 Adelaide St. West, 41st Floor
Toronto, Ontario M5H 4E3, Canada
www.Harlequin.com

Printed in U.S.A.

This one's for Catherine Coulter.
You've given back so much to fellow authors,
a thank-you doesn't seem sufficient. Your advice,
generosity and time are greatly appreciated by me
and so many other writers. Thank you for being you.

TELL
NO
LIES

PROLOGUE

Two months ago
Tucson, Arizona

Billy Nixon had been waiting his whole life to have sex with Emma Perez. Okay, not *all* his life. Two and a half years. It just felt that way since he'd fallen in love with her the day they met in Micro-economics, on his first day of classes at the University of Arizona. Love at first sight is a cliché, and until that moment in time Billy didn't believe in any of that bullshit. His parents were divorced, his older sister had been in and out of bad relationships since she was fifteen, and his friends slept around as if the apocalypse was upon them.

But in the back of his mind, he remembered the story about how his grandparents met the day before his grandfather shipped off to the Korean War, how they wrote letters every week, and how three years later his grandfather came home and they married. They were married for fifty-six years before his grandfather died; his grandmother died three months later.

That's what Billy wanted. Without having to go to war.

It took Emma two years before the same feeling clicked inside her. They'd been friends. They both dated other people (well, Billy pretended to date because he couldn't in good conscience lead another girl on when he knew that he didn't care about her like he cared about Emma). But it was three months ago, when Emma lost her ride home to Denver for the Christmas holidays and he found her crying in her dorm room, that he said, "I'll drive you there," even though he was a Tucson native and lived with his dad to save money.

From then on, she looked at him differently. Like her eyes had been opened and she saw in him what he saw in her. From that point on, they were inseparable.

The morning after they first made love, Billy knew there was no other girl, no other woman, with whom he wanted to spend the rest of his life. Call him a romantic, but Emma was it. He had started saving money for a ring. They were finishing up their third year of college, so had a year left, but that was okay. He did well in school and had a part-time job. He already had a job lined up for the summer in Phoenix that paid well, and he could live there cheaply with his sister—though the thought of spending two months with his emotional, self-absorbed sibling was a big negative. And the idea of leaving Emma for two months made him miserable. But if he did this, he'd have enough money, not only for a ring, but to get an apartment when they graduated. And—maybe—his job this summer would be a permanent thing when he was done with college next spring, which meant he'd have stability. Something he desperately wanted to provide for Emma.

Emma rolled over in bed and sighed. He loved when his dad was out of town and he had the house to himself, since they had no privacy in Emma's dorm. Billy kissed the top of her head. He thought she was still sleeping, or in that dreamy state right before you wake up. It wasn't even dawn, but how could he go back to sleep with Emma Perez naked in his bed?

"Billy?" she said.

"Hmm?"

"Can I ask you a favor?"

"Anything."

"I need to go to Mount Wrightson today. The Patagonia side of the mountain."

"Okay."

An odd request, but Emma spent a lot of time these days in the Santa Rita Mountains and surrounding areas. She was a business and environmental sciences double major who worked part-time at the Arizona Resources and Environmental Agency—AREA, as they called it—the state environmental protection agency.

"For work, school or fun?" he said.

"Last week my Geology class went out to Mount Wrightson and we hiked partway down the Arizona Trail. I noticed several dead birds off the trail. My professor didn't think it was anything, but it bothered me. So I talked to my boss, Frank, at work, and he said if my professor didn't think it was unusual, then it wasn't. But I couldn't stop thinking about it, so went back a couple days ago on my own. One of the closed trails has been used recently. And I found more dead birds, more than a dozen."

"Which means what?"

"I don't know yet, but birds are especially vulnerable to contaminated water because of their small size and metabolism. Remember when I told you my boss got an anonymous letter two years ago? Signed *A Concerned Citizen* and postmarked from Patagonia? The letter writer claimed that several local people were being made sick and that the water supply was tainted. Frank tested the water supply himself after that, but he didn't find anything abnormal. So he dismissed it. But no one has been able to explain why those people were sick."

"And remember—there was no evidence that anyone *was* sick," Billy said. "The letter was anonymous. It could have just been a disgruntled prankster. Didn't Frank talk to the health center about the complaint? Didn't he investigate the local copper refinery?"

"Yes," she said and sighed in a way that made

him feel like he was missing something. "Maybe two years ago it wasn't real," she said in a way that made Billy think she really didn't believe that. "But now my gut tells me something's going on, and I want to know what."

"You told your boss about the dead birds. You said he was a good guy, right?"

"Yeah, but I think he still thinks I'm a tree hugger."

"You certainly gave that impression when you first started there and questioned their entire record-keeping process and the way Frank had conducted that original investigation."

"I've apologized a hundred times. I realize now how much goes into keeping accurate records, and that AREA uses one of the best systems in the country. I've learned so much from Frank. I really believe I can make a difference now, and be smart about it too. All I want is to give him facts, Billy. And the only way I can do that is if I go back up there."

Billy didn't have the same passion for the environment that Emma had, but he loved her commitment to nature and how she continued to learn and adapt to new and changing technologies and ideas.

"Whatever you want to do, I'm with you," he said. He'd follow her through the Amazon jungle if she asked him to.

"It's going to be a beautiful day," she said, as if he needed encouragement to do anything for her. "I just want to check out the trails near where I found the second flock of birds. We can have a picnic, make a day out of it."

"Good call, bribing me with food."

She smiled. "I can bribe you with something else too." Then she kissed him.

An hour later the sun was up and they stopped for breakfast in the tiny town of Sonoita, southeast of Tucson where Highways 82 and 83 intersected. Emma had been quiet the entire drive, taking notes while analyzing a topo map.

As they ate, Emma showed him the map and her notes. "The dead birds I found last week with the class were Mexican jays. The ones I found after that on my own were trogons. I've been studying both of their migration patterns. The jays have a wider range. The trogons are much more localized. It seems unlikely that they just dropped dead out of the sky for no reason. I'm thinking, logically, they might have been poisoned. I don't see any large body of water near where I found them, but there's a pond here that forms during the rainy season." She pointed.

While Billy couldn't read a topo map to save his life, he trusted her thinking.

"That pond, or this stream—" she pointed again "—are right under one of their migration routes. I've also highlighted some other seasonal streams, here and here."

"That seems like a huge area. North *and* south of Eighty-Two? How can we cover all of that in one day? Where are the roads?"

"We can hike."

He frowned. Hike, sure. But this looked like a three-day deal.

"Emma, maybe you should talk to your boss again, show him the map and tell him what you suspect."

"But I haven't found anything yet—just on the map!"

Tears sprouted to her eyes, and Billy panicked. *Don't cry, don't cry, don't cry.* "Okay, what are we doing, then?"

"If you don't want to help me, Billy, just say so."

"I do, Emma. I just need to know the full plan, and I don't understand your notes. I don't even know where exactly I'm going."

"This is the town of Patagonia, see?" She trailed her finger along one of the paths that went from Patagonia up the mountain. "And this is Mount Wrightson, to the north."

Billy had hiked to the peak of Mount Wrightson once. He wasn't into nature and hiking like Emma, but he liked being outdoors, so he took a conservation class that doubled as a science requirement. His idea of being outdoors was playing baseball or volleyball or riding his bike.

"Okay."

"We need to hike halfway up Wrightson. I found a service road that I think we can use to get most of the way to the trailhead. Okay?"

"If you're sure about this," he said.

She frowned and looked back down at her map. He hated that he'd made her sad.

"I'm sorry," he said. "It's fine."

"You don't want to go."

"I do. I just don't want us to get lost."

She smiled sweetly at him. "Stick with me and you won't."

That was the smile he needed. He took her hand, interlocked their fingers. "I trust you."

"Good." She gave him a quick kiss, and they left the café and got back on the road.

Several hours later, Billy wasn't as accommodating. They'd parked at the end of a dirt road near the trailhead halfway up the southeastern side of the mountain and been hiking through rough terrain ever since. The landscape was dotted with some trees and pines, but not as dense or pretty or green as on the top of the mountain. The land wasn't dry—the wet winter and snow runoff had ensured that—so the area was hard to navigate, and the paths they were on weren't maintained. Billy doubted they were trails at all.

The hiking had been fine up until lunch. At noon, they ate their picnic, which was a nice break, because then they had sex and relaxed in the middle of nature. It wasn't quiet—they heard birds and a light breeze and the rustling of critters. A family of jackrabbits crossed only feet from them as they lay on the blanket Billy had brought. Afterward, Billy suggested they head back to the truck. He was tired, and they had already walked miles, which meant as many miles back to the truck.

But Emma didn't want to leave. He was pretty

sure she didn't know exactly what she was looking for, but that she had this idea that if she walked long and far enough, she'd find evidence to support her theory that something nefarious had been happening out here to kill all those birds.

So Billy kept his mouth shut and followed her.

By four that afternoon, Billy was pretty sure Emma had gotten them lost. They had seemed to zigzag across the southern face of Mount Wrightson. He was tired, and even the birds had gone quiet, as if they were getting ready to settle in and nest for the night, even though sunset was still a few hours away.

He stopped next to a tree that was taller than most and that provided much-needed shade. It was only seventy-six degrees, but the sky was clear and the sun had been beating down on them all afternoon. He was glad he'd thought to bring sunscreen, otherwise they'd both be fried by now.

He dropped the large backpack he'd been carrying that contained their picnic stuff, blanket, water, first aid kit and emergency supplies. He knew enough about the desert not to go hiking without food and water to last at least twenty-four hours. Like if his truck didn't start when they got back, they needed to be okay. So he had extra water—but he didn't tell Emma that. It was for emergencies only.

"We're down to our last water bottles," he said. He'd paced himself so he had two left, whereas Emma had gone through all six of hers.

He handed her one of the two. "Drink."

She sipped, handed it back to him. "Thirty more minutes, honey. See this?" She pointed to the damn map that he wanted to tear into pieces now, except without it he was positive they would be lost here forever. "That's the large seasonal pond I was talking about. It'll dry up before summer, according to the topo charts."

How she could stay so cheerful when he was hot and tired and, frankly, bored, he didn't know.

"How far?"

"Down this path, not more than two hundred yards. Three hundred, maybe."

He looked at her. Implored her to let them start heading back.

"Why don't you stay here and wait," she said.

"You don't mind?"

She smiled, walked over and kissed him. "Promise."

Twenty minutes later she was back where Billy waited. She looked so sad and defeated. "I'm ready to go," she said.

"We'll come back next weekend, okay? We'll bring a tent and food and camp overnight."

She looked surprised at his suggestion, a smile on her face. "You mean that?"

"Absolutely."

She threw her arms around him. "I love you, Billy Nixon."

His heart nearly stopped. "I love you, too," he said and held her. He wanted to freeze this moment, relive it every day of his life.

"We're actually closer to your truck than you

think—we made a circle. First we went north, then west, then south, now we're going east again. When we get back to the main trail at the fork back there, we go left rather than right, and the truck is about half a mile up."

He was impressed; he had underestimated her. Maybe they weren't as lost as he thought; maybe he was the only one with a shitty sense of direction. But that was okay, because Emma loved him, and they were going to be together forever. He knew it in his heart *and* his head, and she'd always be there to navigate.

They drove down the mountain, the road rough at first, then it smoothed out as they got near town. They headed west on 82, deciding to drive the scenic route back to Tucson. Emma marked her map to highlight where they'd already walked, when suddenly she looked up. "Hey, can you get off here?"

"Have to pee again?"

"Ha ha. No. There's several old roads that go south. Sonoita Creek, when it floods, cuts fast-flowing streams into the valley. We had a couple late storms this winter. I just want to check the area quickly—we'll come back next weekend. But if I see anything that tells me the streams were running a few weeks ago, I want to come back here first. Okay? Please?"

Billy was tired, but Emma loved him, so he happily turned off the highway and followed her directions. They drove about a mile along a very rough unpaved road until they reached a narrow path. His truck couldn't go down there—there were small cacti sprouting up all over the place, and the chances of him getting a flat increased exponentially.

Emma got out, and Billy reluctantly followed. She was excited. "See that grove of trees down there?"

He did. It looked more like overgrown brush, but it was greener than anything else around them.

"I'll bet there's still water. This is on the outer circle of where the birds could have flown from. I just want to check."

"The path looks kinda steep and rocky. You sure about this?"

She kissed him. "I'm sure. Stay here, okay? I won't be long."

"Ten minutes."

"Fifteen." She kissed him again, put her backpack on and headed down the path.

He sat in the back of his truck and watched Emma navigate the downward slope. He doubted this "path" had been used anytime in the last few years. From his vantage point, he saw several darker areas, plants dense and green, and suspected that Emma was right—this valley *would* get water after big storms.

Emma was beautiful *and* smart. What wasn't to love?

He watched until she disappeared from view into the brush.

He frowned. He should have gone with her. Was he just sulking because he was tired and hungry?

Predators were out here—coyotes, bobcats, javelinas. Javelinas could be downright mean even if you did nothing to provoke them. Not to mention that these mountains bordered the corridor for trafficking illegal immigrants. Billy had taken a criminal justice class his freshman year and they touched upon that topic. He didn't want to encounter a two-legged predator any more than one on four legs.

What kind of man was he if he couldn't suck it up and help the woman he loved?

So he grabbed his backpack and headed down the path Emma had taken. He was in pretty good shape, but this hike had wasted him. Emma must have been fitter than he was, because she'd barely slowed down all day. After this, they'd go to his place, shower—maybe he could convince Emma to take a shower with him—and then he'd take her out to dinner. After all, they had something to celebrate: the first time they said "*I love you*." They'd go to El Charro, maybe. It was Billy's favorite Mexican food in Tucson, not too expensive, great food. Take an Uber so they could have a couple of drinks.

He wished he were there right now. His stomach growled as he stumbled and then caught himself before he fell on his ass.

He was halfway down the hill when a scream pierced the mountainside. Billy ran the rest of the way down the narrow, rocky trail. "Emma!"

No answer.

He yelled louder for her. "Emma! Emma!"

He slipped when the trail made a sudden drop as it went steeply down to a small pond—the seasonal one that Emma must have been looking for. The beauty of the spot with its trees and boulders all around was striking in the desert, and for a split second he thought it was a mirage. Then all he could think about was that Emma had been bitten by a rattlesnake, or had fallen into the water, or had slipped and broken her leg.

But she didn't respond to his repeated calls.

"Emma!"

He stood on the edge of the pond, frantically searching for her. Looking for wild animals, a bobcat that she may have surprised. A herd of javelinas that might have attacked her. Anything.

Movement to his right startled him, and he turned around quickly.

In the shade, he saw someone. He shouted, wondering if Emma was disorientated or had gone the wrong way. But whatever he thought he saw was now gone.

Then he saw her.

Emma's body was half in, half out of the pond, a good hundred feet beyond him, obscured in part by an outcrop of large rocks on the water's edge. He ran to her and dropped to his knees. His first thought was that she had slipped and hit her head. Some blood glistened on her scalp.

"Emma, where are you hurt? Emma?"

She didn't respond. Then he saw the blood on a hand-sized rock on the edge of the pond. And he felt more blood on the back of her skull.

"No, no, no!"

He saw her chest rise and fall. She was alive,

but unconscious. He pulled out his phone, but there was no signal. He had to get help, but he couldn't leave her here.

Billy picked Emma up and, as quickly as he could, carried her up the steep hillside to his truck.

As he drove back to the main road, he called 911. An ambulance met him in the closest town, Patagonia.

But by then Emma was already dead.

CHAPTER 1

Thursday, May 20
Tucson, Arizona

Matt Costa, head of the FBI's new DC-based mobile response team had been in his old office in Tucson for the last month to investigate two possibly connected cases: the murder of college activist Emma Perez, and possible illegal toxic dumping by a copper refinery plant that was the major employer in the small town of Patagonia.

Matt hadn't expected the cases to be over quickly—he'd told his boss that it would take six to eight weeks—but he thought he'd have more information by now. Truth be told, he was antsy. The more time that passed, the less likely they'd find Emma Perez's killer or evidence of Southwest Copper's duplicity.

If the copper company were guilty.

Christine Jimenez, the supervisory special agent in charge of the Tucson Resident Agency, knocked on his open door. "Marshal Wyatt Coleman just arrived. I have him in the break room getting coffee."

Matt glanced at his watch—11:00 a.m. Wyatt was right on time. "Frank here?"

"Not yet."

At the beginning of the investigation, AREA assistant director Frank Block had been grateful that Matt and his team had taken over the case. But for the past week Frank had grown impatient and adversarial. His attitude irritated Matt because Frank, more than anyone, should understand how difficult it was to build a case against a company for illegal dumping—it didn't happen overnight. They needed evidence, of which they still had very little. Until they found the location of the actual dump site, and a witness or something else concretely tying an alleged offender to the physical evidence, their hands were tied when it came to warrants.

Then there was the murder case.

Matt's cell phone rang with a familiar number. "Chris, can you please tell Wyatt I'll be in as soon as I can? We'll give Frank a few more minutes."

"You know why Frank's upset."

Knowing why Frank was upset didn't mean Matt was going to put up with his open frustration and increasing unreliability. Frank blamed himself for his intern Emma's death, and nothing Matt said could change his mind on the matter. But grief coupled with guilt made for bad decision-making.

He held up his phone. "Mind closing the door while I take this?"

Christine nodded and left while Matt answered his phone. "Costa here," he said.

"It's Joe Molina," the caller replied. Molina was the son of Southwest Copper Refinery's owner. "We need to meet."

"What happened?"

"I can't do this anymore."

Like clockwork. Every week for the last three weeks, since Matt convinced Joe that it was in his best interest to cooperate with the FBI in their undercover investigation of his father's refining plant, Joe had second thoughts.

"Joe—"

"You don't understand. I can barely look my dad in the eye. It's eating me up. Why can't you just arrest David Hargrove and make him talk?"

Hargrove was the assistant manager in charge of waste disposal at Southwest Copper, and the primary suspect in their investigation.

"Where are you right now?" Matt said.

Joe was going to blow this investigation if he kept talking about the case over the phone. Matt had repeatedly told him how to reach out to him, what to say over the phone—and what not to say.

"I'm at my house. I'm going to the plant in a minute, but I could hardly sleep last night. You *know* Hargrove is behind this, right? That's what you said."

Matt forced himself to remain calm. "Joe, I explained to you that we *suspect* David Hargrove is involved, and the information you provided about the company's contracts with A-Line Waste Disposal and Trucking has helped us tremendously. But everything we have can be explained away by human error or mismanagement—to bring this to court I need to find the actual illegal dump site or someone willing to turn state's evidence."

"But Hargrove's involved—you can make him talk!"

"How? Put him in an interrogation room and wait for him to spill his guts?" Matt couldn't bite back his sarcasm. That wasn't like him, especially with a civilian. Especially a civilian who wanted to do the right thing even if it hurt someone he cared about. Joe had made it clear when Matt first approached him that he was helping solely to clear his father's good name. There was no evidence that his father, John Molina, knew about any illegal dumping. But because it was his company that officially contracted with A-Line—the trucking company that handled the disposal of their copper slag—the father could be held liable if his employee was found guilty of illegal doings under the company's name.

Matt continued. "I explained to you early on that if Hargrove gets any hint that we're looking at him for taking kickbacks from A-Line—or worse—he could destroy evidence."

"I think I need to talk to my dad."

"We discussed that option, and you said your father would never work with the FBI again after the fallout from the fumbled AREA investigation two years ago. I concurred. Your father is not under investigation, and the agreement between you and me is that your father will have limited immunity, so if an overzealous prosecutor thinks he *should* have known what was going on, he'll be okay. I'm not interested in going after your family business. I just want to put a stop to the serious environmental damage and loss of wildlife that I suspect your manager David Hargrove may be responsible for."

"I know you're right, Agent Costa. I'm just not cut out for this." His frustration was clear in his tone. First Frank, now Joe.

"You're doing fine," he assured Joe. "If I'm right, and the trucking company A-Line is responsible for illegal dumping, we'll be able to trace the shipment and arrest everyone involved—including David Hargrove. And your father will be cleared."

"I'm heading to the refinery now. We have a staff meeting, and the next slag pickup should be scheduled."

"Call or text me when you get that information, and we'll plan accordingly. This is good news, Joe."

"I hope so."

Matt ended the call. It had taken longer than he thought, but ultimately it was necessary to keep Joe on task.

But Joe wasn't the only person Matt had on the inside.

He grabbed his case folder and walked down the hallway to the main conference room. He was relieved to find everyone was waiting there.

On Matt's recommendation, Christine had replaced him as the SSA when he moved to the DC office five years ago. They'd always worked well together, so there was no jurisdictional pushback when Matt was called in to run these cases as head of the recently formed mobile response team. The team's mission was to step in to help solve cases that local agencies might not have enough investigative resources to manage.

Other than Christine, there were four other people in the room.

Zack Heller, a white-collar-crimes expert, was the newest member of Matt's team. The jury was still out on him: Zack was originally from the New York office and a brilliant accountant, the only one of them who truly understood the financial end of hazardous-waste disposal. He'd previously investigated several cases involving graft and corruption in that industry, so he understood the issues. But his communication style was lacking, and his over-eager personality grated on Matt. At thirty-seven, he was tall and skinny, with a shaggy mop of blond hair. The FBI had personal grooming requirements, but Zack's hair wasn't quite long enough for Matt to compel him to get a haircut.

Ryder Kim was the team analyst and Matt's right hand. He was young—twenty-six. He'd served in the military for three years, then went to college and immediately joined the FBI as an analyst. Matt recruited him straight from the Academy, where Ryder had achieved the highest scores across multiple classes. The kid was a logistics expert and was serving as the liaison between the undercover team Matt had placed in the refinery and the town of Patagonia, and Matt. Ryder was also responsible for research. If Ryder couldn't find something, it couldn't be found.

Patagonia's marshal, Wyatt Coleman, was an all-around good cop, but he wasn't experienced in multijurisdictional investigations. As marshal he worked under the sheriff's department. Few towns had local marshals anymore, but Patagonia was a remnant of the Old West. At first Matt had been hesitant to bring him in, but Chris assured Matt that he could trust Wyatt. Matt knew it was important to have someone on the team who personally knew all the parties involved. Wyatt had even agreed to keep the investigation quiet because one of his own deputies had a brother who worked for Southwest Copper, and Matt wasn't positive that Hargrove was the only individual involved in the alleged dumping scheme. As far as anyone outside of the task force was concerned, Wyatt was helping Matt solely with the Emma Perez murder investigation.

And Frank Block, the assistant director who ran the southern AREA office. Matt had casually known Frank for more than a decade. It wasn't until a week after Emma's death that Frank learned she'd collected and sent several dead birds to Game & Fish under his name without his knowledge. Game & Fish performed a necropsy on the birds and determined they'd died of both lead and arsenic poisoning—byproducts of copper refining and other manufacturing processes. The amounts had been too large to occur naturally. AREA immediately inspected Southwest Copper property but found no on-site violations in their storage of hazardous waste.

Frank didn't look at Matt when he stepped in; the dark circles under his eyes told Matt that he wasn't sleeping well.

"Sorry to keep you," Matt said as he closed the door behind him. "I appreciate you making the drive up here again, Wyatt."

Matt didn't want a formal meeting in Patagonia. It was too small a town, and locals might remember him from his time in the Tucson office. Even though Matt had gone down there a few times as the face of the Emma Perez investigation, it would be better not to draw too much attention to himself—especially since he had two agents working undercover.

Wyatt nodded. "Well, you have better coffee."

Christine said, "One of my old army buddies started a coffee business and gives me a hefty veteran's discount. I wouldn't drink the crap headquarters ships us."

"I only have three full-time deputies," Wyatt said. "Maybe you can get me into that program."

"You're a vet, not a problem."

She made a note on her calendar. One of Christine's strengths was building coalitions.

Matt said, "I know everyone is frustrated by the lack of movement the last couple weeks. Joe Molina just told me that the next scheduled A-Line Waste

Disposal and Trucking shipment will be discussed at today's staff meeting. I'm going to work on getting a warrant to track the truck. In open terrain it would be nearly impossible to follow the truck and avoid being seen, even if we worked a tag team. If I can get a tracker on the truck, then we can discreetly follow."

"How soon?" Wyatt asked.

"Most likely early next week. Zack, you have some new information?"

"I need to go to Vegas," Zack said.

Matt stared at him. This was exactly the kind of communication problem he had with Zack. Without showing his frustration, Matt said, "Why?"

"I need to pull A-Line's financial documents onsite, and they are housed in Las Vegas."

Because Matt rarely worked financial crimes, the reasons eluded him.

Christine said, "Is A-Line based out of Vegas?"

"No, they're out of New Mexico, but I traced ownership to a shell corporation that was established in Las Vegas. And that shell corp is under a second shell corp."

Matt waited for more, but Zack was silent.

"Are you talking about the Commercial Recordings Division?" Chris asked.

"Yes. And the recorder's office. They're housed in the same building but are two different entities."

"They can't fax the documents?" Matt asked.

"They did. That's how I know that the first shell corp is under another. But the name on file is the same, and I think that name is bogus. I mean, not bogus—the person is real—but he's a lawyer, a front maybe. Lawyers won't give us shit over the phone, and maybe not at all—"

"Stop," Matt said. "So you are saying that A-Line is itself an illegal corporation?"

White collar was not Matt's strength, which is why Tony Greer, his boss in DC and creator of the mobile response team, wanted to add a financial expert.

"Shell corporations are not in and of themselves illegal," Zack said. "There are a lot of legitimate reasons why a business may want to protect itself, or might want to use one name for one region and another name in another region, for marketing purposes. Plus—"

"I don't need a business course," Matt said. "Bottom line."

"I want to pull the records of companies that have similar attributes as A-Line."

Christine asked, "You mean other waste disposal companies or trucking companies?"

"No, not specifically. I'm looking for shell corporations with the same law firm or lawyer, or corporations with the same principal shareholders or the same filing address. I can do some searches online, but they are not always complete and you can't search by address. The recorder is not going to want to indulge me and pull a hundred files when only three or four might meet my specs."

"Purpose?" Matt asked.

"Information. Who's who. Who knows who. See where it leads me. Every name I've gotten off the paperwork is a dead end. But they all lead some-where. They *have* to. There is a beginning, and I can find it—"

"If you're on-site."

"One day, maybe two. Once I get all the busi-nesses that are attached to the lawyer on record, I can look for something to pull him in on. If we can get him on another charge, we might be able to parlay that into more information on A-Line."

Now Matt understood Zack's thinking. Cut a deal with a low-level middleman to get the big fish. White collar did that far more often than violent crimes, but it was a tactic Matt was familiar with.

"It's an hour flight," Zack said. "If I leave soon, I'll have all day tomorrow. I can even start this af-ternoon."

Matt considered Zack's request. Zack was right—more information might be gleaned if he had access to the physical documents.

"Go. Set it up. Check in with me regularly, with every relevant piece of information you find. It may or may not be important, but I need to know."

"Of course."

"The faster you get there, the faster you get back."

"Now?"

"Do you have anything else to share?"

He shook his head, then gathered his files and practically ran out.

While Zack was obviously smart—with an ad-vanced degree in accounting plus ten years of ex-perience in the FBI—Matt wasn't convinced if he fit on his team. This would be a good opportunity for Zack to prove himself.

"Ryder?" Matt prompted.

"Michael's workplace report has nothing of significance. He's made inroads in befriending several staff and employees, including David Hargrove."

Michael Harris had been working undercover at Southwest Copper for the last three weeks.

Ryder continued. "He's seen nothing unusual or relevant firsthand. But he senses there may be something off between Hargrove and Barry Nelson, the general manager."

"Isn't Nelson John Molina's brother-in-law?" Matt said.

"Yes. Could be nothing, but Michael is watching closely. Since he lives in the garage apartment on Nelson's property, he's become friendly with both Barry and his wife."

"Maybe Nelson also suspects something between Hargrove and A-Line?"

"Michael didn't say."

"Tell him he needs to consider that Barry or John Molina might have their own suspicions about Hargrove. If that's the case, we may rethink approaching them with our investigation. Joe Molina hasn't reported that anyone is suspicious of Hargrove." Matt turned to Wyatt. "Thoughts?"

"Joe is a computer guy," Wyatt said. "He might not be in the loop."

"It's a family business."

"Remember, he wasn't involved on-site until last year when his mom, Clare, came down with cancer. He quit his job and moved down from Phoenix and took over for his dad so John could take care of Clare's needs. Barry is mostly running things until John comes back full time. Joe's book smart—that's the way the long-timers think of him. They like him because he's John's son, but he's not really one of them."

"I don't understand what you're trying to say," Matt said.

"Joe is the figurehead because it's his father's company, but Barry has been running the day-to-day for the past year. John's involvement is starting to increase again, now that Clare is done with chemotherapy." Wyatt paused. "Is this important?"

"Yes," Matt said. "At least to understand the power hierarchy and management structure."

"Joe brought the company into the twenty-first century technology-wise this year, but he doesn't do anything on the refinery floor or with the equipment. He's all about computers and technology. He doesn't get his hands dirty, so to speak."

That made a lot of sense from what Matt knew of Joe Molina and his background in computer engineering.

"Anything else on your end, Wyatt?"

"The upcoming annual Memorial Weekend Patagonia Art Festival is going to keep us busy. The town's population will triple those few days. We only have three deputies, plus me, but our sheriff is loaning us several more to help with traffic and trouble, plus the state troopers will be keeping a close eye on the roads outside of town."

"Do you usually get trouble at an art festival?"

"When you have that number of people in town for anything, things happen. Mostly minor stuff, a lot of DUIs, an occasional fight or vandalism. But this festival funds the town for half the year, so it's imperative things run smoothly."

"Got it," Matt said.

"You should know, too, Matt, that Billy Nixon has been around."

That was not what Matt wanted to hear. "What is he doing?"

"One of my deputies saw him turn off the highway toward the trailhead that leads to where his girlfriend was killed. He's still probably looking for clues, working through his grief."

"As long as he stays away from Southwest Copper. I don't want him asking questions that might make Hargrove or anyone else suspicious."

Matt considered that Emma's murder may or may not be related to illegal dumping. But his gut told him that a random murder in the middle of nowhere was unlikely. The most likely scenario was that someone had tracked Emma and Billy and, when she was alone, snuck up behind her and hit her over the head with a rock. Perhaps the killer intended to push her into the pond where she would drown, making it seem like an accident. But when Billy came running, the killer took off.

But why?

Matt had reached out to both Emma's parents and Billy last month and informed them that the FBI was taking Emma's death seriously, but that he couldn't share anything more than that. Her parents were grateful, and Matt made a point to give them a status report each week, even though he had nothing new to share. At the time, Billy also seemed to understand. Had something changed?

"I'm going to talk to Billy," Matt said.

"I can talk to him," Frank said.

"If I can't get through to him, maybe," Matt said. He wasn't certain Frank wouldn't share too much with Billy about their investigation. He couldn't risk the case and his people in Patagonia because of Billy's grief and Frank's guilt.

Frank said, "I'm taking some time off. So I can talk to him today."

Matt eyed him suspiciously. "Where are you going?"

"Camping," he said. "I need to clear my head. But I can check on Billy before I head out. He'll listen to me, Matt."

Matt weighed the pros and cons, and relented—but he didn't feel good about it. "Make it clear to him—without giving away any details about our investigation—that we haven't forgotten Emma and we are on top of things."

"Are we?" Frank asked bluntly.

"Do you have something to say?"

Frank just shrugged.

After the surprise inspection of Southwest Copper two months ago, Game & Fish and AREA had inspected known waterways and found no sign of contamination. Groundwater had been tested—nothing. There was only so much they could do with the limited information they had, and Frank knew it.

Matt said, "If A-Line Trucking is illegally dumping toxic slag, we'll know next week. If Hargrove is behind it, we'll know that too. I have a good team here, but some cases take longer to develop than others, and we don't want anyone walking away who should be prosecuted—or likewise, anyone blamed who is innocent."

Frank bristled, and Matt realized he overstepped.

Two years ago, an erroneous AREA investigation into Southwest Copper had yielded no violations and created a schism between AREA and the local Patagonia community. Initially, Frank and his team believed that Southwest Copper had improperly dug a well that contaminated the water supply, forcing them to recertify the well and costing the company money. They later learned that a faulty pump in town had led to the rash of illnesses among some of the townsfolk. But the "rush to judgment" by AREA against Southwest Copper had created untold problems, adversely affecting this current, more serious investigation.

AREA's past investigation meant Matt had to be doubly cautious in how they handled these new suspicions. Law enforcement agencies—sometimes justified, sometimes not—were being held to much higher standards now.

He extended an olive branch to Frank because he needed his help—Frank had the technical expertise and knowledge, plus access to specialized testing. The last thing Matt wanted was to bring into this investigation yet another agency. "I need to be able to reach you, Frank, even while you're gone. If we find the dump site, you should be there to lead the environmental investigation."

"I'll check my messages at least twice a day, since cell reception can be spotty."

"Where are you going?"

"Haven't decided yet. Somewhere in the Santa Ritas."

He didn't look Matt in the eye, which told Matt that Frank knew exactly where he planned to go and didn't want to share the information.

He turned back to Ryder. "Michael. Is his cover still solid?"

They used Michael Harris's real identity as a veteran navy SEAL when he was applying to work at Southwest but scrubbed his FBI credentials and created an assault charge that landed him in prison for a year. They knew John Molina made it a habit of hiring veterans, and he preferred veterans who were having a rough go of it.

Ryder nodded. "He's adapted well and doesn't believe anyone is suspicious."

"Good." Matt also wanted to ask about Kara, because her reports were almost nonexistent, but that would have to wait until he and Ryder were alone. Kara Quinn was an LAPD detective on loan to the mobile response team. Matt hadn't told Frank or Wyatt yet about Kara's undercover role as a local bartender. She was there to watch Michael's back, pick up on town gossip and befriend Joe Molina to verify his trustworthiness; apparently, that had been going well.

"Christine, do you have anything to add?" Matt said, ready to wrap things up.

"My office finished the background checks on the Southwest staff, and there are two people we're going to take a closer look at. Nothing that ties them with A-Line, but there's some suspicious behavior in their pasts."

"Send me their names, I'll make sure Michael is aware."

Christine made a note and continued. "Then there's Tanya Hargrove, David's wife." She slid a file over to Matt. "We don't have a warrant to obtain full financial records, but we have her credit reports. Tanya owns a small antiques business. Zack didn't report on this before he left, but he and my analyst think that if there's something wonky going on with the Hargroves, the wife's business might be part of it."

"This seems outside our investigative scope," Matt said.

"Maybe," Christine conceded, "but there were a couple of red flags. Small flags, but worth looking into. For example, Tanya's company credit is out-sized compared to similar businesses, yet it's paid off regularly. She employs one employee, part-time. Hours are spotty."

Matt knew what Christine was suggesting. Possible money laundering. "So if her husband, David, is getting kickbacks from A-Line, Tanya might be running that money through her business."

"Bingo. It might be difficult to prove, but you should keep it in mind," Christine said.

"Is your analyst still looking into it?"

"Time permitting, yes. If anything else comes up, I'll let you know."

They wrapped up a couple minor questions that arose, then Matt said he was done.

Frank left immediately, with a quick good-bye.

Christine turned to Wyatt and asked, "Lunch? Costa isn't big on taking an hour, but I think I can convince him." She grinned over at Matt. He didn't have time for socializing, but he probably owed both Christine and Wyatt a lunch.

"Thanks, but I have plans with my girlfriend," Wyatt said. "Between her schedule and mine, we rarely get to see each other these days, so we both made sure we had lunch free today."

"Tell Lauren I said hi," Christine said. She was grinning at Matt. Then it dawned on him.

Wyatt left, and he said to Christine, "Lauren Valera?"

"Sheriff Valera now, and yes."

"You knew he was dating my ex-girlfriend?"

"Everyone knows. Except, apparently, you. Problem?"

"No."

He and Lauren Valera hadn't parted on the best of terms, but when he heard she'd been elected sheriff three years ago, he'd sent her flowers. Nothing romantic, just a spring bouquet. Since Tucson was in a different county from Patagonia, Matt hadn't felt any need to reach out and discuss the case with her once he arrived in town. But had he known that one of the principal members of his investigation was dating her, he might have done so.

"So no lunch?" Christine said.

"I'll owe you when this is all over, but for now let's order in. My treat, you order. I need to call Tony and get started on the warrant for tracking A-Line's truck."

CHAPTER 2

Thursday afternoon
Tucson, Arizona

Matt often got lost in work, and today was no exception. He ate lunch at his desk while working through logistical details with Ryder. Ryder wasn't undercover per se, but he had rented a small apartment for the month in downtown Patagonia where he could be a resource for both Michael and Kara, plus keep an eye on the general situation. If anyone asked, he was a graduate student working on his thesis.

Matt himself wanted to be closer to the epicenter of this investigation, so he was working out a plan with Ryder to go down to Patagonia and stay there once he had the timeline for A-Line picking up the next slag shipment. He hadn't heard from Joe Molina yet with the details from today's meeting, but he wasn't overly worried. He didn't expect him to reach out until later this evening.

Once they worked out the logistics of where best for Matt to stay in Patagonia, he asked Ryder, "Any other problems?"

"No, sir."

"I've noticed Kara's reports have been...vague."

"She's sending them in regularly."

Kara had been instrumental in establishing the protocols for this undercover investigation. Her knowledge in these matters was extensive. But from the beginning, they'd disagreed about how detailed her reports should be. She claimed she would check in regularly for safety reasons, but no information would mean there was no information.

I'm not doing bullshit paperwork.

He'd put his foot down, though he compromised on formalities. She'd written her report every day, dropping it off each morning at the diner where Ryder sat with his laptop computer. But each report was getting shorter and shorter.

"What does she mean here?" Matt pointed to one of three short sentences.

Sub hooked.

Ryder cleared his throat. "Joe Molina. He's been spending a lot of time at the bar talking to her."

"Keep an eye on her."

"Sir?"

"Just check in periodically, make sure she's covered."

Ryder didn't say anything.

"What?" Matt snapped.

"I don't fit in at the Wrangler."

"Has anyone given you undue attention?"

"No. I go to the coffeehouse every morning as we planned and work on my laptop for a couple of hours. Michael comes between six and seven, checks in. Kara comes between seven and nine. Everything comes through secure text or email, encrypted, and I send to you."

"No one has questioned you? What you're doing?"

"The owner of the coffeehouse has chatted with me a few times. She looked at my University of Arizona shirt and assumed I was a student, and asked me how classes were going. I said I was working on my master's thesis and, at Kara's suggestion, made it a topic that was complex but I knew something about, so I chose physics."

"And you can't just go to the bar for a drink?"

"I don't drink, sir."

Matt felt like no one was watching Kara's back. "Still, check in with her, over and above her morning reports. Make sure she's covered, not having problems at the bar."

"She's not going to like it," Ryder said.

"I don't care what she likes. She is part of my team. I'm responsible for her and her safety."

Ryder said he would check in with Kara at the bar, and that made Matt feel marginally better. When he left, Matt put in a call to Tony Greer in DC, and sat on hold.

Matt asking Ryder to keep tabs on Kara was in

no way a reflection on Matt's confidence in her abilities. She was a good cop with sharp instincts. But they'd only worked on one case together and she hadn't been officially a part of his team. Now that he was her supervisor, he had to cover her at all times.

And now that he was her supervisor, it was going to make the fact that they'd had a relationship—however brief—far more complicated. Especially since he was still attracted to her.

Very attracted to her.

"Matt? Sorry to keep you waiting."

"I'm just doing paperwork. Any word on the warrant?"

"I'm optimistic we'll have it by tomorrow, Monday at the latest. There's precedent, plus we have solid circumstantial evidence from the Game & Fish report."

"Great news," Matt said. "I should know by tonight the exact time the A-Line Truck will be at Southwest Copper."

"Did I see an expense come in for a flight to Las Vegas?"

"Yes, Zack is on his way." Matt filled Tony in on what Zack was looking for. "If he finds something, we'll need financial warrants into those banking records."

"I'll give the AUSA a heads-up. Good work. Maybe this will be wrapped up faster than you thought."

"The waste disposal is only half the case," Matt reminded Tony. "Without physical evidence tying the illegal dumping to the murder, it's going to be next to impossible to prove that they're connected—*if* they're connected."

"One step at a time. If we nail Hargrove or anyone else at Southwest Copper on illegal dumping, I can get almost any warrant you want—and I'll make sure that evidence related to the murder investigation is a priority. I have to go to a meeting, but good work."

Matt wasn't as confident as Tony at this point, but at least they were making progress—slow progress, but still moving forward.

As soon as Matt ended the call, his cell rang. It was Jim Esteban, their forensics expert. He'd been on-site in Tucson for the first two weeks of Matt's investigation—he reviewed all the findings from Emma Perez's death and analyzed the crime scene with an advanced computer model that helped Matt visualize what happened to her. There was no doubt in Jim's mind that someone had intentionally killed her. Though the initial coroner's report listed *undetermined pending investigation* instead of *homicide*, Jim recommended they revise the report to list *probable homicide*. She'd been hit *twice* by the rock, with the force of a baseball bat. There was evidence that she'd been dragged partway to the pond, but that the killer had been scared off.

Jim helped Matt come up with his working theory that the murderer had premeditatedly killed Emma with the intention of making it look like an accident, which is why he ran when Billy approached.

The big question was why? What threat did she pose? Did the killer somehow know that Emma was looking into the dead birds? If so, why would he care?

Billy told him Emma hadn't talked to anyone besides him about her recent suspicions after Frank had agreed with her professor that three dead birds in the area she found them wasn't cause for alarm. Emma had used Frank's name when sending the carcasses to Game & Fish to be discreet, so no one at AREA or Game & Fish knew that she was investigating on her own. The FBI had already run a full background on her professor who'd taken her and her class up Mount Wrightson and nothing suggested he or the class were involved in any way.

Matt and Jim had discussed early on that Emma may have been doing additional research on her own, and may have talked to someone before she went searching for the contaminated water with Billy. But they'd found no evidence to that effect. Her map and notes were written in a shorthand that Frank could only partly decipher, so all they knew was where she had looked and intended to look for contaminated standing water. And while Jim's theory still remained the most likely scenario, Matt couldn't discount that there was another reason she was killed.

Jim said, "I'm done for today. I just wanted to call and check in, see if you needed me for anything."

"Appreciate it," Matt said. "I don't have anything." He gave Jim a brief summary of where they were now. When he was done he asked, "When's your trial over?"

Jim had been the director of the crime lab in Dallas before he joined the FBI's mobile response team and deferred his retirement. He was in his fifties and had been a pioneer in the early days of forensic investigation. He was currently in Dallas testifying on a major case that was one of the last he'd been involved with there.

"I'm hoping tomorrow is the last day for testimony, but I'm not holding my breath. I'm thinking Tuesday for closing statements. I can be back as soon as it goes to the jury."

"I'll let you know, but there's not much you can do here. If that changes, you'll be the first to know."

"I want to be there," Jim said. "There's more I can do—I reviewed the necropsy report from Game & Fish and talked to their lead investigator. They have some new theories on water locations based on storm patterns during the months prior to when Emma found the birds, though I need more time and resources."

"Whatever you can do from Dallas, that's great, but I know this trial is important and that's your first priority."

Matt's phone beeped. He had another call, so he said goodbye to Jim, then answered.

"Costa."

"It's Joe Molina."

His voice was quiet. "You okay?"

"Monday afternoon. That's when the truck is coming."

"What's wrong?"

"Nothing. I have to go."

He ended the call before Matt could ask him any more questions, but at least he had a date. He sent the information to Tony in DC, then, even though it was after six, he went back to work.

He felt like he was missing something important, but he feared they just didn't have enough information to move forward.

It took Frank Block most of the afternoon to track Billy down; the kid finally agreed to meet him at a local college bar. It was late, and Frank wanted to leave at dawn, but he needed to make sure Billy was okay.

"I heard you were in Patagonia this week."

"So?"

"The FBI is investigating Emma's murder now. You need to let them do their job."

Billy just stared at him. The waitress brought over two pints of beer. Frank didn't touch his.

"It's been *two months* since she was killed," Billy said. "Two months is a lifetime in a murder investigation and they still haven't found anything!"

"I know the FBI agent in charge, and he's doing everything he can. More than I can tell you."

"That sounds like a crock of shit, an excuse."

"It's not. They have a lead but it's a delicate situation, and if you start asking questions, their suspect might get suspicious."

Billy's eyes widened. "They have a suspect?"

"I shouldn't have said it that way."

"Either they do or they don't."

"Emma got into something way over her head. I don't think she realized…well, let me just say that the FBI has multiple people covering all angles. Agent Costa needs you to lay low. Please. I know you loved Emma—let them find out who killed her. They will."

Billy drank his beer, looked at Frank. "I miss her."

"I miss her too. I'm following up on a separate lead. I don't know if it'll help, but it's all I can do."

Billy's eyes brightened. "Can I help?"

"No, son."

"Dammit! Why not? I *need* to do *something*!"

"Finals—"

"Are over! I'm done, okay? I can't just sit here and wait for the fucking FBI to figure it out. I need to *do* something! I'm going crazy sitting around just waiting for everyone else."

"You have to sit tight, Billy. Give it another week, okay? We'll know more by then."

"It's been two months. Now I have to wait another week…for *maybe* answers. It's bullshit, and you know it. No one cares."

"I care."

"Really? If you cared, you would have listened to her!"

That hurt, because there was truth in Billy's accusation. Frank had dismissed Emma because she came to him all the time, thinking she uncovered a major environmental disaster. Her theories never panned out. Her heart was in the right place, but she didn't have the experience to know what was serious and what wasn't.

"I did," he said. "I listened. But she didn't tell me what she was up to—"

"Because you never listened to her before. She made one mistake two years ago and paid for it ever since."

Frank couldn't explain that Emma's mistake had caused a lot of problems and expense and nearly got her thrown out of the internship program. He couldn't tell Billy that he'd covered for her, because that was something only he and Emma knew about. No one knew that it was Emma's report that led to the original AREA investigation of Southwest Copper. She had been right about the contamination...but wrong about the source, and it cost Frank dearly—professionally and personally.

But her error was likely the reason she hadn't confided in him more than she had about the dead birds. If she'd only told him her plans!

"You need to back off, or Agent Costa will be talking to you and he doesn't know you like I do, okay? Please, Billy, listen to me."

"Just...go. I'm not going to do anything stupid, okay? I just went down there because I wanted to... I don't know, see if I missed something. If everyone missed something. Not a day goes by that I don't think about Emma. That I don't miss her so much it hurts. I wanted to spend the rest of my life with her. Now...fuck, I don't know what I want to do anymore."

Frank reached out to touch his hand, but Billy

pulled it away, grabbed his beer and went to sit at the bar.

There wasn't anything else Frank could say. He put ten dollars on the table and left, without touching his own beer.

Frank had to leave the investigation to Matt... Frank had no idea how to find a murderer. But he did know how to protect the environment, and he wouldn't let his and Emma's mistake two years ago stop him from doing that now.

CHAPTER 3

Thursday night
Fifteen miles north of Arizona-Mexican border

Bianca did exactly what her brother said, but that didn't stop her heart from racing.

It didn't help that it was the middle of the night and she was scared of the dark. Bad things happened in the dark.

In the dark, her papa was taken from their farm and never came back.

In the dark, her mama cried herself to sleep every night.

And in the dark, bad men came and burned down their little house for reasons that Bianca didn't know or understand.

Her mama told her that her older sister, Juanita, had disobeyed and so they were all punished. Bianca hadn't seen Juanita in over a year. Mama cried, and Bianca thought her sister was dead, like their papa. But she didn't ask because she didn't want her mama to cry anymore.

Mama told her that if the men came for Bianca, she must obey or they would all die.

But they won't take you, my baby, her mother had told her, her hand caressing the gnarled scar that covered the left side of Bianca's face, left over from the fire that had destroyed their home. *God protects us in mysterious ways.*

Bianca promised to obey, though she didn't know what her mother meant. Was it okay that she was ugly because it was God's plan?

But Mama said they were going to America, that they would be free from the bad men who killed Papa and Juanita. Mama had given all her money to a nice man who promised to take them across the border. It was dangerous, but they would be safe as soon as they got across. Mama would have a job and Bianca and her brother, Angel, would go to school.

Bianca allowed herself to dream that this might be true, even though Angel told her it was a lie. Angel was smart; still, Bianca wanted to believe they would be safe and happy. That dream didn't last. They walked for miles and miles and days and days. They started as a small group, but it got bigger and bigger and people were not nice. Angel protected her and Mama. He made sure they had food and water.

But then Mama made the nice man angry, and he was no longer a nice man. He hit Mama and took her away. Then he came back and said she had given Angel and Bianca to him to bring to America. He showed them their birth certificates as proof. But he wouldn't give the documents to them; he told them that if they obeyed, he would give them their papers before they reached America.

And for many months, they did obey. Angel did bad things so they had enough food and water. Bianca didn't know what was happening, but she obeyed because she didn't want Angel to be hurt.

Now they were finally in America and Bianca thought that they would have a home. The not nice man said a long time ago that there would be a house for them and they could do work to pay off their transportation from Mexico. Angel was only thirteen, but he was big and strong; he could do anything. Bianca was almost ten. She could cook and clean, maybe even go to school. She could already read better than Angel because her papa had told her reading was important. He used to be an important man with a job in Oaxaca, not far from their small village. She even knew some English because her papa knew how to speak English.

But instead they were living in a bunker underground, and more people were being crammed into their dark space, boys and girls older than Bianca. Some were hurt. One boy had a broken arm… Bianca squeezed her eyes shut. She didn't want to remember what happened to that boy with the broken arm and sad eyes.

That's when Angel came up with the plan. He said trust no one but him. Do not trust the police, do not trust the bad men, do not trust anyone in the bunker, even if they were crying. And tonight, she had put all her trust and faith and prayers into her big brother.

Angel had never let her down.

She waited until she heard the whistle. Then she crawled *very slowly* across the dirty floor. Angel had warned her not to wake anyone up. Not the bad men and not her friends.

No one is your friend.

She knew that to be true. A while ago one of the girls planned to escape and another girl told on her.

Bianca never saw that girl again.

Bianca didn't want to leave everybody behind. But she didn't want to never be seen again.

She knew what that meant. That would mean that she was dead.

Instead she crawled slowly. She heard the steady breathing of sleep. She heard the snore of the bad man. She was very, very quiet.

Angel said bring nothing. She pushed her tiny stuffed bunny down the front of her pants. Her papa had given her the bunny years ago. It was dirty and stinky, but Bianca would never, ever let it go.

She crawled up the ramp to the opening. The ramp was made from metal and packed dirt. There were rocks that cut into her hands and knees. She bit her cheek so she wouldn't cry. They'd been here for more than a week. Before here, they were in a similar bunker somewhere else. A day's walk, maybe.

They were allowed to go outside only at night to pee, but someone always watched them. She hadn't seen Angel in three days, and she thought that he had been taken elsewhere. Or worse.

That he had been killed, like the boy with the sad eyes.

But then she heard the whistle and knew that her brother had come back for her. She should never have doubted him.

Bianca knew she had to be very, very quiet. The men that had brought them here slept outside, under the stars. They often drank alcohol late into the night, and sometimes they didn't sleep deeply.

No moon tonight. She saw stars everywhere; they were in the middle of the desert. How would they get away from here without a truck or food or water? But she did what Angel had commanded her to do.

When you hear my whistle, leave quietly. Do not wake anyone up. We cannot trust anyone. Turn right. Keep walking and don't stop, no matter what you see or hear. I will catch up to you.

What if you don't? What if they stop you?

Just keep walking, Bianca. Do not stop.

She turned right. She saw no one, but it was very hard to see because it was so dark.

But there were stars, so many! Papa said that the stars were God's glitter to make the dark not as scary. And the fear…it was better to be free and scared than trapped and scared.

So she walked. Behind her she thought she heard something, but she kept walking.

What if there were wild animals?

Suddenly, Bianca tripped over something big and solid. She landed with a thud on the hard ground. She tried to stand up and felt something wet. She jumped away, fell again, got back up.

Someone grabbed her from behind and held their hand across her mouth tightly. She tried to scream, failed and bit the hand.

"Bianca!"

Angel. She relaxed, and he let go. She turned and hugged him so tightly.

"What happened?"

"Quiet. We have to get away from here."

She turned to look at what she had tripped over. It was dark, but her eyes were used to it because of living underground for so long.

It was a man.

He wasn't moving.

"Angel, did you…?" She couldn't ask. She knew he had.

"Now, Bianca. Hurry. They'll be coming for us."

She took her brother's hand and they ran.

CHAPTER 4

Early Friday afternoon
Santa Rita Mountains north of Patagonia,
Arizona

Frank Block knew that it would take hours for his drone to survey the mountain range near where Emma Perez was killed back in March, so he found a place to park, then hiked to a ridge that would give him the best range to fly his drone. He would stay here the rest of the day, eat and sleep, then first thing in the morning head to the next position on the grid he'd marked on his map.

Frank liked Matt Costa, but the FBI agent didn't prioritize protecting the environment like Frank did.

Matt was good at his job. There was no doubt in

Frank's mind that Matt would do everything in his power to investigate whether someone at Southwest Copper Refinery was responsible for the illegal dumping of toxic slag, and he would do everything in his power to find out who killed Emma Perez. But he and his team had already been here a month and they were no closer to an arrest on either of those things.

Time was ticking. Frank's team had already inspected every known creek and river near where Emma had found the birds, and they'd all come up clean. But birds were migratory, and they had to expand the search. If they did that, it could alert the criminals and then they might never catch them. Matt wanted them to stand down temporarily because it could jeopardize the bigger investigation, but he didn't have the authority to order him to do that.

The problem, as always, was resources. They had only so many people and so much time, and after the known waterways tested negative, the case was de facto closed. But Frank couldn't accept that. Birds were the most at risk of poisoning from a contaminated lake or river because they were small, but over time other wildlife—and humans—could be affected. There were over forty threatened or endangered species in the state, and Frank was responsible for helping protect them.

He was doing this on his own personal time, even though he was using AREA's equipment. He would find answers. He'd written up a plan even before he talked to Matt yesterday, but now he put it in motion. He would scour every square foot of the potential contamination zone with his drone, starting where Emma died and going out in a mathematical radius based on the migration routes. If there was anything to be found, he'd find it. And find out how Emma got caught up in it.

Had Emma died because of her investigation, or had she simply been in the wrong place at the wrong time? It didn't make sense to him, and Frank had said as much to Matt. Matt didn't have a response, but he'd seen far more violence and death than Frank ever had. Maybe senseless crimes *were* commonplace to the seasoned federal agent. They would never be to Frank.

Based on what Frank could decipher from Emma's notes, her theory had been good, but roughly executed. She'd forgot to factor in standing water that was virtually inaccessible on foot. The drone would find those areas and then Frank could make a plan to access them.

He set up his tent, secured his food, then climbed up to the top of a boulder overlooking the site where Emma had been attacked. He didn't doubt Billy's belief that he'd seen someone move among the trees. The police at first considered Billy a suspect, or that Emma had fallen and he felt guilty and lied about seeing another person. But there was the bloody rock. And Billy didn't budge from his story. Plus the initial investigation found some evidence of another person in the woods. Unfortunately, the tracks were minimal and led nowhere. When the FBI came in and had an expert review the crime scene and autopsy results, they concluded that she was murdered; it was no accident.

But they still had no solid leads. Frank was as frustrated as Billy, even though he knew more than he'd told the kid.

There was no love lost between Frank and John Molina after Frank had accused him of cutting corners when drilling a new well two years ago. Frank had been wrong, he'd apologized, but Molina hadn't forgiven him.

Frank didn't want to believe that Molina could be party not only to illegal dumping but to murder. Maybe someone else in the company was looking to cut corners. It wouldn't be the first time. But he also had to consider that the birds died of something else—other mines in the area, outside businesses that might bring their waste into the desert thinking no harm was done in dumping it, not understanding that the ecosystem was delicate even here in the vast southwest.

He knew how far some mining companies would go to protect their profits or save their business during uncertain economic times, and how unscrupulous some could be when money was to be had. His job was a balancing act—to protect the environment and at the same time protect the local economy and jobs. It was important that he get it right.

Frank had worked for AREA for twenty-three years. He loved his job, but more, he loved the land. He'd been raised in Colorado—one of the reasons he had liked having Emma Perez as an intern was because they talked about all their favorite places to camp and hike. He had come here for an entry-level opening right after he graduated from college and got married. He'd raised his daughter here, who was finishing her sophomore year at Baylor University. She loved camping and hiking like he did, but she was an athlete first and foremost and had been accepted with a partial scholarship to the Baylor soccer team.

That was another reason he had taken Emma under his wing—she reminded him of his own daughter, whom he missed. He was divorced, his wife had moved back to Colorado but she agreed to let their daughter finish high school in Tucson. Maybe that's why they'd grown so close.

He set up the drone to give him a visual on his laptop. He would record only if he saw something suspicious, because recording would drain the battery faster. He'd recharge the drone overnight, then hike back to his truck and drive to the next location, where he'd set up camp for the day.

As he programmed the drone and made sure it was functional, he thought about how he was feeling a little lonely. Maybe he *was* a little obsessive about Emma's death. He missed his daughter, and though he didn't miss his wife, he missed the companionship, the friendship. Someone to talk to and eat with and hike with. So he became fixated on Emma's death, determined to provide evidence to support the report she drafted under his name for Game & Fish before she came out here that fateful day.

His guilt ate at him. He'd dismissed her when

she found the three dead birds with her professor. Had he been *too* dismissive? If she had just come to him with the additional information she learned—before she started inspecting water sources—he would have listened and initiated a formal investigation into the contamination. Billy said she was "obsessed" with the dead birds, but hadn't shared much about her research and findings.

She wanted more proof, something tangible. She wanted evidence.

So Frank had to look, to know for certain. And while it was painstaking work, he knew exactly what he was doing. They'd already covered the known waterways. Now Frank was working on Emma's theory—seasonal streams or new ponds that formed after the winter storms.

Frank wanted to go through the proper channels, but Matt Costa was right—they had no proof of illegal dumping so far, so Matt wanted an undercover investigation to protect the integrity of the case and everyone involved—AREA, employees of Southwest Copper and the people of Patagonia proper.

We have to do this the right way, or no way at all.

There were many competing interests—the economy versus public health, the environment versus the economy, the innocent versus the guilty. Frank would be devastated if they accused John Molina and Southwest Copper again if they were, in fact, innocent. It could cost Molina his business. The false accusation two years ago nearly did.

Frank sat on the rock and got the hang of the

drone. He'd used it before in the field, but never on an extensive search like this. Once he adjusted for wind and light, he was able to maneuver the device effectively, looking at his computer to see what the drone camera saw. It had rained early this morning, a hard, pounding storm that came in and out in two hours. That might help him find any new streams. Temporary water flows that could very well run over the slag and create a shallow, toxic pond.

He felt almost giddy, like he was twelve again and flying a kite with his dad.

Frank made sure he kept a detailed log of every place he searched and everything he saw, whether relevant to his investigation or not. If he found anything illegal or suspicious, he wanted his case to stand up in court.

But that was really the job of the attorney general, not him. His job would be to clean up any contamination.

Frank slowly relaxed. He could barely hear the drone anymore, but to see what it saw and he marveled at the technology. He leaned back and watched and hoped he could find the source of the contamination.

For the wildlife, for himself, but mostly for Emma.

CHAPTER 5

Friday evening
Patagonia, Arizona

Kara Quinn should have been a bartender instead of a cop.

Two weeks into this undercover gig and she felt as if she'd been here for a year. Everyone knew her name, and she knew all the regulars. She liked most of them. Blue-collar workers, all with a story to tell. They loved her because she was a new face—and, she admitted, because she was a young, cute blonde with attitude. Based on her early recon, that was the persona she determined would work best in this tiny middle-of-nowhere historic town of Patagonia, Arizona.

No one realized that she'd cased the place before

she applied for the part-time job. She needed to understand the clientele, the owners, the overall vibe. Then she created an undercover profile that would guarantee that they not only would hire her but that she would fit in without a hitch. She was *that good*.

She'd been a con artist before she was a cop, and being an undercover cop was, essentially, being a con artist, but with a badge.

The only thing she never pretended to be was a veteran. Veterans had questions that only veterans could answer. Too many little details that could get you hung up. Where you went for basic training, where you were stationed, what your rank was, who your commanding officer was. Details about weapons and jobs and deployment. Acronyms that made her head spin. Colton, her sometime LAPD partner, had served in the Marines for three years right out of high school, and he played the role perfectly. He even went undercover once when a group of active-duty marines was smuggling opium from overseas. She'd played his girlfriend. It was a dangerous gig, intense, but fun.

Yes, she had an odd view of *fun*.

Kara looked over to the three sixty-something Vietnam vets and said, "Another?"

Tom, Russ and Javier nodded and pushed their glasses toward her on the bar almost in unison. They came in late every afternoon, between four and four thirty. They drank three to five drafts each and shared a large pizza or got burgers—pretty much the only items on the menu, other than a club sandwich, which was Kara's favorite. They argued about everything from politics to religion and every untouchable subject in between, but they had one another's backs.

Kara was already half in love with the trio.

She was already pouring their third round. They all walked to the Wrangler, and they all walked home. She didn't have to worry about grabbing keys or calling a ride.

Today they were arguing about Iran. Kara didn't pay much attention. If there was one thing she disliked more than domestic politics, it was international politics.

Honestly, she cared about only two things. Bad guys and catching them.

"We need a surgical strike. Cut off their head," Russ was saying.

"Two more will grow back," Tom said. "Leave them alone. We get involved in too many of these conflicts as it is."

"They'll never go away," Russ said. "They sponsor terrorism around the world, and we need to stop them before they get a nuclear bomb."

Tom snorted. "A lot of good we've been doing these last thirty years. Right, Javi?"

Javi sipped his fresh beer. "We need to do something, but we have to be smart about it."

And so it went. The three didn't agree about much, but they argued good-naturedly.

Too bad the rest of society couldn't learn from them.

Kara took the empty mugs, rinsed them and slid them into the dishwasher under the bar. She wiped down the counter while assessing the other patrons. Friday night, the bar was already half-full and it was only five thirty. By six, it'd be packed.

Employees of Southwest Copper Refinery drank, socialized and blew off steam at the Wrangler. It was their watering hole, the place to hang and relax. In a town the size of Patagonia, there weren't many places to go. The other bar in town, only two blocks away, was attached to the "big" hotel—if you could call a three-story building with thirty-two guest rooms a *hotel*. A sports bar and grill on the edge of town catered mostly to the few young people in the area and tourists passing through. There were a couple of other small hotels, and a motel with twelve rooms next to the sports bar. They'd all be booked for Memorial Day weekend.

No one wanted to be in Patagonia after that, when daily temperatures exceeded 100 degrees through September. Even today at 90 was a bit toasty for Kara, though the bar was comfortably air-conditioned. The art festival brought thousands of people into town, which would sustain the local economy for the four-month dead period when daily temperatures could exceed 120.

Kara really hoped they wrapped up this case before she had to feel those 120-degree temperatures.

"Well, look who just walked in," Tom said.

Kara didn't have to look.

"He's been coming in virtually every night, for the last couple of weeks," Javier said, looking straight at Kara as she wiped down the bar, loud enough to make sure she could hear him.

The trio chuckled.

Kara said, "You all act like a bunch of twelve-year-olds."

Of course she noticed that Joe Molina, the son of the owner of Southwest Copper, came in often. He always sat at the bar and found an excuse to talk to her. Part of her undercover assignment *was* Joe Molina. She was tasked with befriending him and watching his back in case someone was watching him. To gain his trust and confidence. At least that was how Matt Costa detailed the assignment. *Befriend*, he'd said.

She couldn't help it if Joe was attracted to her. And being *friends* wasn't going to get her inside his head. So she flirted when he flirted. It was clear he was preoccupied with everything going on at Southwest Copper, since it was his family's business. She had sympathy for the awkward position he'd found himself in, but she also admired that when the FBI approached him to cooperate with the investigation, he agreed to help. That he was willing to help when the FBI didn't have any real leverage over him—simply because it was the right thing to do—was a rarity in Kara's world.

She was generally skeptical of altruism. In her experience, very few people did the right thing, especially when they had something to lose. Seemed like Joe Molina was one of the rare ones.

He hadn't discussed any of this with her. He wasn't supposed to talk to anyone about being an informant for the FBI. So far he'd upheld his end of the deal.

Still, from the beginning she'd told Matt she didn't think they should alert Joe Molina about the investigation into A-Line and David Hargrove. Matt, to his credit, had considered her argument, but in the end, Matt went with his original plan. There was no guarantee that Michael Harris, who was deep cover at Southwest Copper, would have access to critical information, especially when they would need warrants.

A background check on Joe Molina turned up that he'd had two speeding tickets over the last five years (both paid) and only one small ding on his credit when he was late on a car payment. Hardly anything to garner suspicion. He wasn't particularly tied to Southwest Copper, because until his mother got sick last year, he'd been living and working in Phoenix after graduating from college.

So far, so good.

Joe said hello to the people he knew—virtually everyone—as he walked through the bar and sat down at the end of the long counter. She smiled at him, friendly, just a hint of attraction. She didn't want to make it too easy or suspicious. They'd spent nearly two weeks just getting to know each other through light flirting and casual conversation.

"Hey, Joe, what can I get for you?"

"The usual."

Joe liked the craft beer the bar owners brought in from a microbrewery in Tucson. Most of the regulars drank either Coors or Coors Light on tap. They had a couple of other offerings and the microbrew sales would increase exponentially during the art festival, but 80 percent of their beer sales was in Coors.

Then there were those who tossed back a shot or three of whiskey before they switched to beer.

She poured a pint and put it on a coaster in front of Joe. "It's going to get busy in a few," she said. "Payday."

They hadn't gone out on an official date, though Joe often came near closing and walked her home. Twice already he'd brought her dinner when she was busy. They'd talked a lot about a whole range of things—from her temporary bartending gig through Memorial Day to her quasi-fictional life story—and his *real* life story.

Joe Molina didn't seem to have a lying bone in his body. She didn't need to verify anything, though of course she did anyway because she was a good cop. Kara's old boss in LA, Lex, had often told her she was a human lie detector, and he wasn't wrong about that. It was par for the course, being raised by a couple of con artists. Reading people was in her blood. Coupled with police training and nearly twelve years undercover, and yeah, she could read people better than most cops.

Joe was one of the good guys, and she almost felt guilty about pretending to be someone that she wasn't.

Except that this was her job, and guilt was a useless emotion. The only thing Kara truly felt guilty about—so guilty that she forced herself to push it to the back of her mind—was getting Sunny killed back in LA. No matter what Lex had told her, no matter what went down, she knew deep in her heart that Sunny was dead at the age of twenty-two because of *her*. Kara had manipulated Sunny into helping her take down a sweatshop, knowing full well how dangerous it was for the young Chinese immigrant. Sunny had been trafficked when she was only twelve and forced to work for a decade making knockoff designer clothes until Kara went in deep cover to shut down that operation.

Then Sunny was dead, and her blood was on Kara's hands.

"You okay?" Joe asked.

Joe was perceptive. It bothered her that she'd let her emotions bubble to the surface.

"Nostalgic, I guess," she said, noncommittal.

"You've worked every night since you started."

"How do you know?"

"Small town." He smiled. "So, I was thinking after we talked the other day, about your interest in photography. You mentioned you wanted to shoot the desert, explore one of the ghost towns, that you had a thing for abandoned buildings. It's going to be nice tomorrow morning, not too hot. I'd like to take you down to Harshaw."

"Is that a ghost town or something?"

He laughed. "Not quite. There's still a few people living there. It's not far from town. I thought we could go on a little hike. We could also check out the ghost town south of Harshaw. You'd probably like to take pictures of it, though there's really not much there. A few structures. I think an old church, if it's still standing."

"You were paying attention," she said with a half smile.

"Of course I was. I remember everything you say."

"You do?"

"You don't like anything with mayo in it, but you love mustard, especially if it has horseradish."

She laughed, genuinely laughed, and was slightly impressed. "And my favorite beer?"

"From a microbrewery near where your grandmother lives in Washington, though you'll drink just about anything. If you had your choice, a good reposado tequila straight up."

He *was* good—they had talked about beer the night they'd met because Joe was the first person who'd ordered the microbrew from her, and that was the only time Kara talked about her grandmother. And yeah, she preferred drinking tequila to most anything.

The key to a good cover was to keep it as close to the truth as possible. Unless it was necessary for the job, she never changed certain facts about herself—such as the foods she didn't like, or that she'd been raised (in part) in Washington State. Or that she was an only child. She could call upon the truth more easily than remembering an elaborate cover.

The best lies were based in truth.

"I'd love to go," she said.

"Great. I really need a break from—well, everything."

He wasn't looking at her, and she wondered what

had been going on over and above his helping the FBI in their investigation.

"Are you an early riser?" Joe asked.

Sleep often eluded her, and she generally functioned on four to five hours of sleep a night.

"I can be."

"Five thirty, if that's not too early for you—then we can get down there as the sun's coming up. Should make for some good pictures. Just one caveat."

"A *caveat*?" she teased.

Out of the corner of her eye she saw Ryder Kim walk in. She didn't react, though she was ticked off. Ryder was showing up here at the bar way too often. She didn't blame him—she blamed her *new* boss, Special Agent in Charge Mathias Costa.

She was going to have a word or two with Matt. Soon.

Joe smiled back at her. "Yes, that you'll agree to have a picnic lunch with me."

"That's certainly not a caveat. That sounds like the prize. Do I need to bring anything?"

"Just you. Honestly, Kara, you're the best thing about me coming back home."

She let the guilt flow through her and disappear. She couldn't dwell on it now. "How about a six-pack of that microbrew beer?" she said. "We rarely sell the bottles. They sit there, and believe it or not, beer can go bad. Which is a mortal sin."

"Deal." Joe grinned, then he turned and noticed someone across the room and his smile wavered.

She followed his gaze.

Two Hispanic men—she remembered when they walked in about ten minutes before Joe. They hadn't wanted anything—just went over and sat in the corner. She didn't recognize them—she'd studied all photos of employees from Southwest Copper, and they didn't work there. They hadn't been in the bar before tonight. They were watching Joe now.

"Something wrong?" she asked.

"No, just tired. Long day." He gave her a bright smile. Too bright, she thought, but she returned it.

"I have some other customers who need my attention. You'll have to excuse me a moment."

"Sorry—go. I gotta talk to some of the guys anyway," he said, though he didn't sound happy about it.

She wished she could spend more time eavesdropping, but she'd have to use her eyes more than her ears. Those two men who caught Joe's attention definitely didn't work at the refinery. They were dressed just a bit too nice, and while they were rough around the edges, they were stiff. They didn't belong here, and they knew it. They looked the part of being the first to throw a punch in a bar fight.

Joe put ten dollars on the bar, though the microbrew was only five. Kara put five in the till and the rest in the tip jar next to the old-fashioned register.

She checked on her trio of favorite vets, then went over and took an order for a round at the table where Joe had just sat down. These were guys from the refinery, but Joe's eyes were still on the two strangers in the corner. She served Joe's group, joking with them as warranted.

Joe had more of a white-collar vibe than a blue, even though he'd worked at the refinery part-time while going to college. Based on what Michael Harris had picked up while working there over the past three weeks, some of the staff had issues with Joe because of changes he was implementing. Maybe, Kara had thought—and said as much to Michael— some of the staff were suspicious of Joe because he was poking around, possibly looking for evidence of criminal activity. It was the reason Kara didn't want Matt to bring Joe into the fold: most civilians couldn't lie to save their souls. Not on a day-to-day basis. It was her job to protect his ass. She might have to get closer to him than she'd planned.

Special Agent Michael Harris's job was to figure out what exactly was going on inside Southwest— whether David Hargrove had an accomplice, or if any other person or people knew that the waste disposal firm the company used was illegally dumping. It could be that A-Line Waste Disposal was taking the money from Southwest Copper and not doing their job. Southwest could be completely ignorant of anything illegal. And there was always the chance, however unlikely, that the wildlife found by Emma Perez hadn't been poisoned by copper slag from the plant.

Kara ranked that possibility at the bottom. Usually where there was smoke, there was fire, and those birds had died of chemicals that were found in copper slag. Other possibilities existed but were unlikely.

It could be that only a few employees were involved. Maybe even only David Hargrove, taking a kickback from A-Line and signing off on reports he knew were falsified. Or it could be that this was a much larger conspiracy and the company intentionally violated serious environmental and safety regulations.

Kara wondered if the strangers were with A-Line Trucking. If so, maybe Joe was involved more than anyone thought. Which would be unfortunate. Joe knew a lot about their investigation and could be playing Matt, trying to find out what exactly the FBI knew to protect his own business.

He didn't seem to be the type of guy...but he was clearly uncomfortable.

Despite the seriousness of the assignment, Kara was actually having fun. If she couldn't be a cop in LA, then undercover with this FBI task force was the next best thing.

She glanced over at Ryder Kim again.

Fun *except* for the tight leash her boss Matt Costa had on her. She thought Matt had gotten over his micromanaging thing with her the last time they worked together, but clearly she was wrong.

She walked over to Ryder and said quietly with a smile, "Don't order club soda or you'll draw suspicion."

He blinked at her. "I don't drink."

"I know, Sugar, but fake it."

Ryder wasn't an agent; he was an analyst for the

FBI and possibly the worst undercover cop on the planet. He was also smart, so he caught on.

"Whatever you think best."

She squatted and pulled the bar menu from its stand. She pretended to go over the limited items they served. "And I told you how to reach out. Not here. Especially not tonight. Your cover is minimal, and anyone could have followed you from your meeting in Tucson."

"I wasn't followed." He gave her a slight smile. "I'm not the novice you think I am."

She grinned. Yeah, she liked Ryder a lot.

"Joe doesn't need to see you. He doesn't know who you are, so he might get suspicious and start digging around."

"Matt wants me to keep an eye on you," Ryder said.

He didn't look comfortable in the least, and she didn't blame him. She didn't need an analyst watching out for her.

It took all Kara's training to smile casually at Ryder and not suggest he tell Matt to go to hell. "My place, 1:00 a.m., back door. We need to talk," she said, then put the menu back. She knew full well that health-conscious Ryder would eat nothing that came out of this kitchen.

Kara went back to the bar and fake poured vodka in a glass over ice, then added club soda and a lime. She walked it over to Ryder and winked.

"It's a virgin," she mouthed.

As she walked back to the bar, another large group from the refinery walked in.

Greg Warren, who owned the Wrangler Bar & Grill along with his wife, Daphne, came from the back to help with the influx, but Kara had it covered. She was already pouring six pints and four double shots of whiskey.

"What would we do without you?" Greg said. "Daphne is still nursing that twisted ankle."

"I told her to stay off of it. She made it worse."

"She's stubborn. Hates being laid up like this. I know it's busy tonight, but if you and Neil—" he nodded toward the kitchen to where the cook, Neil, worked "—have this covered, I'm going home to make her dinner, then I'll be back in an hour or so."

"I'm good, Greg. Take care of Little Miss Stubborn."

She walked over to the group and served the drinks, chatting with the guys while keeping an eye on the place.

Kara was a temporary employee through Memorial Day weekend because of the annual three-day art festival. Part of her backstory was that she had been a bartender in LA before her fiancé died. Yeah, they felt sorry for her, but it wasn't a complete lie. Her best friend on the force had been killed two months ago, and she was still dealing with it.

It was people like Greg and Daphne Warren, the sixty-something owners of the Wrangler for the past twenty years, that Kara had a difficult time deceiving. Good, honest, hardworking folks who would be truly hurt when they found out that she'd lied to them. *If* they found out.

But she did it anyway. Kara didn't want to explore what that skill said about her, that twelve years of her life had been focused on being someone she was not.

Twelve years? Try thirty. Try since the day you were born.

Ryder was reading a book. A *book*, in a bar, in Patagonia, Arizona. She wished he would leave. If anyone chatted him up, he would tell them he was a grad student. But it wasn't verifiable. If someone was suspicious, just a few calls and a day or two of tracking would yield his true identity.

At least he looked like a nerdy student. Kara made sure that he dressed down—no impeccably pressed slacks, no tie, no ironed shirt. He wore a University of Arizona T-shirt, appropriately faded, and jeans—new, but passable. She'd ordered him to wash them, get them really dirty, then wash them again with just a touch of bleach.

But *reading*. In a *bar*.

She walked over again when he didn't leave after fifteen minutes.

"Another vodka and soda?" she asked.

"Um, no thank you."

She put the check down. *Hint, hint, kid. Go away.*

Ryder left a ten-dollar bill and walked out five minutes later. She breathed easier. She got it—Matt was worried about this case. This certainly wasn't a typical police investigation. That's why Kara loved it. But she knew how to do her job, and she'd told

Matt that she would call if she needed help. She didn't, so Ryder was a problem.

She poured the trio of vets another round.

Javier said, "I think that kid likes you, but you intimidate him."

The vet was far too perceptive. Why was he watching her?

She laughed. "He's at U of A. A little too young, smart and nerdy for me. Nice guy, though."

"Wonder what he's doing down here. He's been at the coffee shop every morning for a month."

Yes, *way* too perceptive.

She shrugged. "Isn't it, like, finals? Or maybe he's doing research or writing a thesis or something. I wouldn't know. I didn't make it past a year of community college."

"You have street smarts," Tom said.

"That's the only kind of smarts I need," she said.

"That kid is too young. Kara's into guys like Joe," Tom continued.

"Stop," she told him, with a glance at Joe still sitting with the men from Southwest. It didn't hurt if everyone thought she had the hots for Joe Molina.

"He deserves someone like you, Kara."

"And who am I?" she asked jokingly.

"Pretty," Tom said. "Sharp as a whip. You watch the room like you own the place, which is good."

She watched the place like she was a cop pretending not to be a cop. These three old men were definitely too interested in her life.

"You're not happy," Russ said.

"I'm happy enough."

"You pretend, but your eyes—I've seen those eyes before. Sad. You hide it well, but eyes don't lie."

"Stop it, Russ," Tom said. "You're prying."

"It's fine," she said, forcing an edge to her voice. She cleared her throat and intentionally looked down, grabbed the rag and wiped down the bar.

"Daphne said you lost your fiancé," Javier said.

"I really don't want to talk about it," she replied, which was true.

"Leave her alone," Tom repeated.

"I'm not pushing."

"And," Kara said, "I appreciate that."

She raised her hand to another large group that walked in, all from the refinery. Michael Harris was with them—and so was David Hargrove. Michael said something to Hargrove and he laughed, clapped Michael on the back. Good. Michael had done a terrific job getting the rank and file at Southwest to trust him, and in particular their primary suspect. Kara had initially been worried that Michael—a big Black guy, one of only a few Black guys who worked at the refinery—would stick out, but Matt understood the demographics of the area much better than she did. He'd assured her that it wasn't an issue, and considering that the majority of the residents and employees were Hispanic, Matt had been right. No one cared.

"And the rush has begun," Kara said. "You need anything else, holler."

"This is it for us," Russ said. "Put it on our tabs, will you, sweetheart?"

"Of course, sugar," she said with a wink and walked over to the new group.

She left the trio and took orders. Joe had moved tables and was now sitting with the two strangers. Both were Hispanic between thirty and thirty-five, the leaner, older guy about five foot ten and clean-shaven. The taller, bulkier guy had a full moustache and thick five-o'clock shadow. Neither looked comfortable in their casual attire. They weren't cops—Kara would have pegged them as such.

She walked over to them. "Can I get you anything?"

They glanced at each other, then the thinner man said with a smile, "Whatever Joe here is having is fine with us."

No accent.

"Another for you?" she asked Joe.

"No, thank you," he said.

He looked both irritated and worried. At her? At them?

Then as she walked by, Joe reached out and touched her hand, just a brush, and she almost thought it was an accident. She glanced at him, and he gave her a half smile, then turned back to his meeting, his voice so low she couldn't hear him.

But the strangers listened intently.

She served the large group and Michael, then the men with Joe, who stopped talking when she approached. No, not suspicious at all. When she was done, she said to the trio of vets, "Guys, I need to use the ladies' room. Can you watch the bar for two shakes before you leave? I'll be right back."

"Anything for you, Kara," Javier said.

She made sure she walked through the restroom door, but she didn't stay long. She washed her hands and counted to twenty, then left. No one was in the back hall, and Neil was singing to himself in the kitchen as he grilled burgers.

She stood in the hall for a fraction of a second more and discreetly took a photo of the two men with Joe Molina. She didn't look at her phone while she did it; instead, she focused on the other patrons and made sure no one was watching her too closely to see what she was doing.

All clear. She'd find out what was up soon enough. She'd flat out ask Joe in the morning, as well as forward the photos to Ryder to run through the FBI database. After all, she would have their pictures *and* their fingerprints, she thought as she watched them both drink.

Hell, she'd have their DNA if she wanted, though she wasn't certain about the legality of all that. She would bag and tag their drinking glasses and let the legal eagles at the FBI figure out what they could use. At least they could pull their prints.

Her cop instincts were twitching. Those two were up to something, and she hoped Joe wasn't in the middle of it.

But if he was, she'd tie him up with a pretty bow for her boss.

CHAPTER 6

Friday night
Patagonia, Arizona

Michael Harris watched Kara walk away after serving another round of drinks to the group of Southwest employees he'd strategically befriended. The cook came out with two large pizzas that everyone shared.

"Hot, isn't she?" Pedro Vasquez said with a low whistle as he grabbed a slice. "Wish Greg would keep her around full-time. She's much easier on the eyes than Neil in the kitchen."

Appreciative comments spread through the group.

"If I wasn't married, I'd be all over her," David Hargrove said.

"Don't be saying that around Tanya. She'll come

in and whoop that girl's ass for turning your eye," Pedro said.

Michael didn't think anyone could "whoop" Kara's ass unless she let them, let alone David's wife, Tanya.

"Joe has his eye on her," another guy said.

"Who are those two guys he's talking to?" Pedro asked. "I think I've seen them around."

"Saw those same guys out at the old slag field last week. Heard they were from AREA," someone else said. "Don't know why Joe would give those bastards the time of day."

"They're not from that shit bureaucracy," David said. "AREA," he snorted derisively. "Guys from that agency were snooping around a couple months ago, like they always do, surprise inspection or some such nonsense, but found shit, because there's nothing to find."

"Then who are they?" Pedro said, indiscreetly gesturing toward Joe's table.

David chewed his food, chased it down with a long gulp of beer. "They were talking to John a couple weeks ago. They're here trying to buy the refinery, what I heard, or part of John's land. Not quite sure, all I know is that whatever they wanted, John shut them down. So now maybe they're pushing Joe? Why is he dealing with them? Hell, John isn't going to be happy."

Michael hadn't heard anything about John wanting to sell Southwest, though he'd picked up a tidbit over the month he'd been here that a new mine— one still seeking state approval—was interested in buying access rights through Southwest Copper property.

Michael worked closely with Pedro Vasquez on the floor of the refinery. Pedro was his supervisor, but he did as much work as anyone who worked for him. They were responsible for cleaning and maintaining the equipment. David was an assistant manager—in charge of contracts, inventory, and ordering. The other men at the table worked either on Pedro's team or for David. One of the things Michael liked about Southwest was that there wasn't a social hierarchy. David was friends with guys that worked on the floor as well as management. And most of the managers—there were only a handful—were on the floor nearly every day.

Michael was still trying to put some pieces together, but he understood the big picture. Southwest was one of the last copper refineries in the western states. They didn't mine the ore, but three copper mines in Arizona brought them the raw material from which they extracted and processed pure copper. Much of the process was backbreaking and difficult, but it could be a lucrative business.

Mining had its ups and downs, and over the last two decades Southwest Copper had lost half its suppliers to closures. But other potential spots were ripe for mining in the area—just not copper. Michael had heard that there was a new mine southeast of town currently going through the permitting process to mine zinc. But everyone seemed to talk about it with hushed breaths, so he didn't want to show too much interest.

Another guy said, "They don't want to buy the refinery. They're from the *other* mine." Nods of agreement. Michael wondered if this information was important—he'd make sure Matt at least looked into it.

"Then what would they want with John or Joe?" David said.

"Hell if I know," Pedro said.

All good information to put in his report tomorrow, Michael thought. He wondered if Joe was talking to the two because of his father's reluctance to sell or lease his land or for some other business reason. Joe didn't look like he was enjoying the conversation, but he hadn't yet left the table. Michael wondered why Joe would meet here, at the Wrangler, where half the patrons worked for Joe's dad. It seemed…odd.

It would definitely go into his report. Probably Kara's, too, because she was giving the group the eagle eye, as well.

Kara had two things going for her. She was a sharp cop with more undercover experience than the rest of the team combined, and as Pedro pointed out, she was hot—in a sexy, girl-next-door way.

Costa would have his ass if Michael said that out loud, so he kept his opinion of Kara to himself.

Barry Nelson, John Molina's brother-in-law— their wives, Helen and Clare, were sisters—walked into the bar alone. "Hey, guys," Barry said as he approached Michael and the others. "Have a space?"

"For the boss? Of course," Pedro said, and a few of the men shifted their seats to make room.

Barry grabbed a chair from a half-empty table, pulled it over and sat down. "None of that boss crap," he said.

Barry was the general manager of the refinery. He was second in charge, after John. And, Michael knew, he had pretty much taken over most of John's responsibilities when John's wife got sick.

"Everyone coming to the picnic tomorrow?" Barry asked.

A chorus of yeses.

"What picnic?" Michael asked.

"You didn't read the memo?" Barry asked.

"Um, no, I'm sorry."

"It went out before Michael got here," David said. "Annual employee picnic, always the weekend before Memorial Day—up at John's cabin."

Barry said, "Helen's making her famous chili."

"Yeah, Tanya said she was going over there today to help," David said.

"Helen started three days ago, now it's just a matter of putting it all together," Barry said. "They'll probably be drunk on cheap wine before I get home." They all laughed, and Barry said to Michael, "If you don't mind going early, you can drive up with Helen and me. It's hard to find if you're not from the area."

"Or I can pick you up," David said. "So you don't have to get up at the butt crack of dawn." He laughed.

Michael smiled his appreciation. "Great. Thanks."

Another way to get close to David. It was Michael's job, but it made him feel a bit uncomfortable. He didn't like lying. He didn't know how Kara had worked undercover for so long. She seemed to have blended right in here.

As the group chatted and told jokes and talked about football, Michael noticed that David kept looking at his phone. He was texting with someone, and while he didn't visibly show much reaction, every time he looked at a new message, he frowned slightly, replied, then drank his beer. Finally he said, "I've got a few things to do before the party tomorrow."

"I was thinking about getting home myself," Michael said. "I'm beat after today."

Pedro laughed. "And here we all thought that you were the Incredible Hulk."

"Ten years ago you should have seen me. I swear, as I get closer to forty, my muscles feel like they're closer to sixty."

Michael didn't expect David to clue him in on his sudden departure, but he followed him out nonetheless after dropping twenty dollars on the table for his beer and his share of the pizza.

"I'll pick you up in the morning about eleven," David said to Michael. He was walking away quickly at that point, giving Michael no opportunity to chat.

"Thanks, buddy," Michael called after him. Then he climbed into his truck—a beat-up piece of metal that ran amazingly well. He wanted to follow David but couldn't risk being caught. Instead he watched which way David left the parking lot—heading east on 82, the main road in town. Michael also lived in that direction, so he trailed him.

David passed First Avenue, which was where he lived. It was a "new" development by Patagonia standards, built thirty years ago when the town was still thriving.

Where was he going? Certainly not home.

Michael turned down the next street. He was renting the apartment over the Nelsons' garage. They had a house on several acres up in the hills. An older home, well maintained. Michael hadn't wanted to be that close to anyone at Southwest Copper, because it meant he would have to be doubly careful even when in his own space. But when Barry found out he was living out of a motel, he offered the apartment to Michael. It would have been rude to refuse. Besides, Barry was John's in-law, so it naturally brought him closer to the Molina family.

Ultimately, the living arrangements worked out. Barry liked Michael and he would talk to him over beers after work, even when they weren't at the Wrangler. That's how Michael really got to know and understand the people he worked with.

Michael pulled into the carport on the north side of the garage. Two cars were out front, and he remembered that David said his wife would be helping Helen make the chili for the picnic. He wanted to talk to Matt about David's sudden disappearance—that he said he was going home when, in fact, he drove *past* his street. It could be nothing, or it could be important. But he didn't want to risk being overheard, so he sent Matt a quick encrypted message instead before he climbed out of his truck.

"Michael, right?" a female voice said behind him.

He was startled when he turned around and saw Tanya Hargrove standing there. He'd seen her twice at the refinery when she came to talk to her husband, but they'd never been introduced.

"Yes, I'm Michael Harris. I work with your husband."

"Helen said you were renting above the garage. She asked me to come out and fetch you when she heard your truck pull in. How about being our guinea pig? Helen's chili is amazing, but we need a second opinion."

"Don't mind if I do," he said and followed her inside the Nelsons' house, where Helen was cooking—four giant pots covered the stove. The three women were laughing and drinking wine. He saw two empty bottles lined up on the counter, and half of a third was gone.

"Help yourself to a beer, Michael!" Helen called cheerfully from where she was stirring one of the huge pots.

He felt wholly uncomfortable in the mix, but he helped himself to a bottle of Coors Light.

His phone vibrated and he discreetly looked down. Matt had responded with "FUT"—follow up tomorrow.

Good. That meant Michael had made the right call in not tailing David wherever he was headed. Michael wasn't always sure how best to proceed—

he'd never worked an undercover case before. Kara had given him and the others a quick down-and-dirty class she called Undercover 101. The one thing that really hit home was to trust your gut.

If you think you should back off, back off. Blowing your cover can get you killed.

And being here, in Helen Nelson's kitchen with David Hargrove's wife would give him a lot to follow-up on—at least a lot of ways to start the conversation.

CHAPTER 7

There were two things that Hector Lopez valued most: money and family.

You couldn't kill family. No matter how badly they screwed up. No matter how badly he wanted to.

"Is our route compromised? Tell me. It is a simple yes or no question, Dominick."

He wished they were face-to-face. It was easier for his cousins to lie to him over the phone. He wished he could trust them, but this wasn't the first time for a screwup.

"No. The, um, merchandise has been moved, no problem."

"That wasn't my question."

He waited. To think that Dominick was supposedly the smart one.

"No, Hector, our route has not been compromised." Very specific. There was much Dominick wasn't telling him. He may have to cross the border sooner rather than later.

"Did you find the boy?" Hector asked.

"He won't tell anyone."

"Was that my question? Are you an idiot?"

Silence. Silence was never a good answer.

Hector said, "I want them dead. Find them, bring them to the others, kill his sister first in front of everyone, in front of the boy. Then slit his throat. No one betrays me. Their blood will keep everyone else in line. You know this to be true."

"I do. We'll find them."

Dominick sounded so confident, but Hector doubted him. He didn't want to take over the day-to-day management of their operation, but what choice did he have? He would think on it.

"This was more than an unfortunate loss, my cousin. We lose control when they take it. You understand these dynamics?"

"Yes, Hector, of course."

"Are you positive, on your life, that our route is secure?"

"Yes, I swear on our grandmother's grave, our route is one hundred percent secure."

He believed him. "Good. We have a shipment en route. Handle it by tomorrow night. If *anything* goes wrong, clean up swiftly."

"Of course. There may be one other situation."

Hector listened as Dominick told him the one thing he especially did not want to hear.

"And why am I only now hearing about this FBI investigation?"

"We thought they were here about the dead girl. They had no evidence, they left."

"They clearly did not leave."

"We're taking care of it."

"Are you?"

"Yes. This wasn't our operation they found, they don't know about our plans."

"If the feds are around it puts us at risk, whoever they're investigating. There is no room for error. You tell our *partners*," he spat out the word. He would never consider those people his partners or his equals. "Their people, their problem. They need to fix it. If it's not handled by the time my shipment arrives, I will take it out on one of their own. Make that very clear."

"We have a plan."

"You had better solve it. The shipment next week is worth *millions*. I will not lose it. After I deliver it, we'll lie low and see what happens. If there is any hint that the FBI is looking at my network, heads will roll."

Hector didn't give Dominick a chance to respond. He put down the phone, walked over to his bar and poured himself a double tequila.

He didn't want to be on-site, he didn't want to leave his fortress in Mexico, but this shipment was far too important for him to leave the details to Dominick and his idiot brother. Too many mistakes had already happened. Too many problems. And if he didn't deliver, he'd be the one who had to pay.

He had never failed before, he would not fail now.

Hector drained his tequila and walked around his vast office. Volumes of books, priceless paintings. He had first editions of some of the finest works in the world. Originals of great works of art. Seeing what he had, what he had earned, calmed him.

Fear kept most people in line; respect kept the others in line. He had both.

The powers respected him; the minions feared him.

He wouldn't have it any other way.

CHAPTER 8

————

Friday night
Patagonia, Arizona

Patagonia was definitely not LA, Kara thought as she watched the bar begin to thin out rather quickly.

The vets had long left. They never stayed past eight. Michael had walked out with David Hargrove. The two men who had been talking to Joe left only a few minutes later, making Kara doubly suspicious.

Joe came up to her to say goodbye, and she casually asked about the men.

"You didn't seem too happy over there," she said. "Is everything okay?"

"Yeah," he said with a wave of his hand. "It's fine. Just vendors—some are more aggressive than others."

"Vendors? Meeting in a bar? My kind of business." She watched Joe closely. His calm expression didn't give anything away, but she sensed he was tense, maybe angry.

"You buy one thing from someone, they always think you want more," he said, shrugged. "Just business."

It was definitely a way to end the conversation.

"Tomorrow, then?" she asked.

Now he smiled, clearly glad that she had agreed to go with him.

"Can't wait." He squeezed her hand, ran his thumb over her palm. "I might have to show up in the afternoon for the Southwest Copper employee picnic. It starts at eleven, but it goes all afternoon, and I just have to make a brief appearance. I'd love you to join me."

"I have to work," she said. "I told Greg and Daphne I'd be in by five."

"Of course, I get it. If we get back to town in time, we'll go up there, okay?"

"Fair enough."

He squeezed her hand again, seemed reluctant to let it go. "I have some paperwork to do, I really should go," he said.

"And I have customers to take care of. I'll see you tomorrow." She slipped her hand out of his and gave him a smile. He walked out.

Something was a bit…odd about that exchange. She couldn't quite put her finger on it. Or maybe it was simply Joe's preoccupation with Southwest Copper.

She'd pass along to Ryder and Matt the information about the two strangers, then follow up with the drinking glasses with their prints. Maybe it was all innocuous. Maybe it wasn't. But definitely worth following up.

Joe left at eight thirty. The bar remained comfortably busy for another hour or so, but the payday rush was over.

A couple of tourists came in—probably in town for a quick weekend, ahead of the rush of the art festival. A lone man in his fifties with a permanent scowl on his unshaven face entered just after ten and ordered a double shot of their cheapest whiskey on ice, then sat in the corner. He was rough around the edges: she thought ex-military—someone who hadn't had a good experience. Maybe a cop…retired? She wasn't sure. He had an edge that said military more than cop, but sometimes the two were interchangeable. She kept an eye on him, since no one appeared to know him. Anyone who wasn't a local or clearly a tourist always caught her attention.

Like the two men who had been talking to Joe.

A couple of regulars came in after that, not as nice and friendly as the three vets. Two women and a guy, she thought all three of them were jerks. But she chatted with them anyway when they wanted to talk, ignored their veiled insults and cruel jokes about others in town, and shortly thereafter excused herself and pretended to do inventory. She'd already done it, but she wanted to keep her eye on the guy in the corner. He still wasn't halfway done with his whiskey. There was something about him. A familiarity, but she knew she hadn't seen him before.

Undercover cops often nursed one drink.

Greg returned after ten thirty, then Neil closed the kitchen. Greg helped Kara straighten and clean the bar. The three local jerks left after a few drinks. All in all, a quiet Friday night. When it was just the lovey-dovey tourist couple and the stranger in the corner, she called last call.

She asked Greg about the guy. He'd never seen him before either.

So Kara decided surreptitiously to take his picture and grab his glass, just in case, like she had with the two guys earlier.

Something was off about that loner. She knew it in her gut. And she always trusted her instincts.

Kara was staying in an old, run-down two-room house up the hill from the bar. The kitchen and bathroom had both been added around the forties, she figured—and not updated since. She'd lived in better, she'd lived in worse, but the one thing she could say about this place was it was quiet.

It worked for her, because she really didn't care much about where she stayed as long as it was clean—which this place was. But quiet didn't mean privacy. Javier, one of the veterans, lived on the corner down the street and across from her, and she often saw him sitting on his porch smoking a pipe and watching the slow-moving town.

Fortunately, Ryder understood that she meant it when she said to come around to the back. To get there he had to walk along a different road, then down a dirt alley that no one used except the people in the three houses that had garages off the alley. She had a tiny yard with a back gate that didn't have a lock, so he could slip in.

Better Ryder than Matt, she figured. Everyone knew Matt was a fed, and he looked like it too.

She really wished he would trust her to do her job.

When she first met Matt in March, she should have realized he was a control freak. Well, to be honest, she did recognize the trait because she shared it, only she hadn't been on his team before. At that time she didn't actually *work* for Matt Costa, so he didn't pull the boss card whenever she followed her instincts.

Not for the first time, she regretted accepting the offer to work for the FBI's new mobile response team. But she didn't really have a choice.

And then what would you do? You can't go back to your old job; there's a bounty on your head. Hell, you may never be able to step foot in LA again. This offer saved your ass, in more ways than one. You aren't even a fed, you're still an LAPD detective. Best of all worlds.

In some ways.

The truth was that her cover had been blown by an asshole of an FBI agent she had long ago fallen out with. If she could prove that he'd been the one to leak her identity to the press—as well as the identity of her sometime partner, Colton Fox—she would destroy him. Colton was dead and she was exiled. One day she would have her pound of flesh.

Time couldn't heal this wound; it was so deep she would feel the pain for the rest of her life.

She heard his footsteps before Ryder knocked. She quickly opened the back door. "I said to walk in," she muttered.

"I didn't want you to shoot me."

She almost smiled. "Trust me," she said.

He didn't look comfortable.

"It's late," he said. "No one is watching."

"Don't be so sure of that." She grabbed a beer from the refrigerator and opened it. She didn't offer one to Ryder because he didn't drink, and she really didn't want him to stay. Working in the bar, she had no alone time, and she craved one hour to just *be*.

"Spill." She sat on the worn—but clean—leather couch.

Ryder looked around sheepishly. "I could have gotten you a better place."

"Nothing wrong here, and it fits my role. Ryder, we've had this conversation before. I need to stay in character, and when you come into the bar, I risk breaking character."

"Agent Costa is my boss. He wants me to check on you regularly, and he knows I haven't been."

"I pass you my report every morning at the coffeehouse. You see me, know I'm alive and breathing."

"That's not the same thing."

"You should have never have told him you weren't coming into the bar every night."

"I'm not going to lie because you don't like me coming in."

"I didn't want to do regular reports, but I caved. Matt agreed I didn't need twenty-four-seven backup, so he can't renege on it now unless he has a viable threat. And he doesn't."

She waited for Ryder to confirm, and he nodded.

"Michael and I have a system that's working," she said. "Don't jeopardize it."

Ryder looked even more uncomfortable than before.

She didn't want to hurt his feelings—she liked Ryder.

"I'll talk to Matt," she said.

She didn't really want to. Every time she left Patagonia, she risked exposing her cover. She'd think of something else—an excuse. Maybe just take a drive. Maybe because she had to go to a big-box store for supplies. Hell, she could offer to run errands for Greg and Daphne.

Or she'd wake him up in the middle of the night.

Though she didn't want to risk getting shot either.

She said, "I know what I'm doing. I'm writing a daily report for Matt. Joe Molina's taking me down to Harshaw and the surrounding area tomorrow morning. There's a closed mine, a semi-ghost town. I can easily pick his brain when he's relaxed. Because after tonight, I think there's something up with him."

"What happened tonight?"

She told him about the two guys she found suspicious who were talking to Joe, and the older stranger who came in later. She nodded to three paper bags on her table. "Their glasses are bagged and tagged, in evidence bags, the whole nine yards. I also sent you pictures of the three men."

"I got them. I didn't understand the context."

"Now you do. Can you run their prints?"

"First thing tomorrow."

"There's also a company picnic tomorrow. I overheard the men talking about it in case Michael doesn't mention it. Joe wants me to stop by with him later in the afternoon, but I need to be at the bar."

"Matt wanted me to remind you that even though Joe Molina has a clean record, be careful with him."

She ignored the comment. She and Matt had already had that conversation last month when they started this undercover operation. She didn't need constant reminders to be *careful* when she'd been a cop for nearly twelve years.

Ryder got up to leave. "We're all a little out of our element with this undercover assignment, even Matt."

"It's not Matt's first undercover gig."

"But it's the first time he's been in charge of an undercover operation. He didn't tell me that, but…" Ryder shrugged.

Ryder said a lot between the lines, and his unspoken analysis gave cause for Matt's caution. Kara didn't agree, but now she understood.

"He's worried that he doesn't have enough evidence to find out who killed Emma Perez," Kara said.

"How do you know? Did you talk to him?"

"No, not recently, but I read all the initial reports, and Jim's forensic analysis. There's no physical evidence yet tying anyone to her murder. The rock doesn't have prints or DNA. The witness, her boyfriend, didn't clearly see anyone—he thought male, and my guess based on Jim's report is that, yes, the killer is male, approximately six feet tall. So Matt's thinking that the only way he's going to solve Emma's murder is if he solves the illegal dumping, and that's if he can get David Hargrove to turn state's evidence."

"Unless *he* killed her."

He didn't kill her, but Kara didn't say anything. She had been watching David Hargrove from behind the bar for weeks. He didn't have it in him. And if he had killed anyone, he would have broken. He was weak in his gut, Kara was certain of it.

"Matt wants to give her family and Billy Nixon answers," Ryder said.

"I get it. Tell Matt I've got this covered," Kara said. "I'll figure it out. Sell it, Ryder—as best you can. I'll also talk to him and cover your ass, okay? No more stopping by the Wrangler unless it's an emergency. And I told you how I would let you know it was an emergency."

She was reporting daily as Matt wanted—even when she had nothing new to report—yet Matt had Ryder following up on *her* and watching *her* back, not Michael's.

It wasn't because she was a girl; Kara would have ended that bullshit immediately. Matt was certainly an alpha male trying his hardest to be a beta, but he didn't have a sexist bone in his body. Well, maybe a couple—he was a guy, after all—but nothing that gave Kara cause to call him on the carpet.

So why the attention? What was Matt's problem? Did he think she was incompetent? Did he think that her exposure on her last undercover case with LAPD was *her* fault? Her boss had made it perfectly clear that LA FBI and the media were to blame for that fiasco that got her partner Colton killed.

Maybe she and Matt needed to talk again, one-on-one, and clear the air. If Matt didn't trust her to do the job, then this was the last job she would do for the FBI.

Right...then what will you do? You can't go back to LA. You can't go back to your old life. This is the only chance for you to be a cop again.

"I should go," Ryder said.

"By the way, I'm not going to be at the coffee shop tomorrow. I'm leaving here at five thirty, so don't panic. I'll send Matt a report."

She made sure Ryder was gone, then called Matt Costa. It was one thirty in the morning, but she knew cops answered the phone day and night. She would rather have this conversation in person, but that was a risk. She was a lot of things; a fool wasn't one of them.

"Costa," he said on the third ring. He cleared his throat.

Good, she'd woken him up. He deserved it.

"Hello, boss," she said.

"What's wrong?"

She had him fully awake now. "Nothing. I'm writing my report. Had a visit from Ryder at the bar. Again."

He was silent.

"You told him to watch me? Why?"

Again, silence.

"Dammit, Matt, Ryder stands out like a sore thumb. He doesn't drink, he won't eat a burger, he sits there and *reads*. Unless he has something crucial to tell me that he can't tell me on the phone, he needs to stay away from me."

"You're on my team now, Kara," Matt said slowly.

"I know," she said, equally slowly. "Do you think I'm going to blow my cover? Ruin the investigation?"

"What? Of course not."

"Then why the babysitter? You don't have Ryder watching Michael's ass twenty-four seven. Why me?"

"He's not watching you all the time. I just asked that he check in regularly to make sure you were okay."

"And I can't make that determination? Do you think if I was in trouble I wouldn't send an SOS? Do you not trust me?"

"I trust you."

"You're not acting like it."

"I—" He stopped. He was going to say something, but he stopped himself, and damn, Kara wanted to know what he was going to say. "Your point is well taken."

"Then why wasn't it well taken two weeks ago when I first told you not to have Ryder shadow me?"

"You've blown this out of proportion."

"For shit's sake, Costa, knock it off. Don't put this back on me. There are regulars in the bar who see everything, and believe me, they've noticed Ryder. Read my report, you'll have it in ten minutes."

She ended the call. Why had she called him?

Damn, she should have just ignored Ryder—again. Except this was Friday night. Ryder didn't stick out as much when he came in on Sunday afternoon or Tuesday evening—but Friday night everyone who's anyone at the refinery is at the Wrangler. They would have all seen him. And he didn't fit in. Not because he was half-Korean or looked like a grad student, but because he was a physically fit, well-dressed nerd. He looked like a damn intellectual, even in the U of A shirt.

She typed out her memo, her fingers banging on the keyboard with a ferociousness she couldn't take out on Matt in person. She hit Send, then tried to go to sleep. Her heart was beating too fast, so she got up and poured herself a shot of tequila. Downed it. Let it coat her throat, stomach. She sat at the kitchen table and stared into the dark.

She saw Sunny. The beautiful, sweet, scared, brave girl who helped take down the largest sweatshop in Los Angeles.

And got killed.

Because of Kara.

Yeah, she wasn't going to be sleeping tonight.

Ten minutes later her phone rang.

"You're going out of town with Joe Molina? Why?"

"He asked me out. A picnic. It's exactly what we planned."

"I said befriend him. This is going too far."

"It's not like I'm going to jump into bed with him. It's a date. Casual. And didn't you tell me at the very beginning that you weren't one hundred percent certain about Molina?"

"You're going out with him, to the middle of nowhere, after writing that he met with two unidentified, suspicious-acting men at the bar. Shit like this is why I have Ryder watching your back."

He sounded jealous. This was not okay.

She should never have slept with him on their last case two months ago. But then again, she had never expected to work with him again. That had been one investigation, and she had walked away, free and clear.

So she thought.

"What the fuck did I do wrong, Costa?"

He didn't say anything.

"You're right," he finally said. "This is good— I'm just tired. Good work."

"Damn straight. Don't send Ryder to babysit me. If I need backup, for a legitimate reason, I'll take it. If you don't trust me, I shouldn't be here."

"I trust you, K."

K? *K?* Was that like a nickname? A term of endearment? A way to get her to calm down? She hated it.

"Act like it." She hung up.

CHAPTER 9

Early Saturday morning
South of Patagonia, Arizona

"I'm starving," Kara said. She put her camera back in its case and slung it over her shoulder. "Weren't you going to feed me?"

"It's only ten," Joe said.

"I didn't have breakfast."

Joe mocked surprise. "You skipped the most important meal of the day?"

"I opted for an extra half hour of sleep."

"We could have left later."

"And miss the sunrise? No way. That was amazing. I hope my pictures turn out."

"One of the galleries here sells local art on consignment—paintings, photographs, the like. You should consider putting your work there."

"You haven't even seen anything I've done."

"I can tell you have talent."

She didn't have talent; she faked it. She'd read a book on photography so that she would know what everything was on the fancy camera Ryder procured for her, and she could talk about popular photographers, plus she had a basic understanding of framing. But the only real "photography" she'd done was taking pictures of suspects during stakeouts.

"My own personal cheerleader. I'm still starving."

They'd gotten there early enough to first hike up a short hill to watch the sunrise, then they hiked to the other side to explore the old closed mine—not inside, that would have been too dangerous (and contrary to what Matt Costa thought, Kara did not have a death wish). But the area surrounding the mine was intriguing.

"Fifteen minutes," he said as they climbed into his truck. "There's another vista that has an amazing view and a grove of oak trees—rare around here—to provide shade. And then on the other side of that is the ghost town."

"If it takes sixteen minutes, I'm eating my hat." She was truly hungry, but mostly, she wanted to wrap this up so they would have time to go to the Southwest Copper party before she had to be at the bar. While Michael was a good cop, he wasn't used to undercover work and Kara wanted to get a better sense of how the employees treated Joe, and see how David Hargrove acted around the family.

Truth was, it took nearly thirty minutes, but she didn't eat her hat. A fifteen-minute drive over unpaved roads, then nearly a fifteen-minute hike up to the vista. But the view was worth it.

Joe tossed her an apple while he unpacked a picnic. She took a bite, then opened the small cooler she'd brought with beer and water. She popped open a beer and handed it to him, then did the same for herself.

"Beer in the morning?"

"It's like water," she said. "Besides, I've already drank a gallon of water." Not quite, but it felt like it and she'd already peed twice. "And you don't work today, do you?"

"Fortunately, no." He took a swig.

She looked at all the food. "You made all this?"

"Surprised?"

"You can cook."

"This isn't cooking, this is putting together food. But yes, I know how to cook. My mother taught me and my brother, Kenny, everything. Dad can't boil water."

"That's me. I didn't know you had a brother."

"He's followed in Dad's footsteps, at least as far as the military goes. He's career air force, stationed out of Ramstein, Germany. He comes home once a year—he stayed for a couple weeks when Mom got sick, but he had to get back."

"Have you visited him abroad?"

"Once when Kenny got married—I was in college. Mom and Dad stayed for a month two years ago, before Mom was diagnosed. First real vacation they'd had in years. Well, actually, first vacation I ever remember them having that wasn't a camping trip with Kenny and me."

"I hope they went in the spring—I've heard Europe is beautiful in the spring."

"Early spring," he said. "The entire month of March. It rained a lot, but Mom loved it. I think my dad got antsy. He called Barry constantly."

Joe took a bite of a sandwich. Kara had already half demolished hers—she wasn't lying when she said she was starving.

"You know, I admire you for leaving everything you knew in California and just coming out here with no plans," he told her.

That twinge of guilt that sometimes hit her when she worked undercover churned in her gut, but it passed. They looked out at the view, so clear and crisp on this spring day. A bit warm, but a light breeze refreshed her. Though they faced northeast, they could walk around the top of the plateau and see virtually every direction.

Kara said, "Living in LA for so long, I forgot what it's like to be in the middle of nowhere. It's surprisingly peaceful."

She actually hated it. While she protected her privacy and alone time with equal passion, she liked being in the middle of millions of people. When you lived in a big city, no one paid much attention to you. Small town? Everyone knew everyone else's business. Her three years in high school when she lived in tiny Liberty Lake, Washington, had been her version of hell. She'd once considered moving to New York. And, honestly, if this gig with the FBI didn't work out—and since she couldn't go back to LA because every criminal she'd put away as an undercover agent now knew her real identity—she'd see about applying for NYPD. She might enjoy being anonymous in the Big Apple.

"People think that the desert is just hot, dry and flat."

"Definitely not flat," she said with a half smile.

"We have some of the most unique mountain ranges in the country. People look at the Cascades or the Rocky Mountains as mountains because they're green and full of trees, but these are no less spectacular, and we have plenty of trees—just different kinds. Our sunsets are the most colorful, and there is so much animal life—people just think the desert is all rattlesnakes and lizards."

"If we see a snake, I'm outta here."

That wasn't a lie. She detested anything that slithered—criminals *or* reptiles.

"I'll keep my eyes open."

He was serious. She would totally lose her shit if they came across a rattlesnake.

"You're scared," he said with a smile.

"Hell yeah, I'm scared. Those things can kill you."

"They don't just fall from trees and attack."

Unconsciously, she looked up at the grove of spindly trees that partly hung over them, then looked back at Joe to see if he was laughing at her.

He kissed her.

She saw it coming and she didn't stop him. The last two weeks had been leading up to this.

She let herself kiss him back, then took his hands and took a step back.

"Okay?" he asked, concerned.

She nodded. "I haven't been involved with anyone since my fiancé died."

"No pressure, Kara. Anything worth having is worth waiting for, and you're definitely worth waiting for."

The burning heat of her guilt returned, and she squashed it but it was harder than before. Her whole plan was to get Joe to like her. She was supposed to watch his back, plus make sure he didn't talk about the case—or do anything to jeopardize the FBI investigation—but suddenly she didn't feel so good about that.

You've never felt so shitty about deception before. How many men have you led on in your undercover life? Not just criminals you got close to, but honest, law-abiding citizens you used in order to catch a bad guy? Why do you care what he'll think when you leave? You'll never see him again.

"You're one of a kind, Joe Molina," she said and gave him a quick kiss.

"What was he like?" Joe asked as they packed up the remnants of the picnic.

Mixing lies with some nuggets of truth, she said, "Colton was adventurous. He loved the beach— surfing, swimming, boating, you name it." All true.

"You like the beach?"

"I was more of a jog-along-the-beach kind of girl. I liked going out on a boat and water skiing, things like that. But the one time Colton tried to get me on a surfboard, I nearly drowned us both. He said I didn't want to give up control to the ocean and just ride the waves. I told him the waves were trying to kill me."

Again, true story—though at the time they were both undercover investigating a drug-dealing lifeguard.

Joe kept asking questions, but Kara deflected. "It's early enough to swing by your company picnic," Kara said. "Though I'm stuffed."

"Maybe," Joe said.

"Don't you want to go? I mean, shouldn't you make an appearance?"

"I guess so." He shrugged, didn't look at her. She wondered why he didn't want to go. He initially seemed close to his parents—was that not true? Or did Matt's suspicion that Joe felt guilty about lying to his dad mean he wanted to avoid his family?

"Is everything okay?" she asked. If there was something on his mind, he would tell her. She had a sense he really wanted to tell her something, and if that was the case it would be about the investigation, she was almost positive.

"Things are just complicated at work right now. A lot of things going on," he said vaguely. "And I want to be alone with you."

"How's your mom doing?" Kara changed the subject as she put her backpack over her shoulders. She had to tread carefully about getting romantic with Joe.

"She's doing great. Had a checkup a few weeks ago. They got the cancer—the surgery and chemo knocked it out—but she's still not as strong as she was, and my dad is worried about her. He has high blood pressure. I realized I didn't want him taking on all the responsibility for her and running the business too. Especially everything going on at the refinery…" His voice trailed off.

"Like what?" She wondered what he would tell her.

"This is not what I want to do with my life, but Dad needs me right now. He and Barry can't do it all. Dad's in his sixties, Barry's almost there. I heard my mom and Aunt Helen talk about it."

"Helen?"

"Aunt Helen is my mom's sister. It's how my dad hired Barry as the general manager, when he lost his job in Tucson years ago. I've already saved the company thousands of dollars just by upgrading all the computer and accounting programs, streamlining vendors, cutting some wasteful practices. There's more I can do…"

"I hear a *but*."

"I can easily train someone on the new systems and go back to Phoenix. Find a job—my old boss would hire me back, and I'm a computer programmer, there's a hundred jobs that pay better than what I used to make."

"You're torn. Family versus career."

"The refinery was never where I thought I'd end

up, even though I'm not working on the floor. Anyway, jeez, I'm depressing." He gave her a quick kiss. "I promised you the ghost town, and it's not far. Plus, there's an easier way to get back to the truck."

"As long as there are no snakes." She wasn't joking.

He was right—the ghost town was just on the other side of the hill where they'd had lunch. Joe explained that the abandoned mine up the road had built employee housing. The houses were gone, temporary structures that had been demolished by Mother Nature.

"How long ago?" she asked.

"The mine opened at the turn of the century— last century. Was around until mid-seventies, though not at the scale they worked during World War II, which is one of the reasons Patagonia grew. I don't think anyone has lived here since after the war—moved to town and this place died."

Kara dropped her backpack and took out her camera—she figured that's what a photographer would do—and started taking what she hoped would be artistic shots but feared would be bland pictures that didn't say anything interesting.

While the houses were mostly gone, there was a row of what had once been businesses, and they were still mostly intact.

No windows, no doors, some with sagging walls.

"This was the general store," Joe explained. "And a bar."

"A bar? I can just picture myself working behind a bar in the Wild West."

He laughed. "Not a lot of women were bartenders back then, though I'm sure there were a few."

"More likely I'd have been running prostitutes in the rooms upstairs," she said dryly, and was surprised when Joe almost blushed.

She liked Joe, but clearly he wouldn't appreciate her regular sense of humor. She'd have to scale it back.

"Can we go inside?"

"Just tread carefully," he said.

She walked through what had once been a bar. It was filthy; the wind had blown in tumbleweeds and dirt. She could picture what life might have been seventy, eighty years ago when this place was hopping. Working in the mine all day, drinking at night, stumbling down the road to a small house, sleep a few hours, repeat.

Maybe life hadn't changed all that much, though the conditions had certainly gotten better.

A three-legged table had collapsed in the corner. No alcohol in the bar, but the wall behind it had once held a long mirror—on the bottom left corner a piece was still secured to the wall, only a few inches wide. A bunch of beer bottles had been thrown in the corner, most of them ancient, a few that were recent.

"When I was in high school, we'd come out here and drink beer on the weekends," Joe said. "Explored most of these places. Always cleaned up after ourselves, though."

"Kids these days," Kara teased.

They stepped back outside. The covered walk-way that once ran along the front of all these busi-nesses was mostly gone, and they had to step carefully over rotting boards.

It was sad and beautiful and eerie all rolled up together.

An old church stood at the end of the road, the focal point of the tiny, empty town. It was the only structure in sight with a door still intact—in fact, the whole building looked solid, though paint—once white—was almost completely rubbed off from weather and time. Still, it had an almost wel-coming vibe, like the church in that old show her grandmother used to love… *Little House on the Prairie.*

Kara walked down the road because the struc-ture intrigued her in its solid simplicity.

She took a couple of pictures for show—and, to be honest, she wouldn't mind looking at them later and thinking about the Wild West and what life might have been like. She could see herself as a vigilante, righting wrongs because the local sher-iff couldn't—or wouldn't—do anything.

"I wonder why there isn't some historical pres-ervation program here," she thought out loud.

"There's dozens of these abandoned towns all over the Southwest. Some have been preserved. Some are tourist traps. One that I know of east of here was actually converted into a Wild West ex-perience. You dress up and live like the people in the old West—except there's running water and indoor plumbing."

She laughed. "No outhouses? Not very authentic!"

As soon as she got to the steps, Joe said, "Be careful, this wood is rotted, you could break an ankle."

She almost didn't hear him. There were footprints on the stairs. Small, like those of a petite woman.

Or a child.

They were fresh—dust and wind hadn't faded them. A day? Maybe two? She pointed. "Joe."

"Kids. Like I said, I came here a lot as a teenager too."

He was probably right, but she hadn't seen footprints in the bar or store. Just here. At a church. A sign of peace, a sanctuary. A runaway? A criminal?

She wished she had her gun, but that certainly wouldn't have fit in her undercover persona, so she'd left it behind.

"I want to go inside," she said quietly.

"Just in case, let me go first."

It took all her self-control to let him open the door and step through before her.

The footprints went down the center aisle. A couple of pews faced an empty altar. Most were gone; a few others had been knocked over. A cross hung crooked on the wall—Kara was surprised it was still up. Everything was covered with thick layers of dirt; most of the small square windows that lined each wall were broken, and those remaining were so caked with grime she couldn't see out.

She didn't stay behind Joe; she slipped into position at his side.

Then she saw two sets of footprints, one slightly bigger than the other. The bigger one was about the same size as hers—and the other was at least two sizes smaller.

Yeah, they looked like the footprints of kids, maybe young teens, but she couldn't be certain. A petite woman and a child?

She walked along the right side of the church, even though Joe motioned for her to stop. Her cop instincts were twitching. Someone—a kid—had been here recently. Why? Two teenage lovers having sex in a church?

Kara was generally liberated when it came to sex, and she loved having sex outdoors—one of her past lovers who had a sailboat would take her out, and there was something about being under the great blue sky naked but totally isolated that was incredibly erotic. But she would be squeamish about having sex in a church, even an abandoned church. And she wasn't even religious.

Joe was now behind her. The only three pews still standing were at the front, near the altar. She walked around, then turned to face the pews, half expecting to find a homeless guy sleeping, or a dead body.

A stuffed bunny sat in the corner.

It was filthy but didn't have a layer of dust like everything else. More like a well-hugged and often-dropped stuffed animal. The pew had an impression that someone had slept there—a someone who was between four and five feet tall.

A child.

And the child had been there recently, within the last couple of days. Maybe last night.

Kara looked at the pew next to it, across the aisle, and there, too, was an impression. Also about five feet long, maybe a little bigger. Not any bigger than her—she was five foot four. Also on that pew was an empty water bottle and two candy wrappers.

She itched to collect all of it, but it should be Joe's idea.

"What do you think?" she asked Joe.

He shrugged. "Just some kids. Like I said, I used to come here a lot."

"You don't think the footprints are kind of small for teens?"

"There are a few remote houses up in the hills. I don't know any of the people who live around here. They're few and far between and tend to keep to themselves."

He didn't sound concerned.

"What about runaways?"

"I think I would have heard about that. Small town and all."

"Unless they're not local." She hesitated, then said, "We're only a few miles from the border."

"I could call border patrol, but honestly, a few illegal immigrants aren't a big deal."

"That's not exactly what I meant."

She was thinking something far darker than migrants illegally crossing the border.

"Our property doesn't go that far down, but we've had some problems before when coyotes—not the four-legged variety—cut through our property to the main highway."

"Do you own this land?"

"No, but the hills to the east? That's our western boundary, for the most part."

She couldn't see through the grimy windows, but she took his word for it.

"This is all government land," Joe continued, "except for a few parcels that are privately owned. Years ago we had a problem with a migrant camp on our property. They were being smuggled, lying low, I'm not exactly sure the situation. But they started a fire and we lost hundreds of acres of cactus and trees. It could have been a lot worse. But the biggest problem was drug smugglers. We eventually hired a private security company, and once they began to patrol, we no longer had trouble."

"You still have the security company."

He hesitated, then said, "I suppose so. It's not something I'm generally involved in. We should go."

Kara hadn't heard about a security company patrolling Southwest Copper land, and if Matt knew, he would have told her during their initial briefing before she went undercover.

Kara picked up the bunny. It had once been white and now missed an eye. Cute, in its own sad way.

"If there are two kids, runaways or migrants, it's dangerous for them out here."

"You have a kind heart, Kara."

She didn't laugh. She didn't have a kind heart, far from it. But she knew how children could be abused, and she wanted to find the kids who belonged to the two sets of footprints and learn their story…possibly even help them. If they were runaways, they were in as much danger as if they were immigrants from somewhere south of the border.

She knew that kids didn't cross the border on their own. And contrary to popular belief, families rarely crossed in the middle of nowhere. It was the smugglers who promised jobs or transportation that brought them through rough terrain like here, but there was always a hook. Always something to pay back. Always someone exploiting the weak, the desperate.

She wondered if there were smugglers active here now. If so, would that be something they needed to factor into the open cases they were here investigating?

One of her favorite movies was *Casablanca*. She never forgot the line, "In Casablanca, human life is cheap."

Here, too, human life was cheap. Men, women and children were often sold as they labored to repay a debt they would never be able to escape. Some migrants were sold into the lucrative sex industry. Those lives were more valuable to the criminals because the sex trade generated more money…but in terms of raw numbers, most people who were trafficked were used as laborers on both sides of the border.

Those on this side, because they were here illegally, didn't have much recourse. They were taught to fear anyone in uniform or anyone who might be able to help. They were constantly threatened with the loss of their lives or the lives of their loved ones.

And there were many, many more pressed into forced labor south of the border. Most people didn't make it this far.

It was a fucked system.

Kara didn't play politics—she knew border security was important. Drugs, human trafficking, the whole nine yards. The country had to know who was coming into the country, regulate the traffic some way. At the same time, these people had been sold a bill of goods, while many were escaping conditions far worse than they encountered with the smugglers.

It didn't really matter what the story was behind these kids, if that's who these footprints turned out to belong to. Whether they were runaways or migrants, they needed to be found and taken to a safe place. They couldn't just live out here. No food, no water, the hot summer upon them.

Joe said, "I could talk to Wyatt Coleman about what we can do. He's the marshal. I'm sure you've seen him at the Wrangler. He comes in often."

"I know who he is."

"He'll know who to call."

"That would make me feel better." If these kids

were runaways, their prints would be in the system, provided their parents were looking for them.

"Um, maybe I've watched too many crime shows on television—my fiancé was a sucker for detective shows—but do you think that the marshal would be able to do anything with that water bottle? Like, for DNA or something? I mean, if the kids are runaways, they might be able to trace them, right?"

Joe looked surprised, then nodded. "Maybe. At the art festivals, the sheriff's department always has a booth where they take pictures and prints of kids, put them on a card, in case something happens to them. My mom made me do it every year until I was in high school."

He pulled a napkin from his pocket, left over from their lunch, and picked up the water bottle. "We should go."

CHAPTER 10

Late Saturday morning
South of Patagonia, Arizona

Bianca stared at the light-haired woman walking away from their hiding place. The young girl's bottom lip quivered. "Sh-she t-took B-Bunny."

Her older brother, Angel, put his hand on her shoulder and squeezed tight. She stopped talking, but she couldn't stop the tears from falling.

They'd run as soon as they heard the truck and hid in a dry creek bed behind the row of crumbling houses. They waited and waited for the man and woman to leave. At first Angel thought they were the bad men, and he clutched the gun he had stolen. The gun scared Bianca, but Angel promised her it was just for an emergency.

When the truck finally left, Bianca and Angel went back to the church. Angel looked in the small space behind the altar. There were spiders and bugs in there and probably scorpions, too, so Bianca waited by the pew where she'd slept last night. She stared at the place where she'd left Bunny. They'd run so fast she hadn't had time to go back and get him.

Why did that woman take her bunny? It wasn't worth any money.

Angel came back and handed Bianca a water bottle. They had filled up empty bottles from water at a small pond not too far from here.

"We're missing a bottle," he said. "Drink, and I'll go back and get more water. I still have three left."

"Do we have to leave?" she asked. She didn't know what to do. She'd felt safe here until those people came. But they didn't look like the people who had hurt her and Angel and kept them underground.

"I don't think they'll be back, at least not right away. Tomorrow morning, before sunrise, we'll go."

"Go where, Angel? Where will we go? Can we go home? I want to see Mama."

He stared at her for a long time. "I thought you knew."

She felt tears again.

"Don't cry, Bianca. Please."

"Okay," she said as tears dripped out of her eyes. "Is Mama dead?"

"I don't know."

But he didn't look her in the eye. When Angel didn't look at her, he wasn't being truthful.

"She's dead?" Bianca's voice squeaked.

"Roberto gave Mama money, and I saw her walk away."

"So she's not dead?"

Now her brother looked at her. "Mama sold us."

"She did not! Don't say that!" She clenched her fists and tried to stop the tears. "You're wrong."

"I'm not wrong, Bianca. I'm sorry. We're going to get out of here and disappear, okay? I have a plan. I need you to trust me."

"Take it back, Angel! Take it back about Mama."

"You're not a child anymore, Bianca. I need you to grow up and be strong."

She wanted everything to be back the way it was before her papa died. She wanted her farm and the school she went to with lots of other kids and her house and her chickens.

But it was foolish, Angel would say, to think about the past. Or to think about the future. To Angel, the only thing that mattered was today.

He put his hand on her shoulder. "You want to know where we're going—I don't know. But I can get a job somewhere. I'm a good farmer, Papa always said so. I can make money working on a farm. California has a lot of farms. I know what to say, what to do. They'll hire me. I will take care of you. I have an idea how to get a car, but we have to be very careful. If those men find us, they will hurt us. You understand that, right?"

She nodded.

He handed her a candy bar. He'd taken the candy from the men at the camp, but there weren't many left. She was too scared to be hungry, but she ate it, then finished the water.

"When the sun goes down, I'll refill the water. If you hear anyone, you have to hide. You cannot be caught by the police or anyone else. No one is our friend."

"I'll hide, Angel. I promise."

CHAPTER 11

Late Saturday morning
Patagonia, Arizona

Michael Harris stood at the edge of the company party nursing a beer. The gathering wasn't in full swing yet—it was not even noon—but it was clear that John Molina and his brother-in-law had a great thing going here. The building was a large one-room cabin that Barry's wife, Helen, had taken over with a group of women to set up the buffet. Barry was grilling burgers and dogs while John was fretting over his wife, Clare, who had insisted on coming. She looked like she barely weighed ninety pounds and wore a scarf around her head, but her eyes were vibrant. Michael knew that she'd gone through surgery and chemo and was on the mend, but John was very concerned that she not exert herself.

While Clare sat in a cushioned chair on the covered deck, Michael heard her tell John that she was fine, that she wanted to watch the kids play and talk to people, that the fresh air would do her good.

David Hargrove hadn't shown up yet. Michael woke up at 7:30 to a text message from David.

Hey, Mike, something came up and I'm gonna be late to the picnic. You might want to catch a ride with Barry.

Michael had texted him back immediately.

Need help with anything?

David responded a few minutes later.

No, thanks, see you later.

Michael didn't push for an explanation. While David wasn't here, his wife, Tanya, was in the cabin helping Helen set up the food. Michael asked her about David, and she just waved him off. "Dave's just had to help a friend, no biggie."

Michael had sent Matt a message letting him know that David was a no-show. It might be nothing, but after David veered off instead of going straight home the night before, Michael was suspicious.

He wanted to bail on the picnic himself—the only reason he was here was to keep an eye on David. Instead, he volunteered to help Barry with the burgers because David might eventually show up.

"I can manage," Barry said, "but I'll take the company."

"I didn't eat breakfast because Helen said there would be enough food to feed an army," Michael said. "And she had me tasting her chili at regular intervals half the night. That woman can cook. You are a lucky man."

"I am, I am," Barry concurred. "You ever been married?"

"Naw. After the navy I went through a rough patch. Didn't want to put anyone through my crap."

"John said you were in prison for a spell."

"A year, plus a year probation and anger management. Fighting, so I guess I probably needed the shrink."

Michael really hated lying. He wasn't good at it. Kara had told him to stick as close to the truth as possible, and because he had been in the navy, that was easy to talk about. Prison? Not so much.

"It helped?"

"More or less. I haven't been in trouble again, if that's what you mean. I'm grateful for this job."

"We're glad to have you," Barry said. "I have someone I'd like you to meet."

Michael knew what was coming, but before he could object, his boss continued.

"Helen's niece just arrived," Barry said, gesturing to the far side of the cabin where people were parking. "Her name is Shelley. She lives in Tucson.

Helen and I never had any kids, so we spoil Shelley, especially since her dad died."

"Are you trying to set me up?"

He laughed. "Just saying, talk to her, she would like you. She's a defense lawyer and loves success stories."

Defense lawyer. Michael's cover was good, but it wasn't airtight. If a lawyer started looking in the system at his so-called record, they might get tipped off. Just what he needed.

"Sure," Michael said, noncommittal.

Barry laughed. "Don't sound so enthusiastic about it."

"She's the boss's niece. Just as bad as being the boss's daughter, from my perspective."

Barry waved to a very attractive thirtysomething brunette.

She waved back.

"Shelley?" Michael asked.

"That's her."

Hands off, Michael told himself. He liked women. A lot. Sometimes too much, and Matt had made it clear that Michael was not to get involved with anyone while he was undercover. Not only because it was a distraction, but it could put them both in danger if things went south.

At the same meeting, Kara had said: *And you can't trust anyone, no matter how cute.*

"Shelley," Barry said when she was within earshot. "This is Michael Harris. Our newest mechanic. He's only been here three weeks and already has mastered our systems."

"I don't know about mastered," Michael said.

She smiled and extended her hand. "Shelley Brown. Very nice to meet you, Mr. Michael Harris."

"Michael was in the navy," Barry continued.

"A long while ago," Michael said.

"Michael," Barry said, "why don't you get Shelley a drink? And while you're at it, bring this tray of burgers in to Helen."

"What are you drinking?" he asked Shelley.

"What you're having looks good," she smiled. "Find the coldest one in the ice chest for me, will you?"

She was either friendly or flirting. But it was bad either way, because she was attractive and Michael's type—and by his type, he meant female.

Yep, all women were his type. Which was why he often got in trouble.

He took the burgers inside and went in search of an ice-cold beer for Shelley. When he came back out, Barry and Shelley were talking, heads close together, both with serious expressions. When Barry saw him, he smiled, said something to Shelley, and she turned and waved to him.

Was Michael being paranoid, or had they been talking about him? Maybe Shelley didn't like dating Black guys? Or was telling her uncle that she could find her own dates? Or was it something he really needed to worry about? Did they suspect he wasn't exactly who he purported to be? Or maybe they were just chatting about Southwest Copper business. Shelley was a lawyer...but Barry had said criminal defense lawyer in Tucson. Why would she be also working for the refinery? Wouldn't they want a corporate lawyer who specialized in their type of business?

He'd never been undercover before, but Kara had told him stick to the truth as much as possible, and since he was using his name and military record, if anyone googled him and took the time to search through the hundreds of Michael Harrises in the world, they would know that his younger brother had been killed in a drive-by shooting in Chicago when Michael had been a teen, that his dad was nowhere to be found, that his mom died of a drug overdose. He didn't blame his mom for that. She had worked two jobs because his dad was a dead-beat, but when Jerry was killed—she lost hope. Jerry was the best and the brightest of the Harrises. He would have gone to college, left the city and violence behind. But no matter what Michael did or how he tried to protect his family, his brother got killed. If it weren't for the navy, Michael would be dead too.

He owed everything to the military. The system wasn't perfect, but the navy had saved many people like him over the years. A way out. A step up. And damn if he was going to let his government down now. Not when Matt and the entire task force were depending on him to do this job.

Michael smiled and approached Barry and Shelley and handed her the beer.

She smiled brightly. "Thank you, Mr. Michael

Harris. Uncle Barry says you were in the navy. How fascinating."

He stood there, slightly awkward, but then Shelley started asking questions, basic questions he was comfortable answering. Then he asked about her work, and the conversation turned decidedly better.

Okay, maybe he was getting a hang of this undercover thing.

Be yourself, Kara had told him. *Mostly.*

CHAPTER 12

———

Early Saturday afternoon
Desert south of Patagonia, Arizona

Kara had second thoughts about taking the stuffed animal with her. What if the kids came back? What if Kara and Joe had scared them away when they drove up?

Or maybe they left a few days earlier. Not much longer, she didn't think, or the shoe prints wouldn't be as distinct.

She wanted to go back to investigate, but she couldn't do that with Joe. And she would have to be careful about going back alone because she had a cover to maintain. Still, if she was discovered, she could come up with a reasonable explanation. After all, Joe already thought that she was a softy.

"You're quiet," Joe said.

He was driving slow over the rough unpaved road out of the valley, heading north back toward town. They were bouncing, and Kara's stomach churned. She usually had a stronger constitution, but the heat coupled with the bumps in the road and the beer and food they'd had earlier were making her queasy.

She noticed they hadn't been in this area before.

"You're not lost, are you? We didn't come down this way."

"No, we made a big circle. To give you the full experience of greater Patagonia."

"Oh."

He glanced at her. "Are you worried about whoever was at the church?"

"Maybe." She didn't like not knowing exactly where she was. She had a great sense of direction, she knew Patagonia was almost directly north of them, but out here she wasn't confident she'd be able to find her way back to town with ease.

"You don't know for sure that there were kids staying out there. Let's not assume the worst, okay? I'll talk to Wyatt Coleman."

"Okay, you're right," she said.

Joe was wrong.

Maybe because she'd seen so much darkness in her career—and before her career—she automatically assumed the worst. Maybe he was just saying it to make her feel better, but it didn't. She'd seen kids being forced into labor back in LA. Sweatshops, sex shops, you name it, if there was money in it, she'd seen women and children exploited.

She looked out the window, considered her options.

Michael Harris, for one, had to stay out of this part—this probably had nothing to do with their undercover operation. Emma Perez had been killed in the hills southwest of Patagonia, more than a dozen miles from here as the crow flies.

Or, rather, this *most likely* didn't have anything to do with their case.

Matt shouldn't come down here either—that would be foolish of him. The more Kara thought about it, the more she realized she needed to do this on her own. Just make sure she didn't jeopardize the case, hop down here and look around. Maybe bring Ryder along…except she didn't want to be seen with him.

"Penny for your thoughts?" Joe said.

"Just a penny? What happened to inflation?"

"Did you have fun this morning?"

"I did. Thank you. I need to get out and see more of the beautiful desert that surrounds us. I really didn't realize any of this was here."

"So maybe you'll go out with me again?"

"Maybe I will."

"Well, you'll meet my folks at the picnic, but they'll be busy. Tomorrow is our weekly family dinner. I don't want to be presumptuous, and no pressure, I promise. I just thought you might like to join me?"

It was exactly what Matt wanted her to do, get

a sense of the family dynamic, make sure that Joe wasn't spilling the investigation to his father. But this seemed too easy.

"Can I think about it?"

"Of course."

"And I have to talk to my boss, Greg. Daphne will want to fill in, and I think she should stay off her ankle for another couple of days."

"Like I said, no pressure. I missed last Sunday's family dinner, and my mom will be disappointed if I don't show up again."

"You're close to your mom, aren't you?"

"Yeah. I love my dad, of course, but he and my brother always had more in common. My mom... well, I don't know, she's special. She has so much patience, makes up for my dad."

A family dinner would be better than an intimate dinner with Joe alone, Kara figured.

"My mom was the opposite," Kara said.

"You're not close?"

"Nope, and that is A-OK with me."

The road finally started to improve, from dirt with deep holes and rocks to dirt that had clearly been maintained, packed, and any holes were filled with gravel.

Joe glanced over his left shoulder as he slowed down. "Did you see that?"

At first, Kara didn't see anything. Then something shimmered in the sunlight, disappeared, then shimmered again.

"A truck?"

"Yeah, I think so."

He stopped, then reversed slowly. Kara could see it now—a metallic gold GMC truck, practically camouflaged in the desert. If the sun hadn't reflected off it, they might have missed it.

The terrain was mostly flat, but the mountains rose on either side as they wound toward the road. The gold truck was partly off a narrow dirt road that led up the hill.

"That's a private drive," Joe said. "I don't think anyone lives there full-time. Some people rent out their houses for the art festival. They can make good money."

Seeing the truck here *was* odd. Kara was surprised they'd even spotted it, since it was partly obscured by the curve in the road and trees. Since they crossed the highway that morning, she hadn't seen one other person or vehicle.

She looked down at the stuffed animal on the floor. She had to think like a cop, but she wondered if her suspicion was unfounded. Was she being paranoid? Losing her edge, seeing evil where there was nothing but normal people living out normal lives?

She didn't know shit about being normal.

Joe didn't move. "Wait, I know that truck—I think it belongs to David Hargrove. He works for my dad. What's it doing out here?"

Or maybe she wasn't paranoid; her instincts shifted to high alert.

"Does Hargrove live out here?" She knew that he didn't.

"No. He should be at the picnic, anyway—maybe he loaned his truck to someone."

"We should just make sure he didn't run out of gas or something. Maybe he's hiking back to the road."

Joe said, "If he broke down, he'd call."

He was right; her cell had a signal.

Joe put his truck in Park but didn't turn it off. "Wait here."

She didn't want to wait there, and she really didn't like people telling her what to do. She didn't think she'd come off as a submissive woman, even in her undercover capacity as a grieving bartender, so listening to him and staying back would be out of character. But she couldn't jump down his throat or give him a withering stare.

Instead, she said, "I'd like to come with you." She tried to force a hint of worry in her voice, and maybe she succeeded, because he agreed.

He hesitated, then said, "Of course."

He turned off the ignition and waited for her to get out.

Together, they walked up the slope of the narrow road.

Kara saw Hargrove's body lying behind his truck a moment before Joe did. She unconsciously reached for her weapon, which she almost always carried in a holster in the small of her back, but she wasn't carrying today.

Joe didn't notice her hand movement. He had run over to the body sprawled on the ground.

Kara wanted to tell him to wait, they didn't know

what was going on, but she followed silently, batting away flies as she neared the body.

David Hargrove was clearly dead—apparently from a close-range shotgun blast to the chest.

CHAPTER 13

Saturday afternoon
South of Patagonia, Arizona

While Joe called Marshal Wyatt Coleman and reported finding the body and its location, Kara sent a private message to the entire MRT.

David Hargrove murdered. Attaching photo and location. My unofficial TOD is 6–10 a.m. today. Coleman on his way. More soon.

She also texted Greg Warren, her boss at the Wrangler, that she might be late coming in for work. Just in case Joe asked her what she was doing or who she was talking to.

She didn't share the news with Warren that Hargrove was dead—that would get out soon enough.

The marshal arrived fewer than twenty minutes after Joe called him, and brought with him his two deputies—Tom Porter and Rob Vasquez. Vasquez's brother, Pedro, worked at the refinery and was in the bar last night. He would have known Hargrove. Kara kept that tidbit in the back of her mind. Could mean nothing. Could mean something.

She also kept her mouth shut. Most cops itched to get involved, to take over a crime scene, to find clues and answers and work a case.

Not Kara.

Yes, she loved to be involved, but she relished watching from afar. She didn't have to tell people they were doing things wrong; she enjoyed observing. And considering that she wasn't going to blow her cover over Hargrove's dead body—*especially* over Hargrove's dead body—it was best she didn't say anything.

Joe did most of the talking, anyway. He explained to Coleman that he and Kara had gone on a hike and picnic, then drove out to the nearby ghost town so Kara could take pictures because she was a really talented amateur photographer. It was nice of Joe to say that, considering he hadn't seen any of her prints. She had some to show just in case he asked, but he hadn't been over to her place yet.

"We came in on the west side of the valley, then drove around and were heading back when we saw the truck. I recognized it as belonging to David, thought he might have had a flat tire or something, so we went over. That's when we saw his body."

"Did you touch the body? Anything else?" Coleman asked.

"No. Of course not."

"You touched the back bumper," Kara said. "When you squatted down to see who it was."

"Right," Joe nodded. "I forgot."

Wyatt turned to her. "Do you have anything to add, Kara—I never caught your last name?"

"Smith. And no, I don't have anything to add."

She didn't need to tell him that Hargrove hadn't been dead long—if he had, animals likely would have nibbled on his corpse in the middle of the night. And most assuredly, the body would have been in full rigor.

She knew he left the bar before eight last night, so he *could* have been dead since then, but she doubted it. She knew enough about forensics to figure he'd been dead between four and eight hours. It was two in the afternoon now, which was why she'd texted the team a 6:00 to 10:00 a.m. window. Flies responded quickly to blood, but based on how dry the big red hole in his chest was, Kara was pretty confident in her analysis.

"When was the last time you fired that shotgun of yours, Joe?"

Wyatt motioned to the gun that was on the rack of Joe's pickup when he arrived.

Kara had thought it had been a shotgun when she first saw the body; by Wyatt's question, so did he.

"Months," Joe said. "Last time…well, there was a bobcat at the cabin. I think March? I took my mom for a drive up there one day to air out the place, and a cat was prowling around. I didn't aim to kill it, just scare it."

Wyatt nodded. "Wait here." He then went over to talk to paramedics, who had just arrived in an ambulance. Why hadn't he called in the coroner? Maybe they didn't have a meat wagon; it was a small county.

Kara couldn't hear anything they were saying, not from a lack of trying. The light breeze was going in the other direction.

Joe took her hand. "I'm so sorry about this."

"You didn't kill him," Kara said.

"You seem pretty calm after finding a dead body."

"You want me to break down and weep? Maybe have a fainting spell?" She shook her head. "I'm tougher than that."

"You certainly are."

Meanwhile Matt had messaged her back while she'd been talking to Wyatt and said to call him as soon as she was free to talk.

"I texted Greg," she told Joe, "but he didn't respond. I'm going to try calling him at the bar, make sure he got the message that I might be late."

"Go ahead," Joe said. "I have to call my dad." He walked in the opposite direction.

Wyatt was on the radio, maybe calling in the coroner, since the two paramedics got back in the ambulance and drove off. She strode half a football field away—ostensibly to sit on a rock in the shade—then called Matt. She could keep an eye on the situation while avoiding being heard.

Matt answered immediately.

"You still there?"

"Yes. I'm semiprivate, though. Wyatt Coleman is on scene."

"Did you identify yourself?"

"No. Still playing my part."

"Joe texted me shortly after you sent the first message. He wants to know if he can tell Coleman that Hargrove was the subject of an FBI investigation. I told him no, Coleman already knows, but I don't need Joe putting himself in the middle of this investigation. I'm on my way down there. This is really fucked. Hargrove was our only suspect, and hell if we even have a case without him. He must have a partner, but I don't see why he would be killed. Does Joe look nervous? Worried? Do you think he's going to spill the beans?"

She looked over at him. "Not right now, but he was thrown for a loop when he realized that it was Hargrove who was dead. He saw the truck, went to see if he'd broken down. I don't know—I don't know if he was shocked or surprised or if he expected it."

"Expected it? Why would he expect Hargrove to be dead?"

"Wrong word." Maybe it was, maybe it wasn't; Kara just didn't think Joe's reaction was complete and total surprise. "Maybe…because he knew you were looking at Hargrove…he had a thought that his illegal activities got him killed. His reaction was just a little… I don't know. Off, maybe."

"I need to talk to him eventually, but one-on-

one is always better than on the phone. Keep your eye on him, okay?"

"I have to go to the bar in a couple of hours."

"I'll be there by then."

"Just don't come into the bar. You look like a fucking fed."

"Because I am a fucking fed."

"No offense," she said lightly. Sometimes, Matt was too serious for his own good.

"Do you have any other details?"

"Like I texted you, my guess is he was killed this morning before ten. I didn't examine the body, so it's just a guess. We would have heard the shotgun blast if it was after about ten thirty. No critters got to him, so I doubt it was overnight. He left the bar just before eight last night."

"Michael told me David texted him this morning, at seven thirty, that he would be late to the company picnic."

"You sure it was him sending the message?"

"Do we have reason to believe he's been dead longer?"

"It's in the window," Kara said.

Joe was looking at her. When he saw her look back, he raised his hand to signal her.

"I need to get back to Joe," Kara said into the phone.

"And Joe was with you the whole time."

"Yes. He picked me up at five thirty this morning and hasn't left my sight. I can see him now. He's talking to Deputy Vasquez—whose brother, Pedro, works for Southwest Copper."

"Second murder in the Patagonia area recently. Emma Perez being the first."

"But she was in the mountains northwest of where Hargrove was killed."

"Same general area. Do you realize that only one other person has been killed in the greater Patagonia area in the last *decade*? And that was in a bar fight," Matt said.

Kara thought about the two kids she suspected were staying at the church. "Matt, there's something else I really need to talk to you about, but I can't do it over the phone."

"Related to the case?"

"I don't know. Doubtful. Maybe? But it's important."

"I'll call you when I'm done with Joe and Coleman. I'm going to text Joe now. Let me know if he has an odd reaction—or if he says anything to you that he shouldn't."

"He trusts me."

"He was still told not to talk to anyone about the investigation. If he tells you, he could tell anyone."

"Don't be so sure of that. And I got an invite to his family dinner tomorrow and I didn't even try."

"You're always confident, aren't you?"

Before she could think of a retort, he continued. "Keep your eyes and ears open in the bar tonight."

"What about the two guys Joe was talking to last night? And the stranger who came in later? I gave everything to Ryder."

"We're running prints and photos. Ryder's on

top of it. He'll let you know as soon as he knows something."

"Hargrove drove here in his truck. The land is really dry and dusty. Looks like there were other tire marks, but there's no way to get treads. Coleman seems to have noticed them, however."

"He's a good cop, from what I've learned. I'll talk to him—I'm pretty sure he'll call me as soon as he's able."

"Still keeping me out of it?"

"For now. I'll let you know if I have to tell him."

"Ciao, boss." She hung up, called her *other* boss, Greg, and made sure he got her message. She told him she and Joe were out hiking and they found a dead body. After all, it wasn't like it was a big secret. She didn't say who—she didn't want Hargrove's wife to hear it before Wyatt told her.

Then she walked back to Joe and waited for Marshal Coleman to tell them when they could leave.

Matt was right. Wyatt called him fifteen minutes after Matt got off the phone with Kara.

"Hargrove is dead," Wyatt said.

"What happened?" Matt said, not giving away that he already knew.

"Shotgun to the chest. I'll have to wait for the official report, but it's obvious."

"Where?"

"A private road south of the highway. A few houses around there, but not a lot of traffic. The road isn't even paved. What do you think?"

"Send me your report. But if Hargrove is dead, that means he has a partner."

"Why kill him?"

"I don't know. Maybe I'm looking at this from the wrong angle." He was running through all the possible scenarios he could think of, including Joe Molina taking the law into his own hands. But if Kara's time frame was accurate, and Matt didn't doubt her, then Joe had a solid alibi. "Do you have a time of death?"

"No, but the coroner just arrived. Sometime this morning is my guess."

Which concurred with Kara's analysis. Matt said, "I'm coming down."

"You think that's wise?"

"How did Joe Molina seem to you?"

"What do you mean?"

"He knows Hargrove is the subject of an FBI investigation. Did he act off? Concerned? Worried? The timing of this is suspicious."

"He was concerned about his girlfriend."

"What girlfriend?" Why did Coleman think Kara was Joe's girlfriend?

"Kara Smith, the bartender at the Wrangler. She moved here a few weeks ago. They've been seeing each other. Small town, the gossip mill churns twenty-four seven."

"Why was he concerned?"

"That she was with him when he found the body. She seemed fine to me. Calm, not squeamish. I don't know anything about her, to tell you the truth. I should run her."

"I'll do it, we have the resources. I'll let you know if anything pops."

"Thanks. I'm going to head up to the Molina's cabin. Southwest Copper hosts a company picnic every year. I suspect that's where Tanya Hargrove is—David's wife."

"Don't tell her about our investigation, not until we have more information."

"Okay, but why?"

"Because someone killed Hargrove, and it could very well be anyone at Southwest Copper."

CHAPTER 14

Late Saturday afternoon
Northeast of Patagonia, Arizona

Michael had his not-drinking down to a science. He always had a cold beer in his hand—but he would drink only a couple of sips before he'd pour it out or put it down, then get a new one. Michael couldn't afford to be drunk. He had to keep his wits about him. But he couldn't afford *not* to drink either—there wasn't one man here who didn't drink beer like water, though a couple he would peg as serious alcoholics. If he shunned beer—especially at a party like this—he'd stand out, and that was not what he wanted.

Michael felt he already stood out enough because he was one of only three Black guys who worked at Southwest Copper, and besides himself only one was at the party. That guy was married to a Hispanic woman and they had three young kids, so he was keeping an eye on his progeny near the lake.

John Molina had taken his wife, Clare, home an hour earlier because she was tired. Michael tried to avoid Shelley Brown after their initial conversation. He could tell she was a smart cookie and a lawyer and so he decided he didn't want to be around her any more than necessary in case she picked up on the fact that he was a cop.

This undercover thing was going to be the death of him. He hated it.

By three thirty that afternoon, some of the families with younger kids had left, but the party was still going strong. Half the group was swimming or watching their kids swim. Barry's wife, Helen, led a cleanup crew made up of mostly teenagers. And Michael was roped into playing softball with a bunch of the guys—and Shelley Brown. So all his avoiding her that day didn't amount to squat when she ended up on his team.

Never again.

Michael decided he would never go undercover after this. He was miserable. He didn't know how Kara had done it for twelve years. How she was still doing it. Putting on and taking off different personalities and backgrounds and lies. It was enough to give him an ulcer, and most of his story was true.

Michael, as pitcher, struck out the last batter and his team cheered. They'd won, seven to four, and he clapped Shelley on the back. "That three-run double you got in the last inning saved us."

"You're a pretty good pitcher. You must have played in college."

He froze. He didn't remember what he was supposed to say about his college years. He'd enlisted in the navy when he was eighteen, didn't go to college until he got out…but wasn't there something about college that he was supposed to say if asked?

Instead, he just shook his head.

"Where'd you go to school?" she asked.

He was about to answer Michigan State, and hoped the truth was what he was supposed to say, when Shelley looked over his shoulder and frowned.

He followed her gaze.

The town marshal, Wyatt Coleman, was getting out of his truck. A deputy was behind him. Roberto Vasquez—his brother, Pedro, worked for Barry. Michael had met Rob a couple times at the Wrangler.

That's when Michael noticed that Barry and a few other men were huddled by the cabin looking concerned.

Barry walked over to Wyatt.

What was going on? Was Wyatt going to blow Michael's cover? Why?

That's when he realized he hadn't checked his phone in hours, not since he sent Matt the message that David was a no-show at the picnic. He was trying to think of an excuse to pull out his phone, when Shelley said, "Excuse me, I need to see what's going on." She walked toward her uncle and Wyatt without giving Michael a second look.

He checked his messages.

David Hargrove was dead.

Well, shit. How?

He skimmed over all the messages. Kara had been the one to find his body, with Joe Molina. Shotgun to the chest.

This was not good news.

Matt sent him a private message.

Be alert. Check in often. Watch everyone.

He sent Matt a message back that Marshal Coleman had just arrived, then he pocketed his phone.

One of the guys from the refinery who'd hung out at the Wrangler with them last night, Hank Richardson, approached.

"What's going on?" Michael asked.

"It's David. He's dead."

"What? David Hargrove?"

"Pedro heard it from his brother." Pedro had also been with them last night. Everyone liked him; he'd been at Southwest Copper for more than ten years.

Hank continued. "Pedro said not to say anything because the marshal still needs to tell Tanya. She's inside just having a good time, doesn't know what happened yet."

"How? Car accident?"

"He was killed. I don't know what happened, but it might have been a hunting accident."

"He hunts?"

"No, but he was down in the valley, near Harshaw and the ghost town."

"Ghost town?"

"I forget you're not from around here. Yeah, I don't know why David would be out there. Maybe he was doing something for John or Barry."

"Barry?"

"The Molinas own a lot of property, thousands of acres in the area."

"Really?"

"I don't want to be spreading rumors," Hank said. "I don't know what's going on, but yeah, they own a huge spread south of the highway. But get this—Joe and his hot new girlfriend found the body."

"Girlfriend?"

"The sexy bartender at the Wrangler. Blonde. Cute little figure?"

"Right, I remember."

"They were on a hike, I guess. Found the body. Not really a romantic date." Hank laughed, then suddenly stopped as he realized it wasn't appropriate.

Odd, Michael thought. Not only that Hank knew so much about David's murder, but that he thought the situation itself was humorous.

"What do we do?" Michael asked. "I mean, this really sucks. Poor Tanya. I'm glad she's not alone right now."

As they watched, Barry led Wyatt into the cabin.

The story of David's death spread quickly among everyone outside. Some of what Michael heard was definitely embellished; some was accurate. And then Michael heard something that had him suspicious.

"He was playing with fire."

He turned around to see who said it, but a group of four men from the refinery sat in chairs under a tree. He didn't know who said what, but they all looked worried. Pedro was with them.

What did he know? And if he knew something about why David Hargrove went out to the middle of nowhere, did his brother, Rob, know too? What was out there that was of interest to him? Was he meeting someone? Had someone followed him?

Was that why he'd canceled on Michael this morning?

Kara said that David's body was found near his truck, a few miles from Harshaw and an abandoned mining town. Michael knew from his research that there were a few isolated cabins in the area.

Michael felt trapped. He wanted to go inside and hear what Wyatt was saying to Tanya Hargrove. Except the marshal knew that he was FBI. Did he know he couldn't blow his cover? Michael felt so out of his element he wanted to leave right then. He itched to help with the investigation, but if he acted too interested, people might suspect he wasn't who he said he was. Keeping his cover around all these people was becoming harder. He had questions he needed answers to, but if he asked, he'd sound like a cop.

Fifteen minutes after the marshal went in to talk to Tanya, he walked back out with Shelley Brown.

They made a beeline right for Michael. The others he'd been standing with moved away.

Great, he was being hung out to dry.

Except he wasn't. Wyatt knew the truth, right? And he knew to keep quiet, right?

Shelley approached first. "Michael, Marshal Coleman has a few questions for you, since you were the last one who talked to David today. He called you early this morning, right? Uncle Barry asked me to make sure your rights are protected."

What was this about? Michael's first instinct was to blurt out that he was a fed, but he didn't. *Someone* had killed David Hargrove, and likely it was connected to David's illegal activities. Unfortunately, they had no proof that David was involved with illegal dumping. That's why this cloak-and-dagger bullshit.

Michael could just come out and say he had nothing to hide, so he didn't need a lawyer. But the first thing he ever told a friend who was talking to the cops—even if that person had done nothing wrong—was to get a lawyer. But he was a cop. He *didn't* have anything to worry about. Matt Costa had always had his back in the past; this was no different.

Michael must have looked worried.

"I'm on retainer for Southwest Copper," Shelley said. "I help out from time to time. You don't have to pay me for helping you for five minutes, okay?" She smiled both sweetly and professionally at him.

"Yeah. Okay. Right." He cleared his throat and tried to look appreciative of her help. She thought he was an ex-con. Probably thought he was scared of the cops, or intimidated. Worried.

Shelley motioned for Wyatt. The marshal introduced himself, made no indication that he recognized Michael's name. "I'm trying to nail down the last twenty-four hours of David Hargrove's life, and his wife said he called you at around quarter to eight this morning."

"He texted me."

"You didn't talk?"

"No. He texted that he couldn't pick me up. I asked if he needed my help, he said no. That was it."

The marshal made a note on his pad.

"So you came with the Nelsons?"

"Yeah, Helen had already asked me to help her load up her trunk with supplies. I'm renting the apartment above their garage."

"So you don't know why he canceled on you."

"No, I don't. I asked Tanya when I got here and she said he was helping someone, but didn't say anything else."

"Where'd you and David go last night?" Wyatt asked.

"What?"

"How is this relevant, Wyatt?" Shelley asked.

"They left the Wrangler together."

"We left at the same time, not together," Michael said. "I was back at my apartment around eight— I don't remember the exact time—take or leave ten minutes. Then I went to help Helen Nelson in the kitchen. Probably eight thirty or so. Tanya

Hargrove was there, too, and another woman. Her name slips my mind."

He knew it was Crystal Vasquez, Deputy Rob Vasquez's wife, but he didn't want to appear to have total recall of every detail.

"Did he tell you where he was going when he left the bar?"

"No. Just said he'd pick me up by eleven. That's why he texted me this morning, to tell me he couldn't."

Coleman looked at his notes. "Thank you, Mr. Harris. I think that's it. I might have a few more questions. You and David were friends, right?"

"We worked together, we were friendly. I mean, he wasn't my direct boss. I work for Pedro. But David made me feel welcome from the first day, which was nice, so yeah, I guess we were friends, but I've only been here a few weeks."

All true. But he still felt like he was lying.

"Thank you." Wyatt nodded to the lawyer. "Shelley."

"Wyatt."

He walked away, talked to his deputy, then the two got into the sheriff's car and drove off.

"You did great," Shelley said as they watched the officers leave.

"There was nothing to say." He paused. What would an ex-con say? "I, um, I don't really like talking to cops. They're always trying to jam you up. But I didn't do anything."

Shelley put her hand on his arm and smiled at him, though the smile didn't reach her eyes. Did she doubt him? Did she think he'd been lying? "I know that was hard, but thank you."

Thank you? He pushed that out, because maybe that's what a criminal defense lawyer would say. *Thank you for not causing a scene. Thank you for being normal.*

He didn't know. Instead he asked, "What happened to David? Hank Richardson said he was shot. He mentioned where they found his body, but I don't know that area, so I don't know where it is."

"No one really knows what happened to David. My job is just to protect Uncle Barry and Uncle John."

He frowned. "I thought you were Barry's niece."

"Both. My dad was Gilbert Brown, Aunt Helen and Aunt Clare's brother."

"Oh, I just assumed—sorry."

She laughed. "Family, you know? The Browns were born and raised in Tucson. That's where Barry's from too. But when Clare married John, John offered Barry a job, and the rest, they say, is history. But I'm probably closest with Uncle Barry and Aunt Helen—my dad died my senior year in high school and they really took over when I was at my lowest. Helped me with college, applying for scholarships, then law school, the whole nine yards. Found me a place to live so I didn't have to move down here."

"If you don't mind me asking, what happened to your mom?"

"You've heard of deadbeat dads? Well, I have a deadbeat mom. Haven't seen her since I was ten when my parents divorced, and good riddance." A dark sadness filled Shelley's expression.

A lot of anger there, he thought. Anger he understood.

But he didn't want to have a connection with his woman. He didn't know her, didn't know where she fit into this Patagonia world, and he was one big walking lie.

"Chin up, I'm sure Wyatt will find out what happened to David," Shelley said. "But I feel bad for Tanya." She looked toward the cabin.

But she wasn't actually looking at the cabin. She was focused on two men: the same two strangers he had seen talking to Joe at the Wrangler last night. The short, clean-shaven man strutted like he was in charge; the tall, scruffy man looked even more intimidating. Kara had been suspicious—more suspicious than Michael, but his focus had been on David, not Joe. Michael had read Kara's report this morning, where she also included photos of the two men that she'd taken with her phone.

When had they shown up? Why hadn't Michael noticed them earlier?

"Excuse me," Shelley said and left before he could say a word.

Michael watched Shelley approach the strangers and briefly talk to them, then they turned and left. She went inside the cabin. Two minutes later she walked out with her purse and headed straight for her car.

Michael wished he had driven his own car to

the picnic so he could tail her, but he'd come with Barry and Helen. He was stuck.

Instead he immediately sent Matt an encrypted message.

The two suspicious Hispanic males from the bar last night showed up at the picnic immediately after Coleman left. No one seemed to notice them except Shelley Brown, who is a Tucson defense lawyer and the niece of Helen Nelson and Clare Molina. She talked to them, they left, and then she followed. I'm not in the position to tail them.

Maybe Michael was unduly suspicious, but Shelley's behavior seemed odd. What the hell was going on?

CHAPTER 15

Early Saturday evening
Patagonia, Arizona

Joe Molina dropped Kara off at her house, ostensibly to get ready for work because it was too late to go to the picnic—which was probably shutting down after the news of Hargrove's death. As soon as he drove away, she called Ryder. "I'm coming by."

"Aren't you supposed to be at the bar soon?"

"I called in late. This is important. I'll be over in ten minutes."

She needed Ryder to follow up and see if he could find any evidence of the kids she was sure had recently been hiding in the abandoned church and town. Sooner, rather than later. She didn't know when she'd be able to talk to Matt about this, or if he would even think it was important, since she couldn't make a direct link to David Hargrove's murder or the illegal dumping.

The shock of finding Hargrove's body had distracted Joe, and he had completely forgotten about the water bottle and the bunny, so she discreetly put them in her backpack when she got out of his car at her place. Once she was alone, she put each item in a separate evidence bag, labeled and tagged the two bags. Not exactly an acceptable chain of custody, and she wrote that hers and Joe Molina's prints and DNA may be on the items. But if there were missing kids, she hoped this evidence would help find them. Screw any corporate prosecution—finding endangered kids came first.

Kara jumped into her car—not really her car, but one Ryder had gotten for her. She owned only a motorcycle, and that was still in her garage in Santa Monica.

Ryder was living in a small apartment building on the edge of town within walking distance to most of the downtown area. She parked down the block. It was already after five. She didn't see anyone on the street, but since it was still daylight, she was doubly cautious. She sent Ryder a text message: I'm here.

As soon as he opened his door, she walked inside and closed it behind her. Then she shoved the evidence bags toward him.

He took it, looked inside. "What's this?"

"Before we found Hargrove's body, Joe and I

were at an abandoned mining town southwest of Harshaw. A ghost town, empty for decades—you can do some research and find the history, but it doesn't matter. One of the only buildings remaining was a church. I found this bunny and empty water bottle on church pews where two people had clearly been sleeping. Short someones—both under five feet tall."

"Kids?"

"Yes. My guess? Migrants or runaways. Either way, maybe you can send the evidence up the food chain, see if the prints or DNA matches any known missing children. I want to go back to those buildings tomorrow, before dawn. Quietly, in case they returned and are sleeping."

"Did you talk to Matt about this?"

"I told him I needed to talk to him about something unrelated to the Southwest case. But the more I thought about it, the more I realize he isn't going to have the time to tackle this now. There are two kids who may be in immediate trouble. That's why I need your help to cut through any bureaucratic bullshit. If they're migrants who are being trafficked, I need to be there because other than Matt I'm the only one who speaks Spanish on this team."

That was a bit of an exaggeration. She understood a lot more than she could speak, but she got by.

"We should turn this over to the border patrol," Ryder said.

"Run the prints first, make sure they aren't runaways."

"Probabilities are that they're not."

"They're still in trouble. Just do it, okay, Ryder? Please?"

He gave her a half smile. "I have to run it by Matt first, but I don't think it'll be a problem. Phoenix has an auxiliary forensics lab. They can process the evidence. I can scout the ghost town."

"Alone?"

"I can handle myself."

Kara wanted to go herself…and dammit, she should go. But since it wasn't her primary assignment, maybe Ryder *could* handle it.

Except…she felt somewhat responsible for him. Maybe it was stupid, but Ryder was an analyst. He'd been in the military, but not in combat. He was probably one of the smartest guys she'd ever met… but book smart didn't equal street smart.

"I'm going with you. Early, okay? We'll be back before anyone will miss us."

"You need to talk to Matt," Ryder said. "It has to be his decision, Kara. I know you are used to doing things your own way, but Matt's our boss. I can't investigate something unrelated to Southwest, Emma Perez and now David Hargrove without his permission."

"Then tell Matt this—if he says no, I'll go myself. It's about a thirty-, forty-minute drive, mostly on crappy dirt roads. The car you got me isn't really suited for the terrain."

"So you want me for my truck."

"You have a four-wheel drive. So yes, I prefer you to drive."

"Again, I have to clear this. It's out of my hands."

"I'm going with or without you. So if you aren't coming, I'm taking your truck."

"I'll tell Matt what you said."

"Good. Do that. I have to get to the Wrangler. I'm already late."

Matt met with Wyatt at his house just outside of the Patagonia town limits, not at the small marshal's office downtown. While Wyatt was confident that his deputy Roberto Vasquez and Rob's brother, Pedro, who worked at the refinery, were both solid, he understood the need to keep this investigation quiet for now.

Wyatt offered Matt a beer, which he declined. "I have work to do. Joe has been leaving me messages and I'm going over there after this."

"I've put in a request for David Hargrove's phone records. According to his wife, Tanya, he told her that he was helping out a friend and would be at the picnic around noon."

"Was she worried when he didn't show?"

"She said she wasn't, she was too busy to notice."

"You believe her?"

"I have no reason not to, but my gut told me she was more concerned than she let on. She also claimed she didn't know who he was helping or what he was doing. Most of their friends are local, and most of them were at the picnic."

"She knows more than she is saying."

Wyatt nodded. "My impression. But I need more information before I go back and talk to her."

"I'd like to join you."

"Absolutely. She might be more forthcoming with a federal agent in the room than someone she thinks of as a friend. Her best friend is my deputy's wife. Crystal Vasquez."

"Is that a problem?"

"Nope. Crystal is as straitlaced as they come. Both her and Rob are good people."

"Is Michael's cover still good?"

"I didn't expose him, questioned him as part of my job—he was the last person known to have talked to David. Well, they exchanged text messages. Seven forty-five, which is in line with Tanya's statement that he left the house around eight. But no one saw or spoke to him after he sent the message to Michael. Coroner won't give me a TOD yet but says after seven a.m. Based on that, the time the body was found, and witness statements, I'm figuring he was killed between eight and ten this morning."

"Is there anything near where his body was found? Houses? Businesses?"

"Not much. A few houses up the road, but they're vacant or abandoned. There's a rental or two, but when I went up there this afternoon, no one was around and no sign of recent traffic."

"Why was he out there?" Matt mused out loud. "To meet someone? And why so far out?"

"It's only ten minutes south of the highway, so not too remote, to be honest. People like to go out shooting down there because there's no people around, but it's not far from town."

"You're not suggesting it was an accident."

"Nope. No accident. My guess is the killer stood not more than five feet from David."

"What about his truck?"

This was when Matt would have liked to have his forensics expert, Jim Esteban, there—Jim could have processed the truck himself.

"Clean as a whistle. Two things, however. His phone is missing, and he had a receipt in his wallet from a gas station in Tucson from 11:12 p.m. last night."

"Send me a copy, would you?"

Wyatt nodded. "You think he was killed because of the illegal dumping?"

"Yes. I'm just trying to figure out why. Everything was finally coming together. We have my white-collar guy going through records, we have the truck returning on Monday, we have a warrant to track it—and now this." Matt looked Wyatt in the eye. He didn't want to ask the question, but he had to. "Did you tell anyone about my investigation? Even casually, accidentally, someone you trust?"

"No, I haven't said a word. As far as my deputies are concerned, you came down here solely because of Emma Perez's murder. No one questioned it."

Matt believed him, but the information still could have gotten out somehow. Wyatt drove to the FBI headquarters on Thursday; maybe someone involved made an assumption.

Or, more likely, Joe Molina let something slip. He'd been jumpy and paranoid and worried about his family.

"I'm going to talk to Joe."

"You don't think he had anything to do with this? I know he was antsy about the investigation, but I've known him for a long time. I don't see killer."

Neither did Matt, but that didn't mean if pushed Joe wasn't capable of murder. "You said he had an alibi."

"Pretty solid, I'd say, unless his girlfriend is in on it, which is extremely doubtful."

Matt considered telling Wyatt about Kara, but decided to keep it to himself, at least for now. "Let me know if you learn anything else," Matt said. "And when you want to talk to Tanya."

"I'm going to wait until I have more information before going over there. Like I said, something she said told me she wasn't being completely up front. As soon as I can catch her in a lie, I'll be talking to her. And I'm happy to have you join me."

Ryder had left a message for Matt, so he called him as soon as he left Wyatt's house.

He listened as Ryder told him Kara's plan to go back to the abandoned town and search for two kids she thought were in trouble.

It took him a minute to process the information. Why would she risk blowing her cover over this?

"I can't let her do that," Matt said. "I'll talk to you about this tonight, then find a way to talk to

Kara." She would have a fit, but he had to convince
her this wasn't a smart idea. "Whatever you do, do
not let her go out alone."

"Yes, sir."

"What."

"What?" Ryder said.

"That tone."

"I don't have a tone."

"You think she's going to do it with or without
you."

"Yes, I do."

"Fuck. I'll deal with it."

He ended the call. He didn't want Kara to go off
on her own fool's errand. A couple of runaways?
Migrants? What did that have to do with anything?
They were in the middle of a major investigation
and he needed her focused, because something
weird was going on when their primary suspect
in getting kickbacks for illegal dumping ended up
dead.

Matt didn't want to be seen meeting with Joe
Molina, especially in Patagonia, but Joe had left
him several messages and didn't want to talk on
the phone, so Matt arranged to go to Joe's house. It
was risky—Joe lived near his parents, in a separate
house they owned. The last thing Matt wanted to
do was to expose Joe. He didn't know what David
Hargrove's death would mean to the larger investigation, but they still hadn't found the backers of
A-Line Waste Disposal and Trucking, and *someone* had killed David. The timing, the manner, the

location…it told Matt that whoever killed David had set him up. A partner, most likely, but *why*?

Matt feared that Joe had let some details of the investigation spill. Matt had never believed that David was working alone; he didn't have the background to manage something of this magnitude. But without getting David to flip, would they be able to find the people behind A-Line? Would they still collect the slag on Monday? Or had they killed David and then conveniently dissolved the company?

Without the people behind A-Line, they would never be able to prove or disprove that hazardous slag had been illegally dumped. They probably wouldn't be able to find the dump site and clean it up and prevent further contamination and wildlife deaths.

And without David and the people at A-Line, they might never know who killed Emma Perez—and why.

Matt waited until after sunset before heading to Joe's.

Joe was clearly agitated when he let Matt into his house.

"What does this mean?" he asked. "David is dead. He was murdered. Why?"

"Marshal Coleman and I are working together on this, but he's the face of the investigation, not me."

"You didn't answer my question. *Why?* You were investigating David for the contract with A-Line, and now David is dead. You think they're still going to come here Monday? I doubt it."

Matt had his doubts too.

"Why would they kill him?" Joe continued.

"Have you talked to anyone about my investigation into A-Line, or Hargrove or the Perez murder?"

"Of course not."

"Because I can't think of any reason why he would be killed either—unless someone was suspicious that he was being watched by the FBI."

"Maybe he double-crossed his partner," Joe suggested. "Maybe you should have been looking at A-Line instead of David."

"I can assure you, Joe, we're looking at every aspect of this investigation."

"He's dead now. So now you have to go after the trucking company."

Matt said calmly, "We still don't know if Hargrove was acting alone at Southwest. And we don't know where A-Line dumped the slag. We have a warrant to track the next shipment. If that changes, you need to tell me immediately."

"I don't know if I want to be involved anymore," Joe said. "David was killed, Agent Costa. Shot point-blank. Who would do that over a few bucks?"

"This was more than a few bucks." Clearly, Joe didn't know the history of graft and corruption and murder in the waste industry.

"But with David dead, you have nothing. Nothing," Joe said.

"That's not exactly true—"

"Really?" Joe seemed surprised.

"You knew from when we first talked, Joe, that

this might be an uphill battle. But I think it would be best that you step away. I've got this from here."

"You're cutting me out?"

Honestly, Matt didn't trust Joe anymore. He didn't think he was involved with the illegal dumping—he had no motive and there was nothing in his financials to suggest that he was involved in kickbacks. But Joe was clearly on edge, worried about his father, the business, and Matt couldn't discount that he might have said something about the investigation, which could have tipped off David or his unknown partner.

Plus, the two suspicious men in the bar had Matt wondering if Joe had, in fact, done something to put an end to David's duplicity. Matt had Ryder send the glasses directly to Quantico for analysis, put a rush on it, but they wouldn't have the information until Monday afternoon at the earliest. That situation was odd and Matt wanted to ask Joe about it but he couldn't risk Michael's or Kara's cover.

"Let me do my job, Joe. I'm good at it. Watch yourself, okay?"

"How long?" He sounded defeated.

"I don't know. You've done the right thing here, even though it's been difficult."

"It doesn't feel like it, Agent Costa. I feel like shit."

He looked ill.

Matt had to give him something. "Give this another full week. With Hargrove dead, we have another avenue of investigation—his murder. Something must have happened in the last few days that put him at risk, and I'll find it. If *anything* happens, Joe, at the refinery or in town, anything that is out of the ordinary, you need to tell me."

"Just close this case as soon as possible, Agent Costa, okay? I hate lying to my dad, it's eating me up."

"I'm doing my best."

As soon as Matt got settled in the Patagonia motel that Ryder had reserved for him, he checked all his messages. It was late and he was just now eating a sandwich.

Zack was on his way back from Vegas.

I have a lot of information, but didn't have time to put it together before they kicked me out of the office. I'll call you tomorrow.

Fine with Matt; there was nothing he could do on a Saturday night.

Kara hadn't yet sent him a report on her day with Joe or finding the body, and even though he had talked to her, he needed the report in writing. He sent her a message reminding her of such, then added, Do not go to the abandoned town without talking to me first.

It was a direct order, he hoped she realized. He wanted to talk to her face-to-face about it, but she was working and had made it clear she didn't want him showing up at the Wrangler.

Matt put together a timeline of what he knew

so far, but this whole case wasn't making a lot of sense to him.

There was money in illegal dumping, but usually only for the people cutting corners. If he believed that John Molina was in fact innocent, that meant that David Hargrove was conspiring against the owner for profit. Having Molina pay A-Line top dollar, then splitting the money with whoever ran A-Line. Over a year and with multiple clients, it could be a tidy sum, but according to the records Joe Molina had provided early on, A-Line had retrieved only three slag shipments—in February, March, and April. This shipment would be the fourth.

Truthfully, though, for a man like Hargrove, maybe fifty thousand dollars, take or leave, was enough incentive to turn on his boss. But for a company like A-Line, in theory it made no sense—unless they were doing this on a far broader scale. Because they were so new, the FBI hadn't been able to uncover records as to who they hauled. But if he could find something solid here, they would be able to get a warrant for all their records.

They needed the driver. On Monday, Matt was going to make a judgment call based on what happened. He was skeptical that the waste disposal company would show up at all, now that Hargrove was dead. But if they did, they would track the truck and then arrest the driver, compel him to turn state's evidence. To do that, Matt needed something more—something to use as leverage. He hoped Zack had found that piece of information.

Matt stared at the chart he created. Emma Perez murdered, likely because she had learned something related to the illegal dumping. That was all she was researching at that point in time. David Hargrove murdered, likely by a partner or rival.

What about Joe Molina?

Kara was Joe's alibi. Molina couldn't have killed Hargrove. But that didn't mean that Joe hadn't talked to someone, let it slip that Hargrove was stealing from his father's company, or that he was profiting off his contracts, or maybe even more bluntly telling someone that the FBI was looking at him for illegal dumping.

Would John Molina kill him? Out of anger? What about Barry Nelson, his brother-in-law? They would have motive—to protect the company. Or revenge.

Possibly, but Matt put that farther down on the list. It took a cold-blooded killer to pump a 10-gauge into a man's chest.

Yet David must have known his killer. He faced his killer. He didn't try to run. Preliminarily, there were no defensive wounds. His truck was at the scene. Had he driven someone up there? Or had someone followed him? Had he planned to meet someone? Why there, at that spot?

Matt was missing something.

What didn't he see?

Kara opened the back door as soon as she heard Michael walk up the stairs. He entered; she closed the door behind him.

"You shouldn't be here," she said.

"I know."

Michael stared at her in the dim light. She had kept only the stove light on, not wanting to advertise that someone was coming in through her back door. First Ryder, now Michael.

Something was wrong, and her colleague Michael had come to her—not to Ryder, not to Matt. Necessity or convenience? She wasn't used to working with a team. A partner...sometimes. A team? Rarely.

She liked Michael. They'd had a disagreement on the last case, but she liked and respected him. And he was clearly struggling with something. He had a poker face...but his dark eyes were tortured. Maybe that was an exaggeration. Maybe not.

"Beer? Whiskey? Tequila?"

"You've been here two weeks and have a stocked bar?"

"Two and a half weeks," she corrected with a sly smile. "Only the essentials."

"Beer."

She grabbed two from the refrigerator and motioned for Michael to follow her to the living room. Again, she kept only one light on. The blinds were closed. No one could see them...but if someone was spying on her, they might be able to get close enough to hear through the window.

Right. Your neighbor Javi is going to sneak up on your porch, squat his sixty-nine-year-old body under your window and eavesdrop on your conversations.

Still, she motioned for Michael to sit where, *if* anyone tried to peer through the cracks in the blinds, they would least likely see him. She sat in the chair that gave her the best view of both the kitchen—and therefore the rear door—and the front door.

Michael sipped his beer. Kara drained half of hers. It had been a long day.

"You're tired," he said.

"Yep."

"I shouldn't have come."

"Woulda, shoulda. Talk to me."

Michael was silent. She waited. She had nothing else to do except sleep.

"What was your first undercover case?" he finally asked. "Matt said you went undercover right out of the academy."

"I looked young, I had the right attitude, I scored high on the right tests. First job was undercover in a high school to bust a drug-dealing teacher. Prick. Dealt in everything, including Ecstasy, not caring that a shitload of his female students were dosed and raped. Honestly, I wish I still looked eighteen and could do that all over again. It was wholly satisfying."

"How long did it take?"

"Ten weeks. Not only did I have to nail the teacher, I had to get his supplier and his dealers. It was a big network." She sipped her beer, looked at Michael. He wasn't looking at her. He was looking beyond her.

Michael had the whole duty-and-honor thing

going on, and it wasn't an act, she realized. She hadn't *thought* it was an act when they worked that first case, the Triple Killer, together, but she didn't know him well at the time, and they butted heads over some procedural bullshit. Yet she'd liked him from the beginning. He'd been a navy SEAL, one of the best and the brightest or whatever the line was from the commercials. Was that the Marines? Either way, he was a badass. More, his belief in his duty to his country…and now to the FBI…was powerful.

And that's what this was about, she realized. That sense of duty was being challenged. How can you lie to the man you are supposed to be working for— namely, John Molina and Southwest Copper—when you considered yourself loyal and honorable? Even though he was lying and playing the part for his *actual job*, the role was incompatible with how he viewed himself.

Which is why he came to her. Because she lied easily.

Had he realized it was why he was here? She didn't know. She wasn't going to make it easy for him…that wouldn't be fair to Michael. If she told him he was doing the right thing, he would agree, say that wasn't why he was here, try to minimize his confusion. Then he'd be in danger. If she told him to suck it up and deal with it, he'd shut down and question everything he did and said. Then he'd also be in danger. If anyone figured out he wasn't who he said he was, their investigation would be blown—especially if David Hargrove wasn't working alone.

One innocent person was already dead. Emma Perez must have found something—even if she didn't know what it was—that led to her murder. It was the only logical explanation, and the primary reason the FBI was working this case quietly.

Two people. Two people were dead if she counted David Hargrove, and there was no reason to believe he was killed for any reason other than the illegal activities he was involved with.

She drained her beer, put down the bottle.

"Why'd you enlist in the navy?" she asked.

He looked at her, confused. "Why?"

She shrugged, waited for him to talk, which he eventually did.

"It was my way out. I grew up in Chicago, a crap-hole neighborhood. Dad left, Mom worked two jobs, got addicted to painkillers after slipping and falling at her restaurant gig." He paused. "That's not completely true. She did fall, but the painkillers were because my little brother, Jerry, was killed in a drive-by. Trying to numb the pain in her heart. He was playing basketball right across the street from where we lived, gunned down. No fucking reason for it." He paused again, looked at the half-empty bottle in his hand but didn't drink. "The shooters had a reason—Jerry's best friend disrespected the gang leader. It was a lesson. Jerry was the only one who died that day, but every kid on that court playing with him? They're all dead. Every one of them. Either because they joined the gang…or they didn't. I was in a dark place…between Jerry's death and my ma's addiction…the navy saved my life. I'm not ashamed to say so."

"Of course you're not. You shouldn't be." Why would he think she'd think less of him? "If I wasn't a cop, I'd be a criminal. It's the only thing I'm good at."

He looked at her oddly, then smiled. Michael was a handsome guy. Helped that he had the muscles and build of a navy SEAL, broad and lean. "You're a pretty good bartender."

"Yes, I am," she agreed. "But I couldn't do it forever."

"Why?"

"Because it's not me. It's a part I'm playing. The way I talk to customers, what I say and don't say, how I dress—okay, I would probably dress in jeans and a T-shirt most of the time."

"You seem natural."

"Good. I'm doing it right."

He didn't say anything else, but she wasn't sure she'd actually helped him with his struggle. So she said, "I read your report to Matt. About Shelley Brown. She went off with the two guys that met with Joe in the bar."

"I didn't say that."

"You said they showed up at the picnic after Coleman and his deputy left, stood around the fringes for like three minutes and then disappeared…five minutes later Shelley left."

"I didn't see her go off with them."

"But you're a cop, Michael, and you think she did, right?"

"Yes. This could be all on the up-and-up. They could be vendors, like Joe Molina told you."

"Sure. Then why go uninvited to a party and walk off with a lawyer. Lawyer—you said criminal defense, right?"

"Correct."

Now it was Kara's turn to do some heavy thinking.

Michael continued. "She was there as part of the family, not because she's a lawyer."

"Niece, right?"

"Yes. Her dad died, and he was brother to Helen and Clare. It seems that she, Barry and Helen are very close."

Kara assumed that Matt was looking into the lawyer. The whole thing was looking much...*fishier*.

"I don't know how much good I've done," Michael said. "I haven't learned anything that you haven't been able to learn through Joe Molina. All I've done is spy on everyone who works there."

"It's information. It's all important. If you weren't at the picnic yesterday, we wouldn't know that Shelley Brown may be meeting with the two strangers who met with Joe yesterday at the bar. It could be that they were working with Hargrove, or it could be that this crime is a bigger conspiracy. Maybe there's more to it than toxic dumping. Whatever we're dealing with, having you on the inside helps."

"I feel like shit, Kara."

"I could tell you that guilt is a useless emotion, that it's not going to help you do your job, but you know that and it's not going to change how you feel."

"I almost blew it today. I forgot what I was supposed to say about college. I felt like a deer caught in the headlights. Barry even tried to set me up with Shelley—at least that's what it felt like. And I had to be interested but not interested and it was just *wrong*. I don't know how to explain it. I like these people. Most of the guys in the refinery are hard workers. They don't make big bucks, but it's good, honest labor. They have a lot of respect for John Molina and his brother-in-law. They have families and mortgages and I honestly can't say that there's one person I don't like, even David, and I know he could be a killer." He paused. "I don't see it. Some people you can look in the eye and just know they can't kill."

Kara was listening, but she was far more interested in the hookup. "Did it seem odd to you that Barry tried to set you up with his niece?"

"Why, 'cause I'm Black?"

"No, because you're a felon. At least they think so. If I had a sister, I wouldn't care if she was dating you or Ryder or Matt, but I would care if she was dating an ex-con."

"I didn't think of it like that."

"So you and Shelley talked a lot."

"Not about anything serious. We played softball, talked a lot about baseball. That was easy—

I'm from Chicago, I love my Cubs, I didn't have to pretend."

"Lying is the last resort. It's the little things that will always trip you up."

"But this whole thing is a lie!"

"Tell me the truth." Kara waited until Michael looked her in the eye. "Did you blow your cover?"

He opened his mouth to object, then closed it. "I don't know. I didn't say anything to blow it, and when Wyatt interviewed me about Hargrove, he didn't say anything to blow it—Shelley was right there. She seemed to want to protect my rights. It seemed…natural, I guess. I think…it's just that every time I'm with these people, I can't help but think I'm lying to them. That I'm not here just because I need a job. When they find out, they're going to hate me."

She leaned forward. "Okay. I just need to know that you're safe. If you're not, if you think Shelley suspects anything—whether or not she's involved in any of this toxic dumping—you have to walk away."

"That I can't do. I'm the only one in the position to put the tracker on the A-Line truck Monday."

"And you won't be doing that if you're dead."

"I don't think I gave myself away. Not as an FBI agent, at any rate."

"Okay. So I'll tell you the truth. They will hate you when this is over. Just so you know. They will feel betrayed. It doesn't matter if John Molina is as innocent as a newborn and you helped save his company from ruin. He will not like you.

Barry Nelson will tell you to get out of the apartment and never come back. Helen might cry. Joe will be angry—at you and at Matt because Matt didn't tell him about the undercover operation. Matt should never have told him about the investigation in the first place, but that wasn't my call. But think of it this way—Emma Perez is dead. She was killed most probably because she was snooping around into Southwest Copper—or at least asking the wrong questions after she found all those dead birds. What we're doing is trying to find out who is involved in the toxic-waste dumping, where they're dumping—to save wildlife and potentially a more serious contamination—and to find out who killed Emma Perez. She deserves justice. And that's how I do it."

"What? What do you mean?"

"You didn't ask me how I handle working undercover. You talked around it, you talked about your own shortcomings, but ultimately, the reason you came here is you want to know how I can lie to people as a matter of course. How I can walk into a bar owned by good people like Greg and Daphne and pretend I'm someone I'm not. How I can walk away when this is over without guilt or regret. It's because of Emma Perez, and people like her. Getting justice, catching bad guys, making sure they never kill another innocent person or sell another dose of Ecstasy to a pervert or dump toxic slag in the middle of the desert. The teacher I caught my first case? He'd been dealing for *seven years*. Think about that. All the young people he exploited and hurt. That's who I think about when I start feeling guilty."

"Thank you." Michael put his unfinished beer down. "I probably shouldn't have come by."

"You probably shouldn't do it again because I have nosy neighbors, but if you need me, I'm here for you."

Michael got up and walked to the kitchen. Kara followed. At the back door he turned and said, "I'm glad you're part of the team, Kara. I had some reservations at first—maybe I still do—but I'm glad you're here."

He left. He had reservations? Hell, *she* had reservations. But she also didn't have a whole lot of options.

She waited until Michael left her yard, then poured herself a double shot of tequila. Sleep would be a long time coming tonight.

CHAPTER 16

———

Sunday morning
South of Patagonia, Arizona

Kara sent Ryder a message at 4:50 a.m. Sunday morning that she would meet him outside by his truck in ten minutes, then she walked over to his apartment. She saw a figure sitting in the driver's seat and rolled her eyes. She should be the one driving—she knew where they were going. Instead, she opened the passenger door.

It was Matt behind the wheel.

"Did you actually think that I'd let you go to an abandoned town only a few miles from where my primary suspect was shot and killed? And before you comment, I wouldn't let *any* of my agents go alone into an unknown situation."

"Good to see you, too, Matt. Now, can you please drive before someone sees the Wrangler bartender with a federal agent?"

He backed out of the drive.

"At least you lost the suit," she muttered.

Kara had never seen Matt in jeans before. She'd seen him in a shirt and tie, and she'd seen him naked. But casual? Never. She kind of liked it. A little rougher around the edges, and a whole lot sexier than a suit.

"Ryder filled me in on the abandoned church and the items you found there. What makes you so certain they were kids and that they would be returning?"

"I'm not. But I've dealt with runaways before, and I've dealt with human trafficking, and two kids sleeping in the middle of nowhere? That says trafficking."

"Or migrants."

"Possibility. But they had to get there somehow, and no matter what kind of propaganda the politicians put out, two kids don't just walk across the border alone without help. That help usually comes with a whole tangle of strings."

"We're here to investigate the murder of a college activist that we believe is connected to illegal waste disposal," Matt said.

"I didn't ask you to come with me."

"You asked Ryder. I told you not to go out there alone."

"And I'm not. You're here."

Matt didn't say anything for a minute. She directed him to the highway, then to the exit that led to the abandoned camp. "Wasn't Hargrove's body found off this road?" he asked.

"Yep, we'll pass the spot. I'll point it out."

"Do you trust Joe Molina?"

"I don't trust anyone, you know that."

"You know that's not what I meant."

"I have no reason to be suspicious of him, but he doesn't want to be here."

"I read your report last night."

Before Michael stopped by last night, Kara finally had the time to write a lengthy report about her day with Joe, including finding evidence of the kids, finding Hargrove's body and her assessment of Joe, his motivation for staying in Patagonia and desire to leave.

He wants to be the good son, the one that helps, not the one who left the country and never visits. But he feels like he's in his brother's shadow, and that informs his choices.

She didn't know what to make of it—she wasn't a shrink—but she had begun to see Joe as far needier than she had at the beginning.

"What did Zack find out in Vegas about A-Line?"

"He's still putting together information—he had to leave before he could finish his analysis, but he talked his way into the recorder opening up the office to him Saturday afternoon, so he has everything he needs. I'm hoping what he finds will give me evidence that Tanya Hargrove is somehow

involved, so Wyatt and I can compel her to talk."
He glanced over at her. "Nice change of subject."

"What?"

"If anyone found you out here, how would you
explain it?"

"Tell the truth. When Joe and I went to the ghost
town, we found evidence of two kids living in the
abandoned church. I couldn't sleep, wanted to go
back, see if I could help them. I have the whole
story worked out."

He snorted. "And that would work with Joe?"
He actually sounded skeptical.

"Good deeds and all that. Joe thinks I have a
bleeding heart."

She glanced at him. He looked sexier than she
remembered. But that part of their relationship was
over, no matter how compatible they were in the
sack. Not because they were working together—
she didn't have a problem sleeping with a fellow
cop if they both needed to blow off steam—but because Matt was too damn noble and old-fashioned.
He wouldn't do well as a friend with benefits, and
she in no way wanted an actual relationship. When
they parted ways after their last case, they'd left
things open—if they had time off at the same time,
maybe they'd get together, have fun. Then she was
offered this job on Matt's mobile response team.
That changed everything.

She continued to give Matt directions, then
asked, "Do we have IDs yet on those two guys
from the bar? Their very presence raises my an-

tenna. I read Michael's report, they showed up at the picnic."

"We're running the IDs now. We overnighted the bar glasses to Quantico, but realistically we probably won't hear until sometime tomorrow, possibly even Tuesday morning. I put a rush on it and Tony backed me."

"So, when are we going to get the fabulous Esteban RV lab you've been talking about? That would have come in handy about now."

"As soon as Jim is done with the trial he's involved in."

Jim Esteban was the former head of the Dallas Crime Lab and a sworn deputy. He would be joining Matt's team and running on-site forensics out of a new mobile lab.

Kara worked with Jim on the last mobilization and liked the older cop. He was down-to-earth with a Detective Columbo vibe. But he wasn't with them this time because he had to testify on a complex trial from before he joined the team. "The mobile lab is complete, but Jim needs to sign off and make sure it's stocked and ready to go."

"It would help us run prints faster, and it would be totally sweet to bypass all the other cases that your lab has to process."

"For some things, it'll be functional. But it has its limitations. Jim did a terrific job last time working with that lab in Spokane. I'm guessing he could build that kind of relationship wherever we go."

"And Shelley Brown? What do you think about the lawyer niece?"

"No record, completely off the radar, but I asked Christine Jimenez in the Tucson office to quietly dig around. Brown is a local criminal defense lawyer, but I don't know what kind of clients she takes. For all I know she helps rich kids beat DUI raps. For what it's worth, Christine had never heard of her before, so she likely doesn't take anything high profile, and probably nothing federal."

"Slow down here, Matt. I need to make sure we don't miss the turn."

"I don't know how we're going to find this place. It's still dark out here."

"It's almost dawn. Look—you can see a sliver of light to the east."

"Never figured you for an optimist."

She smiled and said, "I saved the maps to my phone in case we lost reception. Slow. Slow…stop."

"We're here?"

"No, this is the spot where David Hargrove was killed. I thought you might want to see it."

He looked at her. "See *what* when it's dark?"

"Boy, you're grumpy. We could check out those two houses at the top of the hill."

"I don't have a warrant."

"I didn't mean break in."

"We're here to look for the kids, Kara. I can't overstep, not just because of the warrant issue. Wyatt Coleman and I are working this case together, and I'm not going to shut him out."

"You didn't tell him I'm undercover?"

"No, I wouldn't do that without letting you know. He knows everything except your involvement."

"And you trust him."

"Yes. He's kept the information to himself. He's a good cop. Now, where am I going?"

She looked at her phone. "The road is all dirt, and it's going to get bumpy. But we stay on this path—it's going to curve a bit west. Then when we hit Harshaw—there's a sign, if we don't miss it—we keep going straight. Joe says only a few people live out this far, and we didn't see anyone when we came through yesterday. About a half mile after we pass the sign, we turn left. The road gets worse. It goes between two hills. Would be a great location to ambush someone if we were still in the Wild West."

"It would be great today to ambush a couple of cops."

"And then as soon as we get through there, the road goes to the right and a hundred yards or so is the entrance to the old town."

She shared a bit of the local history she'd gleaned from Joe and had absorbed from researching online on her phone. It was slow at the bar last night. Maybe news of Hargrove's murder kept people home, or maybe they were all tired from a day of drinking at the picnic. But she hadn't seen *anyone* from the refinery.

"About ten more minutes until you turn," Kara said a few minutes later.

"Did you read my memo about my conversation with Michael?" Matt said.

"Yes, of course I did. What specifically?"

"According to Michael, the rumor among Southwest staff is that the two men Joe met with—and claimed were vendors—work for the new mine, east of Patagonia. We looked into the company when we first started investigating and there were no red flags, but until I have IDs on the men, I can't confirm anything."

"They didn't look like miners," Kara said. "I'll see if I can learn more tonight at Joe's family dinner. Especially since we know Shelley the lawyer is friendly with them."

"It was clear last night when I talked to Joe that he wants out, so I cut him loose. Told him we had what we needed from him." Matt paused, then said, "Maybe he thought killing Hargrove would put an end to this."

"Do you actually think that Joe Molina is capable of murder?"

"I think anyone is capable of murder in the right circumstances."

She didn't say anything because she agreed with Matt on the latter point, but she knew Joe hadn't killed Hargrove. "I was with Joe from five thirty in the morning until he dropped me off at my place at four."

Matt half grinned. "You're a pretty good alibi, then, I suppose. I didn't think he pulled the trigger, but I can't figure out *why* David Hargrove was killed. And hiring someone to kill him would be easier for a man like Joe Molina than pulling the trigger himself."

Kara agreed. "Still, more likely he was whacked

for double-crossing his partner, whoever that is. Stealing. Maybe he wanted to renege on the deal. Any number of things." Kara gestured. "Turn here."

"I would have missed it."

"That's why I told you."

"And Joe took you out here to take pictures?" He was skeptical.

"And to have sex in the old saloon."

He stiffened but didn't say anything.

"Shit, Matt, I'm kidding."

She almost said *What would it matter if we had?* but decided not to push it. Matt could be uptight and surprisingly traditional about some things.

He was looking up at the rocks on either side of them. "I'm surprised they built a town out here at all. This canyon is ripe for flash flooding."

"When we get around this bend, veer slightly left. The road is not really a road, but it's a steady incline up."

"The landscape is interesting out here."

"Rocks. Mountains. Cactus, which are kind of cool. But there's snakes, too, I've been told."

"Lots of snakes. Tarantulas and scorpions too."

She unconsciously shivered and he laughed. "Screw you."

"I don't think I've seen you scared before."

"I don't like crawly, slithery things that bite, sting or otherwise look creepy. Or those things." She pointed to a few large black birds.

They drove out of the canyon and the valley widened. To the east were all cacti and rocks. The sun crept up on the horizon, marred by giant birds.

"Those are vultures," Kara said as they got closer and she'd spotted them circling. "They're disgusting."

"They're nature's garbage disposal. Pretty damn cool when you think about it."

"There's three of them. Must be having breakfast. Shit, now I'm hungry."

"I'd take you out to brunch when we're done, but I wouldn't want to blow your cover."

She rolled her eyes.

"Seriously, Kara, you've done a good job. Michael says your advice has helped him tremendously."

"I know."

"Confident too."

She smiled. "Always. And you don't need to give me a pat on the back to keep me happy. I know when I do well, and I know when I fuck up. I don't fuck up often."

They drove east, then curved back southwest, then finally saw the old ghost town in front of them.

It was sadly beautiful. The sun had lightened the sky, but the whole town was cast in the shadows of a steep hill. To the west, the rock face high behind the church reflected the colorful sunrise. It was quite spectacular, Kara thought. Maybe she should get out here more often.

Except for the snakes and scorpions and vultures.

"They may be kids, but they may also be dangerous," Matt said. "We don't know what we'll find."

She didn't acknowledge the obvious.

This time, she'd brought her gun. She kept it holstered, but she wasn't going out in the middle of the desert unprepared again. She might have to find a way to carry even around Joe. She never carried a purse, not to mention that pulling a gun from a purse was problematic. She didn't like gun fanny packs, but they were generally reliable. She'd ask Ryder about finding her one. Or she could wear an ankle holster. But they could be spotted by someone with sharp eyes or who knew what they were looking for.

They parked, then they cleared the old saloon, which—other than the church—was the only structure solid enough that someone might be hiding inside. It was empty.

They looked around carefully as they approached the church. Something was different... and then she realized. "There's been traffic here since yesterday," she said quietly, gesturing to the ground. The sandy dirt had tire tracks, clear signs that multiple vehicles—jeeps and trucks, by the type of wide tires—had driven here.

"The tracks weren't here yesterday?"

"No. We parked on the other side of the saloon, at the edge of the town. These are definitely new."

"How far from the crime scene?"

"Three miles... Joe said teenagers sometimes come out here to party, but I don't see any beer bottles. And there were multiple vehicles here since yesterday afternoon—at least two."

Matt squatted, inspected the tire treads. "Three, my guess. Could be four."

There could be a logical—and legal—reason for the trucks to be out here, but considering this place was in the middle of nowhere, and the kids were possibly on the run and a homicide took place only a few miles away—Kara was suspicious.

As they approached the church door, Kara put her hand on Matt's arm and stopped him. "This feels...wrong."

He looked at her, waited.

"The door—it was intact when I was here. Someone kicked it in." She gestured to the splintered wood. "The stairs were cracked before. Now they're destroyed."

She and Joe had walked up the side of the stairs where there was more support, but now all the planks were cracked or broken, as if someone had charged up the front without care. "Someone was here looking for the kids."

He opened his mouth, closed it. She knew he was going to say she didn't know that, and maybe she didn't, but her gut told her those kids were on the run and people were searching for them.

Instead, he nodded, motioned that he was going first and for her to cover him. He had his gun out; she did the same. His gun had a light on the top, which he flicked on as he entered the dark church through the broken door.

Yesterday there were missing and broken pews, but the three that had been intact were now upended. A door in the back had been ripped off its hinges, as if someone had been violently searching.

They quickly cleared the church; no one was there.

Kara told Matt about the destruction. There were boot prints everywhere.

"They were looking for someone," Kara said.

"How certain are you that these were kids who were hiding out yesterday?"

"Eighty percent," she admitted. "One shoe print was my size, one smaller. Could have been petite adults, but the stuffed bunny...there was at least one child."

"I have a friend in border patrol. I'll call him. He'd have an idea who we might be dealing with in this area."

Kara stared at the crooked cross still hanging above the upended altar. She wasn't religious. She didn't believe or disbelieve. Religion had simply never been a part of her life. But many people, especially children, found peace in a church. Had they been chased away? Taken? There was no blood here, but there was violence. Anger. Tossing aside the last of the standing pews. Breaking the door. This church had been here for decades—since before World War II, she had read last night when she couldn't sleep. It had withstood time and neglect. But it couldn't withstand violence against children.

"Kara," Matt said softly. "We need to go."

"The vultures."

She turned to him.

"Don't go there," Matt said.

"Don't tell me you haven't thought the same thing! Runaways are treated harshly, Matt. You and I both know that. You may not have worked a trafficking case before, but I have. I know what coyotes will do to the troublemakers. They set examples. We have to check it out, just to make sure it's an animal and not...not a kid."

Matt put a hand on Kara's shoulder, just held it there a minute. It was surprisingly calming, and she felt herself lose a bit of the tension that had built up since she saw the broken door.

"Let's go check it out," he said.

They walked back to the truck, then Matt took several minutes to study a map of the area before deciding on a route that would bring them to the general vicinity where they had seen the vultures.

They weren't circling anymore. They'd found their breakfast. Kara felt sick to her stomach.

Matt said, "I'm not sure we're going the right way."

"They were on the other side of that giant flat rock."

"You mean the plateau." He glanced at her and smiled. "But giant flat rock works too."

She rolled her neck, feeling the tension building up and the fear of what they would find. She appreciated that Matt was calm and trying to keep it light, but usually when she suspected the worst, the worst happened.

"It's probably an animal," he said.

She knew he was placating her, but that was okay. She drank half her water bottle. It didn't do anything to calm her stomach.

"Maybe," she said carefully, still forming her

thoughts, "Hargrove stumbled upon the traffickers. Maybe they shot and killed him and his murder has nothing to do with the illegal dumping and A-Line Waste."

"I've considered that his murder isn't related, but it's too coincidental. We're closing in, we have the warrant to track the next shipment and now our only identifiable suspect is dead."

He was right.

Matt drank some water and added, "Zack Heller says he has something. He's working through hundreds of pages of documents. Without Hargrove, I don't see A-Line coming tomorrow, and that means we won't find the dump site. Or Emma Perez's killer. So yes—I think Hargrove's murder was connected to his illegal activities, and maybe there's a lot more to this mess than kickbacks from an unethical waste disposal company."

"I trust your instincts on this." She paused, glanced at him. "And I appreciate that you trust mine."

"Your methods might drive me crazy, Kara, but I can't argue with your results."

She grinned. "Now you sound like my former boss, Lex."

He said, "Are you adjusting okay? The FBI is a world different from LAPD."

He was clearly trying to distract her from thinking about the two missing kids. Talking about her old life wasn't any better. "I'm fine."

"You haven't talked about what's been happening with your case in LA."

She didn't want to talk about her case, so she kept her mouth shut. Besides, if Matt really wanted to know, he knew who to call.

"I want you to know," Matt continued, "Tony is serious about looking into the actions of the LA FBI office. He has a lot of pull with the regional offices."

"Good," she managed to squeak out, but she wasn't holding her breath.

"I talked to Lex last week."

She didn't want to hear about it. She knew exactly what was going on, and talking about it wouldn't make anything better. But Matt wouldn't shut up.

"He said things have died down, but the hit on you is still active. They're working on tracking Detective Fox's killer—they know who it is, they just have to find him."

She knew that. She had been all up in Lex's face for updates—as much as she could get over the phone. She always got more in person, but going to LA right now wasn't an option.

"They find the killer," Matt continued, "they can get Chen."

"My case was fucked by *your* LA counterpart," she said. Now that she opened her mouth, it wouldn't close. "They blew my cover, they got Colton killed, and they screwed up my case against one of the most violent and notorious sweatshop owners in my lifetime. Chen was handed a fucking *get out of jail free* card! So, sorry if I don't give a shit about finding Colton's killer when he would still be *alive* if that FBI asshole in Los Angeles hadn't outed Colton and me to the press. I should have been there, not on leave in Washington for a bullshit reason. I could have protected him!"

"Kara—I know you don't want to hear this, but you would have been killed too."

"You don't know that!"

She was still so very angry—angry was an understatement. Angry and frustrated and deeply sad.

"I'm just saying, if you need to talk—I'm here."

"Isn't that what we're doing? *Talking?*"

She looked out the side window, effectively turning her back to Matt. She didn't want to talk about it because there was nothing left to say. None of this was Matt's fault, but she still had a hard time thinking about what happened in March without getting angry. Matt didn't hail from the LA office, he hadn't blown her case and he didn't out her identity. He'd given her an opportunity to still be a cop when that had been abruptly taken away from her two months ago. The task force wasn't what she wanted to do with her life—she wanted to be an LA cop until she was dead. That was all she'd wanted for the last twelve years, from the day she walked into the LA Police Academy and felt like she'd found a home.

You're still a cop. Hold on to that.

She had to grasp at it, even if nothing was as she'd planned. There was nothing else she could do with her life. She didn't even know who she was if she didn't have a badge and gun.

And she didn't want to find out.

Matt looked over at Kara, concerned. She was angry, but she was also still shaken by what had happened on her last case in Los Angeles. He knew the whole story—she'd told him some, but not all. One of the first things he did when Tony brought Kara onto the task force was read every page of her last case, then he flew to LA to talk to her former boss, Sergeant Alexander Popovich. The threat to Kara was real; if the FBI didn't bring her onto the task force, either she would be with protection 24-7 or she'd have to leave LA and watch her own back.

Kara cut corners, burned bridges and put herself at great risk in every case she'd ever worked. She also saved lives and closed some of the most complex and difficult cases that LAPD had undertaken. Tony had read her entire file, and Matt planned to, but this undercover investigation in Arizona had moved quickly. What he *had* read had both intrigued and irritated him, and he hoped bringing her onto the task force wasn't a mistake.

Not because Kara was incapable—she was more than capable. But because she was used to working alone. Matt didn't know how she would work as part of a team, which is why he was a stickler for her following protocol, sending him daily reports, and asked Ryder to keep an eye on her.

He trusted Kara's instincts—she'd proven herself the first time they met, working a case together in Washington while Kara was on vacation—which is why he had come out to this ghost town with her. If she thought there was something odd going on at the abandoned church, there was something odd going on—and she'd been right. But she could also be reckless, and there was no doubt that she would have come out here on her own. He couldn't have that. He didn't want to reprimand her or write her up, and he would have to if she violated a serious protocol such as disobeying his direct order not to investigate alone. He wouldn't have been able to look the other way, which is the reason he came out with Kara this morning.

Matt had been in the FBI for sixteen years. He'd graduated from college with a degree in criminal justice and a minor in sociology. He had planned to be a cop in his hometown of Miami. He'd grown up in a rough neighborhood, but his dad was career military and had instilled in Matt and his older brother, Dante, a strong sense of law, order, and tradition. His dad had been born in Cuba, but he was the most patriotic American that Matt had ever met. He never took his citizenship for granted.

An FBI recruiter on campus his senior year approached him, and the rest, they say, is history.

Matt took his job seriously, all the rules that went with it, even those he didn't like. He moved up in the ranks quickly. Landed in the Miami office after Quantico, which had been his number one choice—his brother was his only living family. But a few years later a position came up in Phoenix, and that—combined with some office politics Matt had difficulty threading—had him moving west. A year later he was promoted to SSA and sent to run the Tucson Resident Agency. He did that for five years before he transferred to national headquarters to work on special projects for then newly promoted Assistant Director Tony Greer.

Matt had traveled all over the world with an evidence response team that specialized in war crimes. He served as head of the FBI recruitment and interview panel for a year; and then one night over drinks at Tony's place, they had come up with the concept of a mobile response team. While it was predominantly Tony's vision, Matt helped him develop a practical plan.

Matt wanted this to work, but he was also cognizant of the fact that he and Kara hadn't talked about having slept together. He had thought he'd never see her again...even though he'd wanted to. They'd left it open, but he sensed that she'd be fine if they had a hot couple of nights and went back to their normal lives. Now that they were working together, it was awkward...yet Kara didn't act as if anything had happened. She acted exactly the same, just as he remembered her from the Triple Killer case. Not only had she walked seamlessly into the undercover role, but she helped train Michael, who'd never worked undercover in his life.

"Stop," she said.

He had been focusing on the narrow, rutted path and hoping not to bottom out. He slowed down and she again said, "Stop!"

He did. At first he didn't see what Kara saw. Her focus was on a group of pine trees and low-lying bushes. Everything was surprisingly green here—maybe because of the wet spring, or perhaps a seasonal stream ran through here.

Then he saw a rope. Something that didn't fit.

And then he saw the vultures.

There were five of them picking at a carcass—not an animal carcass, a human.

Kara was already out of the truck, gun drawn, shouting at the vultures.

"Shit!" He jumped out and followed her.

This was the kind of reckless behavior he couldn't allow.

The vultures flew a few feet away but weren't scared of people. Matt and Kara reached the body at the same time.

It wasn't a kid.

Thank God.

The deceased was a Hispanic male in his thirties. At least that was Matt's educated guess—his body was half-gone. If Matt walked away, the vultures would finish the job. It would take only a few hours for the body to be picked down to the bone. Based on the smell of decomp, the corpse was at least a day old. Vultures were attracted to the chemicals in a decaying body, but they wouldn't eat anything that was too ripe, from what Matt remembered in his forensic class. He'd definitely need to call in an expert.

This was another reason why having Jim Esteban here would have been a big help. He wanted his own forensics expert so he didn't have to rely on outside agencies. He didn't know exactly where they were—the abandoned church was county land. Private property dotted the area, and Southwest Copper owned substantial acreage both east and south of Patagonia. He'd need to ask Wyatt who owned this spot and who would have jurisdiction.

Kara was pale at the discovery of the body, but she didn't puke. She looked around the area; he did the same. There had been a campfire. She reached down and held her hand over the wood. "No heat," she said. She broke the charred wood apart with a stick and it crumbled, no sign of embers.

She then walked over to the rope. It was narrow twine with a plastic coating. "There's blood," she said. She gestured to several spots on the rope. "These were used to tie a victim's wrists together to keep them in line, like slaves. I've seen this once before."

"In LA?"

"No."

She didn't elaborate.

"You don't know—" Matt began.

She shot him a look that had him shutting his mouth. She was right. The scene had all the signs of human trafficking. The dead guy could have tried to escape, been killed, left to rot. In days, all evidence would be gone, his bones scattered.

Kara walked away from the empty campfire and squatted next to recently disturbed earth. "Matt, I think this is a grave."

"I have to call Wyatt, find out who has jurisdiction and get a forensics team down here. If this is federal land, I'll have the FBI take over. Don't touch anything else—if there are bodies buried here, they'll bring in dogs and we'll recover them properly."

The nearest FBI evidence response team was in Phoenix, and it would take them hours to get here once he made the call. Border patrol could secure the site until they arrived. If this really was a human trafficking route—and not an isolated incident—then the FBI and border patrol would have jurisdiction.

This was unexpected. And he didn't need this while also trying to find the toxic dump site and David Hargrove's killer. Or were they all connected? If so, how?

He saw movement out of the corner of his eye and glanced back at the dead body.

¡Malditos buitres!

He ran toward the vultures, flapping his arms, and this time they flew farther off—a good thirty yards from the body. But they were watching Matt, and he knew they would be back on the body as soon as he left.

He pulled out his phone to see if he could get a signal. Only one bar, and it went in and out. Shit.

He looked around. He could climb up the nearby hill to call in the crime scene. But he didn't want to leave Kara here alone—in case someone came back. Someone had to stay to keep the vultures from the body. He would call Ryder to come out here and pick up Kara, in order to protect her cover. He didn't know how this crime they'd just stumbled upon fit into the puzzle they had been investigating, but it fit somewhere.

He walked halfway up the cliff and got two

bars. He started typing a message to Ryder when he heard Kara scream.

Matt turned around, gun drawn, and ran down the slope toward where Kara had been inspecting the soil.

Just in time to see her fall into the earth and disappear.

CHAPTER 17

Southeast of Patagonia, Arizona

Almost immediately, Kara knew that she hadn't found a grave—it was too big.

Could it be a mass grave?

She'd never come across a mass grave anywhere before, but she'd seen pictures of enormous pits barely covered with dirt and rocks. The cruelty and inhumanity that went into such a slaughter. The earth was definitely disturbed here, as if someone had dug a wide hole and filled it in.

Maybe someone had buried supplies here. Smugglers often did that—drugs, guns—in an easily identifiable place. Here, in the grove of trees on the east side of a mountain that was relatively easy to get to, close to the border and only a few miles from a highway…yeah, this was that kind of place.

She rose from her squat and was about to step backward when the ground creaked.

She froze. The ground didn't *creak*. This sounded metallic. Weapons? Something larger, like a vehicle? Why would anyone bury a car?

You know why. Remember that gangbanger who had buried his rival alive? Drove his sports car into a hole and had his gang fill it with dirt and sand.

The shit she had seen over the twelve years she'd been a cop. There could be a body here; she needed to tell Matt.

She rose and the ground definitely creaked, as if it were metal. She felt the dirt shift beneath her.

She was about to call out for Matt when the ground gave away completely with a loud *crunch*. She rolled down a metal ramp, frantically trying to grasp onto something to stop her fall. Her arm hit the edge of something hard and sharp—a door?— and pain burned through her. She'd been stabbed before; this felt nearly as bad. She screamed from surprise and shock, then hit the bottom. The floor beneath her was dirt and metal. She couldn't see anything, but a stench of urine and feces and vomit assaulted her senses and she gagged.

She pulled her cell phone from her pocket and turned on the light. Blood dripped down her arm, but she ignored it. The cut hurt, it felt deep, but she had to make sure she was alone before she dealt with her injury, confirm that there was no other threat.

At first she saw nothing, then the shape of the room became clear.

She was in a shipping container—the kind put on trains or ships or the back of semitrucks. She'd fallen through a makeshift door—and may very well have buried herself alive.

Matt's out there. He'll find you.

If he doesn't fall down the hole, as well.

The plus was that she could see a glimmer of light—the door had been pulled up to camouflage the hole...or to lock people in. But she could probably crawl out as long as the earth didn't cave in further.

"Kara!" Matt yelled from the surface.

"Down here! I'm okay. Watch your step. I think I can get out on my own."

She was about to try to crawl out when she heard a breath.

A whimper, really.

Her heart nearly stopped beating.

She shined her light again around the container, this time slowly. The container was eight feet wide and very long, thirty to forty feet, she guessed. Eight or nine feet high. Buried underground.

And another person was here.

No chairs. No blankets. Some empty water bottles. Some with dark liquid in them. A stained mattress in the middle. A pile of shit in the corner. Spiders that scurried from the light. Some clothing. Stained, dirty dresses. Jeans. A lone doll in the middle of the room.

And a child in the corner. A girl.

She turned from the light as if Kara had thrown acid at her, burrowing her head into the filthy wall.

Matt was calling down to her, but Kara couldn't hear what he was saying.

"My name is Kara," she said to the girl.

Kara knew better than to rush over to the child. Even young kids could have a weapon, lash out from fear or pain.

Silence.

"Mi nombre es Kara," she repeated in Spanish.

Still no response.

"No te lastimaré. Puedo ayudar." Kara understood Spanish a lot better than she could speak it, and she wasn't quite sure her message of wanting to help was getting through to the child.

Kara turned her light away from the girl, quickly took in the rest of the room—no one else was there.

Someone had left a child alone, buried in this big tin can underground. For how long?

She couldn't tell her she was with the police. Migrant children were often brainwashed into believing that all police were bad, that they would hurt them or lock them up. They often had experience supporting that belief from their home countries. The smugglers would say or do anything to instill fear into those they moved across the border.

Kara reached into her pocket and pulled out the granola bar she'd taken from Matt's glove compartment.

"¿Tienes hambre?"

Was she making herself clear?

"Here," she said. *"Toma esto. Su alimento."*

Please take the food.

The girl whimpered. Maybe she was too weak, too sick.

"Dammit, Kara! Talk to me or I'm coming down!" Matt shouted.

Kara made her way back to the opening. She crawled halfway up so she could see Matt.

"Give me your hand," he said. "Dammit, you're bleeding."

"I'm fine," she said. "There's a girl down here. About seven or eight years old. She's terrified and possibly injured."

"She's alive?"

"I'm trying to talk to her, but I don't know if she understands me. My Spanish isn't as good as yours. But I don't think having a man come down here and grab her is going to help. I'm going to bring her up."

"Be careful, K. You know how this can go south."

"I'll search her if I can."

"I think I can use the rope to pull open the door, so you can get out easier. Just make it fast."

Kara turned back to the girl. Again, she didn't shine the light directly at her, but near her, so that Kara could at least see enough.

"I want to help you," she said quietly. She'd rescued teenage prostitutes many times before, and half of them had fought her initially. She'd once saved a toddler from his abusive mother, but he didn't know what was going on. He'd been terrified, clung to her for hours until a doctor was able to convince him to let go. She'd been a rookie. The mother had the young boy dangling out the window upside down as punishment. Kara had never been so angry in her life as when she saw that.

But she was getting close right now.

"What's your name?" she asked. *"¿Tu nombre? Yo soy Kara. Usted está...?"*

A whimper. But different.

"¿Qué?"

"Amada," the girl said faintly.

Kara could barely hear her scratchy voice. But she understood her.

"Amada, I want to get you out of here."

How did she say that in Spanish? The girl might not even speak Spanish, or might speak a different dialect.

Kara felt so out of her element.

"¿Déjalo aqui?"

Did that mean to leave? Shit, shit, shit! Kara didn't know.

"Kara!" Matt called, his voice sounding muffled. "I'm going to pull the door up, and that'll give you enough room to get out. But I don't know if I can secure it, so you need to come now."

Kara turned to the girl. "Amada," she said, "now. *Tenemos que irnos.*"

The girl whimpered again but turned toward Kara. *"No puedo."*

"Are you hurt? *El daño?*" Did that mean hurt? She thought so.

The girl nodded.

"Kara!" Matt called.

She saw the metal door slowly rise, and she heard Matt grunting with exertion.

"I'm going to carry you," Kara said. "*Llevar. Transporto.* You, me. *Bueno?*"

She didn't wait for Amada to answer. She walked over and picked her up. She weighed next to nothing. Kara felt bones under her skin and she wanted to cry. She squeezed back the tears. Now she just wanted to hit something. Hard.

Then she slowly climbed up the steep ramp. Matt was pulling on the rope that he'd tied to a handle on the metal door. As soon as Kara was clear, he let it go and the heavy door dropped into the hole, bent, the damage caused by her weight when she had fallen through.

The young girl turned her face into Kara's chest, away from the sun. Kara carried her over to the truck and laid her on the back seat. "She needs a doctor," Kara told Matt.

"So do you."

She looked at the cut on her arm. "No."

"You need stitches."

"And have to explain this?"

"Your health is more important than this operation."

"Ryder was in the army. He can do it."

"You're damn stubborn."

"I'm up-to-date on my tetanus shot, and I don't care about another scar. And it's not as bad as it looks. We have to get the girl to a hospital, and we need to protect that body from the vultures," Kara said.

"Stay here. I got a signal earlier when I was halfway up that slope." He gestured to a hill behind them. "See if you can get some water in her. I'm going to have them bring in a LifeLine chopper. She doesn't look good."

Matt left, and Kara turned to Amada. She looked awful. Her skin was sunk in, her hair was tangled and she was filthy.

Kara opened a fresh water bottle. "Amada, can you drink this?"

The girl didn't even move her head to look at Kara.

"You need water. Just a little water. *Agua*."

Amada was still.

"Amada?" Kara slowly reached out. She didn't want to scare the girl. "Amada, I can help you sit up so you can drink." She put her hand on her arm.

Amada still didn't move.

"Honey? *El trago.* Drink. *Por favor, el trago.*"

And Kara knew. Even before she put her fingers on Amada's skinny neck, she knew the girl was dead.

CHAPTER 18

Sunday morning
Southwest of Patagonia, Arizona

Angel told Bianca to stay hidden while he checked the house. The sun was already up; they were no longer hidden by the night.

Bianca obeyed her brother and leaned against a big rock and made herself as small as possible. But there weren't many places to hide here on the top of the mountain. They had been walking all night, mostly uphill through the cactus and shrubs, ever since the bad men came to the church. Angel wasn't there at the time; he'd been getting more water, but Bianca had done exactly what he said: hide low to the ground behind one of the broken houses. She did. She didn't scream when she saw a giant spider only feet from her face. She didn't scream when she felt something crawl up her leg. And she didn't scream when she heard the bad men breaking things in the church.

Maybe fear made her silent. But mostly, she didn't want to let Angel down. She didn't want to be taken back to the box underground, and she didn't want to die.

It was hours before Angel came back. Hours and hours, but it was still dark. She stayed behind the house, as small as possible. She might have slept. He called for her, but she didn't answer because she didn't know if it was a trick, if the bad men had made him call to her.

He called out again, this time with their secret word, to tell her everything was okay. She tried to get up, but every muscle in her body was sore and cramped. She answered this time, and he ran to her, hugged her. Gave her water, and nothing had ever tasted so good, even though it had dirt in it. He helped her get her muscles working again.

"I thought… I thought they found you," she said.

"I went back to the metal box. I wanted to know what the men were doing. They tied up everyone and took them in trucks under cover of darkness. I don't know where they're going."

"They were here," she said.

"Looking for us. It's not safe. We can't stay."

"I'm scared, Angel."

"Today, we will hide in a house. I found one, it's empty and safe. No one lives there now. I promise, we'll be safe. But we can't use the roads, and we have to go quickly before the sun comes up."

"What if they know about the house too? What if they find us?"

"Bianca, trust me. I can keep watch. We will hear anyone who is coming up, and there are many ways to get out. We stay there today, sleep, eat, then walk at night."

She had to trust her brother because she had no one else. He'd come back for her. He'd gotten her out of the dirty, smelly box buried in the ground. He promised her they would find a way to free themselves from these bad men.

Even if they couldn't go home.

So she waited behind the rock as the sun came up. Angel finally came back for her, took her hand. "There is a bed and there is food. Today, this is our sanctuary."

She followed him. The house was big. There were three rooms! There was even a bathroom and a kitchen and lots of closets. There was dust all over and coverings on the couches and beds, and the windows had closed shutters on the outside, but other than that it was clean. It was like someone had wrapped up everything inside like a present and left. Why would they do that?

Angel said, "There is no power here, but there are cans of food. We can eat it cold. There are jugs I can use to collect the water from the pond so I only have to go one more time. We need to eat, drink, sleep. Then we can go."

They ate cold soup from a can. It tasted weird

but not bad, and they each ate a whole can. They drank water—it tasted much better than the water from the pond. Angel cleaned everything up. "If anyone comes here, I don't want them to see that we were here. You can have the bed. I found a blanket. Just lie on the plastic. I'm going to stay on the couch so I can hear if someone is coming."

Bianca wasn't feeling well, but she thought it may be because she had eaten a whole bunch of food and she'd eaten hardly anything for days and days. Even before they ran away, the bad men gave them only two small meals a day. Bread and water in the morning, and then at night, soup or a sandwich. Once one of the men had brought in small wrapped packages and said they were hamburgers. They all had one and there were a couple left over, so they split them. They were the best thing Bianca had ever eaten. She decided that hamburgers were her very favorite food.

She lay down and fell asleep.

CHAPTER 19

_____

Sunday morning
Southeast of Patagonia, Arizona

Sending Kara away from the crime scene before emergency services arrived was definitely going against protocol, because not only was she a witness, but her prints were going to be all over the scene. She was protected under the court-approved undercover plan, however, so Matt had to make a judgment call. He had Ryder bring his satellite phone when he came to pick up Kara, which he used to give a brief report to their boss back in DC, Tony Greer, and receive approval for his plan. Then Ryder took Kara back to Patagonia before any authorities arrived.

The land was in the county, under the auspices

of Santa Cruz County Sheriff's Department, but because the crime involved a child who was clearly trafficked from south of the border, Tony agreed that jurisdiction would fall to the FBI and border patrol. That cut out all the middle men. Matt's contact in border patrol was already on his way, and he was now waiting for the Phoenix FBI office to send down their evidence response team.

Kara didn't want to talk about the child, and Matt didn't make her. He had her write the facts— what she did in the bunker when she found her, what she said to the child, what she saw. When he read it, the summary was devoid of emotion, just the facts—a perfect police report. But her act of writing had vehemence, and twice she'd ripped the paper with the pen.

For nearly an hour, they took turns watching the truck that held Amada's body while the other walked the area, made sure there were no other bunkers, dead bodies—suspects or victims—and kept the vultures away from the remains of John Doe. Ryder made record time getting to the site and took Kara back to town. Not long after they left, border patrol arrived.

Matt had hesitated to bring in border patrol simply because he didn't want more people involved, but ultimately, if this was a trafficking ring, border patrol would know more about it than anyone. Peter Carillo was a longtime border patrol agent, now second in command. Matt had worked with him during the five years he was in the Tucson office, where they'd served together on a joint task force for years. Peter was one of the smartest, most dedicated agents Matt had worked with, and because this was a sensitive situation, Matt had asked that he come alone.

"Thank you for coming out here," Matt said. "I know I was vague on the phone, but I needed someone I can trust before you bring in a team."

"I'm intrigued, and if it was anyone else, I probably wouldn't have jumped through hoops. You said there's a body."

"Two. That guy over there—I covered him with a tarp because the vultures had already started on his remains—and a young girl."

Matt led Peter to the truck where he'd covered Amada's body with a blanket. Peter put on gloves and pulled back the covering to inspect the young girl's hair, eyes, skin, clothing. Then he closed her eyes and appeared to pray before putting the blanket back over Amada's body.

"My guess is that she's from southern Mexico or northern Guatemala," Peter said. "That's based on her general appearance and the fact that you said she seemed to understand basic Spanish. The coroner will be able to confirm, and if they bring in a specialist, we'll learn exactly where she's from, possibly down to the village. The university has a fantastic program that can pinpoint geography— using primarily DNA and teeth. She's severely malnourished. I can't tell you that's what she died from. But you said she was alive when you found her?"

"This needs to stay between us," Matt said.

Peter raised an eyebrow, but nodded. "National security issue?"

"No—but confidential," Matt said. "I have an ongoing undercover investigation in Patagonia. One of my agents and I came out here for a different reason."

He briefly explained Kara's theory about the two kids staying at the abandoned church, which was roughly five miles to the west, three as the crow flies. When they saw the vultures circling, they tracked them and found the bunker when Kara fell in.

"My partner found the girl, talked to her. Said her name was Amada. She understood basic Spanish—I say basic because my partner isn't fluent but was able to get meaning across. The girl's voice was faint, said she couldn't move. My agent picked her up and carried her out." He paused. "My agent is concerned that moving the girl may have caused her death. I said no, but if you can give me any confirmation before the autopsy, it would help alleviate a modicum of guilt."

"We work closely with the Santa Cruz coroner," Peter said. "I'll make sure he does a thorough autopsy and we find out exactly how this girl died. But I can tell you just by looking at her that I highly doubt moving the child killed her. More likely malnutrition, starvation. I don't think she's eaten properly in months. They most likely left her behind because she was too sick to travel."

Matt didn't know if that would appease Kara, but it might help.

"There's a bunker?" Peter looked around, then frowned. "Where?"

"A container buried underground."

Peter sighed, took off his sunglasses and rubbed his eyes. He took a deep breath, then put his glasses back on and said with surprising emotion, "It's unfortunately more common than you think." He paused, then said, "The earth has to be dug up, and that's generally too hard to do in the desert without equipment, so we see more of these bunkers only partly submerged, or camouflaged by the terrain, not underground. But this area here, there's water, trees, access—they could easily have brought in a backhoe or other equipment. Whose property is this?"

"When I called my people, they said county," Matt replied.

"Unfortunately, much of the desert isn't patrolled by the state or federal government. Even if it's privately owned, most owners don't patrol regularly, especially if it's owned by a corporation or part of a multi-acre parcel. These traffickers know the routine. They know where they can go and when. Depending when they originally buried the container, they could have been using it for smuggling for years. Storage for not only people but drugs, guns, cash. Camouflaging it when not in use."

"Can you tell how long it's been here?"

Peter walked closer but didn't go inside. Matt followed. Peter assessed the terrain, the ground, then said, "My guess is anywhere from one to five years, but my team can narrow it down even more, likely to the season and year it was set up. They're that good."

"ETA?" Matt asked.

"Forty-five minutes. You said you wanted privacy first, so I delayed them."

"And I appreciate it. You have no problem working with my Phoenix office?"

"Our team is small, and your people have access to a better lab."

"What's the next step? We have to get that guy to the morgue—he's only going to get riper out here. I'm not a forensics expert, but my guess he's been dead more than twenty-four hours. Rigor has definitely passed."

"Definitely longer than a day," Peter said. "The vultures aren't going to smell him until he goes through rigor, but it hasn't been weeks, because they prefer fresher meat. Let's go take a look at John Doe."

The vultures watched them from afar as the men approached the body.

Peter put on fresh gloves, squatted, and pulled back the tarp. "You were pretty close on TOD," he said. "Two to four days. Forensics will certainly know more." He retrieved the dead guy's wallet, an old canvas fold-over that was wet from body fluids and blood. He slipped it into a plastic evidence bag. "I don't have a paper bag with me, but this will do in a pinch. Your lab needs to dry this out. I don't know if anything valuable is inside, but if I try to open it, we might lose evidence."

"We can take care of that," Matt said, taking

the bag from Peter. Matt again wished he had Jim and the mobile lab here. They were supposed to have all the basics they'd need on-site, including a drying unit for just such evidence as a wet wallet.

Peter took a couple of photographs of the guy's face, ignoring the foul smell and guts that had been pulled out by the vultures. He walked around the body, then squatted again and pushed up John Doe's sleeve, took a picture of a skull tattoo with words that had been rendered unrecognizable by bloating. He pulled the tarp back over the corpse, then walked over to Matt. He enlarged the photo of the tattoo.

"I'll be damned."

Matt asked, "You know him?"

"No," Peter said. "But this tat? It's a Mexican gang, Los Chicos Sangre, relatively new on our radar, but they've been around for a few years. Gang for hire. They smuggle drugs, people, weapons, whatever anyone needs, both sides of the border. I haven't seen them this far east before—they're primarily in eastern California and Yuma. They're not all Mexican nationals. They recruit American youth into their organization—it's muddying the waters about what we can do. I arrested a group, everyone refused to talk, and then I get a call from one kid's father who's a lawyer, says his son is a citizen and how dare border patrol hold him. Didn't matter that the kid was bringing in a kilo of coke in the wheel well of his car and had a fake Arizona license. That's one of the problems—volume. You have someone drive in with a

US passport, a clean-cut kid, we generally wave them through. Sangre knows that, exploits it. We can't search and question every vehicle. And when we run more detailed inspections—such as searching every vehicle for two hours—they seem to have inside knowledge and back off. It's frustrating, I'll tell you that."

"How would something like this operate?" Matt asked. He knew a bit about border issues from his time in Tucson, but five years in DC and he was not up to speed.

"Sangre operates fairly autonomously. They started primarily as couriers for the big drug cartels. An organization will hire them to transport drugs from point A to point B. Drugs, then guns, then people. They'll do anything for the right price. If we're dealing with human trafficking here— which I think we are—they'll identify a weakness on the border and exploit it. This area, we have a pretty tight fencing unit, but we're always looking for breaches, tunnels. Patrols are good, but not foolproof. And we're also dealing with lack of staff and resources."

"Preaching to the choir, Pete," Matt said. "What do they do when they get these people in? Are these migrants who pay to come in, or is this a true trafficking organization?"

"The kid? My educated guess this is straight-up trafficking 101. They have buyers lined up. Amada is on the young side, but perverts are perverts, and sex trafficking brings in the big money on both sides of the border. But what we're seeing more now is forced labor. Sweatshops popping up. Some legitimate businesses cutting corners by hiring out processes so they can ostensibly say, 'We didn't know.' Some fully illegal operations. A buddy of mine in the DEA led the takedown of a heroin packaging facility in Albuquerque that had ninety people from age seven to seventy working fourteen hours a day and sleeping in a warehouse on wool blankets. All of them undocumented, brought here under false pretenses. But yes, if we're dealing in young women, it's nine times out of ten the sex trade. Move them into big cities where they're swallowed up by the business. Most are dead before they're twenty-five."

Peter spoke matter-of-factly, but his voice cracked at the end. He then said, "Again, Sangre is a gang for hire. They're working for someone much higher up the food chain."

"Any idea who?"

Peter shook his head. "I'll put feelers out."

"How did they transport the others? That poor girl wasn't the only one here. We have evidence of two kids who may have escaped, and based on what my agent told me about what was underground, there were dozens of people held there."

"When I first arrived, I saw some tire tracks, not too many, no heavy rigs, so my guess is that they walked them to a designated pickup point within a five-mile radius in the middle of the night. Last night, or the night before. When my team gets here, they know what to look for. I hope I have answers for you by the end of the day."

"That would be great, Peter."

Matt wondered if Amada was one of the children that Kara thought had been hiding in the church. But he didn't see how a girl that weak would be able to escape and walk miles back here. And considering what bad shape she was in, wouldn't her captors have killed her in the church—or just left her there—rather than bring her back here?

"You know, Matt," Peter said, "the big question is, how did that guy die? Not so much how but *why?* Did someone turn on him? Was it natural? A turf battle? Are we dealing with a CDC issue—did he and the girl die of an infectious disease? We need answers as soon as possible. We may be able to trace the container, though it's most likely a dead end. These things often end up in junkyards or stolen. I can also run through all known associates of Sangre, see if this guy pops anywhere. Find *his* inner circle. But finding other children…if they were transported out of here, tracking them down is going to be next to impossible."

That's what Matt was afraid of.

Peter looked at his phone. "My people are almost here, and so is the Santa Cruz County coroner."

"What's around here?" Matt said. "We came from there." He pointed to the unpaved road—if he could call it that—that wound through the hill, leading back to the abandoned town and Harshaw. "I don't see any other roads."

"This area looks secluded, but it's not." He pointed north. "Around that hill there? Go to the east and no more than two miles and you get to a road twice as wide as the one we came in on. Unpaved, partly fenced. A company owns a couple thousand acres east and north. They might even own this plot here."

"When I called it in, the sheriff said this was county land."

"Probably is, but I'd have to check exactly where the property lines are."

"What company?"

"Southwest Copper."

CHAPTER 20

Sunday afternoon
Patagonia, Arizona

Kara sat in Ryder's tidy kitchen while he stitched up her arm.

"You should have gone to the hospital."

"So you said. Twice."

She downed her third shot of tequila and finally the pain began to dull. At least, the pain in her arm.

"You're good at this," Kara said. She shouldn't be drinking. It wasn't even noon. She hadn't eaten, and Joe was picking her up at five.

"I was premed before I went in the military through the ROTC program," Ryder said. "After my time in the army, I decided I didn't want to be a doctor. They would have paid for medical school and I would have been a career army doctor. Instead, I went back to college and got a master's in business administration."

"To do what?"

"I wasn't sure." He hesitated. "My parents weren't happy that I wasn't going to be a doctor. My dad especially—you know the joke about the Asian F?"

"You mean an A minus?"

He gave her a half smile. "Yes. It's not a joke in most Asian families. I may only be half-Korean, but I've never had a grade below an A. Even in college. After the military—grades didn't seem as important to me. And being a doctor was my parents' dream, not mine. Both my parents are doctors, and my grandfather was a doctor. My mom's dad was an astrophysicist and her mom was a college math professor."

"It's not easy walking your own path."

He didn't say anything, but he didn't have to. She could see it in everything he did, how he managed with ease what could be a stressful job.

"For what it's worth, I'm glad you're on this team," she said.

She reached for the tequila bottle, but Ryder grabbed it first and put it behind him. He finished the last stitch. She looked at his handiwork and grinned. "Beautiful. It probably won't even leave a scar."

"You'll scar, but hopefully it'll be small. It was a deep cut, but not too long. What are you going to tell Joe Molina?"

She was about to give a sarcastic answer but closed her mouth. It was a good question. "I'm not working today, so I can't say I broke a glass in the bar—and this is on my forearm, so that wouldn't even be likely. Probably can't hide it—or shouldn't hide it. Wearing long sleeves all day? Nope." She closed her eyes and pictured herself doing a variety of tasks and if in those tasks she might cut her arm right at that spot.

"Bingo!" She smiled. "Checking the oil on my car."

"How would you cut it?"

"Well, it's going to be bandaged, so he doesn't need to see the size or shape. But I would put up the hood. The oil cap is kind of in the middle of the engine, to the right. I'm short, so I would probably stand on the fender to lean in to reach it. So the story is I slipped and my arm got sliced on—" she pictured a standard engine, though she could look at her car and make sure she got it right "—the crankshaft. Or a bolt. That would work."

"Would he believe you'd check your oil?" Ryder asked.

"Why not, because if I owned a car, I'd know how to maintain it. I ride a bike, and I don't mean a people-powered bike. I know how to change a tire, check my fluids, the whole nine yards. I can check oil on a damn car."

Ryder didn't smile or comment. Instead, he handed her a water bottle and a sandwich.

"This isn't a tofu-alfalfa-spinach burger, is it?" She eyed the plate suspiciously.

"Turkey, avocado and cheese. Mustard, no mayo."

"You remembered! My new best friend." Okay, maybe she should stop drinking. She hadn't eaten since last night, and usually three shots didn't make her sound like an idiot.

She'd drink tonight, when she was alone, to erase the memory of the underground bunker that had been a prison for children. Try to forget poor dead Amada who was scared of the light.

"Eat, then you should rest," Ryder said.

"I need to go to my place. Joe is picking me up at five."

"It's not even twelve. I'll wake you up in plenty of time."

She ate the sandwich, drank two water bottles and then lay down on the couch.

"You can go to my room," Ryder said.

"I'm good here. Don't let me sleep more than two hours." *If* she could sleep.

She was glad she'd showered when she first arrived. She'd thrown out the clothes—they were a disgusting mess—and Ryder gave her a pair of sweatpants and a T-shirt. She doubted she would sleep.

As soon as she closed her eyes, she'd see Amada. *Why'd you have to die, kid?*

It would be easier if Kara had found her dead. But Amada had been alive. Breathing. Talking.

Scared. In pain.

And then she was dead.

She had to get her head on straight. She had to *think*. Get back in the program, refocus on David

Hargrove and illegal dumping. Find the dump site and throw those bastards in prison. That would make her feel better.

Finding trafficked children wasn't her damn job.

She drifted off to sleep, wondering about the young owner of the stuffed bunny she'd found in the church.

CHAPTER 21

Shortly after the FBI evidence response team from Phoenix arrived, Matt left the crime scene in their capable hands. They knew Peter Carillo, so the transition would go smoothly. He appreciated it when different agencies and jurisdictions could work together to get the job done. One reason Matt had been tapped for the mobile response team was because of his ability to delegate. He valued people who had the training and experience to do a job right, and Peter was among the best and brightest.

Matt headed over to Wyatt Coleman's office in Patagonia. He'd sent him a message that he had some information on Hargrove's murder. Matt hoped that if they solved Hargrove's murder, they'd also solve Emma's murder.

As soon as Matt got a strong signal on his phone,

he called Ryder. He wanted to check on Kara, without making it seem like he was checking on Kara. He filled Ryder in on who was taking lead on the case, gave him a list of follow-up calls he needed to make with the coroner and the border patrol, then he asked, "Were you able to stitch Kara's wound? Or should I drag her to a hospital?"

"I was able to manage," Ryder said quietly. "It'll be a small scar. Hold on."

A second later Matt heard a door close, then Ryder said, "I stepped outside. Kara is sleeping on my couch."

"Is she okay?"

"She seemed a bit out of sorts. Anytime there's a dead child…well, I don't blame her."

Did Ryder think that Matt would hold Kara's reaction against her? Did he come off as that heartless?

Matt asked, "Do you think she should cancel her dinner with Joe Molina?"

"I don't think she would."

"That wasn't the question. Honest opinion here, Ryder—can she handle it? What we found was more than a little disturbing. I know Kara has a background investigating trafficking in LA, but this was bad."

"Based on what I know of Detective Quinn, she will handle it no matter what. Some people cope better with these situations by working."

Matt was reminded again that Ryder was quietly perceptive. He rarely gave his opinion unless asked, but when he was asked, he nailed it.

"I'll talk to her later, make sure she's okay." Matt had kept his motel room in town so he wouldn't have to drive the hour back and forth to Tucson, especially now. His phone beeped, and he looked at the incoming call. "Hey, Ryder, Zack's calling me, I need to talk to him."

He ended the call and switched to Zack Heller. "Costa."

"I have it," Zack said. "It's so simple I didn't see it at first. A-Line *is* David and Tanya Hargrove."

It didn't take long for that to sink in.

"You mean they own the company."

"With Tanya's brother, Roger Kline. Kline's a long-distance trucker, has had his license for more than a decade. I'll need to extend the warrant to dig into his finances. I called Tony Greer to speed up the process—I hope that's okay. I don't know if Kline's the ringleader or what, but the connection is crystal clear from my research. Kline owned a company called RSK—his initials, *really* dumb. He dissolved RSK in the middle of an audit."

"How did that work? Wouldn't the principals be investigated and questioned?"

"All I have is that it was disbanded, no disposition, but it's definitely the same Roger Kline. Another resolution might have taken place in Colorado. I have to deal with that jurisdiction for answers. It took me a while to unravel how Kline set up his shell corporations. It was not initially apparent from the filings. Brilliant, really. All his companies link to a central hub—one that's buried and

protected beneath layers of documents and paperwork. Organized like a beehive."

Matt didn't need the analogy. "You're saying the
three principals intentionally hid the information."

"Yeah, there's no other reason to create so many
levels of corporate filings unless you'd want to ob-
fuscate who is in charge. Kline and both Hargroves
all signed the initial paperwork. The signatures
were notarized, as well, so Tanya Hargrove had
to have known what she was signing, or she's a
trusting fool."

Not all people who trust their spouses are fools,
Matt thought, but he would have to assess that when
he talked to Hargrove's wife. "This is great, Zack.
I need your report in writing. Could you shoot it to
me? I'm heading to the marshal's office now. We're
planning on talking to Tanya this afternoon." He
thought a second, then added, "So Hargrove is actually at least a partial owner of the waste management company that he himself directly contracted
with to remove hazardous slag from his own employer's business. Sounds like an obvious conflict."

"Yes. It's highly unethical, especially because
waste hauling can be very lucrative when the waste
is hazardous. But if he disclosed his ownership to
Southwest Copper, it wouldn't be illegal," Zack
said.

"He didn't disclose it." Matt didn't know for certain, but when he'd first approached Joe Molina,
Joe showed Matt the contract with A-Line, and
nothing in there indicated Kline and the Hargroves

were the owners. "And they would profit even more if they didn't dispose of the slag properly."

"Yes. It was clearly a scam," Zack said. "And if you find the dump site, we can prove it's a scam. A hauling company is paid good money to truck the slag away and dispose of it properly. Slag waste can be resold—in the research I've been doing, I see that it is used in roadways and other legitimate projects. The toxic elements—like the arsenic and lead—can be neutralized. It's a supply-and-demand issue finding who needs it, when and where to store it in the meantime. Would probably be easier and more profitable to just dump it illegally and keep the money."

Southwest Copper thought they were paying an outside company to take care of that headache, not realizing they were paying their own employee.

Definitely possible.

"The contract specifically hired A-Line Waste to haul and properly dispose of the slag. My guess is that Kline and Hargrove took the money, then dumped the slag illegally nearby in the desert. And they probably weren't just contracting with Southwest Copper. Add in a half-dozen other businesses? Yes…they'd be making a nice profit. So where's Roger Kline?"

"He lives in Phoenix."

He could very well be with Tanya now. Wouldn't he want to see her, comfort her after learning about David's death?

Or would he bolt, thinking that someone might be after him too?

"Send your report to me and Ryder, ASAP. Ask Christine to contact the Phoenix office to send two agents to pick up Kline. Once they have him in custody, let me know—I might send you up there to interview him. But first I want to talk to Tanya Hargrove. He may in fact already be here."

Roger Kline would know the location of the dump site. Did he kill his brother-in-law? Did they have a falling-out? If so, he would have bolted. Or were they both mixed up in something more dangerous? In their illegal games, did they stumble across the human trafficking ring? Maybe saw something they shouldn't have seen?

"I can go to Phoenix right now." Again, overeager, but this time he had a point. It was a two-hour drive from Tucson.

"Okay, head there, meet up with the agents, talk to Kline in his home. If he's not there, track him down. I'll have Tony start working on a search warrant—but hopefully by the time you get there, I'll have information out of Tanya Hargrove and you'll have cause to arrest him. Let me know when you're there and we'll discuss how to proceed."

"Okay, I'm on my way." He sounded unnaturally excited. Maybe Zack spent too much time at computers and reading accounting reports.

"Send the report first."

"Right, on it." He hung up.

Matt would normally let a seasoned agent work the case as he saw fit, but he'd quickly realized that Zack Heller had rarely been in the field. He was brilliant when it came to technology and paper crimes, what warrants he needed, how to find financial information no one else could find—and understanding the meaning. But Matt didn't know how well he would do in an interview. He *would* have two other agents with him. Matt wished he could be there himself, but he had a feeling Tanya Hargrove would be more likely to talk than her brother.

He sent a quick message to Christine about what Zack found and asked that she get two solid agents to go with him.

But none of this that Zack learned explained why Hargrove was dead.

As Matt pulled into the parking lot behind the Marshal's office, his phone rang again. He looked down. Joe Molina. Shit, Matt didn't want to talk to him, especially after his borderline panic attack last night...but he might have more information. He answered.

"Anything?" Joe said immediately. "Have you found out what happened to David?"

Matt grew immediately irritated. "I'm working on it, Joe."

"I'm going to my parents' for dinner tonight. I was hoping you'd have some answers so I can stop this charade."

"Calm down. I know this is hard on you, but we just touched base yesterday. It's an active investigation. There's no need for you to panic."

"Easy for you to say. Someone has not been murdered in your family's business, and you're not lying to your father about what you know."

Matt hesitated, then decided he wanted to know exactly what Southwest knew about A-Line. He asked, "Did you know or suspect that David Hargrove had a personal financial interest in A-Line?"

"What? No. He did? Are you sure?"

"He hid it well, but yes, we've traced the company back to him." Matt didn't mention the brother-in-law or wife—not until he could talk to Tanya.

"That little shit," Joe said.

"We're getting closer, Joe. So just hold tight, and I hope that we can wrap this up tomorrow night."

"Really? That soon?"

"I don't want to jump the gun, but we have a plan if A-Line picks up the shipment of slag tomorrow on schedule, and a plan if they don't. So hold tight."

"I can't wait until this is over, Agent Costa. I just want to get on with my life."

Matt shared with Wyatt Coleman everything he'd learned about A-Line, the Hargroves and Roger Kline. Coleman said, "Nothing surprises me anymore." He went on to say he planned to interview Tanya Hargrove that afternoon but was waiting for David Hargrove's phone records.

Then Matt told Wyatt about what he'd found in the desert southeast of town. He was honest about everything, except that Kara was there. While Matt trusted Wyatt, he didn't want to jeopardize her cover, not unless it was absolutely necessary.

"A dead little girl?" Wyatt shook his head. "Shit. I've heard of those bunkers, never come across them. Where was this again?"

Matt pulled out a map and showed him.

"Why were you down there?"

"I wanted to look at the crime scene—where Hargrove was killed. Just to clear my head, I suppose, as I try to put all this together. I saw vultures in the distance and decided to investigate." It was plausible, but Matt didn't know if Wyatt fully believed him. "I called my people and Peter Carillo from border patrol."

"Good. Peter is one of the best we have down there."

"You know him well?"

Wyatt nodded. "We have breakfast once a month."

"That makes things a lot easier. In addition to the deceased female minor, we found one deceased Hispanic male, approximately thirty, with a tattoo indicating membership in a gang called Los Chicos Sangre."

"They operate primarily out of Yuma, best I know."

"That's what Peter said. We believe, based on the evidence at the scene, that a lot more people were kept in that bunker."

"Migrants? Were they living there? I had to break up a camp southwest of here, closer to Nogales, last year. We raided it with the sheriff's department and border patrol."

"We don't think this was a simple case of illegal immigration—the evidence all points to human trafficking."

"Well, shit. And are you thinking that Hargrove

stumbled across this? That he was killed because he saw something?"

"I can't discount the timing."

"I'll help get whatever information you need, Matt. I'll talk to Peter, the coroner, the sheriff—if these people are using my town to traffic kids, I'm going to shut them down."

That was exactly what Matt wanted to hear.

Wyatt continued. "Patagonia is a small town, and strangers stand out, which is probably why these people were staying in the county, using unpopulated areas to move about. But it's certainly not unheard of that we get traffickers passing through. They don't stay. My jurisdiction may be small, but it's tight. I know everyone in town. I can't see any of them—even David Hargrove, if he's guilty of illegal dumping or kickbacks—aiding and abetting those people."

"Now that you mention strangers," Matt said and pulled out his phone. He scrolled to the photos that Kara had taken of the two men in the bar talking to Joe Molina and handed the phone to Wyatt. "Do you know who these two men are?"

Wyatt looked closely, then shook his head. "I haven't seen them before that I remember. The Wrangler gets a lot of tourists and drive-throughs."

He handed Matt back his phone.

"The reason I ask is that they showed up at the picnic yesterday afternoon, less than fifteen minutes after you left."

"They don't seem the type to work for Southwest Copper."

"Joe said they were vendors."

"That's certainly possible."

"I'd like confirmation on that, but I need to do it quietly."

"Understood. Can you send me the photos?"

Matt did, then pocketed his phone. "What can you tell me about Shelley Brown?"

"I don't know her well. We've met a few times. She was at the picnic yesterday. She's a relative and a lawyer who works pro bono for John—and when AREA came down two months ago for the surprise inspection, she got here quickly—angry as all get out. She had helped resolve the legal situation two years ago when AREA inspected every inch of Southwest Copper after accusations arose that the new well they dug had contaminated the water supply. You know about that, of course."

"Yes, it's the primary reason we're handling this investigation quietly."

"Not only were John and his people cleared, but the original accusation was anonymous—and that really angered a lot of people here. Southwest Copper is the largest employer. Half the people in this town work for the company or are married to someone who works for the company. The other half are split between those who retired from Southwest, or own a small business here—where their customers are Southwest employees. They consider them family."

"I get it."

"Why are you asking about Shelley? She doesn't

live here, and she doesn't work for Southwest officially."

"She's John's niece?"

"Technically, she's Clare and Helen's niece. Their older brother's kid. Gil was killed twelve, fifteen years ago? I don't know the story. Her family is from Tucson. Shelley still lives there, works there. All I've heard is that John and Clare Brown met at U of A. John dropped out of college when he enlisted in the army near the end of the Vietnam War. They married after he served for three or four years. John bought Southwest Copper from the original owners, turned it into a bigger, more focused business."

"I was under the impression he owned it with Barry."

"No, not to my knowledge. John is the sole owner of the company. He brought Barry on ages ago—I couldn't even tell you when. I remember hearing that Barry had lost his job, couldn't find anything, and when John's general manager retired, he hired Barry. Barry is invaluable, for sure—when Clare got cancer and John took her to Tucson for chemo, Barry pretty much took over. Why all the questions?"

"Michael reported that Shelley left the party immediately after those two strangers."

"With them?"

"No. But the timing has me looking into her. Now, if those men really are vendors, and maybe she's negotiating a contract or something, then fine. But I need to know."

"Did you ask Joe?"

"No. I'd like to wait until I know exactly who they are, then talk to him."

"You're not thinking that Joe is involved with any of this?"

"No." He hesitated. "Maybe. He was willing to cooperate at the beginning when I approached him. He provided valuable information, and I believe he's very concerned about his dad's reputation and company. But the last week he's been off. I can't explain it any other way. We ran him early on, before I approached him. He has great credit, no unusual expenses, no criminal record, he had a good job in Phoenix that he voluntarily left when he came here last year to help his family. So I was comfortable. Now I fear I made a mistake."

Matt couldn't help but remember that Kara hadn't wanted to read Joe into the investigation.

"Would you have been this far along if you hadn't brought him in?"

"No. Michael would have had to be the one to obtain the A-Line contracts and schedule for us, and that would have more risky, and possibly taken much longer."

"Then don't second-guess yourself. This situation is sensitive. But we might want to talk to John Molina, now that we know that David and his brother-in-law owned A-Line. He has a right to know. If he doesn't already."

"You're right, but let me think how I want to approach it, okay?"

"Your call. I have to follow up on a report anyway, preferably this afternoon. When do you want to talk to Tanya?"

"I want to read through the financial information that my agent sent me to make sure I understand exactly how the operation was set up. Two, three hours?"

"Is five p.m. too late?"

"That's perfect. I'll meet you outside Tanya's house. Thanks, Wyatt." Matt shook his hand and left.

CHAPTER 22

Hector listened to his cousin explain that the authorities had found their most recent camp.

"But," Dominick continued, "we were long gone. They didn't find anything important."

"What did you do with the bodies?"

"What do you mean?"

"Did you take them? Bury them?"

"Vultures were taking care of Vince."

"And the girl you left behind?"

"She was dead."

Sometimes Hector had a difficult time believing that he shared blood with this man. His father and Dominick's father, brothers and friends, had run an empire for three decades. And yet, now Hector was the only one who seemed to have any sense of business and self-preservation.

"So," he said slowly for even the idiot to understand, "the authorities have her body."

"Um, yeah?"

"Is that a question? Do you not know the answer?"

"Well, I guess they do. I told Rondo not to get caught, so he left as soon as he heard the truck coming."

"Do you see the problem?"

Dominick didn't answer.

"The problem," Hector continued, "is that had the bunker been empty, the authorities wouldn't give it much thought. Another abandoned camp, no practical way to gather evidence. They would be irritated, not angry. Now they have a body. A child. And that will give them motivation to keep looking. They look too much, they might find something. Something that will hurt *me*. *Now* do you understand, *cousin*?"

He was losing his temper. He took a deep breath to calm himself, but that didn't help. He poured a double shot of tequila. Stared at it. He would not be his father and drink too much, too often. But it was times like this that Hector understood why his father drank tequila like water. When the people who were supposed to do a job failed in spectacular ways.

"Yeah, I see your point," Dominick said.

"Where are the others?"

"Secured. They'll be gone by tonight."

"I'm sending up the last big shipment tomorrow. You understand? Tomorrow. I have buyers that I cannot disappoint. Then the Nogales pipeline shuts down. We move out of the area until the authorities back off, go back to Yuma as our base. If anything else goes wrong, I want no one alive who knows our operation. Do you understand?"

"You can trust me, Hector. I'm on top of it."

"You are?" Hector said, his hand tightening around his phone. "If you are on top of it, where are the runaways? Are they dead, as I ordered? Or are they still out there?"

"We're close."

"Close is bullshit!" Hector downed the tequila, letting the alcohol burn his throat, his gut. "Find them, kill them!"

He slammed his phone down. The screen cracked.

His network had been running smoothly for *years* until one of his men had been caught and he'd made a deal with the devil. A *lawyer*.

Never again.

He left his beautiful office and found his most-trusted employee. "I'm going to Nogales. I need to make sure the exchange goes smoothly. Make the arrangements."

CHAPTER 23

———

Sunday afternoon
Patagonia, Arizona

Kara woke up on Ryder's couch with a splitting headache. Could have been the three shots on an empty stomach, or the fact that she had gotten very little sleep in the last few days. Days? Try months. Sleep was not her friend, but she crashed for the last two hours. She clearly needed it.

After grabbing three aspirin, she said goodbye to Ryder, then slipped out and walked back to her house. As she rounded the corner, she saw Javier from the bar sitting on his front porch. Though she saw him often rocking on his glider, this time it startled her. She had to get her mind back into her undercover role. Her focus had been diverted to the underground bunker and the dead little girl.

Shut it out, shut it down.

Her negative emotions would seriously affect her job tonight when she was with Joe if she didn't get them under tight control.

She waved to Javier when he lifted his arm.

"Not working today?" he called down from his porch.

"I asked for the day off. Kind of drained."

"You left early this morning."

Nosy neighbor. She gave him a sly smile. "Did I?"

He gave her an odd smile and nodded. "Want to come in for a beer? Got a cold one."

"I'm having dinner with Joe and his family. You and the boys can gossip about *that* tonight."

Javier laughed, but it didn't quite reach his eyes. He was thinking about something, and she didn't know if it was about her. She was going to have to be doubly careful around him now.

"I'll be back behind the bar tomorrow," she said and waved as she crossed the street to her house. She glanced back as she unlocked her front door. Javi was still watching her from across the street.

Dammit, she didn't need this prying. There wasn't a whole lot she could do, except be careful. And certainly not have Ryder or Michael come over to her place anymore.

She sent a message to the team that she had a nosy neighbor and no one was to come by her place until further notice.

Even though she'd taken a shower at Ryder's, she took another one, trying her best to keep her bandaged arm dry. The cut still hurt like hell.

Standing in her room naked, she looked at the clothes she had. Not much. Three pairs of jeans. Twice as many T-shirts. Couple of pairs of shorts. And one dress. A casual sundress she'd worn for her interview at the Wrangler, white with small black dots. She'd bought it on clearance at one of the shops in downtown Patagonia. Hadn't worn it since because she was definitely *not* a dress girl. But this one wasn't all that bad. Simple. And comfortable. Not as comfortable as her jeans, but cool, which was a plus. She'd be able to hide her gun on her thigh, too, if she wanted to—though she wasn't going to do that. Couldn't risk Joe finding it; he'd gotten very touchy yesterday. But because of the dress, she could carry a purse, and so she stuck her small 9 mm inside. Not the Glock the FBI issued her, or her larger .45 that was her weapon of choice. They both looked like cop guns. The 9 mm looked like what a single girl might have, and she had loaded it with hollow-point bullets, which she preferred for concealed carry and home defense.

Kara drank half a pot of coffee before Joe picked her up. That, plus the aspirin she took earlier and the sandwich Ryder had fed her, made her feel half-human.

He gave her a light kiss and took her hand. "I almost called you to cancel because my cousin Shelley decided to come to dinner. I'm glad I didn't—you look beautiful."

"Don't get used to it—I don't like dresses."

"You should." He kissed her again. Yes, he was definitely getting touchy. That was good…and bad.

"If it's a family thing," she said, "I don't mind if you have to cancel."

He opened his truck door for her. "It's not that. It's my cousin. Sometimes she drives me up a wall. So if I'm not myself, you'll know why."

Shelley Brown. Kara's cop sense went on alert. The same two strangers that Joe had talked to in the bar had shown up at the Southwest Copper picnic yesterday and talked to Shelley.

He looked down at the bandage on her arm and frowned. "What happened?"

"My own stupidity," she said. "I was checking the oil in my car and I cut my arm on a bolt. It's fine, really. I put the bandage on mostly to keep the germs away."

He closed her door and got in his side. Kara wasn't big on chivalry; she always felt there was another angle to it. But Joe seemed to be genuine.

Still, she wasn't sold that he was a saint. It all went back to those two men in the bar. Joe had said they were vendors…but now? She couldn't help but think it was a lie. Or obfuscation.

Something was going on. Just because there was nothing in Joe's background that suggested he would do anything illegal didn't mean that he was clean.

But toxic dumping? Working with David Hargrove to defraud his own father? For what purpose? A little extra money? Then why agree to work with the FBI in the first place? Why give them the contracts or information about slag shipments and finances?

Dammit, she was jaded. Par for the course in her life, but she'd never doubted her instincts before.

Just keep your eyes open, like always. Joe is probably as straight as they come, but if your instincts are telling you something different, just pay attention. Doesn't mean you're right.

Today…today was a shitty day. That could be clouding her judgment. She'd faced misery before. Death. Violence. But today had hit her harder than she expected, even though she'd faced these horrific crimes before. Crap like finding a bunker of human waste and suffering and carrying a dying girl into the sun for her last few minutes of life.

Finding Amada this morning had thrown her off her game. In LA when she was dealt with an unspeakable crime, either she went to the gun range and fired hundreds of rounds, or she went to the gym and punched a dummy until her hands bled, then drank her frustration away with a bottle of tequila. Maybe not the healthiest of coping mechanisms, but she had to do something so she could get up the next day and go back on the job.

Here…she didn't. She couldn't run until her lungs burned and her legs were rubber. She couldn't shoot at targets or get completely wasted and nurse a hangover the next day. She was in the middle of an undercover job and she needed to grow the fuck up and play her part.

People sucked. The best way to get out of this

mindset was to find the bastards who had left poor Amada to die. That would make her feel better.

Then she could take a day off and beat up on dummies.

"Penny for your thoughts," Joe said as he drove.

"Nothing. Just tired."

"You're frowning."

"Resting bitch face."

He laughed. "That's the last thing I would say."

"I actually needed today off, so thanks for that. I think I slept too much, though, and that has made me more tired."

"Are you okay? After yesterday? Finding a dead body wasn't my idea of how to end our date."

"It was...weird." What could she say? What would Kara the bartender say? She didn't break down yesterday; she wasn't going to break down now.

"You say the word, I'll take you home."

"No Uber out here?"

He laughed. "I don't think there's much demand, but I'm sure there's a couple people around here who might drive for one of those services." He paused, grew serious. "You're not serious, are you? Because I am very happy to take you home whenever you want."

"I'm fine. Nothing a cold beer and good food won't fix."

"That, I can do. My dad is barbecuing and Uncle Barry brought over the leftover chili from the picnic yesterday. They almost canceled tonight because of what happened to David... My dad is heartbroken. David's worked for him since high school."

"Yeah, it sucks. Like I said, weird. Do the police know yet what happened?"

"I called Wyatt this morning, but so far, they have no leads or suspects. Maybe they do and aren't telling me, but Wyatt is a good cop. I'm sure he's doing what he can."

Hmm…this might be a more productive night than she'd expected. Originally she planned to go to the dinner and meet his parents—which was uncomfortable, because she wasn't in a relationship with Joe, even though it was clear that he was pushing in that direction. But she needed to keep an eye on him. Now? She could pick John Molina's brain about David Hargrove, plus she could assess Shelley Brown. Michael was suspicious of her. That was good enough for Kara.

Maybe there was more going on with David Hargrove and A-Line Waste Disposal and Trucking than even Matt suspected.

"Don't worry, Kara. You're not scared, are you? I'm pretty sure David was killed in an accident. Or maybe he was robbed and fought back. I don't know. Do you realize that we've only had one murder in Patagonia in ten years?"

"The college girl who was hiking?"

"What? Oh—no. That wasn't here—that was east of town, in the county."

"Sorry—I heard someone talking about it in the bar."

"It was still awful—I don't think they've solved

it yet either. But I was talking about a bar fight, nine years ago. The fight was there, not the murder. That night one of the two involved went to the other guy's house, shot and killed him."

"Did you know either of them?"

"No—well, one I went to high school with, but he was older than me by a couple of years. My point is that this area isn't prone to crime. We get more thefts and whatnot in the tourist season, but when you only have a thousand year-round residents, everyone pretty much behaves."

Joe pointed out a house set far back from a road off the main highway. "That's my place," he said. "My parents own it. They lived there when they were first married. When they built a bigger house up the mountain, they decided to keep this one too. It's not really my idea of independence to be living off my parents."

"You came home to help your mom, right?"

"Yeah, and I'm glad I could, but I'm ready to go back to Phoenix now."

"I hear a but."

"No but. My dad understands, I think… I don't know. He's starting to think about retiring and how, now that I am here, maybe he can pass it off to me."

"But it's not what you want to do with your life."

"Not even close."

"Have you asked him if that's his plan?"

"Not exactly."

"A little unsolicited advice. Not that I'm the best person to be giving anyone advice, but generally when you want to know what someone is think-

ing, you need to ask them. Your dad might surprise you."

"I don't want to disappoint him."

"I doubt that's even on the table. From every-
thing you've said about your dad, he's a good guy.
He must know you don't want to run the refinery.
He's not going to guilt you into staying."

"Maybe."

"You know what my grandmother Em used to
tell me? *Don't borrow trouble.*"

A wave of nostalgia rushed over Kara, surprising
her at its intensity. She hadn't talked to her grandmother in weeks, and she felt like crap about it. She
last called her right before she went undercover,
said she was going on a case and wouldn't be able
to talk every week. But the truth was she'd avoided
her grandmother since leaving Liberty Lake two
months ago. Now that Em knew more about Kara's
job than Kara had ever wanted her to know, Em
was worried all the time—and Kara didn't want
to listen to it.

*You're a crappy granddaughter. Em doesn't de-
serve you.*

Maybe Kara needed to take a bit of her own
advice, and after this case take a few days up in
Washington and show her grandmother she was
fine. Lie if she had to. She was good at that.

"You're right," he said. "I'll talk to my dad.
Sometime. This week, maybe."

"You don't sound optimistic. Everyone goes
through rough patches, right?"

"Sometimes my dad makes everything harder

than it needs to be. He's very prideful. Not a bad thing, of course, but he can be stubborn."

"Stubborn pride. Yeah, I've heard of it before. There are worse sins, I suppose."

He had turned up a long driveway to a small, beautiful cabin that looked like it had more deck than house.

"Wow. This is really nice."

"My dad pretty much built it himself," Joe said as he turned the engine off. "Took two years— my brother, Kenny, helped him a lot—I was too young, but I remember wanting to help so badly. Dad started when I was seven, and Kenny was twelve. I was lucky to be able to hand them tools and fetch water."

He sounded bitter, then it passed. Just like the conversation yesterday when they were hiking, when he was telling her about his family and his brother. Before they found Hargrove's body.

"Let's just have a nice dinner, okay?" Kara said.

Joe looked at her, put his hands on either side of her face and kissed her.

It was a more emotional kiss from Joe than Kara wanted, but she let Joe drive that train. The more he trusted her, the more he would share with her…and her gut was still talking to her. There was something she was missing…or Joe was hiding something.

It might be innocuous.

It might not be.

"You know, if you stay around Patagonia, it might give me incentive to stay too."

That last remark definitely made her uncomfortable. She said, "I like you, Joe, but as I told you from the very beginning, I don't know what I'm going to do after Memorial Day. I don't want to plan that far in advance."

"If Patagonia isn't right for you, maybe you should try Phoenix. Especially if I end up going back sooner rather than later. My condo is in Old Town Scottsdale. There's a view, three pools, baseball, lots of restaurants and shops and bars. You'd fit in. I think you'd like it. You'd easily be able to get a job."

"Maybe," she said, trying to sound noncommittal.

But Joe didn't take it that way. He smiled and kissed her again, this time with even more passion and urgency, and with what Kara thought of as a possessive promise of what bed would be like.

She could not—would not—sleep with Joe Molina.

She was no prude and certainly no saint. She couldn't say that she'd never slept with a target or a witness while undercover. But the times were few and far between; she tried to avoid it because the emotional entanglements were difficult to navigate.

It was worse for the mark, because they never knew she was faking it. Faking emotion, faking affection, sometimes faking passion. But the guilt scratched at her conscience. She tried to convince herself she didn't care, and sometimes she really didn't.

But when she had to con a guy like Joe—yeah, it bothered her. So she vowed she wouldn't sleep with him, especially since he seemed to be falling hard for her.

Even though she didn't completely trust him.

It's what you wanted. You wanted him to like you, rely on you, half fall in love with you so he'd tell you everything.

Well, shit.

CHAPTER 24

Sunday evening
Patagonia, Arizona

Matt sat outside David and Tanya Hargrove's house in a tract neighborhood on the east side of the town. Though one of Patagonia's "newer" neighborhoods, it was more than thirty years built out. In the eighties one of the mines east of town had a government contract and increased production, creating hundreds of jobs. Unfortunately, it slowed production down only a few years later when the government didn't renew the contract. Then the mine closed down completely shortly thereafter. In the six years it was at full production, a 110-home development called Vista Shores—which made no sense to Matt since there was no lake or river in the area—of small houses on narrow, deep lots had been built. They were virtually identical, different only in paint and trim and three different floor plans.

Many of the homes had fallen into disrepair; many had become rentals as their owners left to find work elsewhere but were unable to sell the property. The Hargroves owned their house, the largest model (at nineteen hundred square feet) in the development, on a cul-de-sac that backed up to the mountain. They'd bought it just after they were married eight years ago and took out a second mortgage three years ago.

Wyatt Coleman had texted him that he was on his way, but Matt was early. He was trying to wrap his head around what the couple had been up to, and why they'd gone this route. He finally had the warrants for David and Tanya's finances, and Tony had come through with a ton of information. Matt was still trying to put it all together, but it was clear that there had been a lot of money going through their accounts for a short period of time.

But why the A-Line scam? Had Hargrove thought it would be easy money? Did he plan to take the money and run after a year, before anyone realistically would catch on? Try to prolong the scam? It was unfathomable to Matt that someone who lived in this beautiful, isolated desert landscape would want to mar it with toxic waste. Bring harm to not only the wildlife but potentially the people who lived here. Even if the poisonous slag didn't end up in the groundwater—the desert was exotic and full of life. He thought about how most people who didn't live here, or hadn't visited often, didn't understand the raw, stately beauty of the plateaus, the variety of species, the vast open space and towering mountains.

With few exceptions, Matt had rarely seen a sunset more beautiful and vivid than that which fell over the desert. Lack of urban lights and pollution made the blues bluer and the oranges oranger. Though the summer heat made his backyard unbearable when he lived here, during the rest of the year he would sit by his small pool for hours with a beer or two and watch the sky deepen. It was one of the few times Matt could actually relax.

That the Hargroves, or anyone, would coldly damage this beautiful place Matt considered his home angered him immensely.

No fucking reason would justify that.

Wyatt Coleman arrived a few minutes later. "You have to see this." He handed Matt a printout.

"What am I looking at?"

"Phone records for both Hargroves. I needed a warrant, which wasn't hard to get—the guy is dead, I'm investigating his murder—but it's the weekend and everything moves a little slower. I'm lucky I got them before Monday."

Matt skimmed them. Hargrove had received two missed calls from the same number on Friday during the time he was at the Wrangler, then called the number back at about the time he was leaving. "Whose number is it? Did you run a reverse directory?"

"A burner. Purchased up in Tucson is all I could

learn. Maybe your people can trace it further. I hear the FBI has better resources for the pay-as-you-go cells."

"We might be able to trace the burner to the location where it was purchased, but that would be it."

If they learned the day and time it was activated, they might be able to talk to a clerk or get surveillance cameras, but it could have been bought months ago. And if it was a busy location, next to impossible to find someone who might remember a one-time customer. They could get lucky, or it could be someone local, but Matt wouldn't hold his breath. "The best option would be when we have a suspect checking this number against any in his possession."

"The number ending in 37 is Hargrove's wife—he called her Friday night, which matches what Tanya told me—that he'd called her when he was leaving the Wrangler. He also called her just before midnight—so where was he during those four hours?

"And this," Coleman continued as he pointed, "that ends in 02? That's his brother-in-law, Roger Kline.

"He talked to him Friday night for thirteen minutes before he called his wife, then briefly Saturday morning—for two minutes—before he called this other number, which I traced to your guy Michael Harris. I got his statement yesterday, just to have it on record and because it would be expected. Did Harris find it odd that David canceled on him?"

"Yes, but he got a ride, then stayed at the picnic because Tanya Hargrove said he would be there by noon. But David was a no-show."

"Tanya also called Roger—Saturday night and again this morning. But here's the odd thing," Wyatt continued. "Tanya tried calling David multiple times between noon and three p.m.—which was when I notified her that he was dead."

Matt counted. "Sixteen unanswered calls. She was worried about him."

"She expected him to be at the picnic by noon. When I talked to her, I asked that exact question. She said she thought he'd be there around noon, but she didn't really notice because she was so busy."

"She lied."

"How do you want to handle this?" Wyatt asked.

"The way we originally planned. You be gentle, I'll come in with the A-Line corporate paperwork, the list of shell corporations, and ask the hard questions. I'd like to use this, as well, if you don't mind." He held up the phone records.

"It's all yours."

They walked to the door together and Wyatt rang the bell. A woman answered—not Tanya Hargrove.

Wyatt knew her. "Crystal. Good to see you." He glanced at Matt. "Crystal is Deputy Roberto Vasquez's wife."

Matt would have preferred to interview Tanya without anyone else present, but he'd make it work.

"Crystal, this is Special Agent in Charge Matt Costa with the FBI. We need to talk to Tanya about David's murder."

"Did you find out who did it?" she asked. "Did you arrest the scumbag? Who is it? Do we know him? Is it a tourist?"

"We need to talk to Tanya," Wyatt said.

"Right. Of course. Come in."

One benefit of having someone related to law enforcement is that they usually cooperated with law enforcement, which could be a plus when talking to Tanya.

Crystal opened the door wider, and Wyatt took off his hat and stepped inside. Matt followed.

The house was both clean and cluttered. The furniture was too big for the space, chunky, oversize pieces. Every wall had pictures—landscapes and framed photographs, mostly of Tanya and David together or with groups of friends. Fishing. Camping. A beach vacation. A large wedding portrait centered on the main wall, but it looked out of place because of all the photos surrounding it. Knick-knacks on every available surface. A lot of stuff everywhere.

Matt could never live in a place like this.

Tanya's dyed-blond hair was pulled back into a stringy ponytail, revealing dark roots, her face devoid of makeup, eyes red from crying. She was sitting cross-legged on the oversize sectional couch staring at a blank large-screen television.

Her grief appeared real. That didn't mean she wasn't privy to what her husband and brother were up to. But Matt had to handle this carefully.

He let Wyatt take the lead.

"Tanya," Wyatt said. "This is FBI agent Matt

Costa. We'd like to talk to you about David's murder."

She slowly turned to look at them and blinked. She didn't say anything.

Crystal said, "Can I get you guys water? Coffee?"

"No, thank you, ma'am," Matt said.

Crystal motioned for them to sit down on the couch across from the sectional. The pieces of furniture—with a square coffee table between them—felt crammed into the room.

Wyatt said, "We're sorry to disturb you today, Tanya, but it's really important that we have all the information we need so we can find out who did this to your husband."

Crystal sat next to Tanya and took her hand. "Of course, we understand. Tanya's still in shock over this whole thing."

"Do you have family, Mrs. Hargrove?" Matt asked. "Anyone who can come stay with you for a few days?"

Tanya didn't respond but looked down.

Crystal said, "She called her brother. He'll be here tomorrow. But I can stay as long as Tanya needs me."

Good to know, Matt thought, though why Tanya didn't answer made him suspicious. Right now Zack Heller should be talking to Kline. They'd coordinated the timing earlier, once the agents were in place—Zack was to wait until five fifteen to approach Kline's house in Phoenix, so Kline couldn't call his sister and alert her to a line of questioning, at least not without Matt knowing about it. Tanya's phone was faceup on the table in front of her. If anyone called her, Matt would be able to see the name or number.

Matt glanced at Wyatt, who said, "Tanya, I have a few questions. I know you're upset, but if we want to find who killed David, I need to do this. Do you understand?"

"No one would hurt David," she said. "You know him, Wyatt. He's fun and funny and a good man. He would never hurt anyone. He doesn't even like to kill spiders. He scoots them out of the house. He hit a bunny once on the road and he was very upset about it. Who would do this to him, Wyatt? I don't understand."

"That's why Agent Costa is here. He's going to help me find out exactly what happened. Okay?"

She nodded again, and Crystal put her arm around her friend.

Wyatt said, "Yesterday you were upset when I told you about what happened, so I'm going to ask some of the same questions because you might remember something different now."

"It's so unreal."

"You said that David left the house early yesterday morning. At about seven thirty, correct?"

"Yes. I was still in bed. I was up late making chili at Helen's house, and we drank a lot of wine. Except Crystal—she drove me home."

"I did," Crystal confirmed. "It was just before eleven."

"Was David here?" Wyatt asked.

Crystal frowned. "I don't think so. I didn't see his truck."

Tanya said, "I was mad when David left yesterday because he said he would be late to the picnic. I shouldn't have been, I wish I wasn't. I wish I'd said *I love you.* I wish I'd gone with him. I wish—"

"Honey, that kind of thinking is going to twist you up inside," Crystal said. "David knew you loved him more than anything."

Wyatt steered her back on track. "Michael Harris, who works with David at Southwest, said that David texted him at quarter to eight on Saturday morning to tell him he couldn't drive him to the employee picnic. Harris said that you told him that he had to help a friend. What friend would that be?"

"A friend? I don't know. I don't think I said that."

"You didn't tell people at the picnic that David was late because he was helping a friend?"

"I may have, I don't know. It's not important, is it?"

"Then why did David leave so early on a Saturday when you had plans?"

"I don't know!"

She didn't look at them, and Matt couldn't be certain whether she was lying or not. She was grieving, she was exhausted and emotionally spent, but her demeanor was off.

"What did David tell you?"

"I… I don't really remember. I think… I think he said he had to check on something."

How many times could this woman say "I don't know?" Matt wondered, growing irritated.

"On what?" Wyatt asked. "What was he checking on?"

"I don't know, really. I was mad because he came home really late, later than me, and he was upset and told me everything was fine, but I knew everything wasn't fine. And...well, I was mad. And now he's dead and he died thinking I was mad at him and, and, and—"

Tears started to fall.

Matt didn't think she was faking the emotion, but he knew she wasn't telling the whole truth. Not lying...just avoiding the important details.

Matt glanced at Wyatt and gave him a slight nod. Right now, they needed Tanya comfortable and talking, and if Matt pushed too soon she might clam up.

Wyatt continued being understanding and kind. "I know this is hard for you, Tanya, but it's really important that you think back to Friday night. Do you know where David went after he left the Wrangler? Before he came home."

She frowned, her brows furrowed as she stared at her clasped hands. Was she trying to come up with a lie?

"He told me that he was meeting a friend in Tucson. I told him he shouldn't be driving all the way there that late at night and that's what we were arguing about."

"You talked to him after he left the Wrangler?"

"Yes—he called to say he would be home after midnight. I said don't go all the way to Tucson, that's ridiculous."

"Who was he meeting?"

"I don't really know."

Dammit, she knew. She knew and didn't want to say; Matt could practically read her mind.

"Did he go to a restaurant? A bar? Someone's house? Tanya—this is very important. Whoever he met in Tucson may know why he changed his plans. Other than you, they were one of the last people to see him alive."

As Wyatt spoke, the truth of the situation fell on her. She opened her mouth, closed it. Then shook her head. "I didn't ask."

"Did you have an idea of who he might be meeting with, just didn't ask him to confirm?"

"No. I don't know what you're getting at. David didn't do anything wrong."

"I didn't say that he did. At this point, we have no leads. We don't know who he met with Friday night. We don't know who he went to 'help' Saturday morning. All we know is that he was killed after he sent the text to Harris."

"I don't know!"

Matt looked down at his phone. He'd been watching Tanya closely, trying to find a way to get her to tell them what they knew to be true, and as a result he had been ignoring several text messages.

They were all from Zack Heller.

5:12 p.m.: Roger Kline is not here. Checking the property.

5:16 p.m.: Car missing.

5:25 p.m.: Neighbor says Kline left before dawn Saturday. Hasn't seen him since.

5:35 p.m.: Warrant just came through. Searching property now.

Matt showed the messages to Wyatt, who frowned.

"What?" Tanya said. "What's going on?"

"When did you last talk to your brother?"

"I called him after you told me...told me that David had been killed. He said he'd be here as soon as he could."

"That was yesterday?"

"Yes."

"Was he at home?"

"I don't know. I guess. Why?"

"Did you talk to your brother this morning?"

"No—I mean, yes. I think so."

"You think so or you know so?"

"Why are you being so mean, Wyatt?"

"I'm trying to find out who killed your husband."

"You're confusing me!"

"Did David and your brother have a business together?" Matt asked.

The question clearly caught Tanya off guard, and she stuttered her answer. "I—I—I don't know. I mean, they like each other, they always talk about doing something together, they... I..."

Matt took off the gloves, so to speak.

"Mrs. Hargrove," Matt said in a calm, firm voice, "we know that you, David and your brother, Roger, started a business late last year based in Las

Vegas called RSK, Limited. That business was an umbrella for other related companies, including one called A-Line Waste Disposal and Trucking. In January the Southwest Copper refinery contracted A-Line to haul slag—hazardous waste—from the property for either lawful resale or proper disposal. To date, A-Line has removed three truckfuls of slag, with a fourth expected tomorrow, but we have hard evidence that the waste was neither sold nor disposed of properly."

The *not sold* was his guess. Matt's guess was that there were no records and would be no records because this entire thing was a scam to make money from Southwest Copper and likely other refineries in the region by just dumping the haul in the middle of the desert.

Tanya's eyes were wide and she looked terrified. She should be. Her husband was dead. Her brother Roger was in the wind. Either Roger killed David, or Roger was in hiding because of David's murder. Either way, David's death and Roger's disappearance were connected to A-Line.

Or Roger could be dead and they hadn't found his body yet.

Matt had been working on a theory since he talked to Zack, though he retained an open mind because there were too many questions. He felt that A-Line was bigger than Roger and David and Tanya. That they had been used by someone else to create these entities and got in over their heads, and then a dispute between the parties resulted in David's murder.

But from the minute Wyatt started questioning David's widow, Matt suspected she knew far more than she had said. More about A-Line, and more about who her husband had been meeting with Friday night, and why he changed plans Saturday morning.

"I… I don't know what you're talking about," Tanya said with a dismissive wave of her hand. "What does any of this have to do with my husband's murder?"

Matt pulled out his phone and showed her a copy of the original RSK paperwork that Zack had sent to him. "Is this your signature?"

She didn't say anything.

"It was notarized by a bank manager in Las Vegas. You and your husband traveled to Las Vegas on December thirteenth and were there on the date that this was notarized."

"How do you know that?"

He flipped through his phone and showed her the warrant. "We have a warrant for your and your husband's financial records, which includes credit card and banking statements."

"What? But don't you have to ask me for that information?"

"No. The warrant was duly signed by a judge. For the last month, your husband has been the subject of an FBI investigation for his association with A-Line Trucking and alleged illegal dumping that culminated in the loss of wildlife. Through that investigation, we learned that you may have been privy to the illegal dumping—at the minimum, you benefited financially from the contracts that A-Line has with Southwest Copper and any other entities. Your business here in Patagonia saw an unusual increase in cash deposits that has led our white-collar crimes unit to believe you may have been laundering money through your business for A-Line or other entities associated with that business. We have our best people analyzing the files and accounts, and we'll know exactly how it is structured and who profited from this illegal activity."

They didn't have proof of money laundering—and based on the structure of A-Line, he didn't see how—but Zack had a clear analysis that Tanya had a huge influx of money into her business that didn't correspond with any known changes in inventory. It could have been a red flag as soon as she filed the appropriate tax paperwork, but that wouldn't have to be legally done until next year.

And who had she been laundering money *for*? A-Line? Another business? Zack had explained several types of scams that could be going on, but ultimately, the money had to come from *somewhere*, and the only place it could have come from based on the information they had was A-Line or one of their entities.

And if the money was legally received for transporting waste, why was it filtered through Tanya's antiques shop?

"I haven't done anything wrong," she insisted.

"A college student was murdered two months ago while investigating poisoned wildlife. Now your husband is dead. Why."

"Stop."

Matt kept pushing. "Tanya, where is Roger? He's not at his home in Phoenix. My people are putting an APB out on him right this minute for questioning related to the murder of your husband."

"No. No. No, no, no! Roger and David are as close as brothers. Roger just—just—you're wrong. How dare you!"

"According to my agent who is right now at Roger's house, his neighbor said that he left home early yesterday morning—before dawn—and he's not answering his phone. We know that Roger talked to David on Friday night, and again yesterday morning right before David changed his plans about the picnic. Do you know where Roger is right now?"

She shook her head.

Change gears. Matt asked, "What was Roger's reaction when you called him yesterday afternoon and told him David was dead?"

"Why are you being so mean? My husband is dead!"

"And the marshal and I want to find out who killed him."

"It's not my brother."

"What did your brother say in your conversation?"

"Nothing."

"You told him David was dead and he said nothing?"

"I mean, he was upset. He asked if I was sure, and I said of course I'm sure, the police were here and they said…they said David had been shot. In the middle of nowhere. And I asked him to come here, that I needed him."

"And what did he say?"

"He said he would. But first he had something important to take care of. But he promised he'd be here by tomorrow."

"What did he have to do that was more important than consoling his grieving sister?"

Crystal frowned. She wasn't happy about Matt's questioning of her friend, but she didn't interrupt.

Tanya didn't answer.

Wyatt spoke up. "Tanya, did Roger's business have something to do with A-Line? If this business venture of theirs got them in trouble with the wrong people, your brother could also be in danger."

Smart, Matt thought. Good cop, bad cop almost always worked.

"This is all a misunderstanding," Tanya said.

"What is?" Wyatt asked.

"Just—this! Nothing has to do with A-Line."

"Does John Molina know that you and David have a financial interest in the company's waste disposal contract?"

She bit her lip but didn't answer.

"What did your husband tell you about his plan for Friday night?" Matt pushed. Sometimes asking the same question repeatedly could rattle a suspect and they would open up and tell the truth. Didn't seem to be working with Tanya, but they were close.

"Nothing, I told you."

"Where's Roger?"

"I don't know. Just give him time to fix everything."

"Fix what?" Matt asked.

She bit her lip, didn't answer.

This was getting them nowhere, and Matt was frustrated.

"Were Roger and David working with anyone else? Did they borrow money? Maybe someone who wants their money back?"

"I... I...well, Roger borrowed money for the truck. He used to be a long-haul trucker, so he knew who to go to. And we had lots of contracts. We were going to branch out and hire more drivers and it was going to be great."

First actual admission that Tanya was involved in A-Line and their contract with Southwest Copper.

Matt asked, "Do you have a list of these contracts?"

She shook her head. "David took care of all that."

"Did he have an office here?"

"No, he had his laptop. He did everything on that thing."

"We have a warrant for any computers or paperwork."

"He never went anywhere without it," she said. "It's not here."

Matt glanced at Coleman. Wyatt said, "His laptop wasn't in his truck."

"If Roger and David were into something potentially dangerous, Roger might be in danger," Matt told her, appealing to her concern about her brother.

Tanya bit her lip.

"Tanya," Matt said, calm but firm, "your husband is dead. Your brother is in danger. Where is he?"

"I was really upset yesterday, so I didn't know what my brother meant about fixing things. All Roger said was to stay home, not go anyplace, and he'd be here as soon as he could."

"He didn't tell you what he was doing?"

"No, and I was upset!"

As soon as he could.

"So he didn't say he'd be here on Monday, did he?"

"I—no, but he will be!"

"Where did Roger take the slag that he hauled away over the last three months?"

"I don't know. That wasn't my job."

"What was your job?"

"Nothing. I run a gift shop in town. Antiques, mostly, Southwest items. All they wanted was my signature, and David and I are married. It meant that we were all equal partners, that's it. I didn't do anything. Is Roger okay? You have to find him. He's all the family I—I—I've got left!"

She turned to Crystal and started to cry.

Matt didn't know how much of this was an act. Tanya knew more than she was saying, but he couldn't compel her to talk unless he arrested her, then she'd get a lawyer, and then he'd be hours—days—in negotiations about what she may or may not know. He suspected she knew more than she said but had no idea about the trucking end of it.

Wyatt said, "Tanya, you need to think about this long and hard. Because if Agent Costa and I walk out of here without the information we need, you're going to be in a heap of trouble."

"I have thought about it!"

"I think you know exactly where David was going yesterday morning. You didn't expect that anything would happen to him, but the *sixteen* calls you placed to his cell phone between noon and three tell me you were worried when he didn't show up at the picnic by twelve. Yet you told me yesterday afternoon that you didn't realize he was late because you were so busy."

Matt was impressed with how Coleman called her on the carpet.

"That's not what I said."

"Sixteen phone calls, Tanya."

"I thought he was still mad at me because of our argument."

"Which was about…?"

"Nothing! Him getting in late the night before. Then having to go off early. I don't know. Just—why are you doing this to me?"

Wyatt looked at Crystal. "We've been friends since I started this job," he said to her. "I have a lot of respect for your husband, Crystal, and I know you want to do the right thing. Convince Tanya that she needs to be honest with us if we're going to find out who killed David."

Crystal looked torn.

"Tanya, honey…"

"Don't! Don't turn on me too!"

"I would never. I love you, sweetheart, but Wyatt just wants to help. He just wants to find out who killed David."

"No one wants to help! You don't care about David, you only care about what he might have done. He didn't do anything wrong. *We* didn't do anything wrong. And he's dead and you don't care!"

She jumped up and ran upstairs.

Wyatt turned to Crystal. "I'm serious, Crystal. Tanya is in over her head, and until we know who else David and her brother were working with, she and Roger are in danger."

"Let me work on her," she said. "I'll stay here and see what I can do."

"If Roger shows up, call or text me immediately," Wyatt said. "We need to talk to him."

"You don't really think that Roger killed David, do you? They were so close, the three of them."

"I don't know what to think, but Roger left his house early enough to drive down here by the time David was killed. Or he and David were trying to fix whatever Tanya alluded to and couldn't, and David took a bullet to the chest. Whatever it is, it's important we find the truth—because we need to find out where they dumped the toxic slag, test it, see if it's what's been killing wildlife in the area. It could be the cause of a potential environmental disaster that would take years and millions of dollars to clean up."

Matt said, "Crystal, be careful here. If you see anyone unfamiliar, or if you get a bad feeling, call 911 immediately. Or your husband. Or Wyatt. We don't know what David and Roger were doing, but even if Tanya doesn't know the details, whoever killed David might not know that. She, too, could be in danger."

Crystal opened her purse and revealed a .45. "My dad taught me how to shoot when I was ten, and my husband and I go to the range every month. I'll be okay. And I'll call Rob—I can tell him what's going on, right?"

Wyatt deferred to Matt. "The information about David and the trucking company is going to get out," Matt said. "We need to talk to John Molina."

Wyatt said to Crystal, "Yes, I wouldn't ask you to keep anything from your husband, but ask him to talk to me before he talks to anyone else."

"Of course I will," she said. "Do you really think that Tanya is in danger?"

"I don't know," Wyatt said. "Just do what Agent Costa said and be careful, do not hesitate to call 911."

Crystal locked and bolted the door behind them when they left. Wyatt walked with Matt to his car.

"What do you think?" Wyatt asked.

"Tanya knows more than she's saying."

"Scared?"

"I don't know if it's fear… I think it's partly denial, partly self-preservation. She doesn't want to think that this business venture they cooked up had anything to do with David's murder, but she'll be thinking about it now. I'm going to have my people find out more about this truck loan of Roger Kline's. Maybe there's something there, though loan sharks don't usually go around killing people who are behind on their payments, and when you have collateral—like a truck—they'll just take the truck. Maybe break your legs, maybe kill your dog, but they don't kill the person who can give the money back."

"Unless killing David was the threat."

"Could be," Matt agreed, though that didn't feel like the most likely scenario.

David was killed halfway between Patagonia and the ghost town outside of Harshaw, an unincorporated town with a handful of homes. If it were him, and he were making a statement, he'd leave the body where the statement would have the most impact. That David Hargrove's body had been found so quickly in a remote area was luck for them, because likely the killer didn't expect anyone to find him soon.

And his laptop was missing, which suggested that the murder was about A-Line, unless Hargrove was involved in other schemes. At this point, Matt would buy into almost any theory.

"Kline didn't go through a bank for a loan," Wyatt said.

"That's not necessarily the sign of a guilty man. If he couldn't get a traditional loan, he might go to a friend. There's something here, but I haven't quite figured it out—and I can't for the life of me figure out how Tanya's local antiques business fits in and why she's recently had a large influx of cash. It's set up as if she's laundering money, but from who? And how does it fit with A-Line?" Matt couldn't see the endgame. He usually could, especially when he had this much information, but there were still too many questions. "So, Wyatt, how trustworthy *is* Crystal Vasquez?"

"She and her husband are native Patagonians. Born and raised here. Good people. She's a little flighty, but she isn't going to help anyone with a crime. She's a deputy's wife. If anyone can get Tanya to talk, it's Crystal—and she'll call me."

"Good. We need to do one more thing, and I don't know if you're going to like it."

"Tell me straight."

"Search David Hargrove's desk and locker at Southwest."

"Now?"

"I'd like to do it tonight. We now know we're missing his personal laptop. It has information that could be relevant to this case—both the toxic dumping and possibly even Emma's murder—and may shed light on why Hargrove was killed."

"Which means we need to talk to John Molina tonight."

Matt had been thinking about the same thing. "We can't get around it, and he might be willing to cooperate if we share this information. I don't want to out Michael, not yet—Roger Kline may still show up tomorrow with the truck. I want to explain to John that he has to let Kline take the slag so we can trace it."

"I think I can convince him."

"Me too. Because right now, Kline is the only one who knows where he dumped the slag. But if he can produce paperwork, names, locations of legal disposal, we're back to square one."

"Because then we don't know why either Emma or David were killed."

"Exactly."

Wyatt said, "Let me get a warrant, just to cover my ass. After the AREA overreach two years ago, John isn't going to let me—a friend—let alone a federal agent in to search his business."

"You can make it very specific—we just want to search Hargrove's desk, locker and common area for his laptop, cell phone, documentation related to A-Line or any of the other shell corporations he and Kline had their names attached to. And even though Joe already gave me copies of the contract, we should officially ask for it, as well."

Wyatt was taking notes. "Okay. I think I can get this tonight, but it might be late."

"How about if you get it by ten, we'll go tonight. If not, first thing in the morning."

"Agreed."

CHAPTER 25

Sunday evening
Patagonia, Arizona

One of the pluses of working undercover for so many years is that Kara was used to being the person she was expected to be. Even in more intimate situations, like the Molina family dinner, she could handle herself. It was all a matter of becoming your character while never forgetting that you had a job to do.

John and Clare Molina had welcomed Kara into their home. They were friendly, warm and genuine.

"How are you?" John asked Kara when Joe went to the kitchen to get her a drink. "Joe told me you were with him when he found David's body."

"I'm okay, thank you for asking," she said. "It

was a shock, to be honest. We'd had a lovely hike and picnic, and then...well, I'm sorry you lost a friend. I know he worked for you."

"David was one of my managers. A friendly sort, everyone liked him. My human resources manager knows a lot about insurance and whatnot, to help his wife, Tanya, work through the paperwork. But we'll give her a few days to grieve first."

Clare said, "Poor girl. I don't even think the police know what happened, do they, John?"

"Not that I've heard," John said. "I was going to call the marshal in the morning, see if he had any news. I'll be addressing the staff tomorrow. Everyone knows, but they need to hear something from me. Like I said, David was well liked."

Joe joined them on the deck and handed Kara a cold bottle of beer. "I'm hoping all this talk hasn't scared Kara off."

"I'm a bit tougher than that," she said.

"Patagonia is a great place to live," John said, "but it's a bit slow for young folks. I know Joe is hankering to get back to Phoenix."

"I'm fine," Joe said.

Kara couldn't help but notice that Joe's assessment of his father was all wrong. Clearly John didn't mind if Joe left. He would miss him, she was pretty sure, but he saw that Joe wanted to leave. And Joe brushed it off.

"It's a relaxing community," Kara said. "I really like Greg and Daphne, but I knew coming in the job was temporary."

"Daphne was a godsend when I was first diagnosed," Clare said. "Joe told you I went through cancer treatment? All is good."

"She just needs to take it easy," John said, "which she doesn't like to do."

Clare smiled and waved his comment away. "I spent the last fourteen months being coddled and tired. Daphne came over near every day just to talk to me. Didn't treat me like a fragile flower, which I appreciated."

"Me too," John said and took his wife's hand. He looked out at a car coming up the long driveway. "Barry and Helen are here." A second car was behind them. "And Shelley. Joe, get the barbecue started, would you? I'm going to get the steaks ready. You like steak, don't you, Kara?"

He said it in a tone of *You're not one of those vegetarians, are you?*

At least that's how she took it. "Love it," she said.

He nodded approvingly.

Kara chatted with Clare about the house and the view as she watched Barry and Helen wait for their niece, then the three walked up the porch stairs.

"Kara the bartender!" Barry said boisterously as he took her hand. "Glad you could come. Helen, Kara is helping Greg down at the Wrangler for a while. And this is our niece, Shelley, from Tucson."

"Nice to meet everyone."

Shelley barely acknowledged her. "I need to talk to Joe. Give me a second."

Kara watched as Shelley crossed the large deck to the corner where Joe was adjusting the gas barbecue and cleaning off the grates.

Barry started asking Kara questions, while Helen went inside with two bags of food she'd brought.

Barry's questions were innocuous, and a few minutes later Joe came back over to her. "Don't scare her away, Barry."

"I'm not. You don't scare easily, do you, Kara?"

"No, sir."

"See? I'm going to help John with the steaks. He likes them mooing, and I need to make sure they're at least warm. Excuse me."

"You have a nice family," Kara said to Joe.

"Thank you. I love them. Just worry about... well, just everything."

"Why worry? Your mom seems to be doing great. She looks good." She mentioned his mom specifically, though she suspected Joe was worried about a whole lot of things that weren't related to his mother's cancer.

"She is, gets tired easily, but is really doing great. Just...business isn't as good as it used to be, and with regulations and new rules and compliance issues, Dad just sometimes...well, you don't need to hear all the miserable details. It'll all work out."

Interesting. Kara filed that away to talk to Matt about later.

They chatted while cooking, then ate on a screened patio to avoid bugs. Shelley basically ignored Kara, which was both good and bad. Good because it was clear Shelley didn't think Kara was anyone important, but bad because Kara couldn't get a good read on her.

After dinner, Kara helped Helen clear the table

and rinse the dishes. She praised Helen's chili, and Helen talked for fifteen minutes about her tricks and tips for the kitchen. Kara listened even though most of the advice went over her head. She had a lot of skills; cooking wasn't one of them.

Through the window, as Kara was drying a pot, she saw Shelley and Joe talking—arguing, by their expressions and Shelley's clenched fists. She couldn't hear what they said, but body language didn't lie—Shelley was angry about something.

She glanced at Helen, then made sure no one else was in the kitchen. "Is everything okay with them?" She gestured out the window. "They're fighting like brother and sister."

Helen stared for a moment, then frowned. "I don't know what's up with them," she said. "But it's rude."

"I shouldn't have said anything."

"You came here for a nice dinner. Joe said you don't get a lot of time off. He shouldn't be arguing with his cousin." She sighed, put a wine glass away. "But they've always been like that, since they were kids."

"I don't have a big family, so I really wouldn't know."

Shelley suddenly pulled out her phone and started talking, walking away from Joe. He immediately turned and came into the house.

"You good?" Joe asked, leaned over and kissed her. His whole body was tense, his face flushed. Yeah, he and Shelley had gotten into something.

"I'm good. Are you?"

"Fine." He looked out the window, must have realized she could see him and Shelley arguing and said, "I told you how Shelley always gets under my skin."

Helen said, "I thought you outgrew that, Joseph."

"I did, Aunt Helen. But Shelley knows all the buttons to push."

"That she does," Helen said with a light laugh.

Kara waited for Joe to explain more.

He didn't. Instead, he grabbed two more beers and handed one to her. "Thirty minutes, then we're outta here, good?"

"Whatever you want," she said, "though I really like your family."

That seemed to make him happy. "Yeah, I'm lucky."

They sat in the family room and chatted with Barry and John—Helen and Clare were doing something in another room, and Shelley hadn't come back in from her call. Kara tried to assess if there was any strain between the people here, but other than Joe and Shelley, she didn't sense anything. Barry was chatty; John was quiet. That was likely more driven by their personalities than by any problems between the two. They both seemed comfortable with the other.

She heard a car pull up in front of the house; John said, "Joe, see who that is, would you mind?"

Joe rose and left the room. A few moments later, he came back with Marshal Wyatt Coleman.

Kara tried to make herself as invisible as possible; Matt had told her they might have a warrant to search Hargrove's locker. Was he here? Or was Coleman handling it alone?

"John, Barry, I'm really sorry to disturb you on a Sunday evening," Wyatt said, his hat in his hands, "but I wouldn't be here if it weren't important."

"Of course," John said. "Please come in."

Wyatt nodded to everyone who was in the room. "It's about David Hargrove's murder."

"Sit," John said. "Can I get you anything?"

"No, I'm good." He remained standing.

"Do you know who killed him?" Barry asked.

"No, Barry, sorry—we have a lead, and I'm following up on it. In fact, I just obtained a warrant."

"A warrant," John said bluntly.

"To search David's locker and desk at Southwest Copper. After my interview with Tanya this afternoon, I learned that his laptop is missing. Not only that, but she claims not to know where he went Friday evening or Saturday morning. I'm hoping that I'll find something in his locker or his calendar that can help me."

"And it can't wait until tomorrow?" Barry asked.

"It could," Wyatt said, "but I'll be honest with you—I'm a bit stumped on this one." Shelley came in from the kitchen and Wyatt nodded to her, then continued. "I can't rule anything out. Tanya was emphatic that he had his laptop with him when he left Saturday morning, and it wasn't in his truck when his body was found."

"What's going on?" Shelley asked.

"Wyatt has a warrant to search David's locker and desk," John said.

"It wouldn't be at the offices," Shelley said, "if his wife said he left with it from home on Saturday morning."

"Maybe not, but he could have stopped by there Saturday before he was killed. Or he could have a backup drive in his desk."

John nodded. "I remember his laptop. He always brought it in with him."

"I really hate to ask, but if you could let me in this evening, I promise to be quick. The warrant is very specific—David's work space, his laptop, his work computer, any company vehicle he used, and his locker."

"He didn't use any of our trucks," Barry said, "at least not regularly. John, you can stay here. I'll take Wyatt over."

"Nonsense," John said. "My company, my employee, my responsibility."

"I'll go with you, Uncle John," Shelley said.

"No, you have a long drive ahead of you tonight. I don't want you having to worry about this."

"Can I at least look over the warrant for you?" she asked. "To make sure this isn't a fishing expedition."

John nodded and gestured for Wyatt to show Shelley the document.

Wyatt handed Shelley a printout of the warrant. She read it slowly and carefully, then said, "It's in order. But why do you need to take his work computer too? That's Southwest property."

"He used it, so yes, I'm going to take it. Everything will be returned as soon as we don't need it.

This case is my number one priority. I didn't want to make a big scene tomorrow when everyone is at work," he said. "I want to resolve this quickly."

"I appreciate that, Wyatt," John said.

"Do you have any suspects?" Shelley asked.

"I can't really talk about the case right now," Wyatt said. "We're beginning to narrow our focus, but it's still a work in progress."

"Are you sure you don't want me to handle this, Uncle John?" Shelley asked.

"I've got this, honey. You stay, there's still dessert. Pack up a doggy bag, you're too skinny. Work too much," he mumbled.

Barry walked out with them, and Shelley went into the kitchen.

Joe hadn't said a word. He looked worried, but what would he have to be worried about?

Kara walked up to him and lightly touched his arm. "What's wrong?"

"My dad doesn't need this bullshit. I'm going to check on my mom. Can you excuse me for a second?"

"Of course," she said.

Suddenly she was alone in the room and the house was surprisingly quiet. She didn't even hear Shelley in the kitchen—had she left, as well? She heard two cars drive off and thought maybe Barry had left with John, until he walked back into the house. "Sorry about that, Kara," he said.

"It's not your fault. He's just doing his job, right?"

"I don't know what the police think they'll find at the office. Would you like another beer, Kara?"

"I don't know—maybe I should go. You have a lot on your plate right now."

"Nonsense. Joe has been under a lot of stress. Having you around has been a bright spot for him."

Kara didn't know what to say to that; tonight was the first time she'd met Joe's family, other than seeing Barry at the Wrangler a few times.

"I've made you uncomfortable."

"No. Maybe a little."

"Don't be. He told John and me a couple weeks ago he was going to ask you out. I think it was the day after he saw you at the bar, when you first started. Was a bit nervous about it, I think—which tells me he's smitten." Barry smiled. "That's an old-fashioned word, but it fits."

"I like Joe. But—I just lost someone close to me. I'm not ready for anything…you know." This was becoming uncomfortable. She actually liked these people. But breaking Joe's heart was the least of her concerns right now.

"He told us. Your fiancé. And truly, I'm so sorry. But you'll like it here. Don't let David's murder dissuade you. In fact, until poor David was killed, there hasn't been a violent crime here in a decade."

Except for Emma Perez. No one seemed to care about what had happened to Emma outside of town, except Matt and the FBI, Kara thought.

"Joe told me. I like Patagonia. It's much slower paced than LA. I needed it."

"But you're not staying," Barry said quietly.

She shook her head. "I'm not leading him on or anything. I told him."

"I know. He's a romantic at heart. And maybe you'll find that you need Patagonia more than anything else. It's a good place to relax, to heal, to find peace."

"That's what I've been doing," she said, doubly awkward with this conversation.

"Joe's a good man who's had to go through some shitty things of late. It's enough to…" His voice trailed off. "Anyway, nothing depressing. I'm going to get you that beer, okay? Just one more, promise."

"Thank you. I'll be out on the deck, if that's okay. It's a beautiful night."

She walked outside and took a deep breath. It *was* a lovely night, but her primary reason for going out there was because she heard a door close in the kitchen. Someone else was out here. She was suspicious by nature.

Kara stood at the edge of the deck, arms on the railing, ostensibly looking at the thin orange line that was the last of the sunset. One thing she loved here more than LA was the stars. They were everywhere, shining bright because there was no smog, no city lights. Even now, at twilight, she saw dozens of stars. In an hour there would be thousands.

Then she heard the voices.

Shelley and Joe. They were standing on the deck, but on the north side, outside the kitchen door. If Kara walked ten feet to the right, she'd be able to see them—and they'd be able to see her. Instead, she remained perfectly still and hoped that they didn't know she was out here.

"If this comes back on my dad, I swear, I'll never forgive you," Joe said.

"Get a grip. It's going to be fine," Shelley said.

"It's not *fine*. I can't believe you. I can't believe any of this. How *dare* you—"

"Stop. Okay? It's under control. And next time—"

A door opened and closed behind her. "Here you go, Kara," Barry said and handed her a cold beer.

She smiled and tapped her bottle to his. "Thank you." She pretended to drink. She never drank a beer she didn't open herself. She had swapped out two that Joe had served her with dinner and no one had suspected. She didn't think that anyone here would drug her, but when you worked undercover as long as she had, you had to be cautious. Even to the point of paranoia.

Shelley and Joe came from around the corner. "Uncle Barry. I didn't know you were out here," Joe said.

"It's too lovely to stay inside. Everything okay with you two? You hardly spoke at dinner."

"Same old stuff—Joe doesn't want to tell his dad he wants to go back to Phoenix."

"Shelley, I said stop with that. My parents need me here. It won't be forever."

"You're a good son, Joe," Barry said. "But your father will understand. You had a life there, and you visited all the time. It's not like you abandoned your family."

That was not what they were talking about, Kara knew. Not only because of the comments John had made earlier about understanding that the small town wasn't for young people. It was clear that Shelley and Joe were arguing about something else—but was it relevant to the David Hargrove murder? If Barry had waited just two more minutes before coming out, she might have known what their conversation was really about.

"I'd better head back. Have to be at work early tomorrow," Shelley said. "It was good to meet you, Kara. Kara what?"

"Smith," she said.

"That's common."

"You're a bitch," Joe said.

"What? It *is* a common name." Shelley smiled. "But seriously, it was good to meet you, Kara Smith. I hope to see you next week for family dinner."

"Thank you," Kara said.

Shelley kissed her uncle, then walked back inside.

"Ignore her," Joe said.

"She's right. Smith is common."

One reason she always used a common name when undercover was because it was almost impossible to trace, just in case, and very easy to lay a cyber trail. If anyone looked, they'd find an old Facebook page for Kara Smith with a photo of her—not too close-up, not too far—that was private but had a public profile that said she'd been engaged to "Colton Foxgrove." A photo of her and Colton from behind was also public, on a beach in LA. Everything else was private, and she hadn't updated the page in more than a year…even though they'd created it a month ago.

It was nice when the FBI had people in private business to backdate for them.

"I can take you home if you want," Joe said. "I don't know when my dad will be back. Let me just say goodbye to my mom."

"Go," Barry said. "Helen and I will stay with Clare and wait for John. Don't worry about a thing, Joe." He clapped his nephew on his back.

Kara didn't know why she had the impression that everyone was trying to make Joe feel better. She wondered if something had happened with his mother—Clare had seemed tired during dinner—or if finding David Hargrove's body had unnerved him. It should—most civilians didn't see a dead body ever in their lives, and rarely someone they knew who had been violently murdered.

Or it was something else. Like the "vendors" he met with the other day. His argument with Shelley. Kara's gut that Joe was acting distinctly different from when she first met him three weeks ago. Kara had a feeling that Shelley had been watching Joe closely all night. Maybe for no specific reason, but it seemed odd.

Odd enough that Kara made a note to send Ryder a message tonight to look deeper into Shelley Brown. She knew that Michael had raised the flag…now she was.

CHAPTER 26

Sunday night
Patagonia, Arizona

Joe walked Kara to her door. He wanted an invite in, but Kara had to put up a barrier. If Joe came in, he'd expect to stay the night. He'd been subtly leading up to it all night, and her conversation with Barry just about clinched it. The whole night had given her a weird vibe, and not just because the marshal came to execute a search warrant after dinner. Matt had told her it might happen, so she was prepared; what she wasn't truly prepared for was knowing that Joe had fallen for her to the point that he was talking to his family about trying to get her to stay in Patagonia. They'd met only three weeks ago; this was their second "date."

If she'd known that Joe Molina was clingy and possessive with his girlfriends, she would have planned this out completely different.

The conversation between Joe and Shelley bothered her, but it didn't seem to be in context to anything they'd previously discussed. And Shelley telling her and Barry that it was about Joe wanting to go back to Phoenix—and Joe going along with it—didn't ring true either. But admittedly, Kara heard only part of a conversation. Something might be off, but it might not have anything to do with David Hargrove's murder or the FBI investigation into illegal dumping.

Except...what if Joe had talked to Shelley about the FBI investigation? She was a lawyer; he might want to consult with her. He wasn't good at keeping secrets; he'd told Matt multiple times how uncomfortable he was keeping the information from his father. But what would it mean if he had talked to Shelley? Probably nothing.

Except... Shelley and Joe had talked to the same two men at the bar, a day apart. Two men who were suspicious in how they presented themselves. Yeah, she shouldn't judge a book by its cover, but twelve years as a cop and she couldn't help it.

None of this added up.

She had told Matt not to bring in Joe Molina. She wished now that she had pushed harder. Because while she didn't want to think that Joe was party to murder, now...she was thinking.

She was squeamish. She needed to do her own

investigation to find the truth. Her gut told her Joe had a secret.

Might not be murder. Might not be illegal dumping.

But could be.

Not you. That's why you have a team. You need to tell Matt.

What if she was wrong?

You're not wrong.

Her instincts had saved her life more than once.

She unlocked her door but only cracked it open. "I really enjoyed dinner, Joe. Thank you."

"I'm sorry about that whole thing with Wyatt. I should have expected that they'd want to go through David's things. I just didn't think they'd come on Sunday night."

"It's a good thing that they're taking his murder seriously, right? And if they're looking through his things, they must have an idea of what happened."

"Maybe, but my dad doesn't need this right now."

"Is your mom okay? You seem worried about her."

"She's tired. She has a doctor's appointment this coming Friday, and we're hoping that he'll adjust her meds and she'll regain her energy. I hate seeing her like this."

She touched his face because it was the right thing to do. "It's hard on you and your family. I hope they figure it out."

He nodded, put his forehead on hers and whispered, "I don't want to go."

"I know. But if I invite you in, you may not leave and I don't think I'm quite ready for that."

He pressed his body against hers, firmly kissed her, increasing his intensity, the urgency. And if this were last night, if this were before she had doubts about Joe, about his emotional state of mind, about possible secrets…she might have given in. Because sometimes, sex was just sex. It didn't have to have an emotional attachment; it didn't have to mean anything except release. Satisfaction. Lust.

But not now.

Still, she didn't pull away. She had to get as close to Joe as possible so he didn't suspect that she was suspicious about anything. And she might be wrong.

She hoped she was wrong.

She was rarely wrong.

Her thigh felt his phone vibrating in his pocket.

You're right.

Dammit.

"Do you have to get that?" she whispered.

"No. You're more important than any call."

She put her arms around his neck, and he took that as a sign that she wanted more, which he was primed to give. He pressed her harder against the door frame and kissed her again. A full-body kiss, and if they were naked, it would have been deep penetration. The door swung in and he was slowly, steadily, pushing her inside her house. He'd gone from light and sweet to dark and passionate in a blink, and she got that little thrill she always did when she anticipated that sex was going to be fun, wild, cathartic.

Just not here, not with Joe.

His phone vibrated yet again.

A moan escaped his throat, and she put her hands between them. "Joe."

"Sorry. Sorry."

"No apologies."

He stepped back, ran a hand through his hair. "I really like you, Kara. I hope—I don't want to blow it."

"You didn't. I'll see you tomorrow, okay?"

"Promise?"

She smiled, nodded, watched him walk down the rickety porch steps and get in his truck.

She itched to follow him, find out who was calling him, but that would be foolish. She wished she could have bugged his truck, but she didn't have the equipment, and if she left her phone in the cab set to record, he might have found it. That wouldn't have been smart.

She stepped back through the doorway and paused.

Someone was in her house.

She reached into her purse for her gun.

"Close the door."

The voice was quiet, low and familiar.

"Fuck you, Costa."

She slammed her door and flipped on a light.

Matt stood in the doorway of her bedroom. The place wasn't big—living room, kitchen, bedroom. And Matt's presence practically overpowered the space.

He stared at the gun in her hand.

"I sent you a message that we needed to talk."

"And I told you that coming here was a problem. My neighbor has his eyes on me."

"The sixty-nine-year-old vet."

"His eyesight and his brain are intact, and he gave me a look today. He's watching. I don't think for any reason other than curiosity, but I have to be careful. Just, why, dammit!"

She went to her kitchen and grabbed a beer from her fridge. She didn't want to offer Matt one, but she did anyway. Not *offer* so much as shove it in his hand.

He didn't smile, but he opened the beer and drank half of it.

She glared at him. "What the *hell* were you thinking? What if I invited Joe in for drinks?"

"I would have hidden in the bedroom."

"And what if I decided to take him to bed?" she snapped.

A darkness crossed Matt's expression. She didn't know where it came from, and for a split second she was almost scared.

Almost.

She opened her mouth to speak, to accuse him of being *jealous*, but the words didn't come. And as if he knew what she was going to say, and that she couldn't get it out, Matt stepped toward her.

There were a thousand ways this could go wrong. They'd had a connection two months ago…but it was out of lust, of mutual attraction, of opportunity. She needed to say no, she needed to take a step back because Matt Costa wasn't Colton Fox. He wasn't a cop who was happy with a mutually satisfying friends-with-benefits arrangement. He might not see that in him, but Kara saw it. She read it down to his DNA.

Yet.

She lusted. It was as simple as that. And from the minute she'd landed in his bed two months ago, she wanted Matt Costa to completely let go. He hadn't. He simmered. He *wanted* but refused to take. He *ached* but refused to give in to his passion. He held back, even when he let go.

And she wanted him fully.

And *damn*, she would use his jealousy to get that out of him.

She slammed her beer down on the table, and two steps later she had him against the wall. He was shocked, surprised. Really? After the electricity that sparked between them, even when they were ten feet apart?

He groaned, a deep, guttural moan that had Kara on the verge of orgasm just from the sound of his desire. And that was when she knew she had him undone.

Matt had never been jealous before in his life, but listening to Kara and Joe making out in the doorway, he became angry and annoyed. With her, with himself, with the entire situation. This was exactly what they'd planned…yet he didn't want it.

Wanting Kara was wrong. Two months ago it was borderline. She didn't work for him. They'd been drinking (the first time); they had a mutual attraction. It had…well, it had happened and had been exactly what he'd needed in that moment. What Kara wanted. But now? She was on his team. She was part of his work life. He was responsible for her safety, her career, her well-being...and he wanted her in bed. Now.

He stepped away. Kara was flushed, her eyes opened, and she said, "Stop thinking and take me to bed. Now, Mathias Costa. I want you."

She was so demanding, so enticing, she knew exactly what he wanted and she gave it willingly.

Slow down. Savor this. It's going to be the last time. It has to be the last time...

He picked her up, carried her to the small bedroom and dropped her on the bed. He stared at her in the dim light, doubting himself, questioning this decision.

You're not questioning it. You know it's wrong. Walk away. Walk the fuck away right now...

She pulled off her dress. All she wore was a thong and a thin bra. The white bandage on her arm, from the cut she sustained this morning, practically glowed in the dim light. Her scars, from cases long ago, long before he met her, marred her trim, muscular figure. Each scar had a story to tell. He wanted to know the history of each mark.

Dammit, staring at her, he was horny.

He'd been horny from the minute he heard her walk up the porch steps.

It was more than sex, but he didn't want it to be. He didn't want to think about it.

But for the last two months, since she walked out of his life, he had wanted this moment again. Maybe to convince himself that it was just sex, just a moment in time, a way to release tension with a very willing partner. A partner he had complex personal and professional feelings about. A partner he respected and admired even when he was frustrated with her.

She wasn't smiling, she wasn't frowning. Her light eyes flashed with intensity. Lust. Reflecting everything he felt.

"Come. Here. *Now*."

It was a command.

Walk away, Costa.

She closed her eyes and put her arms above her head in the ultimate sign of trust.

"Just let go, Matt," she whispered.

"Kara—are you sure?"

She opened her eyes. Didn't say a word, but the way she looked at him…damn. There was no other place he wanted to be. No one else he wanted to be with. Sleeping with her now, while she was on his team, was wrong on every level…but he didn't want to resist. He craved her, plain and simple. From the day he saw her jogging around Liberty Lake, before he knew her name, he had wanted her.

Against his better judgment, he let go.

Matt and Kara were dressed again and sitting at the small kitchen table. It was well after midnight, but Matt had wanted to fill Kara in on what he'd learned from Wyatt.

"The search at Southwest Copper went off without a hitch. Wyatt and I decided that it was best if he went in alone, with his two deputies, because Molina knows them. Wyatt uncovered a flash drive in his locker."

"That was fast."

"John Molina was cooperative. He wants answers. Wyatt and I went back and forth about telling him about A-Line, but based on what we know of the man, he would likely confront the driver tomorrow."

"Do you think they're even going to show? If the company was just David and this Kline guy, why would Kline show up?"

"I don't think anyone will show, but I can't be certain, so this way keeps as much information contained as possible."

"Okay. And? What was on the flash drive?"

"A copy of Hargrove's files, likely from his missing laptop, last downloaded Friday. Copies of all the financial statements and shell corps. Other names, payments and copies of emails. Based on information I read, we think that David and Tanya got in over their heads financially, and Roger connected them with a loan shark. They couldn't pay back the loan and the interest, so they came up with this idea for A-Line. Roger borrowed the money—from the same loan shark—for the truck. But there's some other files that don't support that theory. We sent everything to Zack to analyze with the documents he has from Las Vegas."

"Have they paid any money back? Because there's no reason to kill someone who owes you money."

"Zack agrees. This isn't about the loan shark—it's about what David and Tanya did for him. Zack thinks they're the figureheads of a major money-laundering scheme, but he needs a little time to analyze the new information. Wyatt and I are going back to talk to Tanya first thing in the morning. With this information we might be able to get her to tell the truth. I'm going to push—we don't have enough for an arrest warrant yet, but money laundering is serious, and the big question is who were they working for. None of the three has any background in finances to put together something like this. If anything, we can get her for obstruction of justice if she lies to me. A small charge that won't stick, but it'll get her under my thumb for the next few days."

"And Roger Kline's still in the wind."

"We're looking for him. Tanya said she talked to him this morning, but I'm not certain."

"You think he might be dead too."

"It's crossed my mind."

"Again," Kara asked, "why kill Hargrove?"

"Million-dollar question. Finding Roger Kline is now our number one priority, and I think—I know—that Tanya knows more than she's telling. Nothing here so far tells us exactly where they dumped the toxic slag, at least that we could figure out in a couple hours. They have records that they sold the toxic waste to a company in Kansas, so we need to follow up on that because the company doesn't have a digital footprint and may not even exist. If it's part of the paper trail, it would expose them pretty quick—within a year or two— so either they are complete idiots, or they had no intention of keeping the scam going for long."

Matt reached out and touched her hand. Ran his thumb up and down her palm, slowly, erotically. He skimmed over her forearm, lightly caressed her bandage. Consciously or unconsciously, he was turning her back on. Hell, he had never turned her off. She was well satiated, but still she'd go back for more…

Except now she was in work mode. She said, "That would mean they planned on running. Leaving the country, getting new IDs, and nothing about the Hargroves tells me that they'd survive like that."

"Tanya seems entrenched here, with her friends and her antiques business," Matt concurred. "So you vote for idiot."

"I vote that they thought they could bury the paper trail and no one would be the wiser. Maybe keep the company going for a year, collect money to pay off their debt and shut it down."

"I think," Matt said slowly, "that whoever they went into business with is using them. And yes—they are idiots—willfully being used." He paused. "What I don't see is murder."

"You don't think any of them killed Emma Perez."

Carefully, he said, "I don't think David or Tanya have the capacity to hit a girl over the head with a rock and act like nothing happened. Jury's out on Roger Kline."

"Where does Amada come in? The bunker? The trafficking?"

"I don't think it does."

A big fucking coincidence, she thought, growing angry. She pulled her hand away from Matt's and got up. Grabbed another beer. She didn't want a beer, but she needed something to do before she jumped down his throat. Because Amada was important. The missing kids were important. She didn't give a flying fuck about toxic dumping or greedy criminals. She wanted justice.

"Kara—" Matt began.

"No. Do *not* placate me. These people are criminals. They just don't care. They don't care about the environment, they don't care about a flock of dead birds, and they don't care about dead kids."

"We have nothing to connect the Hargroves to trafficking children."

"They deliberately avoid thinking about it." She paused. "I told you my parents were con artists. When I was a kid, I helped them run cons all the time. I didn't think about it because the guilt would sink in. I didn't see a way out when I was young. When I was thirteen or so, I began to sabotage some of their cons. This was after my dad went to prison and my mom eventually hooked up with an asshole. I didn't fuck with all of their scams— they would have known—but enough that eventually my mom's boyfriend figured it out and sent me packing. That's how I ended up at my grandmother's at fifteen."

"Nothing you did as a kid is comparable to what these people are doing," Matt said sharply. "How can you even think that way?"

"I'm not saying it's comparable—I'm saying it's surprisingly easy to *not* think about the repercussions. To *not* think about people you hurt. So either they really don't care, or they honestly haven't thought about their actions. Maybe they convinced themselves that they weren't hurting anyone. I'm not cutting them any slack—I'm just suggesting that they aren't thinking about what *could* happen, only the benefits of their scheme. So yeah, I think that the bigger picture goes beyond their greed to defraud Southwest Copper and make a quick buck dumping slag in the desert. That maybe they could have hit Emma over the head with a rock and justified it because she was getting close to figuring out what they were doing. And little Mexican kids? Who are they to anyone, right? Just…commodities, to be bought and sold and traded. Not their problem, not anyone's fucking problems!"

Matt walked over to her. He took the unopened beer from her hand, then put his hands on her shoulders and looked her in the eye.

She was agitated and angry and she didn't want him to pull out some fucking justice card. She knew justice was selective. She knew they couldn't save everyone. She knew it was an uphill battle. But dammit! What about Amada? Who was going to grieve for her? Who was going to miss her?

"I'm not going to walk away from what we found this morning. I think we're looking at two different cases, but as far as I'm concerned, they're both mine."

"They are both *ours*," she corrected.

Matt nodded, smiled. "Ours."

She felt herself relax, just a fraction. She believed him, that he wouldn't walk away.

"But right now," Matt continued, "we have Roger Kline on the run, and Tanya Hargrove knows what's going on...even if she doesn't realize exactly what she knows. I'm going to force her to look at the reality of her situation. She'll tell me everything she knows."

"She doesn't seem to be the type to care about dead wildlife."

"No, I don't think she is. But I have an idea." He leaned over and kissed her. She was surprised, and she didn't get surprised like that. But the kiss was... comfortable. That was odd for her. "Thank you."

"I didn't do anything."

"You gave me the idea."

She had no idea what she'd said, but if it got them the answers they needed, great.

He kissed her again, his body as close to hers as possible without touching anything but her lips. "I'd better leave," he whispered.

Her mouth parted and he took more. He wanted more. She felt it. She craved it, just like he did.

She leaned against him, and if they were naked, they'd have been having sex against the counter. That sounded like a lot of fun, a perfect way to clear her mind.

Matt groaned, then stepped back. "I don't want to go, but I have to. I don't know how this is going to work, Kara."

"Stop overthinking everything," she said. "I'm not going to be an albatross around your neck. We have fun together, Matt. We need to blow off steam.

At least I need to, and I needed this tonight. *You* needed it."

He stared at her. Yeah, they both needed it.

Maybe you need each other.

No, she wasn't going to go there.

"Remember, I promised," she said. "I don't kiss and tell."

He didn't look satisfied with her answer, but again, he really had to get out of his head sometimes. "Trust me," she said.

"I do."

That, she realized, was all that really mattered.

He walked to the back door.

"Matt." He turned and looked at her. "Did you run Shelley Brown?"

"So far, nothing of interest. She's a criminal defense lawyer, as you know, so I suppose anything is possible, but most defense lawyers aren't the scumbags you see on television."

"I haven't had much luck with them," Kara said, "but I'll take your word for it."

"The Tucson office is looking at her, but there's nothing on the surface."

"Dig deeper."

"Why? What happened?"

"I met her tonight. Got a vibe. She's calculating. I don't have a better word for it. And I need to keep a better eye on Joe."

"Kara—"

"He knows something he hasn't told you. He's wrestling with it, and I don't know what it is. I think I can find out. Originally I thought it was guilt about wanting to return to Phoenix, thinking he would disappoint his parents, but that's not it. He and Shelley were arguing about something else, and *she* lied to me about what it was, not Joe. He didn't say anything. I can't prove any of this—hell, I don't even know what *this* is—but it was enough to have me suspicious."

"I'll talk to Christine first thing in the morning and put Shelley Brown at the top of the list. But why would she be involved with Hargrove and scamming her family?"

"It might have nothing to do with him. But she's up to something, and I keep circling around to the so-called vendors both she and Joe met with. I don't know what her demeanor was yesterday at the picnic, but Joe was nervous and concerned when he was talking to the same guys on Friday."

"Okay. You sold me. Your instincts are usually good."

"Good? They're the best," Kara said with a smile. "Go, you have a busy day tomorrow."

"You know, Kara, you're really bossy." Then he winked and left, and she burst out laughing.

She and Matt were going to get along just fine.

CHAPTER 27

Monday morning
Desert south of Patagonia, Arizona

Frank Block was getting too old for camping.

He never thought he'd say that, but even though he had a mat under his sleeping bag, getting up each morning revealed more aches and pains than the day before. For fifty-two years old, he was in great shape—he jogged regularly and hiked nearly every weekend. His job at AREA required him to be fit and spend a lot of time outdoors. The heat didn't bother him, but he hadn't been camping in years and sleeping on the ground three nights in a row was showing his age.

He was up before dawn and double-checked his notes and his map. For the last three days he'd covered more than a hundred square miles with his drone, using aerial maps from each season over the last two years, topographical maps, and his expert knowledge of bird migration. He had a list of every site that AREA and Game & Fish had tested in March and April after Emma's murder, but he looked at each again to see if he could spot any dead wildlife.

Nothing. No dead birds, no untested ponds. He hadn't found any unexpected streams or pools of water in any size.

Early Monday morning, he broke camp and moved to an area near the old town of Harshaw, south of Patagonia. From here he could check the vast area of plateaus, ravines and canyons all the way to the San Rafael State Natural Area. He didn't expect to find anything too far south—not only because that would be out of the range of the birds that Emma had found, but because it would be difficult and impractical to dump slag that far into the desert.

He'd considered that the dump site could be anywhere here, with a seasonal stream flowing through it, causing contamination downstream in standing water. He also considered that the water could be gone by now, so he was particularly looking for an indication that pooled water had recently dried at an unmarked site. He could bring in a team to test the soil, sand and foliage in the area to see if there *had* been any contamination in the area. Then they could follow the presumed path of the stream to where it may have crossed through the toxic slag.

He understood copper refinery enough to know that the only way the slag would be toxic would be if the water actually went through it but not in enough quantity to dilute the arsenic and lead. Both were naturally occurring in soil and safe amounts of arsenic were often found in ground water. The reason the birds had died was because of their size and metabolism.

The primary problem was if there was a buildup of toxins over time and the runoff went into a major watering hole for wildlife. They'd start seeing larger game getting sick and dying, including endangered species, like the pronghorn, a deer that was native to the area. The species he was more concerned about were birds, like the bobwhite, that were just now beginning to see an uptick in their numbers. They would be vulnerable to high levels of arsenic in the water.

But in the end, while he cared deeply about the animals and the desert environment, he desperately wanted justice for Emma. It was a laborious process, but Frank was determined.

He was frustrated he hadn't heard anything from Matt Costa yet. The FBI agent said he would call if he had any news—so Frank assumed no news meant Matt and his team hadn't found anything. He'd checked his phone regularly, sometimes having to hike a mile to get reception. Still, nothing.

By the time he arrived in the valley he planned to survey for the next day or two, it was dawn. He secured his truck in a spot that should get afternoon shade, then hiked with his drone, laptop and lunch to a plateau that would give him the best range. He set the coordinates, sat back and navigated the drone.

It was peaceful watching the land from the drone's camera. He saw a family of mule deer cutting through a canyon. They were all over Tucson, but they didn't have many this far south, so he felt lucky to catch sight of them. He followed them for a while—they might have a water source he wasn't aware of. If they found the contaminated water, the adults would be large enough to survive, but the young offspring trekking on their spindly legs would be more vulnerable.

He tracked them to a known water source, one that Game & Fish had already ruled safe. He watched for a while, then realized he was wasting time.

He flew the drone back along the canyon, then over a hill. There were two cabins near the top of the hill, which boasted pines and cottonwood among the cactus. He'd often thought about retiring to a cabin in the middle of nowhere. He'd considered Flagstaff—not as hot in the summer—and it was close to the Grand Canyon, which Frank had always enjoyed exploring.

Movement caught his attention. It was a person, a young male, cutting through a path near one of the cabins, not coming up the road. Did he live there? Frank set the drone to record. He came in closer, and the boy looked up. He was Hispanic, twelve maybe, wearing ragged clothes. He looked terrified when he saw the drone.

He was carrying two-gallon jugs of water.

Something was not right.

Frank had seen the same kid yesterday through the drone but hadn't thought much of it—a few families lived south of 82. People on vacation who wanted to get away from technology and civilization for a few days. Frank had a friend once who was writing a book and came up to a one-room cabin in this area with no indoor plumbing in order to find peace and quiet to finish his project.

But this kid was wearing what looked like the same clothes as yesterday that hung loosely on his thin frame. Same clothes, different day…different area. How many miles away? Five? Maybe fewer as the crow flies.

What was he up to?

Frank brought the drone back and packed everything up. The kid was scared, but was he scared of the drone or something else? He looked like a runaway…dirty, disheveled, uncut hair—but why here? Was he in trouble? In hiding?

He could be a migrant from across the border; it wouldn't be the first time someone had broken into a vacant house for shelter. But he was just a kid… a scared kid.

He should call Marshal Coleman, but Frank didn't want to turn a child in to the authorities. He should—he was a state employee—but first he wanted to know the story. If this was a kid in trouble, he could get help. If he wasn't? If he was a gang member or runaway, Frank would call the authorities.

Frank had a good sense of direction, and he'd been studying the area maps for days, so he knew exactly where the cabins were that he'd seen on camera. He hiked down to his truck and fifteen minutes later was driving up a winding road. He passed one vacant cabin—it was boarded up—and stopped at the second. This one wasn't boarded but looked empty. A vacation house, possibly. Small, functional, a good place to get off the grid for a weekend. Didn't look like there was any electricity up here, but there might be a generator around back.

He got out of his truck. "Hello!" he called out. "My name is Frank. I'm not going to hurt you. I want to help."

He cautiously walked up to the porch. He had left his rifle in the car—he didn't want to scare the kid—but now he wished he'd brought it. His daughter would call him a bleeding heart, a foolish old man who saw only the good in people. Which wasn't true—but he tended to focus on positives. His instincts told him this boy was in trouble. Frank couldn't turn his back on anyone in trouble.

"The drone is mine. I saw you yesterday and again this morning. I can help you, son."

He tried the door. It was unlocked. He knocked. "I'm coming in. I mean you no harm." He repeated that in Spanish as he opened the door. *"No quiero hacerte daño."*

He didn't speak Spanish well, just enough to get by.

He pushed open the door.

The boy stood there with a gun aimed at him.

"*¡Vete! ¡Vete!*"

"I'm not going to hurt you. *No daño.*"

He kept his hands up.

"Put down the gun, please." He nodded toward the weapon.

The boy had been crying.

"Are you hurt? *¿Lastimas?*"

He looked into the second room. His hands were shaking, and Frank hoped he didn't accidentally fire the gun.

He pointed to himself. "My name is Frank. I'm camping. I want to help you. *Quiero ayudarte.* What is your name?" He pointed to the boy. "*¿Nombre?*"

His bottom lip quivered. "*Mi hermana. ¿Mi hermana está muy enferma y la ayudas?*"

He spoke too fast for Frank to keep up; all he understood was *sister.*

"Your sister? *Hermana?*"

The boy nodded and looked at the doorway again.

Frank walked slowly to the door, his hands still up, palms out. The boy didn't stop him.

On the bed, under several blankets even though the cabin was warm, was a young girl. She couldn't be more than ten. She was flushed, and the foul stench of vomit came from the room. One of the gallon jugs was on the nightstand next to her. The boy spoke rapidly, but Frank didn't understand anything except that this was his sister and her name was Bianca.

The girl moaned.

Frank went to her side. She was burning up and her skin appeared swollen.

"Bianca, my name is Frank. *Nombre* Frank." He had only basic first aid training. He had no idea what was wrong with her.

He smelled garlic.

He looked at the water jug.

"Where did you get this water?" he asked the boy.

The boy didn't answer.

"This is important! Where did you get the water? *Agua?*" He picked up the bottle and held it out for the boy.

Bianca said something in Spanish to the boy, and he responded, then she said to Frank in broken English, "We found a pond. I'm thirsty, all the time."

She sounded weak, her words labored and soft.

"I need to know where the pond is," Frank said. "Bianca, you have been poisoned. You need a hospital. Tell your brother you need a doctor."

She did, and the boy shook his head and raised the gun.

"Bianca, what is your brother's name?"

"Angel."

"Angel," Frank said, "your sister has arsenic poisoning. From the water." He pointed again. "She needs immediate medical help." He turned to the girl. "Tell him you will die if you don't go to a hospital."

She did, tears in her eyes, and Angel started crying, but he didn't lower the gun.

Frank needed someone to help him. "Can I call for help? Please? One person?"

Angel didn't want to, but Bianca was talking to him, and after a couple of minutes, he put the gun down at his side and nodded.

Bianca said, "He's scared the bad men will come find us. Please help, but no bad men. They will kill us."

What had these kids been through? Frank took out his phone. He walked outside far enough until he found a signal on the edge of the front porch. He dialed Matt Costa's number. Angel watched him closely.

"Costa." He sound gruff and busy.

"It's Frank."

"I don't have time to—"

"I found someone who knows where the contaminated water is. But it's a complicated situation. I need you to meet me. Do you have medical training?"

"What happened? Are you hurt?"

"I'm in the hills south of Eighty-Two. Southwest of Harshaw, which is a tiny old community south of Patagonia—I can send you exact coordinates. I'm with two kids, brother and sister. They found the pond, drank from it, and one is very sick, but they don't want to go to the hospital. They are terrified. I don't want to say more than that. I trust you, Matt. You speak Spanish. I need you to come here alone."

Matt didn't say anything for a long minute. "Are you one hundred percent positive?"

"Yes." He hoped.

"I have someone with medical training on the team. I'll bring him with me."

"A man?"

"Yes, why does that matter?"

"The sick child is a little girl who says she is terrified of bad men. If you understand what I'm saying."

Again, silence. Matt understood, Frank was certain. "Hold on." He muted the phone. Frank hoped he had done the right thing, but he was certain that if he did nothing, Bianca would die.

Matt came back on the phone. "Are you sure you can't get the kid to a hospital?"

"I'm positive." Frank didn't want to tell Matt everything, but it looked like he didn't have a choice. "Her brother has a gun. He's scared, Matt, not dangerous, but I promised him I would only bring in one person."

"Shit, Frank. Okay. Tell me your exact location. I'll be there as fast as I can."

CHAPTER 28

Monday
Patagonia, Arizona

Matt ended the call and immediately called Ryder. "What do you have by way of medical supplies?"

"I have a well-stocked first aid kit."

"We have a possible poisoning."

"They need to call the poison hotline. Or go straight to a hospital."

"We can't—not yet. I'll explain on the way. Just be ready. I'm at Tanya's house. I have to talk to her, but I'll pick you up as soon as I can. Is Michael set?"

"Yes, sir," Ryder said. "He has the tracker, and two agents from Tucson are prepared to follow as soon as it's activated."

"Good. Kline probably won't show, but Michael

needs to be prepared." Matt had briefed Michael last night. Wyatt hadn't told John Molina about A-Line and Hargrove's involvement because they concurred that if Molina knew his employee had defrauded him and committed serious environmental crimes, he wouldn't be able to keep a poker face. Plus, there was still a chance—a good chance, in Matt's mind—that someone else at Southwest Copper was involved. Michael was keeping eyes and ears open in the hopes of learning who that person might be.

Matt ended the call, and Wyatt Coleman pulled up behind him. His phone beeped, and Matt looked at Frank's location. Now that they had a possible location for the dump site—if Frank wasn't jumping the gun—Matt didn't really need Tanya's cooperation. But he still had to find her brother, Roger Kline.

Matt stared at the map, enlarged it. He knew this area—it was on the hill near the place where David Hargrove had been killed.

What the *hell* was going on? Could one of those kids have possibly killed him?

He sent Frank a message to be careful, that the kids may be dangerous. It didn't matter how young they were; age had nothing to do with violence, not anymore.

Matt met Wyatt as they walked up the driveway to Tanya's house. "I'm going to play hardball, because I'm tired of this game she's playing, and Frank Block has information about the dump site.

I'm putting all the cards on the table and telling her she's an accessory to murder."

"Good cop, bad cop again, I see," Wyatt said with humor that Matt didn't feel right now.

Wyatt knocked on the door.

No answer.

He knocked again. "Tanya? It's Wyatt Coleman."

He glanced at the driveway and said to Matt, "That's Crystal Vasquez's car. They should be here; it's only eight in the morning."

He knocked again. "Crystal? It's Wyatt. I need to talk to Tanya."

Then Matt stepped up and knocked louder. "FBI, open the door. We have a warrant." Wyatt raised his eyebrows at the tone, and Matt said, "I told you, no kid gloves."

Still no answer.

Coleman tried the door. Locked. "I'll get a locksmith out here."

Matt didn't have time for that. He said, "I'm going to walk around the house, see if anything is unlocked."

"*Do* you have a warrant?"

"Yes—to search any and all property belonging to David or Tanya Hargrove, and Roger Kline."

Matt walked down the side yard and around to the back. Two sliding glass doors opened up into the yard, and neither had closed blinds. He tried the first; it went into the kitchen. Locked. The second led to the family room. Also locked. But when he looked through the window, he saw Crystal Vasquez asleep on the couch.

Matt pounded on the glass door. "Crystal Vasquez! Law enforcement! Open up!"

At first she didn't move, and Matt feared she was dead. He pulled his gun out, uncertain what he might find or who was inside. He didn't see any blood or signs of violence through the window.

Wyatt joined him at the door, saw the gun in Matt's hand. "What happened?"

Matt was about to break the door when he saw Crystal move.

Wyatt rapped loudly on the glass. "Crystal! It's Wyatt! Open the door!"

She was moving slowly, as if she were sick. One hand went to her head. Matt pounded on the door some more.

"Crystal! FBI!"

She sat up, looked at him, blinked. It took her two tries to stand, and then she staggered to the door as if she were drunk. She fumbled with the lock and it finally opened.

"Where's Tanya?" Matt demanded as soon as she slid the door open.

She didn't speak right away, then said, "Sleeping?"

She leaned over. "I feel sick. I'm sorry. What time is it?"

"Eight fifteen in the morning," Coleman said.

Matt ran upstairs, gun out, looking for Tanya. He searched every room; she wasn't here. Her bed hadn't been slept in.

He came back downstairs. "When did she leave?"

"Leave? She's upstairs. Sleeping. We...we had a

glass of wine, and she said she was tired. I called Rob and told him I was going to stay overnight to keep Tanya company, then I fell asleep…" She looked at the couch. "I… I don't know why I didn't wake up sooner. I'm so tired."

Coleman said, "She's gone. You don't know where she went?"

"Tanya? No." She frowned.

Matt called Christine. He'd spoken to her earlier about digging deeper into Shelley Brown, based on his conversation with Kara last night, so he wasn't surprised when she sounded a bit irritated. "I just got to the office, Matt. I'm working on it."

"Not that. It's Tanya Hargrove. She's in the wind. She drugged her friend last night and disappeared sometime after…" He looked at Crystal.

"Drugged?" Her eyes widened, and she sat heavily back on the couch. "We had the wine at ten…"

"She left sometime between ten last night and eight this morning, but my guess it was last night after— Crystal, what time did you talk to your husband?"

"Before the wine. I mean I… I only had half a glass. I'm pregnant. Oh, God, drugged? Are you sure?"

Wyatt immediately went to her side. "I'll get you to a hospital."

Matt said to Christine, "She left last night, likely before midnight. We need to find her."

"I'll get on it immediately, planes, trains, automobiles."

"Don't forget border patrol, but if she crossed last night, it's going to be a bitch to get her back."

"I have it covered."

"Thanks, Chris."

"Why would she do this?" Crystal asked them. "I don't understand."

Matt asked, "Did she talk to her brother yesterday?"

"I don't know. She was upset after you left, and I tried to console her—she could have," Crystal admitted. "But not in front of me."

Matt said, "Wyatt, can I talk to you in the other room?"

Wyatt looked at Crystal. "I'm okay, I think," she said. "I need to call Rob, is that okay?"

"Call him, have him pick you up and take you to the doctor, just to make sure everything is okay. Congratulations—I didn't know."

"Fourteen weeks. I didn't want to say anything until I had my next appointment, just to make sure, you know? We've been trying for so long... oh, God, why would she do this to me?" Her hand went to her stomach as her other hand picked up her phone.

Wyatt followed Matt to the other room. "Frank Block called me and may have found the contaminated water, but it's a complicated situation and I need to be there."

"Do you want me to go with you?" Wyatt said.

"No—I have Christine tracking Kline and Tanya, but you're local. You know everyone they know. Check her business, her best friend, any fam-

ily in the area. Find out if she said anything to anyone. Look at her search history on her computers."

"I have some ideas."

"I'll call you as soon as I know about the dump
site, and let me know if you find them."

The A-Line truck was scheduled to arrive at
Southwest Copper at nine that morning. It didn't
come. Michael wasn't surprised. Matt had said he
felt there was little chance that it would show up.

Michael made an excuse to go into the admin-
istrative building shortly after the truck didn't arrive when scheduled. He was talking to Ginger, the
HR person at Southwest, about the 401(k) plan that
the company offered, pretending he didn't quite
understand the paperwork. The girl was very nice
and patient with him while he asked rather obvious questions.

The only people with private offices were Ginger and John Molina, but he never closed his door
and was rarely in his office as it was. Today he was,
and Barry stood in the doorway. Michael made a
point to keep Ginger's door open, and while only
half listening to her, he focused on John's conversation with his brother-in-law.

"I called A-Line and no one answered. No voice
mail, no anything," John was saying.

"Maybe the number was entered wrong."

"I'm looking at the business card in David's
file. It's right here. I dialed twice. No one is there.
They're nearly an hour late. I have six men just

waiting around to load the truck when it gets here—this isn't the way to do business."

"I'll see what I can find out."

"You know what I also found in—"

"Michael?" Ginger was saying. "Do you understand?"

"Excuse me? Oh, yes, that helps. Thank you." He rose and took his folder from her.

John was still talking. "—for a year! Why would David authorize payments up front?"

"I'll talk to the accountant," Barry said.

Michael walked out of the HR office. As he left, John said, "Don't bother, I have a meeting with them in Tucson tomorrow morning."

"Maybe we should talk to Shelley about this first."

"She means well, but this is above her head," John said. "Every time I have a concern about something, she waves it off. This is serious. Something's fishy here, Barry. I don't want to speak ill of a dead man, but I had a feeling Wyatt wasn't telling me everything he knows about David's murder."

Michael left the building, thinking about what John said—and what he clearly suspected.

He went to the men's room and locked himself in a stall, the only place he was guaranteed not to be interrupted. He pulled out his phone and sent a message to Matt about what he'd overheard.

He ended with Please advise.

Then he went back to work, mindful that there was more that they didn't know about this case than they did know.

CHAPTER 29

Monday
South of Patagonia, Arizona

Matt picked up Ryder at his apartment on the way to the remote cabin. He told him everything that happened at Tanya's, plus what Frank Block had told him about the two kids and possibly finding the contaminated water.

As they turned up a steep dirt road and passed the spot where David Hargrove's body had been found, he said, "Be prepared for anything. I don't know who these kids are, or how dangerous, but Hargrove may have been killed for being in the wrong place at the wrong time. It might not have anything to do with A-Line."

"What was he doing out here in the first place?"

Ryder asked. "We're a good twenty minutes from the highway, and these aren't real roads out here."

A valid question.

The road up the mountain was rocky and rutted. Matt slowed down. At the top, a cabin to the right was boarded up and a truck to the left was parked in front of a long drive that led to a small home.

Ryder had a medical bag with him. Once again, Matt was reminded that Ryder always seemed to be prepared for whatever he was needed for. Matt was glad for it. He wished he could have called in Kara—the victim was a young girl. They didn't know if she'd been assaulted—or if the boy was really her brother. Traffickers often used young teens to recruit or keep their other victims in line. But Kara had her own line of investigation today with Joe Molina, and Matt wasn't ready to pull her out yet.

Plus, Matt didn't even know where these kids had come from. Runaways or from south of the border. Trafficked or not.

Or if they were the two kids who'd been at the abandoned church.

Frank stepped out onto the deck as soon as he heard Matt approach.

"Thank you for coming," he said.

"What in the hell were you doing out here? This was your camping trip?"

Suddenly, Matt realized exactly what Frank had been doing.

"It was, wasn't it? You've been looking for the dump site on your own."

"Yes, I'll explain everything later."

"Now, Frank."

"Look, yes, okay? I have a drone and equipment and the experience to find the contamination because I understand it's not your priority right now."

"It *is* a priority, but I also have to build a case against Hargrove. Now that he's dead—"

"*What?* Since when?"

"How long have you been out here?"

"Since Friday morning. I took a week off from work. I told you. What happened?"

"David Hargrove was killed at the base of this hill sometime Saturday morning."

Shit. Did that mean that Frank was now a suspect?

"Were you here?" Matt gestured to the cabin.

"No. Friday and Saturday night I was west of here, camping on the east side of the fire road that goes up Mount Wrightson. Sunday I was closer to where Emma was killed. Then last night I camped about a mile south of here, between Harshaw and the abandoned town."

Matt didn't know how Frank would be able to prove any of that, but he had no real reason to suspect him. "We're going to have to talk about this later, Frank."

"I have logs, and my drone has GPS. I've downloaded all the data because if I do find the site, I need to be able to get to it and document it. So yes—I can prove my whereabouts all weekend."

That gave Matt some relief. Then Matt saw movement in the cabin.

"The boy has a gun," Ryder said.

"Move!" he told Frank as he drew his weapon.

"Stop, Matt—"

Matt focused on the boy who had come to the doorway. He appeared to be twelve or thirteen, skinny, about five foot five, with thick dark hair that hung in his eyes. He was holding a gun at his side. "Put it down." He repeated the command in Spanish.

The boy stared at him and Ryder but didn't raise the gun.

Frank said, "Matt, he's scared. He hasn't threatened me, but he doesn't want to put down the gun."

Matt wasn't going to yield this point. *"Baja el arma o no podemos ayudar a tu hermana."*

He hoped he got the message across. Gun down, or no help.

"¡Ahora!"

A weak female voice said from another room, *"Ángel, por favor, haz lo que él dice."*

The dialect was different from what Matt was used to—definitely not Cuban, street Spanish, or Americanized Spanish. Most likely Central America or far southern Mexico. Peter from border patrol thought that the dead girl they'd found was from Guatemala, but that didn't mean that these kids were. Yet, even though it was a rough translation, Matt understood that the girl wanted the boy, Angel, to cooperate.

"Lento pero seguro," Matt said, his eyes on Angel's gun hand.

The boy put the gun on the table. It was a basic 9

mm, scuffed and dirty. Ryder immediately picked it up and checked the magazine.

"Holds ten, two bullets missing. Hard to say if it's been recently fired."

"Bag it. We'll send for ballistics."

Ryder unloaded the gun and put the empty firearm and the bullets separately in two evidence bags he'd pulled from his medical kit.

"Bianca," the boy said, his voice gruff.

Ryder said, "Is that your sister's name?"

Angel didn't say anything but pointed to the other room.

Frank said from the doorway, "This is Angel. His sister is Bianca. Bianca speaks English fairly well. They escaped from somewhere in the desert—that's all I could ascertain. Angel found a pond and has been going out at night to replenish their water, there's no electricity or running water here, but I think the water is contaminated. Bianca has signs of acute arsenic poisoning, including extreme thirst. So my guess is it must be a concentrated source. I wanted to bring her right to the hospital, but they're too scared to leave," Frank said.

Speaking in Spanish, Matt told Angel that Ryder was a medic and was going to examine Bianca, then Ryder took his medical bag and went into the room.

Matt stood in the doorway, watching closely, while Ryder looked over the girl. The room stunk of vomit, but the kids had tried to clean up the mess. They'd washed their hands and faces. The clothes they wore were stained and dirty, but they didn't have much choice—the small house appeared empty of anything they could have changed into.

Bianca was young. Not much older than Amada. Her long dark hair was loosely braided. A burn scar marred the left side of her face, from her forehead to her neck, and one eye was partly closed with scar tissue.

A deep anger grew inside Matt. Had someone done that to her? As a punishment? As an example? He considered the underground bunker where Kara had found Amada.

Ryder spoke softly to the girl, asked her questions in English—and if Bianca didn't understand, Matt translated.

Ryder turned to them a moment later. "She needs a hospital or she will die."

Matt explained to Angel.

The boy shook his head and spoke in rough English for the first time. "They'll find us!" He looked around for something to use as a weapon but found nothing.

Matt said in Spanish, "Angel, listen to me. You need to pay attention to my words. Bianca will die if she doesn't get to a hospital as soon as possible. All this that you have done will be for nothing if your sister dies. Do you understand that?"

Angel was clearly torn.

"I found the bunker. The hole you and Bianca were kept underground. Were you with a girl named Amada?"

The boy was surprised, as if he didn't believe Matt. Thought it was a trick. Said nothing.

"Did you come here from Honduras? Guatemala? Against your will?"

In rapid Spanish, as if the sudden freedom in telling the truth gave him energy, Angel explained. They were originally from Oaxaca, a small village in southern Mexico. They lived on a farm and their father worked in a city. He made the wrong people angry, and bad men came to their farm and burned it to the ground. That's how Bianca was hurt—she nearly died in the fire. Their father was killed in front of them. They were left alone, but their mother couldn't work or feed them. She made an agreement with the same bad men who killed her husband.

"Our mother did bad things. She had to. They made me do bad things. For months and months. Then our mother—she gave us to someone else. And that man took us away, and we came here. I had to do things—bad things—but to protect my sister."

"I know you did," Matt said calmly. "Tell me the truth, Angel. I can help you if you tell me the truth."

He didn't believe this kid had killed David Hargrove. First, he had a handgun, not a shotgun. That didn't mean he didn't have access to one. He was also thin, hardly more than skin and bones. Would Hargrove have just let the kid aim a gun on him? The evidence suggested the killer was no more than a few feet away as the bulk of the buckshot hit Hargrove dead center mass.

But Matt had to be sure.

"Did you use your gun on anyone?" He gestured to the evidence bag.

The boy looked scared.

"Tell me the truth, Angel."

"He was holding us prisoner. I gave Bianca the signal to escape, a whistle we had practiced. She crawled out of the hole when the man was asleep. I told her bring no one, say nothing. Not to trust anyone, because they will turn you in. And she was very quiet. But after I gave the signal, the man woke up. I fought him, and he had a gun. I got it. I don't know how. I just knew if I didn't, he would kill us. He said I was trouble, he didn't want me with them because I was trouble. But they had Bianca and I couldn't do anything but what they said. And so I fought him and shot him. I had to. And then we ran. It was dark, but we ran into the darkness."

Matt frowned. That didn't make sense...unless...

"How many days ago was this?"

"Four nights. We found the old church early the morning we ran. Stayed there another night. To make sure it was safe to leave. A man and woman came and found our hiding spot, so we stayed invisible, hiding, and watched. The woman took Bianca's stuffed animal."

Was this man and woman Angel saw Joe and Kara? They'd gone to the church Saturday morning...that fit the time frame. And Kara had the bunny.

"Then I had to get more water... Bianca hid in

the church but ran when the bad men came looking for us."

"The man and woman came back?"

"I don't know, I wasn't there, I was getting water.
Bianca hid. She said it was a lot of men. But we
were there for two days, how did they find us? I
knew I should have left sooner, moved faster, but
Bianca wasn't feeling well, and I thought she just
needed more water because we were dehydrated.
The desert is hot. I found this place and brought
my sister here until she could feel better. But she
just got worse."

Ryder interrupted and said, "Matt, if we don't
get her to a hospital, she will die. That wasn't hy-
perbole. She may die anyway. Her condition is very
serious. The faster we get help, the better chance
she has of surviving."

Matt told Angel exactly that. "Listen to me,
Angel. Ryder works for me. He needs to take Bianca to the hospital and get her the help she needs.
A doctor there can make her better, but you need
to understand that she is very sick, okay?"

Angel nodded and said, in English, "Just do it.
Please pray, help, Bianca is my family. Only family."

"I'm going to have Ryder leave with Bianca
right now, and you need to show Frank and me
where you found the water that made her sick." He
frowned. "Did you drink the water too?"

"Yes."

"Do you feel sick?"

He shrugged.

Dammit, the boy probably needed medical attention, as well.

"I'll show you if you save my sister. But please, please do not send her back home without me."

On a hunch, Matt said, "I'm going to show you a photo of a tattoo, Angel. You tell me if you've seen it before, okay?"

He showed the kid the Sangre tattoo, a cleaner version that Peter had sent him earlier after they realized the dead man at the bunker had one of the tattoos.

Angel's eyes widened and he nodded. "They are bad men."

"Have you seen them? Their faces? Would you be able to identify the men who brought you here?"

He nodded. "I will. I will point my finger at who did this. You save my sister, I will do anything you want me to do."

Matt turned to Ryder. "Take her to the children's hospital in Tucson. Tell them she's under federal protection as a witness to a felony. Stay with her. Do not leave her alone for anything, okay? Call Peter in border patrol—only Peter—and tell him what has happened. He'll know what to do, what paperwork needs to be filled out on the kids, the whole nine yards. I'll meet you at the hospital later."

He handed Ryder his car keys, then explained to Angel what was going to happen. "I can help you and your sister. I can protect you. We will meet Bianca at the hospital later, where you will also be checked by a doctor. But first you have to take my friend Frank and me to where the water is that you've been drinking from, and you have to tell me the truth. From here on out, no lies. The whole truth, the good and bad, okay? We will find these bad people and they will be punished for what they have done."

Angel looked at his sister as Ryder carried her out to Matt's car. Then he nodded. "I help you."

They drove as far as possible down dirt roads before Angel said they needed to get out and walk the rest of the way.

They'd driven past the abandoned church, then turned east. This kid apparently had walked four miles each way to get water for his sister. He was strong, in body and soul, Matt thought. So much like those of his relatives who had escaped the Cuban dictatorship. Fought, survived or died fighting. Matt had a great respect for this kid who survived so much, so young. It was a difficult situation, but Angel was a witness, and if he could help put these criminals away, Matt could help him in return. Matt had some experience in Florida with Cuban refugees, but that was a different situation. A different time. He knew that if these kids were truly orphans, however, it might be easier.

Easier? Nothing was easy these days.

Matt, Frank and Angel walked another half mile until they came to a valley. Matt looked at his map. The underground bunker was northeast of their location, about a mile.

Matt couldn't see a road anywhere near them and was skeptical that this was the actual toxic dump site. But a small stream flowed slowly into the valley now from recent rains. If Frank was right—if water was flowing over the toxic slag, it would carry the poison downstream.

Frank stared at the stream and the area, then looked at his map. "This is it!"

"How can you tell? No truck would ever make it down here. Not through this terrain."

Frank didn't respond. He was staring at a dead mouse on the edge of the water. He took off his backpack, put on gloves and took a picture of the mouse, then put the rodent in a paper bag. He walked slowly up the stream to where the water had pooled in an impression about twelve feet across. Matt followed him, noting several other small rodents lying dead on the water's edge. Frank took photos, and so did Matt—just for his own information.

Then Frank walked to the deepest part of the stream. Only damp earth south of the watering hole showed that the water had once flowed farther. Without another rain, in days it would be completely dry.

Matt watched as Frank removed a test kit from his backpack and extracted water, put it in a test tube. He labeled it, then took out another test tube and repeated it.

"Frank, where is the water coming from? A big rig can't get through the desert," Matt repeated.

Frank didn't say anything but handed Matt the map he'd been using.

It took Matt a minute to read the map, but now he saw what Frank saw.

The topography showed that this water was flowing mostly east to west. An unpaved road went from State Route 82 at a southwest angle, then cut directly south and went through a small mountain range, then turned west again. It stopped—or appeared to—but there was nothing out here. It was all open space.

Frank said, "This is all part of the state preserve where any kind of dumping is illegal. But no one comes down here. If they're camping or hiking, they're going to be doing it west of here, where we were, or north up Mount Wrightson and Madera Canyon. The Southwest Copper land is both to the north and east of us, so whoever was dumping the toxic slag had to first go through Southwest property to get out here. It's the only way."

"I don't see it. Show me." Matt handed the map back to Frank.

"In this area." Frank circled his finger. "Okay, we're here." He pointed to a spot. "The truck would have driven this way." He moved his finger from the highway down to where they were. "It's accessible to a good driver but would be almost impossible for us to find. And truly, after a season or two of wind, monsoons, dust storms—the slag would be so spread out it would take time and research to pinpoint the exact toxic dump location. But because of the rainstorm late Thursday night, I can find it. And we'll be able to clean it up—as long as this is the only site."

Frank looked at the two test tubes. "Positive for arsenic and lead, well over natural limits."

Matt turned to Angel. He didn't know how much the kid understood about what they were doing, but he had been watching them closely.

"We take Angel to the hospital, and you call this in on the way," Matt said. "And don't come back out here without backup."

"I need to call in the park rangers and Game & Fish. We need to collect the rest of this wildlife, have it tested, confirm what I think happened. Then we'll need to canvass the entire area, make sure we find the slag, that this is the only place it was dumped. And clean it up before the next storm. Monsoon season is coming—we have to get on this as quickly as possible."

"We'll call on the road."

"I'm going to stay."

"No."

"You can use my truck to get back to town. I'll just grab my supplies and call it in."

"I said no, Frank. I'm not leaving you out here for even a couple hours until a team can be assembled."

"You don't have any authority over me, Costa."

Matt wasn't giving in. He held up the map.

"Here—" he pointed "—less than two miles from this spot, my partner and I found an underground bunker and evidence of human trafficking. The body of a dead gang member—I now believe the same man Angel fought and killed—and a deathly ill child, who succumbed minutes after we rescued her. A little girl, couldn't have been more than eight, had been trapped in a buried cargo container for God knows how long. The same container Angel and Bianca escaped from. The gang has been trying to find these kids—they tore apart the abandoned church sometime on Saturday night. And someone killed David Hargrove Saturday morning not far from where the kids were staying. Maybe by the same people looking for them. I don't know if he came across the gang, or if he was killed because his partner got cold feet, or hell, if he was involved in multiple illegal activities. And until I know exactly what happened, no one is going to be out here alone. And that includes you."

Frank stared at him, maybe because he sounded impassioned, or maybe because he'd finally connected the dots.

"You're right. I didn't realize..." Frank frowned at the pooling water. He took a few pictures with his phone, then they silently walked the half mile back to Frank's truck.

CHAPTER 30

Monday afternoon
Tucson, Arizona

With Ryder at the hospital with Bianca, and Matt needing to bring Angel there as well, he had to leave his team—Kara and Michael—in Patagonia. He talked to the two agents who would have been tracking the A-Line truck—had it shown up—and asked them to stay in town and be available if either Kara or Michael needed help. He then sent his team the other agents' contact information.

Frank was driving them to Tucson. He talked to the park rangers about the location of the contaminated water. It would be too late to put a team together tonight, but they and Game & Fish would be all over it tomorrow at dawn. That meant everyone would learn the truth soon enough.

But first, Matt had to tell Kara. Matt wished he could talk to her in person and tell her about the kids, but she was already at work. Instead, he called her. He could have texted, he probably should have, but felt a call was justified.

"Yep," she answered. He could hear the clank of glasses.

"We found the kids from the church. They're alive."

Silence. She didn't say anything. Was someone sitting there? Someone she couldn't talk around? Had he made a mistake calling her?

"Good," she said. "One sec."

He heard her tell someone to watch the bar for a minute. Then a few seconds later she got back on the phone. "Where? Are they okay?"

Matt gave her the basic information—the kids were alive, the girl was very sick with arsenic poisoning and they had found the contaminated water.

Again, she was silent, and Matt thought she might not have privacy again. "You have to go?" he said.

"How sick?"

"I don't know yet. I'm on my way to the children's hospital in Tucson with the boy. You were right about what happened."

"Sometimes," she whispered, "I hate being right. Thanks for telling me. I gotta go."

She ended the call.

Matt closed his eyes and considered the possibilities. He could pull Kara and Michael now, but they still didn't have all the answers. Michael was looking for anyone who acted out of the ordinary or suspicious in light of David's murder—he needed to be at Southwest to do that. Kara was working on Joe; she planned to discreetly push him for more information about the alleged "vendors" he'd met with on Friday night.

Matt's boss, Tony Greer, back east in FBI headquarters might want to pull the plug, but they still hadn't solved Emma Perez's murder, which was the primary reason Matt's team was here. It had been so easy to fall down the toxic-dumping rat hole once they tied David Hargrove to A-Line, because it was tangible. They had some evidence and knew what to do to find more. But there was no evidence in the murder investigation. She'd been attacked in the middle of the woods. Matt believed based on everything they knew that she was killed because she was looking for the toxic dump site and may have inadvertently tipped her hand to the wrong people, but they had no evidence.

He had to get Roger Kline in a cage and rattle him. That would be the only way he might get some of the answers they needed. Phoenix FBI was searching his house, and Zack Heller was going over all his finances, so there might be something there they could use to leverage for more information.

But until they found him, or Tanya, they were stuck.

Matt glanced back at Angel in the back seat. He'd fallen to sleep. The poor kid had been walking eight miles every night to get water for his sister, only to learn that the water was making her sick.

But they'd come from Oaxaca. How far was that? Nearly two thousand miles? How long had it taken them? Months, most likely. Had they driven part of the way? Walked?

Matt would do everything in his power to keep them safe.

Ultimately, though, the entire trafficking case would be handed over to border patrol working in conjunction with other local and federal jurisdictions. But until Matt knew how all these things fit together, he wasn't going to walk away.

He'd promised Kara he wouldn't back down, that he would find the people who left Amada to die in that filthy bunker.

It would greatly help if Angel could give a good description of everyone he saw at the bunker. It might be tilting at windmills, but every arrest helped. Every coyote taken off the streets was one less predator. It was an imperfect system, but Matt would do everything he could to make sure that girls like Amada no longer died in shit-infested bunkers in the middle of nowhere.

Matt called Wyatt Coleman. They had a decision to make.

"Costa? Weren't we going to meet this afternoon?"

"I'm on my way to Tucson. I'll be back late tonight." Matt told him a quick version of how they found the contaminated water. "AREA will be down in the morning to clean up the water and locate the dump site, which Frank thinks isn't far from the pond. We need to talk to John Molina—either we wait until tomorrow when we have more information, or you can talk to him now, give him a heads-up."

"You know more about this case than I do."

"But you're his friend. He deserves to know. I don't think he was party to this, I know you don't, and it would be worse if the press gets hold of it tonight—Frank just got off the phone with the AREA director. It could leak."

"Okay, I'll talk to him. I'm going to give him your number if he has questions I can't answer."

"That's fine. The only thing—don't tell him about Michael, or that Joe was helping us. I promised Joe he could tell his dad on his own terms. Everything else is fair game."

"I'll do it now—I agree, if he gets a call from someone else, it'll be much worse."

"Remind him that he's not under suspicion, but he might have to make some records available, answer a few questions."

"Knowing John, he'll want to help with the cleanup. I'll let you know how it goes."

"Thanks, Wyatt."

Matt didn't want to pass off the task of talking to John Molina to the other cop, but the truth was it would be better coming from a friend than from a federal agent out of Washington, DC.

Frank made good time to Tucson. "If you don't need me, I need to go into the office and turn over all my documentation to my boss."

"You did good, Frank. I hope they don't give you any shit for going off the rails on this."

"They will, but I think I'll be okay. If not? Well, I'm getting close to retirement age."

Frank left Matt and Angel at the emergency room entrance and drove off.

Matt helped Angel through the admission process. Once Matt made it clear to hospital security and the nursing staff that Angel was a witness in a federal crime and no one was allowed to visit him who didn't have a federal badge, he told Angel he had to go.

"The doctor needs to check you out. They'll probably take blood, maybe an X-ray."

"Don't go."

"I have to," Matt said. "These people know what to do. They'll take care of you and your sister. We have a guard here to protect you. And tomorrow morning Agent Christine Jimenez, someone you can trust, will be here to take down what you know—that basically means you tell Christine everything you told me—and then you can work with an artist who will draw the faces of the men who brought you and Bianca here according to the descriptions you give. Anything you remember, anything you know about their plans or where they might be hiding, you can tell the agent."

"Will you come tomorrow too?"

"I'll be back, I don't know when." Matt showed Angel his badge. "Do not talk to anyone who doesn't have a badge like this, okay? There will be a policeman outside your door, but you're not in trouble. He's there to protect you."

Angel nodded, but he didn't look happy. He glanced at the nurse, who looked annoyed that she had been kept waiting to take care of him, then leaned forward. He took crumpled papers from his pocket and handed them to Matt. "These—these are my papers. And Bianca."

Matt unfolded the wrinkled documents. They were birth certificates, from Oaxaca, splattered with blood.

"The man had them. They're all we have."

Angelo Jesus Herman Aguilar. He had turned twelve at the end of last year. *Bianca Margarite Aguilar.* She would be ten next week. Matt wondered if she knew her birthday was coming up.

"I am going to make copies of these, then give them back to you. Okay? Thank you for trusting me."

"How is Bianca? Is she…is she going to be okay?"

All Matt had learned was that Bianca was still in tests. "The doctors are with her now, and you'll be able to see her soon."

Two agents were already on-site, thanks to Matt's Tucson office, and he assigned one to Angel and one to Bianca. He found Ryder sitting outside the dialysis room in the basement. Matt sat next to him, relieved to relax for five minutes.

"Angel is upstairs. The doctor agreed to put him

and Bianca in the same room, which will make it easier to protect them."

"I don't speak much Spanish, and Bianca doesn't speak much English, but she managed to tell me what happened to them. At least as well as she could." Ryder stared at the closed door, spoke matter-of-factly, as was his way. But Matt could tell by a few slips that Ryder had been affected by this situation in much the same way as Kara. "Bianca thinks they've been traveling for over a year. The fire that scarred her was before Christmas. Not last Christmas, but the Christmas before that. The men shot her father, then set their farm on fire. Her mother tried to survive on their own, but she didn't have a job or any way to get one. Bianca believes that her mother gave them to the men who brought them here, and Angel told her that their mother sold them and was dead. No one who she and Angel started traveling with was still with them when they crossed the border."

"You need to write this all up."

"I did. I'm gathering some more information and will send it in. There's more—her information might be very valuable. For example, they came through a tunnel that was one day's walk from the bunker."

"Peter with border patrol can help there. How is she? I told Angel she was going to be okay, but I don't really know."

He almost didn't want to ask. Had his delay this morning jeopardized the child's life even more?

"They don't know," Ryder said. "If they can

detox her system, she might get through this with minimal side effects. But she'll have to go through dialysis, and depending on the extent of the internal damage, she might need dialysis for the rest of her life. They won't know for a few weeks. After this procedure, she'll need a red blood cell transfusion. Her immune system is weak, she's likely never had any vaccinations, so they're testing her for everything. She's young, which is both good and bad. Good because she's strong and she can heal, but she's extremely underweight."

Matt glanced at his phone, then said to Ryder, "Christine sent two agents from her office to relieve you. One for Bianca and one for Angel."

"Would you mind if I stay for a bit, at least until she's settled into her room with Angel?"

"Of course," he said. "I'm going to the office and checking in with Zack and Christine, then I'm heading back to Patagonia. Since you have my car, how about if I call you when I'm ready and you can swing by headquarters and pick me up. It'll be a couple hours."

Ryder called him as Matt was walking into FBI headquarters fifteen minutes later.

"I just got off the phone with Tony Greer's office. They have been helping me work with the lab to expedite the prints and IDs of the men Kara flagged on Friday."

"Anything we can use?"

"No IDs on the two men Joe Molina said were vendors. However, one set of prints showed up in an unsolved carjacking in El Paso from four years ago. The victim was beaten unconscious and has permanent nerve damage. The local authorities believe that the crime wasn't a simple carjacking. They have evidence that the victim may have been an unwilling partner in the sex trade."

"Someone who was trafficked?"

"No, the victim was a fifty-six-year-old man, naturalized citizen, with a family and small business. The authorities believe that a trafficking organization forced him to allow them access to his property."

"And he didn't go to the police?"

"Based on what the detective in charge of the investigation told me, he feared for his life and his family."

Matt believed it. "I know how these criminals operate. Go on."

"He never told the authorities exactly what he did or didn't do that resulted in his beating, but the detective thinks that he said no to using a specific property they wanted for their criminal activity. Either because his clients were getting suspicious, or because he had a change of heart or simply couldn't give them what they wanted."

"So they beat him, took his car as payment or to cover up the motive. Are you suggesting that's what's going on here?"

"I went back to Michael's initial report about the two strangers in the bar. It was all rumors and secondhand information. One employee thought the two men were from a new mine and John Molina had been in an argument with them. There was speculation in the group, but what if they were on the land without permission?"

"Or without permission from John," Matt mused.

What if these two men were trying to leverage Southwest Copper for access to their property? They owned more than two thousand acres. The bunker was on the edge of Southwest land, but very likely they would have had to have crossed it to get to the bunker.

Kara was suspicious of Shelley Brown, who also met with the same two men on Saturday. Could Joe also be privy to the illegal operation? If so, why would he have helped Matt in the first place? And if he or his dad was being threatened, why not come to Matt at the very beginning?

Joe had an inside track to the FBI; Matt would have jumped on the information.

"I asked Christine to dig deeper on Shelley Brown since Kara had a twitch about her."

"A twitch? Is that a technical law enforcement term?"

Matt almost laughed. "For her, it is. I'm adding Joe Molina to that. Kara thought he'd lied to her about something, and her instincts are usually good on that. Anything else?"

"Yes. Kara sent a third set of prints. Remember the old guy in the bar? He nursed a drink for hours and Kara had, I guess, a twitch about him. His name is Garrett DeYoung from Texas. I have nothing else on him other than his driver's license and make and model of a truck in his name. And he's a licensed bounty hunter."

"A bounty hunter?" Matt repeated. "Could he be after the guy from El Paso?"

"Possible," Ryder said. "There's nothing else on him, not even who he works for—the analyst who ran him thinks that his files have been scrubbed or sealed. He can get into the next layer, but it'll take another day or two."

"If the guy is from Texas, he might be in a motel in Patagonia or the surrounding area. Find out where he's staying, his cell number, anything you can get. I want to talk to DeYoung as soon as I get back there. Where does he live?"

"Odessa."

"That's not far from El Paso." It clicked, made complete sense to Matt.

"The detective in El Paso was very cooperative. I'll ask him about DeYoung and get back to you if he knows anything."

"Call Kara and tell her that if she sees DeYoung or either of the two men in the bar to call me immediately. Let her know everything you told me. Plus, send Wyatt the information as well and ask him to be on alert until we know more. Good work, Ryder. Any word on the kids?"

"Still in tests."

"I'll let you know when I'm leaving."

Matt touched bases with Christine, then wrote up a detailed report for Tony Greer in DC. Then he walked into the small conference room that Zack Heller had taken over. He looked and acted like he'd been living on caffeine for the last seventy-two hours. The room was organized chaos, with stacks of paper, spreadsheets, two laptops and a whiteboard with numbers that meant nothing to Matt.

"They were laundering money for someone... I'm going to find it," Zack said. "It's here, I can feel it. I can tell you this, Matt—whoever set this up knew exactly what they were doing. They're good. I'm better. I'm going to get it."

"Zack, you need to sleep."

"I'll lose the momentum. Just—give me this afternoon, okay? I'm going to sort the information in a different way. There is a pattern, there's *always* a pattern, even if it's random."

Matt was concerned about his new team member. He sent Christine a text message to keep an eye on him.

Christine replied: He drives me crazy, but he's growing on me.

CHAPTER 31

Monday evening
Patagonia, Arizona

Though virtually everyone at Southwest Copper had heard by now that David Hargrove had been murdered on Saturday before they arrived at work Monday morning, John Molina took a few minutes to announce David's death in person and share his condolences. By the end of the workday, they also knew that he and his wife were suspected of defrauding Southwest through the waste disposal company, and that Tanya and her brother had disappeared. So when Michael was invited to go with some of his coworkers to the Wrangler after their shift, he agreed. He was eager to hear what everyone thought and assess whether someone knew more about the situation than was public. David had a lot of friends, which might mean that Tanya had a lot of friends. Someone who might be willing to help her hide out.

Michael had assessed each of David's coworkers, and he couldn't pinpoint anyone who was party to Hargrove's illegal activities. Matt had told Michael earlier that he wasn't sold that Roger Kline had killed his brother-in-law.

It came down to motive.

Michael wasn't as sure as Matt that David's brother-in-law *wasn't* involved. He'd seen families torn apart by greed. Until Tanya and her brother were questioned, Kline was considered the primary suspect in David's murder.

Michael walked into the bar with his coworkers Pedro Vasquez and Hank Richardson, and they joined another group from the refinery that was already there. Kara was behind the bar. Vasquez was particularly upset because it was his sister-in-law Crystal whom Tanya had drugged. "Crystal is pregnant!" he said, not for the first time. "You know what drugs like that can do to a baby? And Tanya knew! She and Crystal were best friends, and she drugged her anyway!"

"You didn't tell me Crystal was preggers," Richardson said.

"Rob wanted to keep it quiet until they knew everything was okay. They didn't tell anyone, but Crystal had a miscarriage last year at twelve weeks. They wanted to wait, make sure she got through the first trimester. But he's my brother, he tells me everything."

He tells me everything. Did Rob tell Pedro anything about the investigation? Wyatt Coleman, the marshal, had promised Matt he would keep the investigation on a need-to-know basis. But that didn't always mean the same things to different people.

They pulled a table over to the larger group and sat down. Vasquez was heated and made sure that everyone knew exactly what he thought of Tanya and the whole situation.

"I mean, what was she thinking? Tanya doesn't have the brains to up and disappear like this. Why?"

Kara came over and took orders for drinks. She held Michael's eye for just a second longer than he expected. Was she trying to give him information? What did she think he was, a psychic? Then she was back behind the bar drawing beers and pouring whiskey.

"You think she and her brother killed David?" Richardson asked.

"No. Hell, I can't imagine… But I don't know," Vasquez said. "My brother says they're wanted for questioning—made me promise to let him know if I hear if Tanya reaches out to anyone. But so far as I know, she hasn't, and I bet she's not going to, not after what she did to Crystal. Everyone loves Crystal."

That was true, Michael realized. Crystal Vasquez was not only a cop's wife; she was a Patagonia native. She was the first to bake a casserole if someone got sick, the first to volunteer to help if someone needed anything, and she was genuinely kind. She was the friend who offered to stay with Tanya so she wouldn't be alone after David's murder.

"She's okay now, though, right?" Michael asked.

"Yeah, Rob made sure she went to the doctor today and got checked out. Valium, it was. And the baby is okay, heartbeat strong, but they're going to monitor her some more, I guess. Make sure there's no, like, side effects or something. And it's a girl. She's fourteen weeks and they said for sure it's a girl. I'm going to have a niece!"

After a round of congratulations and toasts, and offering his own toast, Michael said, "It's just surprising to hear all this. I was with Crystal and Tanya on Friday cooking chili. I wasn't cooking, I was tasting, but they seemed to be close."

"They are—at least, everyone thought so. And no one knows what Tanya is thinking. Hell, maybe she just snapped after David was killed."

"Maybe Tanya's in trouble," Michael suggested, waiting to see how the others would respond.

"The way she spends? And it's all junk. Well, to me it is." Vasquez shrugged. "I don't know what to believe anymore, but that David would scam John and Barry? I just don't understand. What kind of trouble? Credit debt, probably. But that doesn't mean you bite the hand that feeds you."

"What have you heard?" Richardson asked. "Word is they own A-Line and got paid to take away the slag. What's with that?"

"I think it was worse," another guy said. "I was

in the office today and overheard John talking to his accountant on the phone. It seems David authorized a prepayment for the waste disposal. So they took the money…but didn't even pick up the slag today."

It didn't seem that anyone knew about the illegal dumping yet, but they were all angry that David had defrauded their boss.

"Rob said there's a fed who's been working with Wyatt on the murder of that college girl," Vasquez said.

"A fed?" another guy said, skeptical. "They're a bunch of assholes."

"Rob says he's okay. Wyatt's been spending a lot of time with the guy and keeping things close to the vest. I was thinking, maybe, you know, the feds have been looking at David a long time. Rob wouldn't say squat when I asked, but I can read between the lines."

"I don't like the feds much," Richardson said, "but Wyatt's always been a stand-up guy."

General consensus around the tables was that, yes, Wyatt was one of them.

"What the fuck does David know about waste disposal?" one of the guys piped up.

Everyone looked at him. What was his name…? Reggie, Michael thought. Michael didn't work with him—he handled the actual pure copper coils.

"I mean," Reggie said, "waste disposal is a serious business. It's a, like, major business, not a side job."

Richardson said, "One of my cousins who lives

right off the highway said that there's a lot of shit going on south of Eighty-Two right now."

"What?"

"Like, I don't know, there were park rangers heading out there, and three sheriff's cars. There's like, what, a dozen Santa Cruz County sheriff's trucks, all told? What were three of them doing out there?"

No one said anything.

"Shit, what's going on in our town?" one guy said.

Michael looked from face to face. These guys loved their jobs, loved John Molina and loved their community. They weren't involved…they might gossip and criticize, but they weren't party to any crime.

"I wonder if Joe suspected something was up," Richardson said suddenly.

"Joe? Why? And why wouldn't he say something?"

"I don't know. But he was acting weird today."

"Maybe because of the accounting bullshit John's dealing with," another said.

"Everyone's been acting… I don't know, preoccupied lately," Richardson said. "And Shelley has been showing up a lot the last few days."

"You're such a girl," one of the guys said, and they all laughed.

Richardson didn't think it was funny. Neither did Michael.

Joe swore to Matt that he hadn't told anyone about the investigation into David Hargrove, but if he did…that opened up the suspect pool. What if someone killed David to protect the Molina family? If Barry and John knew that David was committing fraud that could hurt their business, could one or both of them conspire to kill him? Maybe confront him…and things got out of hand?

It was a stretch, Michael thought, but maybe one that needed to be explored.

He couldn't forget that Shelley might be involved, and she'd been seen talking to the two strangers last Saturday after the picnic. Ryder had sent him information that one of the men was wanted in El Paso for carjacking and assault. Could *she* have hired them to kill Hargrove? Why? To protect her family? Joe had been assured by the FBI that his family had limited immunity—the company was marginally protected provided they weren't directly involved in the illegal dumping, and nothing Michael had learned suggested that they would be okay with it.

"Hey, Harris, you zoned out."

"Sorry. I'm more tired than I thought. I'm going to leave, hit the hay early." He drained his beer and said goodbye. "But I'm going to take care of you guys first."

"You don't have to do that," Vasquez said.

"Just the one round, you get the second, free-loader."

They all laughed.

He walked up to the bar and waited for Kara to have a moment. Gave her his credit card and told her to charge one round on him, making a show of it.

She did, then when he signed, he leaned over and said quietly, "Joe may have talked to Shelley. Watch yourself."

She smiled, nodded. "Yep, I'm pretty certain." Slightly louder, she said, "You sure you want to pay for those three, too?" She jerked her thumb toward the three Vietnam veterans at the end of the bar. "They can get rowdy."

He blinked, then just smiled.

"Credit where credit is due, sailor," she said. She poured three fresh drafts and walked down the bar, placing them in front of the veterans. "Michael— Michael, right?—he says he was in the navy, wanted to buy you fellows a round."

Michael ended up going over and chatting with the vets for a minute, then he left.

It wasn't until he left that he understood. It was Kara's cover. She didn't want anyone to see them whispering together. Why hadn't he been more careful?

He was not cut out for undercover work.

Michael drove straight home—home being the apartment he rented over the garage of Barry and Helen Nelson. It was barely seven, but there were two cars in the driveway—Shelley's and Joe's. Helen's practical sedan wasn't in the garage, where it usually was. Was Barry in there with them? Or had Barry and Helen gone out together?

Michael wanted to go inside and see what they

were up to, but that would be awkward. Instead he
went up to his apartment and called Matt. Filled
him in on what he heard in the bar. "I don't know
if it means anything, but now Shelley and Joe are
here at Barry's house. They're family and all that,
but…it just feels odd to me, and Joe hasn't been out
here, that I know about, since I moved in."

Matt didn't say anything for a minute. "We're
running a deep background on Shelley, but so far
nothing has popped. But her association with those
two outsiders is suspicious, and if Joe told her about
our investigation—and she didn't say or do anything—that also makes me suspicious."

"Could be the same reason," Michael said.

"Kara ID'd another suspect—I have a lead on
him. I need to go. But send Kara a message telling her exactly what you told me. She's meeting
up with Joe later. She can do a better assessment."

Michael did what Matt said, then watched the
Nelson house from his window, keeping the lights
off so no one could see him looking.

Fifteen minutes later, Helen came home. She
was alone—so that meant Barry was likely inside
all along. Five minutes after she arrived, Joe and
Shelley left the house. They argued outside—not
loud enough for Michael to hear—before Joe got
into his truck and sped off alone, clearly angry.
Shelley immediately pulled out her phone, got in
her car and drove off.

CHAPTER 32

Monday night
Patagonia, Arizona

Monday was always a slow night at the Wrangler. Tonight was no exception. There were still two separate tables of Southwest Copper employees kicking back; the three vets had left earlier than usual. Two tables of tourists were left—a couple, and two women who looked like the artsy type, possibly here as vendors for the fair. Just after eight, a group of four college students walked in. Two of the kids looked high, and they all looked young enough that she carded them. They were all twenty-one or twenty-two.

Kara wasn't a fan of drugs under any circumstances, but she usually let the potheads go about their business as long as they didn't bother anyone and weren't driving. She'd watch these four, and not just because they made her twitch, but because of something she'd overheard one of them say.

When are we doing another run?

A *run*. Common slang for moving drugs across the border. If these four were smuggling in crap, she would pound heads.

Right. You're going to announce you're a cop; just let the world know you've been lying for the last three weeks.

The kids were too loud, too obnoxious, and had eaten two orders of French fries and a double hamburger each. As soon as they were served, Greg came up to her and, with a nod to the boys, said, "Do you want me to stay?"

"I can handle them. Go home and make sure Daphne isn't walking around making her ankle worse."

"She's coming in tomorrow," he said. "She's much better."

"Good."

After Greg left, she got the tourists and one of the Southwest groups another round of drinks, then spent longer than necessary cleaning off the tables near the four boys.

They'd definitely been down in Mexico. Might have been innocuous, but she still had a feeling they were up to something.

She went back behind the bar and considered her options. Cut them off or ignore them.

She decided to call the Patagonia marshal's office nonemergency line.

"This is Kara Smith at the Wrangler," she said from the phone in the back of the restaurant.

"Hello, Kara Smith. This is Marshal Coleman."

"The marshal answering the phone?"

"I was working late, so I picked up. Is something wrong?"

"I've been a bartender for quite a few years, and this group of college kids—I carded them, they're all legal and the IDs were real—came in here. At least two of them are high. Based on their conversation and their attitude, they just came up from Mexico. First, I don't know who's planning on driving, but they're all drinking, and second, I don't know what might be on their persons." She didn't want to say that she thought they were running drugs, because that wasn't something she figured an average bartender would be up on. So she went with vague. "I'm not one to rat someone out for getting high, but this feels different, I don't know."

"I'll swing by. They leaving?"

"No, I just served them another round. I'd guess they'll be here thirty to forty minutes."

"Haven't done a field sobriety test in a while. Might be fun to play with some college kids. Thanks, Kara."

"Don't mention it."

She finished loading the bar dishwasher and ran it. She wanted enough time to empty it and run the final load.

The tourists paid and left, and shortly thereafter Joe walked in. He sat down at the bar, looking both frazzled and angry.

"Hey," she said, "what's up?"

When he looked at her, he breathed easier. "You are a sight for sore eyes."

"Thank you, I think. You look upset."

"Did you hear that the police found out that David Hargrove, the guy we found dead, was illegally dumping slag in the desert?"

"No—they were talking earlier about him and a waste company or something like that. I didn't quite understand what it meant, but your people from the refinery were pretty agitated."

"Well, it just happened this morning—apparently the FBI and one of the environmental directors found water that had been poisoned by copper slag. Well, we're the closest refinery, so of course they think it was from ours. I guess it was—Wyatt told my dad that David owned the waste disposal company that David had contracted with to dispose of our slag. And then…well, long story, but my dad said that David authorized prepayment for the year. Which means all the money is now gone. When my dad found out that David actually *owned* the company, he practically fell apart. I'm glad I was there with him when he heard—he's not taking this well at all."

"It's not your father's fault, though, is it?"

"No! But he trusted David, and I should have stopped it a long time ago."

"Did you know? How could you have stopped it?"

He stared at her. "No, I didn't know, but I should have, you know what I mean?"

"I do." She put a microbrew beer in front of him, even though he didn't ask for it. "Unless you'd like something stronger?"

"Thank you. This is fine. Honestly, I just wanted to see you. You're the only bright spot in my life right now."

"That's sweet, but it can't be that bad. Excuse me one sec, I need to close out your guys over there." She gave him a smile and squeezed his hand.

Joe didn't let go right away—an action that would normally annoy her, as it practically screamed of possession—but then he released it and she didn't have to intentionally pull away.

Though she couldn't comment to him, Joe was clearly frustrated because he knew about the FBI investigation and agreed not to say anything about it. She could see how that secret—especially with Hargrove dead and every agency seemingly out in the desert now investigating the dump site—could grate on him.

Or he had a secret, something he hadn't told her—or Matt. She knew he wasn't telling the complete truth about the two men he met with on Friday. Now that she knew that at least one of them was wanted by law enforcement, she wondered why Joe was talking to them at all.

Matt was already aware of her suspicions regarding Shelley and Joe. She just wasn't certain how it all fit at this point.

By the time she returned to Joe after closing

out the tabs for the Southwest table, she noted that
he'd barely touched his beer. Before she could talk
to him about anything else, the shorter of the two
men Joe had talked to on Friday walked in and sat
at the bar.

Joe noticed him immediately, but he was trying
not to react. He stared at his beer. Joe seemed nervous. Had the guy threatened him? If he had, why
wouldn't he tell Matt?

Kara started down the bar toward him, and Joe
awkwardly reached for her across the bar. "Hey,
Greg's in the back, right?"

"No. He left. I'm closing tonight."

"That isn't safe."

"Patagonia is a pretty safe town, the recent murder notwithstanding."

"Still. You're an attractive single girl leaving a
business late."

She tried to keep her cool. "I've been a bartender most of my adult life, Joe. I am very savvy
and aware of my surroundings. Don't be so possessive, okay?"

Maybe she shouldn't say that to someone she
was supposed to be flirting with, but she couldn't
imagine any woman putting up with that kind of
bullshit.

"I'll stay."

"You don't have to."

"I know. I want to."

She walked over to the stranger at the bar. "Same
as last week?" she asked.

He stared at her. "Tequila, straight up."

"Man after my own heart," she said with a half smile. "We have house or the good stuff."

Now he gave her a smile. "Good stuff."

She poured, put it in front of him. Out of the corner of her eye she saw Joe watching them closely.

She left the bar area, walked over to the college kids and cleared their plates. "Another round?" She looked at one of them who was clearly intoxicated. "Except for him."

"Aw, he's not driving."

"Who's driving?"

The blond in the group said, "That's me." He definitely was the most sober, and he did look a bit concerned that his friend had drawn her attention.

"Where you heading?"

"Tucson, ma'am."

"You, no more. I'll serve your other friends if they want, but I'm closing early tonight."

"We're done." He handed her a credit card.

She ran the card, made note of the name. They were up to something, she was positive now, and the blond definitely didn't want to be on anyone's radar.

Coleman hadn't shown up, but Kara couldn't police the world. She'd done her due diligence, and at least the blond had only one beer and didn't appear to be on anything else. Two of his friends were definitely flying—their eyes glassy, their movements slightly off. Maybe her admonition would keep them alive on the drive back. Or Coleman could be waiting for them to leave, follow them a bit to see if they had a problem. That's what she would most likely do in his position.

The boys left her a pretty good tip, considering she just chastised all of them. She watched them walk out, much quieter than when they walked in.

Not thirty seconds later, the suspect drinking tequila left.

She didn't like that at all. It raised her antenna.

She'd seen kids used as mules, and if the Wrangler turned into a swap—a place where the mules met the dealers—that would be bad for Greg and Daphne. Except…in the three weeks she'd been here, there had been nothing like this before.

Sometimes, a coincidence is just a coincidence.

Damn. This isn't a fucking coincidence.

One of the biggest problems working undercover was that when you saw a crime about to happen, you couldn't do one damn thing about it. Yes, if it was in front of her, she would have an obligation to step in, but just *thinking* there might be a crime didn't mean you should blow your cover.

She glanced over at Joe. He was partly watching her, partly watching the door close on her new suspect. She looked over at the table. The boys hadn't left anything behind. But she had a wallet behind the bar—left months ago, apparently— that she palmed, then she ran over to the table and "found" it.

"Well, shit, they won't be getting far," she said, for anyone who was within earshot. "Hey, Joe, watch the bar for one sec," she said and ran out before he could argue with her.

ALLISON BRENNAN

The boys were driving a four-door Ram pickup truck. They were already inside. The stranger was getting in a rental car—evident from the sticker. She memorized the license plate, then watched the two vehicles leave. Had they already exchanged the merchandise? Or was she wrong?

Then she remembered that the blond had gone to the bathroom for quite some time, for longer than ten minutes, shortly before the stranger came in. The back door wasn't alarmed; the Wrangler was a small, family pub. He could have easily slipped out then, returned.

Smart. She would tell Wyatt Coleman about the suspected operation, once she left undercover. She didn't want the Wrangler to end up with a bad rep or attract more criminals.

As she was walking back toward the door, she saw the marshal's truck pass by. He followed the Ram. Good. He must have been waiting on the street and jumped on the situation immediately.

Her job was done.

She went back inside and walked straight into Joe.

"What the heck?" he asked.

She held up the wallet. "One of those kids forgot his wallet. I couldn't catch them in time." She stepped behind the bar and put the wallet in the drawer. "I'll have Greg mail it to him tomorrow. No harm, no foul."

Joe sat back down on his stool. "I was thinking about taking tomorrow off," he said. "Maybe

we could get out of town for a day or two? Just…
I don't know, relax?"

"Sounds fun, but I can't take time off, not this
week leading up to the art festival. It's the whole
reason Greg and Daphne hired me."

"You're right. I'm sorry. I'm just…everything
that's been going on. My dad. What that traitor
Hargrove did. And we don't really know what the
fallout is going to be—financial or otherwise, especially with the environmental agency all over
the place, then there'll be more people—rangers,
cops, the FBI, the EPA, hell, I don't know, probably
every alphabet agency on the planet. It's stressful."

"I'm really sorry that you and your family have
to go through this. Anything I can do to help, let
me know."

"Thanks," he said and took her hand again. "I
hope when the police realize this was all David
Hargrove's scam, they'll just go away."

During the hour drive down from Tucson, Ryder
had located Garrett DeYoung, the bounty hunter
from Texas, staying at an RV park just outside the
Patagonia city limits. Matt dropped Ryder off at
his apartment, then drove to the RV park himself
when they got back to town late Monday evening.

Sometimes Matt marveled at how good Ryder
was at getting information.

Unfortunately, no one seemed to know why DeY-
oung was in town or whom he was looking for. He
was licensed, but Matt approached his RV cau-

tiously anyway since it was dark and he didn't want to be taken for a trespasser.

He wasn't there.

Matt talked to the park manager. DeYoung had come into town on Wednesday and paid up front for a week. He drove a 1990 beige Ford pickup truck with Texas plates—Matt knew that information from the Texas DMV. The RV was small and not hooked up to water or electricity, but the park had community showers and bathrooms for guests.

"Do you know when he left today?"

The manager shrugged. "I work noon to midnight. He wasn't here when I arrived. Last night he came in just as I was leaving, so around midnight."

"When he returns, would you please call me?" Matt asked. He handed the manager his business card and wrote his cell phone on the back. "Anytime. It's important."

"He in trouble?"

"No."

The manager was skeptical.

"I need to talk to him about a job. Like I said, it's important—so let me know, okay?"

"If I'm here, I'll call." He pocketed the card.

Matt wasn't going to hold his breath on the manager doing any favors for him. Besides, his team was on the lookout for DeYoung and so was the Patagonia marshal's office. When someone spotted DeYoung or his truck—and Matt was certain it would happen sooner rather than later—he'd get the call.

Matt called Wyatt to see how his conversation

with John Molina went, but his cell phone went
to voice mail. Matt told him about DeYoung, then
asked him to call if he had a chance. Matt went
back to his hotel room to decompress. It had been
a long week.

He pulled out the Emma Perez case files again.
Could he tie David Hargrove or Roger Kline to
her murder? He had to be missing something. Few
criminals were so good that they didn't leave a
trace of evidence.

Her murder had been fast. No defensive wounds.
She'd been surprised by her killer, screamed, hit
twice, fell unconscious. Died en route to the hospital.

The location wasn't anywhere near the contaminated water. Emma had been killed several miles
southwest of Patagonia; a mile south of the highway. The contaminated water was found southeast
of Patagonia, with two mountain ranges and at least
ten, fifteen miles between them. Yet…she had been
looking for the cause of the bird poisonings. There
had to be a connection, otherwise her death would
be random.

And it was clearly *not* random.

The original police reports included a map of the
region. Coleman had marked the area where Billy
said he and Emma had been hiking, both north
and south of the highway, following the migratory
path of the Mexican jays, based on Emma's research. The birds were found on Mount Wrightson,
and Billy and Emma had hiked there in the morning, had lunch and made love, then drove south of

82 and hiked in the valley closest to the highway, southwest of town.

The map looked familiar, Matt realized.

He brought up a Google map of the area so he could zoom in and out. Emma was killed almost directly west of Harshaw, the tiny town outside of which David Hargrove was killed. There was no road between the two locations, but when you have two murders within two months in a town that hadn't seen a homicide in a decade, you had to consider that they might be connected.

Staring at the map, he frowned. Going east from Hargrove's murder was where he and Kara had found the underground bunker. It was roughly ten miles as the crow flies from where Emma died, but it wasn't possible to drive between the two points— well, possible, but there would be a lot of winding around, it would be easier to go up to the highway, then back down to each site.

He took out the map that Frank had given him, from his survey this weekend. He looked at all three maps together—Google, the police report, Frank's.

Matt remembered what Peter Carillo from border patrol said to him the other day.

I've seen abandoned bunkers like this before... they're way stations...they move around to avoid detection...

He called Peter, not caring that it was after ten at night.

"Carillo," a gruff voice answered.

"Peter, it's Matt Costa. Sorry to call so late. I have something to run by you."

"Shoot."

"Did you hear about the Emma Perez murder a while back? She was a college student at U of A and was killed ten weeks ago while on a hike with her boyfriend."

"I remember getting a bulletin on it."

Matt explained why he was interested in her death, the dead wildlife she'd found and the recent discovery of the illegal dump site.

"I'm looking at a map of the region and almost directly east—about ten miles away—is where we found the bunker with the young girl."

"I'm not following."

"I was going on the assumption that either the Perez death was an accident, or someone killed her because she was looking for the illegal dump site. But she was nowhere near the dump site, which is about three miles southwest of the underground bunker."

"Okay," he said slowly.

"She was supposedly searching in a circular pattern, but she wasn't a trained wildlife biologist, just an intern."

"You're losing me, Matt, and I've been working since five this morning."

"You said the other day that traffickers often maintain multiple bunkers. Hidden from sight, underground or in an area not normally traveled. Emma Perez was hiking down an overgrown path looking for a water supply that may have been contaminated. Billy, her boyfriend, was behind her on the trail. He said he heard her scream, but when he reached her, he saw out of the corner of his eye someone running. When he looked again, no one was there. He was focused on getting Emma to his truck."

"Did the police go out and look at the scene?"

"Yes, but I don't know how far they looked or what they were specifically looking for. I know it's been two months, but the area is pretty remote. Inaccessible by vehicle, but I can send you the exact coordinates. You and your people know what to look for."

"You mean if it's an area known for trafficking."

"Exactly. I'm thinking a mile radius, plus or minus. Some of the area wouldn't be feasible."

"Send me what you have. Is this time critical?"

"The only suspect I have is in the wind, and I'm still having a hard time wrapping my head around opportunity. They would have to track her, I don't know how they could feasibly have done it. I need something more."

"I can put together a small team tomorrow morning and head up there."

"Thank you."

"By the way, I'm writing up a report for my boss tomorrow and I'll send you a copy, but I have some preliminary information on the bunker you found," Peter said. "It's been buried for eighteen months. There's evidence of both recent and older biological matter. We'll have more details when the full reports come back on that. But so far, everything confirms what we thought initially."

A little voice piped up, "Daddy, why are you working?"

"PJ, it's after ten, why are you out of bed?"

"I'm not tired."

"Go to bed and I'll come in in five minutes and read you another book."

"Promise? Five minutes? Not six minutes or seven minutes?"

"Go. Now."

A giggle in the background made Matt smile, then he said to Peter, "I am sincerely sorry to bother you at home."

"Work never leaves me alone. I'm pretty sure you're the same way."

"I'm single with no kids. I don't have another life."

"My wife's a saint. And, though we both work hard, we do two things that help us maintain our sanity. First, once a month we go away for the weekend. Leave the kids with her mom in Phoenix, and either drive to Flagstaff where my brother has a cabin, or fly anywhere that we can get a direct flight. It gives us much-needed alone time. Second, we never go to bed angry. That one I learned from my parents, who've been married for forty-six years and counting."

Matt didn't know what he would do with time off. He didn't know what he would do if he didn't have work. Maybe he was a lost cause. How many women had he dated who said he was preoccupied?

That he always brought his work home? That he couldn't turn it off?

Maybe he couldn't. Maybe he didn't want to.

"How do you turn it off?" he asked Peter, surprised when he heard the words come out of his mouth.

"The job? It's hard. Especially when I have something like this bunker and now that unsolved Perez murder. It's heartbreaking. And maybe I don't completely turn it off. Some of my colleagues don't bring their work home at all. They're able to shut it in their lockers and be with their families. I've never been like that, not completely. Gina knew that when we married, and she's the world's best listener. Sometimes I hate telling her things because I know they're tough, but if I couldn't share with her, so she knows what's in my head, I don't think I would have survived this long. I would have quit or we'd have divorced.

"I'll tell you what. I'm staring at these maps, and I have some satellite images I need to look at when I get to the office in the morning. You might be onto something, and if I see what I think I'll see, I'll go out there with a team tomorrow. We know what we're looking for, and if it's there, we'll find it."

"Thank you, Peter. I owe you big-time."

"What you owe me is finding the ringleader of all this mayhem. Do that, we shut them down for a while."

"A while?"

"You're seasoned, Costa. You know it's all playing whack-a-mole. Take one player off the board, another pops up. But they won't pop up here again anytime soon if I can help it. And at some point, we'll get ahead of them for good. I have to believe that or I would quit tomorrow. And, I think, so would you."

Kara was waiting for a couple to finish their drinks and leave so she could close the bar. She'd called last call fifteen minutes ago but was giving them time before kicking them out.

The door opened, and the old guy in the cowboy hat walked in.

Garrett DeYoung, bounty hunter.

She almost told him she'd already called last call, but she knew Matt wanted to talk to him. He sat down at the bar and Kara walked over. "What's your pleasure?"

"Scotch, neat."

"House?"

"Fine."

She poured, put it down in front of him. "Last call," she said. "But take your time. I still have to close up."

He put a ten-dollar bill on the bar. "Can I ask you a question?"

"I may not have an answer."

One side of his lips twitched up, then he pulled out his phone and showed her a photo. "Seen this guy?"

It was the "vendor" Joe met with on Friday night, the Hispanic guy with a smooth face, the same one that had sat two stools over from where DeYoung now sat.

"You a cop?" she asked.

She had to decide what to tell him about the stranger, and she had to do it fast. Otherwise, no matter what she said, he'd think she was lying. So she kept the conversation going while she figured out what to say—and how to keep him here long enough for her to contact Matt.

"Bounty hunter," he said.

She nodded toward the picture on his phone. "What'd the guy do?"

"He's wanted in Texas."

"That doesn't answer my question."

"Was he here tonight?"

"Came in maybe an hour ago, ninety minutes? Had a shot of tequila, the good stuff. Left. Who is he?"

"Thanks." He drained the scotch, tipped his hat and left.

Shit. She immediately texted Matt but doubted that he'd get here in time.

CHAPTER 33

—

Tuesday morning
Patagonia, Arizona

Matt hadn't slept well. He'd missed DeYoung at the bar. He'd wanted to go in, talk to Kara, but instead called her and they debriefed over the phone.

When he couldn't sleep, he'd contemplated going over to Kara's place in the middle of the night but decided against it. He wasn't certain how he felt about their time in bed the other night. On the one hand, he craved her. He could work with her, talk with her, argue with her, but when they were alone, he wanted her in bed. That she was an enthusiastic partner—pushing him in ways he hadn't been pushed before, urging him to fulfill his fantasies— was intoxicating. He realized that Kara *was* his fantasy. That knowledge made this attraction, this *affair*, ten times worse.

This, simply, couldn't end well.

His track record with women was pathetic. He could dismiss his early relationships as failing because of immaturity—his high school girlfriend, the girls he dated in college—he had clearly wanted different things in life but didn't recognize then that you needed a partner who shared at least some of your own dreams and desires.

But even his relationships over the last five years, when he should have been mature enough to learn how to love someone, he'd screwed up. Lauren Valera, now the sheriff of Pima County, which included Tucson, they'd been good until he left for DC and she was stunned. He didn't understand why she was surprised, and it wasn't like he expected her to give up a promising career to follow him. But they had parted on not-so-great terms. And Beth… Matt had truly cared for Beth, but he hadn't loved her. She'd split it off, officially, but told him that he had walked away mentally before she had the courage to walk away physically.

Beth had been far too good for him in many ways…but he should have known there wasn't a future. He thought about what Peter said about his wife, Gina, and how he shared both the good and the bad with her because she needed to have all of him or none of him. Matt would never have been able to talk about the darkness with Beth when she was so…*light*.

And now Kara. If he was a federal agent in LA

and she was a cop in LA, it would be different. Same line of work, different departments. But they were on the same team. He was her *boss*. Kara had made it clear that she considered this stint temporary, until it was safe for her to go back to LA. But Matt knew—and Kara *had* to know, even if she hadn't admitted it to herself—that she'd never be able to go back to the way things were. That she didn't acknowledge that fact bothered him. But it bothered him in a different way than he thought it would.

He didn't want her hurt.

He shook his head, pulled himself out of bed and made the crappy coffee from the in-room motel coffeepot. Looking at his track record, all he could see was him screwing something up with Kara, and then them hating each other. It didn't matter how easygoing she was about sex; sex always changed relationships.

Fuck, fuck, fuck.

He drank his coffee, showered, made another cup while he dressed, then headed down to a diner on the corner. More coffee and food, and at eight thirty Matt read a text from Christine giving him an update on Angel and Bianca. Both kids had restless nights, and Bianca woke up with a nightmare. But the staff was great, and the kids seemed to be doing well medically, at least as well as to be expected. Christine left at eight in the morning when two agents came to relieve her. She was checking in at the office, then said she'd go home to shower and take a short nap, then return in a couple of hours to officially interview Angel.

The kids are having a hard time trusting anyone. I didn't want to pressure Angel to make a statement, and the doctor said he was extremely fatigued and malnourished. I spent the time talking to him, getting him to trust me. This afternoon will be soon enough, and we'll get better information.

That's why Matt had wanted Christine to replace him in Tucson five years ago. She always weighed every situation to determine the best course of action.

Christine had a way of instilling devotion. She was as calm as Zack was hyper. He responded to her text, thanking her.

I know I promised you my case wouldn't take too many of your resources... I owe you one.

She immediately responded with a laughing emoji. You owe me more than one, Costa.

Zack was calling him. "Costa," he answered.

"I found stuff, lots of stuff," Zack said. "I'm typing it up now—" Matt could hear the clicking in the background "—and I have more stuff to find."

"Have you slept?"

"Yes," he said.

"No," Matt heard in the background.

"Who was that?"

"Agent Jimenez," Zack said.

There was some noise, then Christine got on the

phone. "Matt, it's Chris. I stopped by here to check on the office and realized your guy hasn't slept. Maybe an hour at his desk, but he's wearing the same clothes he was in when I left last night to go to the hospital. The guard said he was here all night. Your office smells like body odor and stale food."

"Put him back on," Matt said.

Zack said, "Boss?"

"Tell me what you learned, then go to your hotel, take a shower and sleep. That is an order."

Matt appreciated the dedication, but not the stupidity. Not sleeping one night—Matt understood. But multiple nights? He knew Zack had been putting in far too many long hours.

"Okay. Okay. Listen."

Matt rubbed his eyes. Zack was really annoying him. He didn't know if this was going to work out. But he couldn't discount his skills. There were few people who could see connections like Zack. "Talk."

"I tracked A-Line and every layer of corporation between it and the parent company owned by Kline, RSK," Zack said, talking fast. "Like I told you yesterday—I mean Sunday—there are multiple levels of companies, but A-Line is the *only* actual business, meaning the only company that is being used to earn income. There are no employees, just the principals—Kline and the Hargroves. If they even kept records, I have no idea where they are. Nothing's been filed with any state or federal agency. They could be paying under the table, which is what I would do, but—"

"Zack! Bottom line."

"So A-Line is the front-facing business, and RSK is the holding company that everything comes from." Zack continued as if Matt hadn't yelled at him. "Once I was on-site and could look at the files and time stamps, then put everything into my computer, I could see exactly what was going on. And it's *simple*. So very simple, no one would get away with it."

"They didn't, Zack, but I don't know what you want to tell me."

"Right. Well. These companies are set up to be pass-throughs—it's money laundering, pure and simple, though I don't have all the bank records—yet. But Tanya Hargrove's antiques business is front and center. She has far more cash flow last year than any other year—in fact, since she opened the business eight years ago, she has more cash flow last year than the first seven *combined*."

"Money laundering. For who?"

"Well… I'm not quite sure, but the same lawyer is attached to all these filings *except* A-Line's. Robert Duncan, with Fosco, Britton and Lourdes out of Las Vegas. Pure corporate law. I think the Hargroves and Kline worked with the lawyer for at least two years—basically, they were just names on paperwork. Tanya is buying and selling a lot of merchandise…but I don't think it exists. I think it's all on paper. That cleans the money. I mean, really well. None of them have the background to cook the books, that's the lawyer."

"Where is the fucking money coming from?" Matt snapped.

"I don't know. *Yet.* I'm getting there. Because a lawyer set this all up, I'm pretty certain one of his clients is the beneficiary."

"How much money?"

"Based on Tanya Hargrove's business returns, one million the first year, two million the second year and I can only imagine it being the same or more this year. And the Hargroves aren't living that kind of life. But there's one other thing—and, uh, I think this is how you're going to find them. Property is also a great way to launder money, and one of the shell corps is buying up property, has been for a couple of years. Much of the money that Tanya was washing was used to purchase property in the name of a company, not an individual, which is much harder to trace, but I'm working on it."

"Send me the list and get some sleep."

"But you missed the main point!"

Matt almost threw his phone across the restaurant. His anger was already causing undue attention by the few other customers. He lowered his voice. "What did I miss, Zack?"

"A-Line. I think the Hargroves and Roger Kline created A-Line using the same structure that the lawyer used to create these dozen shell companies, but they used it as an actual business—the business to haul waste. Only, they really didn't know what they were doing and that's why they ended up on our radar. If we never found out about them, we would never have learned about this multilevel shell corporation that's laundering money. I'm telling you, Tanya Hargrove's business isn't the only one that's funneling money into these companies."

"Great. Now sleep." He ended the call and called Christine directly.

"Chris, make sure Zack gets to his hotel safely, and if he returns to the office in less than six hours, arrest him."

"You sound serious."

"I am serious. What do we know about this lawyer, Robert Duncan?"

"I would say that I'd ask Zack to find out, but I don't want to be arrested."

"Can you send what Zack has to Tony? I'll call him and get him to light a fire under the Las Vegas office to get everything they can learn about the guy."

His email refreshed and he saw the list of addresses that Zack just sent.

"Chris, I'm looking at the addresses Zack just sent. One is here outside Patagonia. I'll go there. Two are in Las Vegas, one each in Phoenix, Tucson and Saint George."

"I'll send someone to the other properties and contact Las Vegas and Phoenix."

"You're the best. Sleep."

"One hour to set this up, then I'll be crashed."

"Thanks, Chris."

"Anytime. Sometimes you drive me crazy, Mathias, but the last couple weeks have been a lot of fun."

"You have an odd view of *fun*."

She laughed and ended the call.

* * *

Matt did something he never allowed his agents to do—go to a potential crime scene alone. But Wyatt Coleman was busy, and Matt needed Ryder in Patagonia to brief Michael and Kara on what they'd learned, while simultaneously protecting their cover.

The Phoenix FBI office had warrants to search the properties Zack had identified as likely being bought from ill-gotten gains—Matt was surprised at how quickly Tony was able to get a search warrant, even though it was limited to documenting and visual inspection. Meaning, they couldn't look in cabinets or computers, but they could photograph and document anything in plain sight.

One property on the list was near the small town of Elgin, thirty miles northeast of Patagonia. Google Maps showed two structures on the property, both appearing to be barns. Matt approached slowly, didn't see any other vehicles, but still when he exited his vehicle, he had his hand on the butt of his gun, watching and listening for any movement.

The first barn was made of wood and falling apart. A quick search told him no one was inside. The larger barn looked like a warehouse, made of a combination of aluminum siding and wood, and while it had seen better days, it was mostly intact. The large barn doors were latched but unlocked. Impressions in the ground indicated a large truck had gone in and out through these doors.

Cautiously, he flicked the latch. One left door didn't budge; the right side moved slowly inward.

He pulled his gun and pushed open the right door, then stood back against the wall.

Silence.

He entered, immediately assessing the cavernous space, making sure there was no one inside.

No person was inside, but the A-Line waste disposal truck filled most of the space.

"I'll be damned," he mumbled.

But the truck wasn't all he found.

As he walked inside, he saw odd rays of light coming from holes in one wall. After doing a thorough search of the building and the truck, and ensuring he was in fact alone, he inspected the wall.

Someone had fired hundreds of rounds from a semiautomatic rifle from the outside into the side of the barn. Based on weathering—or rather, the lack of weathering around the holes—these were new.

He looked closer at the truck. It, too, was riddled with bullets. He searched but found nothing that looked like blood anywhere on the truck or in the barn.

By a rough estimate, he counted over two hundred holes on the north-facing wall. At least a third of them hit the truck.

Someone shooting up a barn? This wasn't target practice, and the price of ammunition told him no one but an idiot would spray more than two hundred rounds into the siding. Was someone trying to get rid of evidence? That made no sense—if they wanted to get rid of evidence, it would be easier to set the truck on fire. Were they trying to blow up the gas tank? Clearly, it hadn't worked.

Matt went outside and walked around the perimeter. He found spent brass—whoever did this didn't collect their brass. Definite possibility for fingerprints. There were multiple vehicle treads—not clear enough to get any real imprint, but clear enough that Matt knew at least two trucks had been here.

Could Roger Kline believe that shooting up the barn would destroy evidence in the truck? Was he trying to blow it up? If so, there were far better ways to make a truck explode. Or was this the handiwork of the same person who killed David Hargrove? Had David been here when the barn got shot up? If so, why not kill him here?

Matt leaned to the second option, but David's murder had been almost…perfect. And Matt didn't use that word lightly.

There was no evidence. Autopsy and forensics had come up with zip. You couldn't run ballistics on a shotgun even if they found it. David was shot and killed on a rarely used road in the middle of the desert where eventually he'd be found…days or weeks. Why was he there? That was the million-dollar question.

Based on the timeline Tanya had given them—which Matt wasn't holding his breath was accurate—David had left at quarter to eight to "help a friend." What if he was out here, getting the truck ready for Monday…because that's when A-Line was scheduled to pick up the slag from Southwest Copper. Was he attacked? Forced somehow to drive his truck back toward Patagonia?

But why there? Out here was a far better place to kill someone. Why take him anywhere? General rule of thumb for bad guys: if you want to kill someone, kill them. Don't pussyfoot around, talk to them, move them. You kill them and leave—it was the best chance of getting away with it.

Unless they needed David to *do* something for them. Or maybe he hadn't been out here at all. Perhaps the shooting was meant to intimidate him. It could be that someone lured him out of town and killed him...someone he knew. Trusted.

"What the hell were you into, Hargrove?" Matt muttered as he stared at the sad barn. "And where's your wife and brother-in-law?"

At this point, Matt feared again they were dead and they may never find their bodies.

But you found David Hargrove, and quickly, he thought to himself.

They found Hargrove quickly because Joe Molina drove right past the body. A coincidence, but plausible. Hiking, picnic, return and find a body...

Joe had been worried on Thursday morning when he called him...on Friday he had been both upset and angry that Matt hadn't arrested Hargrove, even though all the evidence against him was circumstantial. Joe knew that they needed to wait until the A-Line pickup on Monday to track the truck... Joe knew that they had the warrant to track the vehicle electronically. And yet he was still adamant that Matt "do something."

Why?

"Dammit, Joe. Did you take the law into your own hands?"

Except that made no sense. Killing Hargrove would make Joe a murderer, and why would he kill someone when he knew they were *this close* to ending the operation?

And the autopsy confirmed that Hargrove had been killed between 8:00 a.m. and 10:00 a.m. on Saturday morning. Joe had been with Kara.

He was getting a headache thinking about it. Because the more he learned, the more the motive eluded him.

Matt went back into the barn and, after slipping on a pair of gloves, searched the cab of the truck.

Bingo again. He could now directly tie A-Line to Roger Kline and the parent company, RSK. Inside the center console was the trucking license for Roger Kline, listing his known home address in Phoenix. The truck was registered to RSK, Limited—out of Las Vegas. Which was more proof that Kline had been involved in the multilayers of shell companies. A copy of the receipt signed by David Hargrove for picking up fourteen tons of slag last month from Southwest Copper—and thirteen tons in March, and fourteen and a half tons in February. The truck was currently property owned by another company under the RSK umbrella.

After taking pictures of everything, Matt climbed out of the cab and called Wyatt Coleman. He told him about the discovery. Not for the first time, Matt wished he had Jim here on-site to process the scene. Fortunately, Wyatt agreed his deputies would handle the scene, which relieved Matt so he wouldn't have to call in yet another jurisdiction. He'd much rather let Wyatt work with other local cops.

"Consider it done," Wyatt said. "And some news—Phoenix PD found Tanya Hargrove's car parked at a mall. They checked with mall security and learned the car was there both Sunday and Monday nights."

"Did they search the car?"

Maybe they'd get lucky and find out where Tanya had gone.

"I sent them the warrant. They'll let me know if they find anything, and impound the car. But get this—the mall is only two miles from where her brother lives."

"So Sunday night she drugs Crystal with Valium, leaves her house and drives to her brother's home. But we had Phoenix PD sitting on the place." Matt snapped his fingers. "I'll bet Kline picked her up at the mall without going home. Knew we were watching his place, went elsewhere."

"Sounds plausible."

"The faster we find Tanya and Roger, the better. They're the main stumbling block now to putting all the pieces together."

Other than Emma Perez. But if Matt's theory was right, then she may have been killed by one of the same traffickers who had held Angel and Bianca in the underground bunker.

Was that the endgame of Hargrove and Kline? Were they laundering money for gangs like Sangre that were trafficking in humans? It seemed far too unrealistic, but it was the only thing that made sense with what he knew right now.

He still had a lot of questions, like why jeopardize exposing a profitable trafficking organization to haul and dump hazardous waste? Maybe A-Line was just one more company used to launder the money.

It was beginning to make sense now. Except for one thing.

Everything he knew about Kline and the Hargroves told him they weren't smart enough to run this kind of operation. That meant someone else was pulling their strings.

And that person was extremely dangerous.

CHAPTER 34

Late Tuesday afternoon
Southwest of Patagonia, Arizona

Peter Carillo was waiting for Matt at a trailhead about a mile south of Highway 82, several miles southwest of Patagonia. He looked at the map of the area. This wasn't the same trail that Billy and Emma had used, but as Matt studied the map, he realized they were on the western side of the same hill. They were on the edge of a huge quarry—one that had long ago been excavated and then shut down. You wouldn't be able to see the scar on the earth except from the sky, or walking here, along the rim. Several vehicles were on the narrow road that had once been maintained by the quarry but was now in disrepair. It looked like Peter's team was packing up as the sun was getting low. Two park rangers—this was state land—stood sentry at the head of another gravel road that went east.

As soon as Matt got out of his car, he felt the moisture in the air. A storm was coming. He looked out at the horizon. Northwest, huge gray clouds were forming in the distance. It might not hit them here, but it would definitely sweep through Tucson by tonight.

"You didn't tell me what you found," Matt said as he approached Peter.

"You need to see it. This is an old quarry. I didn't put two and two together until I looked at the map more carefully. This road here has been recently used—trucks, it seems. We could drive down there, but I don't want to mess with any potential evidence, and it's a short walk."

The road they walked ended in two hundred yards, where a small abandoned warehouse made of cheap materials stood barely intact. The sides were bowed, but the roof appeared solid. A four-wheel-drive late-model Ram truck with Arizona plates was parked next to the warehouse. It seemed out of place.

"This was used for storage of equipment and extra supplies during the initial excavation for the quarry."

"Why didn't the original investigators find this?"

"We're about a mile from the pond where Emma Perez was found. And when I read through the material you sent me last night about her murder investigation, it indicated that Billy used the main trail to hike in here—that's on the other side of the mountain. There's no maintained trail between there and here, though it's fairly easy to navigate. While old-timers know about the quarry, it shut down thirty years ago. The only reason I knew it was here—after I studied the maps—was because I looked at old land-use maps."

Distant thunder rumbled. Was this storm going to delay the toxic cleanup on the other side of the valley?

"Have you looked at the weather reports?" he asked Peter.

"It's not going to reach us this far south, but Mount Wrightson is going to get three to four inches overnight. We'll get some moisture—not the torrential downpour they'll see in Tucson—but the winds will gust up to forty. Flash-flooding watch starting at eight tonight, until 2:00 a.m. I'd keep your eye on it—you're not going to want to be driving near any of the creeks around here. I'm not looking forward to the drive home, so the sooner we get out of here the better."

Matt made a move to enter the building, and Peter stopped him.

"What's going on?" Matt asked.

"I've already called the coroner. He's on his way. The sheriff and their crime scene team should be here any minute."

"Just tell me, Peter."

"I'll show you."

One of Peter's people was walking around the

area; Matt hadn't seen him at first. He looked a little green, his mouth in a thin line.

Matt braced himself for the worst.

He stepped through the door. At first he didn't see much of anything; it was the smell that assaulted him. The smell of blood and death. As his eyes adjusted to the dim light, he stared at the rear wall. Four dark red splotches, each between five and a half to six feet up from the ground. He looked at the base of the wall. Four bodies lay there. All adult males. All dead.

He turned on his flashlight and walked carefully over to the bodies. Shined a light, then quickly turned it away.

The victims were practically faceless. Matt had seen the aftereffects of these types of gang-style executions before, but they were usually a firing squad in foreign countries. A group of people forced to stand against a wall, shot in the back, their bodies removed and the next group of people led in.

This was different. The men had been shot in the back of the head with a bullet that created maximum carnage. For show? Or because that's what the killers had on them? The victims weren't restrained in any way. One of the men had been shot farther to the right of the group, as if he'd tried to run.

Brutal and efficient.

"Gang revenge killings?" Matt asked, his voice gruff.

"We did a basic inspection. None of them have gang tats."

Peter and Matt went back outside.

They'd been young, from what Matt could tell. In their twenties. Looked like retaliation. Execution. It had been brutal.

Peter said, "The truck is registered to a Jeremy Rapport, out of Tucson. I didn't pull the wallets of any of the boys—wanted to wait until the sheriff gets here. This truck came across the border yesterday evening at seven forty-five. We log every license plate electronically, so when I ran the plates, it popped. I pulled down the photo—we log a photo of the driver—and it was Jeremy. There were three others in the truck with him. I don't have a good image of their faces. They were waved through. Two Caucasian, one African American, one Hispanic. College age, clean-cut, truck not flagged—no reason to stop them.

"Sangre uses kids just like these boys to run drugs and people across the border," Peter continued. "I've seen it before. This place hasn't been on our radar, but they're not coming back. They left the bodies here. They didn't care who found them or when or even if they were found."

"Did they come here directly from the border?" Matt asked. "Maybe to meet up with a supplier?"

"Most likely," Peter said. "But it's not on the way to Tucson from Nogales, so it was a planned meet. They'd had to have been here before—no one just stumbles onto this place. I'm thinking they've brought in drugs with them over the border—there's no human-smuggling compartments in their truck, I looked—no false bottom in the back where people might lie down and are locked in for hours. But a full forensics sweep will tell you if there had been drugs or weapons in the vehicle. There is a compartment behind the rear seats. It's locked, and I didn't want to contaminate any evidence—now that this is clearly a murder investigation—so I didn't break it open. But based on the sound when I knocked, I'm guessing it's five feet long and two feet high. The type we typically find that is used for smuggling drugs."

"Why kill them now?" Matt asked. "If they were useful to the gang, why get rid of your mules?"

"Any number of reasons," Peter said. "They didn't bring back what they were supposed to, they were robbed, they tried to get out of the business—like telling the gang that this was the last time they were doing a run. Or maybe Sangre picked up chatter in law enforcement and these kids were whacked because they knew too much about the operation. Whatever it was, gangs like Sangre are vicious."

"Shit," Matt muttered. "And this is close to where Emma was killed, at least on the map." He looked at Peter for confirmation, since the border agent knew the area better than he did.

"She was killed less than a mile from here, but on the west side of the hill. There's no trail to get there from here, but it's easy enough terrain to hike. This warehouse was used by traffickers as a way station—there's human waste behind the building, garbage, clothing—no one trashed the inside, so it was probably used for multiple reasons, including storage and drug exchanges. There's evidence that a lock had once been on the door."

Peter turned on his flashlight, since the sun was setting so fast they couldn't see much anymore. A new metal hook was on both sides of the door, but there was no padlock.

"If you know this place is here, have you inspected it before?"

"To be honest, there are abandoned buildings all over the region, and we focus closer to the border. Local law enforcement might patrol, but if they don't see anything suspicious, there's no reason to dig deeper. This place?" He jerked his finger to the old quarry outbuilding. "It's practically hidden, can't even see it from the road up there, and like I said, this place shut down more than thirty years ago."

Dammit, Matt thought. These college kids didn't deserve to be executed. He didn't care how stupid they were, or what crimes they committed, to be murdered like this was downright evil.

Peter's radio beeped.

"Carillo."

"Sheriff and coroner are here."

"Send them down."

Matt spent thirty minutes with the assistant sheriff of Santa Cruz County while the coroner photographed and secured the bodies—mostly to keep the peace between the FBI and the local jurisdiction—and was happy to hear Wyatt Coleman had said positive things about him. That made a world of difference, he realized, having a local agency smooth the way.

The wind was picking up, but so far no rain—maybe Peter was right. But the periodic thunder seemed to be getting closer.

The coroner came out with the identification of all four men.

Rapport was twenty-two; the others were twenty-one. They all had University of Arizona student IDs in their wallets. Rapport was the only Arizona native—two came from California and one from Idaho. They all lived in the same house near the university.

Matt was happy to let the sheriff handle this case but offered his help and resources if they needed it.

He walked back to his car with Peter. "Thanks for calling me, Peter. I need to fill in my boss, and we'll have to juggle jurisdictional issues. I told the sheriff that I need everything—reports, photos, suspects. But this is clearly a smuggling-related murder, correct?"

Peter agreed. "This is right up Sangre's alley."

"I still don't know why Emma Perez was killed, but I can't discount that these four students were found not far from her murder. Was it the same gang? Did she see something? She wasn't executed—maybe her death was spontaneous. Maybe she saw something, heard something and one of the gangbangers panicked." Maybe her death had nothing to do with the dead birds or toxic dumping.

"If they were using this place to store supplies—guns, drugs or people—and they saw her in the vicinity, if she made any indication that she saw them or that she was heading in their direction, then yeah, they might kill her and not think twice about it."

Matt considered that Billy had been spared. He'd been taking a break, letting Emma go down to the pond without him. It reasoned that Emma saw someone there who killed her without hesitation—likely for the reason Peter said. This warehouse was used for smuggling, and the smugglers feared exposure. But when Billy came running, the killer ran. Maybe they didn't have a gun on them at the time and didn't know if they could fight Billy off, or if he was carrying a weapon.

Matt would find them. He would track down every Sangre gangbanger if he had to and find the bastard who killed that girl.

Matt drove immediately back to Patagonia and was almost to his hotel when Wyatt called him.

Wyatt said, "I just saw the bulletin. Four dead college students. Said you were on scene."

"I was. They were executed."

"The truck found at the scene—registered to Jeremy Rapport. I pulled him over last night."

"What time?"

"Ten fifteen. The new bartender at the Wrangler called it in, said they seemed impaired. A couple of them were, but the driver passed a field sobriety test. I let them go. I added the information to the bulletin but wanted to know what else you knew about the case."

"Not much more." Matt told him what Peter had said about the likelihood of the boys being drug mules for the Sangre gang. "My interest in the case is because they were executed less than a mile from where Emma Perez was murdered."

Wyatt was silent, then said, "Well, I'll be damned. I'm looking at the map now. You think they're connected."

"I think," Matt said cautiously, "that we had the motive for Emma's murder wrong. We assumed because she'd been searching for the toxic dump site that was the reason she was killed. It appears that she was killed because she may have gotten too close to one of the Sangre gang's storage facilities, or saw something going on that made her suspicious."

Matt pulled up to his motel and saw an old Ford truck with Texas plates. "Wyatt, I have to go. Call me if you learn anything. I'll do the same."

He pulled up and cautiously got out, not knowing what to expect.

Garrett DeYoung was leaning against the hood of his truck, looking like he didn't have a care in the world. He looked at Matt. "I hear you've been looking for me."

"I think we need to go to the marshal's office and have a conversation."

He laughed. "Invite me in."

"Like hell."

"Maybe I should introduce myself." He reached into his back pocket.

"Slowly," Matt said, hand on his gun.

"Really? You think that's necessary? One federal officer to another?"

DeYoung slowly pulled out his wallet and tossed it to Matt. Inside was a badge.

Alcohol, Tobacco and Firearms.

Opposite the badge was DeYoung's identification. The photo was a little younger, but just as rough around the edges. Garrett A. DeYoung from Dallas, Texas.

Not a bounty hunter from Odessa. A federal agent.

"Can I come in before you blow my fucking cover, Costa?"

Reluctantly, Matt let DeYoung into his hotel room, but he didn't take his eyes off him.

"Thank you," DeYoung said.

"What are you doing here?" Matt demanded. "What's with the bounty hunter cover? You should have informed the local FBI office that you were working undercover."

"No, I should have—and did—inform the local ATF office that I'm working on a case. I have no obligation to report to all the alphabet agencies. And now I'm telling you to back the fuck off."

Matt bristled, kept his cool. "I meant, what are you doing in Patagonia?"

"It's not the FBI's concern," DeYoung said.

"I'm working a major case, so yeah, it's my concern."

"It's complicated."

"I have all the time in the world," Matt said.

"I don't."

Matt remembered everything Kara had said about her encounters with DeYoung. That the two strangers who'd come to the bar and met with Joe, whom Joe called "vendors"… DeYoung had entered the bar after they left. And per Kara's report, he'd also shown up last night after the "vendor" left the bar, asked her questions about him—gave her nothing but his standard line—and left.

"You're looking for two men," Matt said. He needed more information, but if he acted desperate, DeYoung wouldn't tell him anything, and he didn't want to burn Kara. If DeYoung knew Kara was working for Matt, he might not go back to the bar.

"My case," DeYoung said. "Not yours."

"ATF doesn't work human trafficking."

"Neither does the FBI."

"Tell that to my boss."

"Okay, yes, you deal with that bullshit, but that's not why I'm here. The Lopez brothers are for hire. They work for whoever pays them."

Lopez. That was one more piece of information for Matt. He wished he didn't have to go through hoops with DeYoung, but he'd met mavericks like him over the years. They did what they wanted until they were fired or killed. They didn't give a shit about helping other cops do their job.

"I found one of their underground bunkers," Matt said. "I know what they do."

DeYoung shook his head. "You know nothing, Costa. They're US citizens, free to move back and forth across the border. I have been tracking them for two years because I need to get at their leader.

Their boss. He rarely comes to the US, but he's coming now, and I'm going to nail his ass to the fucking wall."

"You are one person."

"I need confirmation that he's where we think he is, then with a snap of my fingers, I'll have ATF SWAT on-site. If you grab either brother, I'll lose everything I have worked for. Two years, gone."

"When I ran you, it came back bounty hunter."

"How'd you get my prints?"

He didn't answer. "So you're ATF with a cover of bounty hunter. This is bullshit."

"It's not." He handed Matt a card. "That's my boss, call him. Just stay out of my way."

"Did you know about the four students who were killed?"

"I was too late."

"Would you have saved them if you weren't?"

DeYoung didn't directly answer. Instead he said, "One of those victims, Jeremy Rapport, has been running guns down to Mexico for the Lopez brothers since he was eighteen. Bringing back pseudoephedrine, primarily. He recently had a come-to-Jesus conversion, I don't know what— he wouldn't say—and he agreed to become an informant for the ATF. He's the reason I'm here. I don't know if they found out he had informed on them, or if one of the kids Jeremy was with did something stupid, but unfortunately now they are all dead. When your people dismantle their truck, you'll see how they were smuggling arms. It's extremely easy to get guns out of the country. It's big business south of the border, as I'm sure you know, since you used to work in Tucson."

DeYoung had researched him, Matt realized.

DeYoung continued. "But if we take out the Lopez brothers now, too early, nothing changes. I need to get to Hec—" he cleared his throat, not wanting to give the name to Matt "—the honcho who runs it. That's the only way we can make an impact."

DeYoung almost slipped. He knew exactly who the target was and was keeping everything to himself.

"Fuck that," Matt said. "Who is it? We do this together."

DeYoung looked at his watch. "I'm done."

"You need to talk to the local marshal. You're running a dangerous op here in his jurisdiction, and he needs to be aware of that."

"Naw, he doesn't. And neither do you. I've got this under control."

"Bullshit! Your informant is dead, that's how much fucking control you have!"

DeYoung bristled. "Get off your high horse, Costa. I did some research on you when I found out you were running me. You're not all that different from me."

"I am nothing like you," Matt said. He had no idea what DeYoung was referring to. "This solo operation you have here? You're getting people killed."

"I answer to my boss, just like you answer to yours."

"I need to know what's going on—I have people

here, a case I'm running. I need details of your operation so we don't screw each other."

"I'm here—you need to leave."

"Not going to happen."

"Then if any of your people get caught in the crossfire, that's on you."

DeYoung opened the door. A rush of rain swept in. He slammed the door shut behind him.

Matt itched to follow the ATF agent but doubted he'd be successful. DeYoung had that edge; he'd know a tail and know how to throw it.

His informant was dead; he was in over his head. And he didn't care about any other operation.

He was toast. Matt would do whatever it took to get DeYoung fired, or at a minimum pulled from the field. There were so many things wrong with what he was doing! Legally, ethically.

Matt called his boss, Tony, forgetting that it was after midnight in DC.

"Greer," a sleepy Tony said.

"It's Matt. I had a visit from an undercover ATF agent telling me to back off."

"Back off what?"

"The Lopez brothers. He gave me a bone—didn't know I was fishing—the two men that Kara tagged at the bar that we've been running are the Lopez brothers. He pretty much confirmed that they were involved in the human trafficking situation Kara and I uncovered but claims they're for hire, most recently working with college kids to run guns down to Mexico, drugs back up. He's not backing down. His twenty-two-year-old informant is dead, he damn well knows where the Lopez brothers are and he isn't sharing. I need information. And mostly? Why the hell was Joe Molina meeting with these two men?"

"You woke me up, so I'm lost."

Matt reminded Tony where they were in the investigation, and that Kara had tagged two Hispanic men at the bar on Friday night because they made her suspicious.

"So I'm thinking," Matt said, talking as the thoughts came to him, "that either they approached Joe about their illegal business and Joe turned them down, or Joe has been working for them all along."

"Why would Joe Molina agree to help our investigation if he was doing something illegal?"

"I don't know. To find out what we know? Or maybe because he didn't know David Hargrove's waste disposal scam was going to collide with gunrunning?"

It didn't make sense to Matt that Joe would be party to gunrunning or human trafficking, but he needed to talk to Kara ASAP. If Joe even suspected that Kara was a cop, she was in immediate danger.

"I need to talk to my team, and Tony, you need to put a leash on Garrett DeYoung. I'm going to send you his badge information now."

"I'll look into it."

"I don't think you understand, Tony. He's dangerous not only to himself but to my team. I offered to work with him, and he warned me not to get caught in the crossfire. Something else is going on with him and this investigation. I'm not backing down."

"I'll get answers. Hold tight. It's two in the morning, Matt—I don't know how fast I can get those answers, but I'll get them."

"Thank you."

Matt called Ryder first, told him everything he'd learned and asked him to fill in Michael immediately. Then he called Kara.

Her phone rang. And rang.

Dammit, was she still at the bar? Eleven thirty… she could be. But she knew he wouldn't call her if it wasn't important.

He immediately sent her a message.

911.

She knew that meant to call in immediately.

He counted the seconds.

Call me, Kara, dammit!

He waited one minute for the callback that didn't come, then ran out into the rain and headed to the bar.

CHAPTER 35

Late Tuesday night
Patagonia, Arizona

Kara unlocked her door and was about to push it open, relieved to get out of the rain, but hesitated at a small, unfamiliar sound.

Someone was in her house.

For a brief moment, Kara thought it was Matt. But he'd promised he wouldn't sneak in again—she might be tough and trained, but no one liked to be surprised like that. They'd be done on every level if he did that to her again.

She turned away from the door—she was a well-trained cop, and that meant never go into a dangerous situation without cause. Better safe and embarrassed than dead and buried, especially since she'd made the decision not to carry a weapon—which she would never make again. Sometimes, she got so in character that she forgot her training.

She was about to bolt down the steps when a man stepped into view from the corner of the house and rushed her. At the same time, the person she'd sensed was inside her place came out to the porch, grabbed her from behind, and pulled her back in through the doorway.

The man outside immediately stepped in and closed the door behind them.

She spun around and kicked one in the balls, then used her elbow to smash the second guy's nose. Though it was dark—the light she normally kept on in the kitchen was out—she realized these were the two strangers from the Wrangler last Friday who'd been seen talking first to Joe, then Shelley. She'd served the shorter of the two the tequila last night. Joked with him.

Who did they think *she* was? Did they know she was an undercover cop? She wasn't actively investigating them. She hadn't blown her cover. She'd never blown her cover unintentionally.

No, that wasn't it. They thought she was Joe Molina's girlfriend.

Suddenly, everything in the last twenty-four hours shifted into focus. Joe's concern for her safety last night. The way he looked at the short guy drinking tequila. Did he know they were going to try to grab her? Fear for her safety? And hadn't said anything to her?

In the fight, the men shifted positions to try to

get a better hold on her, effectively blocking the front door. She ran toward the back. She had three guns hidden in the house, but she couldn't risk taking the time to extract them—one was under the couch cushion and she couldn't easily get to that, the other was in her bedroom, and there was no way she wanted to be trapped in her bedroom with these two guys on her tail. The third...well, that was in a kitchen drawer; she might be able to get at it.

She wasn't an idiot—she ran through her options and decided in less than a second that running was her *only* option. If she had enough momentum, she'd be able to run out the back door and leap over the backyard fence without a problem—it was a drill they had performed over and over again in the police academy, and something she was particularly good at.

But she didn't get that far.

She apparently had broken the second guy's nose—he was the taller, broader asshole—and that served to anger him. He caught up with her as she reached the back door and pulled her backward toward him. He banged her head against the refrigerator hard enough to leave a dent.

Dizzy, she reached behind her to claw his eyes, but he grabbed her wrists and twisted them up and behind her.

"¡Maldita perra! Puta!" The guy she'd kicked in the balls, Mr. Short Tequila, came over to her and hit her in the face. She tasted blood, and his ring cut her cheek.

The guy holding her used rope to tie her hands

behind her, then pushed her out the back door. They were talking rapidly now in Spanish. She caught bits and pieces, but little made sense to her.

That's when she saw the body outside her door. It was a man she didn't at first recognize; in the dark she could only make out his general shape, and the fact that he was facedown. He was moving on the ground, and as the two thugs pulled her down the stairs, they kicked at him and he groaned. A puddle of water was already forming on the ground around him.

Was it Matt? Ryder? No...the guy wore jeans and his build was different than either of her team members.

Before she could figure out who it was, one of the thugs said something that she thought was *Hold her still*. Definitely had something to do with her.

Kara knew she couldn't go anywhere with these two thugs. She struggled against the ropes they had tightened around her wrists. She screamed at the top of her lungs; the short guy with the broken nose slapped her. She screamed again and the tall guy pulled a bandanna from his pocket and stuffed it in her mouth.

"One more sound," he said in perfect English, "and I will slit your throat, bitch."

He picked her up and threw her over his shoulder. He may very well slit her throat, but she also knew that being prisoner was not an option. She tried to bite him but couldn't get a good angle. She kicked hard, but he held tight. She tried to spit out the bandanna, but it was literally gagging her. Less than ten seconds later, he pushed Kara roughly into the trunk of a car. The short guy reached into her pocket and grabbed her phone as he did so. He smashed it on the ground.

Well, shit. There goes plan B.

The trunk came down fast and hard. A beat later, two car doors slammed shut, the ignition turned, and they were speeding down the street.

She rubbed her face on the trunk carpet to work the bandanna out of her mouth so she could breathe. She gasped, eager for fresh breath. She was wet and soggy from the downpour.

They'd tied only her hands, not her feet. So she moved her body around as best she could to see if she could find anything to push out the taillight or to fashion as a weapon. A crowbar, a hammer, anything to use against her captors as soon as they opened the trunk.

She didn't find anything. The car smelled new and surprisingly fresh. A rental car? Really? Two guys used a rental car to kidnap her? Who were these people?

But if it was a rental car, there should be tools in the wheel well. She bounced a bit, found it under her. Now, if she could just work up the floor to get to the tools, she'd be in business.

Easier said than done, she realized as the ropes cut into her wrists.

She would just have to improvise.

CHAPTER 36

Tuesday night
Patagonia, Arizona

Before Matt even got to the Wrangler—the bar was less than five minutes from his hotel—Tony texted him with the names of the Lopez brothers.

Dominick, 29, and Rolando "Rondo," 25, Lopez. Last known address Phoenix, AZ. More soon.

Finally he had names, but that didn't do him any good if he couldn't find them, or didn't have cause to arrest them.

He texted Tony: I need an arrest warrant. Get me something. An unpaid parking ticket.

Matt forwarded the information to Wyatt and the

rest of his team and considered his options. He had no reason to arrest them. Meeting with Joe Molina wasn't cause. Showing up at the Southwest picnic wasn't cause. The word of ATF agent Garrett DeYoung wasn't cause, because Matt had no evidence of their crimes—and he didn't know *what* DeYoung had. But Matt was very good in interrogations.

Men like the Lopez brothers, if they've been in this business for any length of time, aren't going to cave even under a great interrogator.

By the time Matt got to the Wrangler, it was closed. No cars in the lot, only security lights on. He didn't want to blow Kara's cover, but at this point, he feared it had been blown and she was now in trouble.

The bar wasn't far from her house.

He turned out of the parking lot and headed up the street. Parked right in front of her house, pulled out his gun and ran up the stairs as the rain pounded down.

The front door was unlocked.

He knocked, then opened the door.

The living room was a shambles. There had been a fight here. Both lamps broken. The couch on its back. "Kara!" he shouted. "Kara, it's Matt!"

No answer.

He feared he'd find her body, but he searched the small place quickly.

No body.

Some blood. A little in the living room, a smear across the refrigerator. And a bloody handprint on the counter. A handprint that was too big for Kara.

They left a print. A damn good print.

The back door was partly open. More blood here, a couple of drops.

He cautiously opened the door, braced for an attack.

None came.

He saw a body lying facedown in the wet yard. Too big to be Kara. Had she killed her attacker? One of them?

Matt cautiously approached, not knowing if the man had a gun. He heard a groan, then he recognized the worn jeans, jean jacket and plaid shirt.

"DeYoung?"

"Costa. Didn't. See you. Follow. Too late."

Matt squatted, not caring that he was already drenched. He carefully maneuvered DeYoung to his side; that's when he saw the blood on his chest.

"Were you shot?"

"Knife."

DeYoung's face was bloodied; he'd been beaten and stabbed.

"The Lopez brothers?"

DeYoung started to lose consciousness.

"Don't you dare," Matt said. "Who did this?"

"They took Joe Molina's girlfriend."

Kara.

"Why?"

"Leverage."

"What the fuck is going on?"

Again, DeYoung faded. Matt called 911. "This is FBI agent Mathias Costa." He gave his badge number, then said, "I need a bus at 3390 B Street.

Male in his fifties has been stabbed and beaten. We're in the backyard."

He ran inside, grabbed towels and a blanket, and came back out. He used the towels for pressure on DeYoung's stomach where he'd been stabbed, then covered him with a blanket to try to keep him as dry as possible, but it was nearly impossible. He maneuvered so he could keep pressure with one hand and call Wyatt Coleman with the other.

He told him what DeYoung just told him. "I called for a bus, but I need a forensics team here. Kara Quinn has been kidnapped. You know her as Kara Smith, the bartender."

"She's one of yours?"

"Yes. I didn't tell you because it was need to know. Now you need to know. I'll explain everything when you get here. But we're time sensitive. She was grabbed by Dominick and Rolando Lopez. There's evidence here, bloody prints, I want an APB out immediately."

"Did they know she was a cop?"

"If they did, she'd be dead. They think she's Joe Molina's girlfriend. Wyatt—I had good reasons to keep her identity secret. She's a great cop, she put up a fight and I need to find her ASAP. I'm calling my people because we can trace her phone if she still has it."

"Okay, I'll get everyone out there ASAP. And Matt—it's okay you didn't tell me. I get it. Anything else?"

"No. She was my eyes and ears. And now she's gone." *And I need her back.*

He called Ryder next and told him what happened. "Did you reach Michael?"

"Yes, he's at his apartment. He's standing by."

"Good. I'm going to need all hands. But right now I need to find Joe Molina. He's not answering his phone."

"Do they know she's a cop?" Ryder asked.

"No—I don't think so. Before DeYoung lost consciousness he called her Joe's girlfriend and said the Lopez brothers grabbed her for leverage. I need to talk to Molina immediately, but I have my hand on DeYoung's gut, trying to stop the bleeding."

"I'll drive by his house," Ryder said.

"Do not engage. Just let me know if he's there, or if there's any activity in his house. Be careful. The Lopez brothers could very well be there, maybe holding him hostage as well. Check in immediately after. On your way, call Phoenix and have them run by Molina's condo up there."

Leverage. DeYoung thought Kara was Joe's girlfriend. That meant the Lopez brothers likely thought Joe cared what happened to her...that they wanted Joe to do something? What the hell could it be? Why Joe? What did he have that the Lopezes wanted?

Matt called Michael Harris.

"Harris, where are you right now?"

"Home. I just talked to Ryder about the suspects—"

Matt interrupted him and told him everything he'd told Ryder.

"Ryder is heading to Joe Molina's house to see

if he's there. If he's not, I need you to find him. Check his parents, his uncle, the refinery, any place he might be. Keep me informed every step of the way. As soon as Wyatt arrives, I'll meet up with you. If you find Joe Molina, don't let him out of your sight."

CHAPTER 37

Late Tuesday night
Patagonia, Arizona

When Ryder first called him, Michael Harris had changed into khakis and a black T-shirt. Now he strapped a gun on his thigh and put on his shoulder holster for his primary service weapon. He had his badge and his federal ID, and he wished he could have told Barry Nelson any other way that he was a federal agent, but that wasn't an option. Not when his partner's life was in danger.

He left his garage apartment and went out into the light rain. It had been pouring not thirty minutes ago, sheets of water coming from the sky; now the storm seemed to be passing.

First thing was to make sure Molina wasn't here.

He didn't see his car. He crossed over to the main house and rang the bell, gave them time to come to the door.

He didn't hear anything. No movement, no sound. Both of their cars were in the garage.

He rang the bell again, pounded on the door. "Barry Nelson! This is Michael Harris! It's an emergency!"

He listened. No sounds, no movement. The last time he'd seen them was when they greeted their niece Shelley Brown at the door for dinner several hours ago.

He pounded on the door. "FBI! I'm coming in!"

He tried the door; it was unlocked. Though Patagonia had a low crime rate, the Nelsons always locked their doors at night when they went to bed. Something was definitely wrong. He pulled his gun.

"Barry? Helen? It's Michael Harris! Are you okay?"

Silence.

Michael flipped on the lights. He quickly walked through the small one-story house. The kitchen had been cleaned after dinner, but the bed was still made in the bedroom. In the family room— a comfortable space off the kitchen that boasted a large-screen television mounted on the wall, two couches for guests, and the two recliners that Barry and Helen used—was untidy. Not as if there was a struggle, but as if they'd left quickly. A bowl of half-eaten popcorn had been upended. The popcorn was on the floor, but someone had picked up the empty bowl and put it back on the table.

Two half-empty glasses were on the small end

table that sat between the two recliners. Michael leaned over and smelled the drinks. Helen and Barry, when they were enjoying an evening alone, always had a drink together. Helen liked vodka and cranberry juice; Barry liked whiskey and lemonade. Helen had talked about it when they were making chili the other night, about how Barry drank beer around the boys, but when just with her, he liked whiskey with a couple of ounces of fresh-squeezed lemonade.

The ice had melted, but the glasses were still cold. If Shelley was here before ten…that would make sense. They would have had dinner, settled in for a show, had a drink… Helen was meticulous. She never left any dish unwashed or a floor unswept. She wouldn't have allowed popcorn to stay on the floor.

He called Ryder. "Helen and Barry are gone, but their cars are here. I saw Shelley Brown come for dinner. She left about an hour later, then…" He paused.

"What else?"

"Actually, she returned just before ten. I assumed she'd forgotten something…but thinking about it now, she lives in Tucson… If she forgot something, why drive nearly an hour to get it? I don't know if that means anything. There's no sign of a struggle at the Nelson house, but they appear to have left quickly—yet, the television and the lights were off. I'm going to drive over to the Molinas' house, make sure they're okay."

"I'm sitting outside Joe's house. His car isn't

here, lights are off. Doesn't appear to be anyone home. Agent Costa wants me back at my place to be the repository for information, but you should call him before you go to John Molina's. He'll want to go with you."

Ryder sounded upset and he wasn't one that generally showed any strong emotions.

"I'm on it. We'll find her."

"I know you will." He said it with conviction, as if speaking the words out loud made them true.

Kara knew she had a concussion. Her vision was off, and her head ached and she suspected she had a cracked rib to top it all off because her chest was sore. She had to get out of this mess and save herself, because she couldn't expect anyone else to save her.

They'd driven for fewer than ten minutes, and she was certain they'd turned right onto Highway 82, which led to Nogales—and the border crossing. If their car slowed at the border, she could alert someone to her presence. Unfortunately, they turned right before they hit the town—they didn't stop at any lights or stop signs, and she heard only two or three cars pass them. She did manage to get out of the ropes—took her every ounce of patience she possessed, but she did it.

They didn't drive long—maybe two minutes—when they turned again and stopped the car. The ignition cut off. They didn't get Kara out of the trunk, however. She heard voices—the two men who grabbed her and a woman. Their voices were too low for Kara to make out what they were saying.

Then she heard a voice she recognized all too well.

"What have you done?"

Joe.

"There's no excuse for this! Dammit, Dominick, you didn't have to kidnap Kara. She's innocent in all this—she doesn't know anything!"

I know a lot more than you think, asshole.

One of the men spoke. In English, slight Hispanic accent. She remembered that while the two men had communicated in Spanish with each other, when the short tequila drinker spoke to her, he spoke in perfect English and she sensed he was American.

The group must have moved closer to the car, because Kara could clearly hear them.

"Mr. Molina, as I explained to Ms. Brown, and I will explain to you, you are very lucky to be alive. Ms. Brown and I have come to an agreement, and you will do well to listen to her. Your job is to make sure she returns—if you care about your girlfriend and your family. But rest assured, if you run or go to the police or talk to that FBI agent you have been working with, I will kill the pretty bartender, then I will kill your family."

"Joe, let's go," Shelley said.

That *bitch*. Kara had doubts about her at the dinner on Sunday, but she was a defense lawyer, and Kara had some issues with defense lawyers. That's one reason she'd asked Matt to dig around into her life, to make sure her gut instincts were right.

And dammit, they were.

Joe said, "I need to stay. You go, Shelley, bring back whatever it is they want, I have to make sure Kara and Barry are safe."

Barry Nelson? They kidnapped their uncle, as well? Why? Maybe to keep Shelley in line, because the woman probably didn't care squat about Kara.

But they don't know you're a cop. That's a plus.

"As I said, and this is the last time I will repeat myself, once I have what's mine, I will release your girlfriend and your family. *After* we are safely away. You only have yourself to blame, Mr. Molina. If you didn't bring the FBI here, we wouldn't have this issue."

"I didn't bring them! The agent was already investigating David about dumping hazardous waste. Not you, not Shelley, I told you that!"

"I don't believe you. David Hargrove was already on our payroll."

What? Did she hear that right? Hargrove was working for these guys? How could they have missed that?

"I don't know what this waste disposal bullshit was, and I don't fucking care," Dominick continued. "The agent and the marshal have seriously damaged our revenue stream. They've uncovered two of our storage units. It's only a matter of time before they find the tunnels on *your* property. Tunnels you have graciously allowed us to use."

"I never did!"

Joe sounded panicked. Good. Kara hoped he was suffering.

"Joe, let it go *now*," Shelley said.

"Yes, Joe, do it," Dominick said. "Because I answer to more important people than *you*. You're truly lucky that your cousin is persuasive. Because I was ready to kill you all."

"I want to see Kara first. I need to make sure she's okay and you're not lying to me."

A moment later, the trunk popped open. Kara resisted the urge to immediately come out fighting. If they knew she was a cop, she was dead. She'd dealt with assholes like these two when she was an LA cop. She also knew that they would never let any of them walk away from this. They were all as good as dead. That Joe and Shelley didn't know or understand that was irresponsible and stupid.

Joe rushed over to the open trunk. "Oh my God, Kara—are you okay?"

"Wh-what's going on?" She forced fear into her voice. Okay, she didn't have to force it. She was scared, and she *hated* being scared. She was also angry. *Very* angry.

"Rondo, I told you to tie her tight," Dominick said.

"I did, bro."

"Please, let her go," Joe said. "She has nothing to do with this! Barry and Helen are here. We'll get whatever it is you want—just let Kara go."

What the hell? He was going to throw his own aunt and uncle under the bus to save *her*? She wanted to pummel the bastard.

The taller, hairy man—Rondo—roughly pulled Kara out of the trunk. She winced as her muscles ached after the fight at her place, then cramped in the trunk.

"She's feisty, Joe. I see why you like her." He kissed her on her neck, then sucked hard. She fought back, her right arm came loose and she elbowed him in the ribs. It was involuntary, an automatic reaction to being manhandled.

He turned her around and slapped her, pushing her to the shorter Dominick.

Joe stepped forward. "Don't! Don't touch her!"

Dominick pulled her to him, holding her arms so tightly she could feel the bruises form under her skin. He looked her directly in the eye. He was questioning her reactions…she wasn't scared enough, she realized. Fuck! She *was* scared, for herself and everyone, but her instincts always had her fighting back.

She averted her eyes, looking down, trying to be docile. She couldn't force herself to shake, but she let out a whimper and tried to get out of his grasp using only a fraction of her strength.

Because what she saw in this man's eyes *did* terrify her. He would kill without hesitation, without remorse.

Dominick laughed and shoved her toward the bulkier Rondo. "Take her inside. Tie her up."

Joe began, "Let me—"

"You saw her, she's alive and kicking. Now go, before I lose my patience."

Shelley said something, but Kara couldn't make

it out as Rondo gripped her arm and led her into a small cinder-block house. All the lights were on inside, but no other houses were in sight. In the distance she saw a city of lights—had to be Nogales, she figured—but here, they were in the hills off the main highway, and there were few other people. The houses were few and far between.

Inside, she saw Barry and Helen Nelson sitting together on a worn couch, hands clasped. Helen had a bruise on the side of her face.

Which bastard had hit an old woman?

Wait...no... Shelley brought them here. That's the only thing that made sense.

How the hell did that work? Who was Shelley Brown really, and why would she voluntarily bring her aunt and uncle to be held hostage by these pricks?

"Are you okay?" she asked them before she stopped herself. It was a cop question. But it was also a concerned-citizen question. She turned to Rondo. His nose was swollen and slightly askew—she knew she'd broken someone's nose back at her house. He was not as smart as Dominick, she surmised. Didn't mean he wasn't dangerous, and he'd given her a damn hickey on her neck, she felt it throbbing. "You hit her?"

He looked surprised. "No."

"Helen tripped getting out of the car," Barry said quietly. "If you have ice? It would help."

Rondo pushed Kara down on a straight-backed chair, then pulled several zip ties out of his pocket. He pulled her arms behind her around the back of the chair and tied her wrists. Then he secured each ankle to the chair separately.

"No one is able to hear you talk or scream or cry," he said, "but if you do, I'll hit you or gag you because I don't like it, okay?"

She nodded.

He glanced over at Helen and frowned. "I'll find you some ice. Sorry about that."

When he left, Kara whispered, "Are you sure you fell?"

She nodded. "I did. I was so nervous and scared and didn't know why we had to leave our house. I tripped getting out of Shelley's car." She squeezed Barry's hand. "She's in trouble, isn't she?"

Barry didn't say anything. He just stared at the floor, and that's when Kara realized that he knew about Shelley. He might not have known exactly what was going on, but he knew that his niece Shelley was involved with some bad people.

He didn't have a chance to say anything before Rondo returned a minute later with a dirty towel. "I folded it around some ice I scraped off the freezer. Maybe it'll help. I don't like to see nice women hurt."

"Thank you." Helen took the rag with her shaking hands. Barry helped her hold it to her cheek.

Rondo turned to Kara. "You're not a nice woman. Just remember that."

Rondo went back outside. Kara heard a car drive away, but it wasn't the men—she could still hear them talking on the front porch. One was smoking a cigarette, the smell drifting in and making her crave a puff. She wasn't a regular smoker, but she took it up once for an undercover gig and smoked daily for the better part of three months. Every once in a while—especially when she smelled tobacco—she had a sudden desire for a hit.

Kara could escape—at least she was pretty certain she could. She would head straight to town and find the police station, or a phone and call for backup. But Barry and Helen wouldn't be able to make the trek. They were near sixty, and while they seemed physically fit, they wouldn't be able to run for a mile or more in the dark. The lights Kara saw were at least two, three miles away, but the terrain was desert—and she couldn't use the road because they'd be looking for her.

If she escaped, they might hurt Barry and Helen. She wasn't going to have that on her conscience.

But if Dominick and Rondo left, an escape attempt was definitely in play. She could get help. She wanted to tell the Nelsons that she was a cop, that they needed to listen to her, but they might be too scared to keep her secret. They might believe that when Shelley returned, they would get out of this mess, when Kara knew that they would all have a bullet in the brain even if Shelley did everything Dominick told her. Because it was clear that he was angry.

She hadn't put it all together, because she didn't understand what David Hargrove was doing for Dominick or Shelley. More was going on than the FBI had thought when they first came down here to investigate the murder of Emma Perez.

If Joe was involved, he didn't know the details, because he had willingly helped the FBI. If he hadn't been involved… Why was he involved now? Because Shelley told him the truth? What truth? That she was working with smugglers?

What had Dominick said to Joe?

It's only a matter of time before they find the tunnels on your property. Tunnels you have graciously allowed us to use.

Joe denied it… Shelley didn't.

Tunnels. For smuggling.

Angel and Bianca.

Amada.

Kara would kill them.

She took a deep breath. She couldn't kill them, though she wanted to. But they were traffickers, and Shelley had been helping them. Barry? Did he know? Was he in the dark until recently?

She said, "What's going on? Those men grabbed me when I was walking back from the bar. I saw Joe and Shelley outside. What did I do?"

"You didn't do anything," Barry said. "I'm so sorry about all of this. Nothing like this should have happened."

Her suspicions were confirmed. Barry knew about the trafficking.

Helen held out the makeshift ice pack. "You need this more than me."

Kara knew she must look a mess—her face hurt, but she didn't think anything was broken, other than maybe one of her ribs that still ached like a bitch.

"I'm okay," she said. She frowned, pretended to be scared. "I just don't understand. Is this a ransom thing? I don't have any money. I mean, I have five thousand in my savings account…" She let her voice trail off.

"Honey, I'm really sorry that you got mixed up in our family problems," Barry said. "But it'll be okay. Shelley will return in the morning with everything those men want, and we'll be able to leave."

"Really? They're just going to let us leave? But we know who they are!"

"But we're not going to the police. They know that."

She frowned, visually urging Barry to continue talking, but he didn't.

The only reason Dominick would believe that Barry wouldn't go to the police was if Barry had committed a major felony.

"I'm sure nothing Joe and Shelley did is as bad as kidnapping," Kara finally said, lying through her teeth. She was positive Shelley was up to her eyeballs in criminal activity. "I'm sure the police will take that into consideration, right?"

"I wish I could explain everything—even I don't know exactly what happened—but it's better for you if you don't know."

Dominick and Rondo walked in. "That's right," Dominick said. "Just keep your mouth shut." They walked through the house, and a minute later she heard a television and the cheers from a sporting event drifted through the house.

Dammit, they weren't leaving.

But Kara wasn't going to sit back and wait for dawn. Because there was no doubt in her mind that she was dead as soon as Shelley returned.

She hoped that Joe did the right thing and called Matt.

She wasn't holding her breath.

CHAPTER 38

———

Very early Wednesday morning
Tucson, Arizona

When Matt and Michael were talking to John Molina at midnight, Christine called Matt with the first good news of the night: her team had located Roger Kline and Tanya Hargrove at a property on the list Zack had identified. Matt told Christine that Kara was missing, that he needed to talk to them immediately, and she said she'd move mountains to have them in an interview room by 2:00 a.m.

It took some quick talking and arguing with the county prosecutors to get a limited immunity agreement on the table in two hours, but Christine was good. Matt definitely owed her more than one.

Matt and Michael had talked to John Molina

late last night. Hell—it was only two, three hours ago? Matt was running on fumes, but he couldn't slow down now.

John had no idea that Barry and Helen were missing, he didn't know where Joe was, or what Shelley was up to. As Matt and Michael had talked over the information they had, the more they agreed that Shelley Brown was involved in something illegal—and Joe Molina could be involved, as well.

John had given them more information about the accounting discrepancies that Michael had overheard John talking about on Monday.

"My accountant is conducting a full audit, but there are some oddities. Nothing with our actual bank accounts, but our books—the books that Barry has been responsible for over the last two years since Clare got sick—are a mess. I don't know if it's because he didn't know what he was doing, or if there's something else going on."

Matt's bet was that there was a whole lot of something else going on, and he didn't believe that John Molina had any part of it. The man was crushed when Matt left—and he didn't even tell him that he suspected that his son was involved.

But John wasn't surprised when Matt had asked about Shelley Brown.

"I've known Shelley since the day she was born. I loved her like a daughter, but she's always had... well, her mother left when she was young, her father had wild dreams, none of which worked out. Gil—that's Clare and Helen's brother—I told him if he spent as much time building a business as working his get-rich-quick schemes, he'd be better off. He didn't speak to me after that. A few years later, he was killed—drunk driving."

"I'm sorry," Matt had said.

"Don't be. He was drunk. He was driving. He put a mother of three in a wheelchair for the rest of her life." John took a deep breath. "But Shelley seemed to do better after her grief. Barry and Helen took care of her. They're good people. They loved her like she was their own daughter. She had been seventeen at the time, then earned a scholarship to U of A, went to law school. She did a lot of pro bono work. But…she still has that hard edge, I guess you can say. And she represented some unsavory people. Everyone deserves a second chance." He looked at Michael. "You were never in prison."

"No, sir. But I was in the navy. Navy SEALs, ten years."

"I knew you were military. That is a lot harder to fake."

"I'm sorry, sir."

John looked at him, nodded, then turned to Matt. "I'm going to lose everything, aren't I?"

Matt shouldn't have said this, but he'd felt he needed to. "No. I don't know about the business—I don't know what Barry was doing—but I have no evidence and no suspicion that you were involved in anything criminal."

"My life, my freedom, is more important than my business. But I love my company and the people who work for me. If the company fails…a hundred ten men and women will be out of work. That impacts their families, my suppliers, other businesses."

"Don't make assumptions. Let's find Kara and get through this."

That's where they left it with John. Michael stayed in Patagonia to help Ryder coordinate, and Matt drove straight up to Tucson and was now waiting to talk to the two people who might have answers.

Roger Kline's attorney was already at the jail—not the Vegas attorney Duncan, who'd signed all the paperwork for the multiple corporations, but a public defender who was young and eager to please. He seemed to understand the seriousness of the situation—that an undercover cop had been abducted—so he agreed that the limited immunity deal was good. Nothing Roger said here would go on record, but that didn't mean that they *couldn't* prosecute Roger for a crime he admitted to—they just agreed not to use his confession or statement, and he couldn't be charged as an accessory to any crime against a law enforcement officer.

Matt had several suspicions he wanted to confirm, but the most vital was whether Shelley Brown had a role in A-Line, and if so, what specifically did she do.

"Thank you for agreeing to talk to us, Mr. Kline," Matt said after introducing the prosecutor.

He didn't know what to expect—defiance, maybe—but Kline looked terrified.

"My client has asked me to inquire about witness protection for him and his sister."

Should have been done before agreeing to talk, but Matt didn't say anything.

"That's not protocol," Matt said, "but if your client has cause to believe that his life is in danger and he has information that may lead to the prosecution of a felony, then I can bring his request to my boss and he'll discuss it with the US Marshals and Department of Justice. I can promise you that while he is here at this jail, he will be safe." He glanced at the prosecutor for agreement.

She said, "I can authorize Mr. Kline and Mrs. Hargrove be put in special holding, where they won't be with the general population."

"As long as no one knows we're here, we should be okay," Kline said. "But I'm serious—they'll kill us. They killed David."

"Who is they?"

"I, uh, maybe I'd better explain from the beginning."

"That would be good."

"Um, well, a couple years ago—"

The prosecutor asked, "Can you be more specific? Two years? Three years? Longer?"

"Um, nearly three. Three years this September, I think."

The prosecutor made note. Matt wished she wouldn't interrupt yet—he wanted Roger to be comfortable, to tell him everything he knew, as fast as possible, and frequent interruptions often put the suspect on the defensive.

"I was in a bit of trouble, financially, and Tanya was about to lose her store in Patagonia. The antiques shop. David made okay money at Southwest Copper, but nothing to really support my sister, you know? Well, I was down there helping her with the big Labor Day festival—Patagonia has these two big art things, bring in a lot of local money. And Shelley came in."

Matt's heart nearly stopped. Was it going to be this easy? "Shelley Brown?" Matt asked for the record, calmly, as if he already knew everything.

"Yeah. I mean, I didn't know her then, but Tanya did. I guess Tanya had done some work for her, you know, kind of off book."

"What kind of work?" the prosecutor asked.

"Um, I don't know if I should say."

Matt refocused the conversation. They'd find out exactly what Tanya did for Shelley when they talked to Tanya. "You met Shelley Brown at Tanya's antiques store in Patagonia."

"Yeah. And she said she needed someone she could trust to be the head of a company she was starting. Just on paper, you know, and she paid us five thousand dollars for our trouble. So yeah, we did it. It wasn't any trouble, really. She just wanted Tanya and David—they being married—but Tanya knew I needed money, so Shelley agreed that we could all be on the paperwork. We asked for six thousand and got it. Easier to split the money three ways.

"Then a couple months later, she said she had another company. Just basic stuff, you know? To help her clients. Another six thousand dollars."

"Did you ask her what these companies did? The

companies of which you and the Hargroves were so-called figureheads?"

"Well, sort of. She said it was all consulting, and to get her clients the best tax breaks, she needed to establish separate businesses. It made sense when she explained it. She's a lawyer, she's really smart."

And Roger was definitely not the sharpest tack. "Go on."

"So, there were a bunch of these. Eight, nine, maybe. She paid six thousand for each one. I mean, that's a lot of money, you know? But it's, like, one-time money, we split it three ways, and I had to get out of debt. Well, I started getting mail for one of the companies. And, um, one day, in September, I think, last September, David and I were talking. Because you know, we figured out how to set up the paperwork because we did it with Mr. Duncan— he's the lawyer who did all the paperwork and stuff that we had to sign. It wasn't that hard. We created this company for A-Line Waste Disposal because I used to be a trucker, still had my license, and it was a good way to make some extra money. David said the company that had contracted with his boss was going out of business, so he sent out bids and told John that we were the best bid."

"Did David actually send out a notice for bids?"

"No, but he made it seem like he did. I mean, I got a truck at a good deal, and he knew the business. But when I picked up the first load, well, it was a lot harder and more expensive to dispose of than we thought. We couldn't do it for what we said we could, so we kind of decided after that that the desert is a big place and no one would notice…

"Well, I guess someone did, eventually, because all of the sudden, Shelley called David and said he needed to come right up and talk to her. So he went. Then he called me in a huge panic. The FBI was sniffing around and we had to lie low, disband A-Line, just pretend we never knew anything about it."

Shelley knew about the investigation. The only logical way she could have heard about it was through Joe. Matt asked, "When was this? When did Shelley call David?"

"Friday. He called me Friday night."

"Let me get this straight. What you're saying is that you agreed to go into business with Shelley Brown, on paper, without knowing what business and without seeing any income from the business."

"We were signatories, like a flat-fee consultant."

That sounded like something Shelley would say to get three people who had barely passed high school to think they were important.

"Did you ever meet with the lawyer, Robert Duncan, whose name is on all the paperwork?"

"Yeah, to sign everything. He's a notary, he had to authorize it. We went to Las Vegas. Shelley gave us a bonus so we could stay in a nice hotel and have a little fun."

Again, half-truths, but Matt didn't think Roger was lying. It was a bill of goods that Shelley sold him.

"But A-Line was your and David's company."

Roger nodded. "We knew exactly what to do. We

just had to file an amendment—the registrar in Las Vegas walked us through how to do it. Because it was our company, on paper, we didn't need to go to Shelley. We just wanted our own legitimate business to have a steady income, because we didn't know when we'd see another six thousand."

"Did you have any other clients other than Southwest Copper?" the prosecutor asked.

"We were trying…it's just a hard business to break into."

It was an important question, but Matt had a stronger sense of urgency because he had no idea where Kara was.

"What happened on Saturday?" he asked. "David called you Saturday morning—he was killed between eight and ten."

"I don't know! He was supposed to meet me at the truck. I got there, he wasn't there. I was late, yeah, but not *that* late. Then I heard a car, thought it was him, but these two creepy-looking guys got out so I hid. They just started shooting at the barn!"

"How did you survive?"

"I hid in the hay loft. Jumped on the top of the cab and into the loft. There isn't a ladder or anything. And just prayed and prayed. They fired like a thousand rounds. And then they came in and looked around. They talked about burning the place down, but one of them said it would be better to just leave this for the cops to find. And they left. I waited for hours before I got down, then I called Tanya. She said you'd been to her place, to talk to her, and she was freaked. So I said to lie low and we'd figure out what to do. We decided we needed to disappear for a while, you know? Until things all calmed down. I tried to access one of the companies, to see if we could get money from one of them, but I didn't have any of the banking information, I realized."

Matt asked, "Can you identify the men who shot at you?"

"Yeah, I think so."

Matt pulled out a sheet that had six photos, two of which were of Dominick and Rolando Lopez.

He looked, then pointed first to Dominick Lopez, then Rolando Lopez.

"You're positive."

"Yes. And I saw one of them driving a black car down the main street in Patagonia on Sunday when I was on my way to Tanya's. So I hightailed it out of there and called Tanya and told her not to leave her house, that I'd come up with another plan and come get her."

"Had you ever seen them before?"

"No, not until they shot up my truck."

Matt said, "Go back to what Shelley told David about the FBI investigation into A-Line."

"I wasn't there, you know. He just was freaking out, which is why I said I'd meet him on Saturday."

"But you said that David specifically said that Shelley knew about the FBI investigation into A-Line."

"Yes," Roger said. "She was really angry, David said. Like, spitting angry. He thought she was going to kill him…oh my God, did she kill him?"

Matt was pretty certain that the Lopez brothers

killed David, but he couldn't prove it yet. "We're still investigating David's murder," he said. "Did David talk to her on the phone? There was an unknown, untraceable number he called on Friday night."

"No, I mean, yes, Shelley called me and then he called her when he got to Tucson. They met at a bar."

"Name?"

"I don't know, really. He said they met at this dive bar and she was spitting angry, those were his exact words. Shelley told him that she'd been informed of an FBI investigation and she wanted to know why the FBI was investigating him and A-Line. She, um, I guess she'd done some research and knew that we started up the company, and so she like, um, got mad about that because we weren't supposed to mess with her project. She was really mean about it, though. Like, we were just supposed to do as she said and keep our mouths shut. She said that she would figure out what to do, but she wanted to see the truck. That's why David and I were going to meet her out in Elgin, but like I said, David never showed."

"Hold on—before you didn't say that *Shelley Brown* was going to meet with you in Elgin."

"Oh. Yeah. That's why David wanted me to come down. She wanted to talk to both of us and find out a way to get rid of the truck. If A-Line never showed up at Southwest Copper, and the FBI couldn't find the truck, then they'd—I mean you—would go away."

"Do you know Emma Perez?"

"Uh, no, I don't think so."

"She was a college student at U of A."

"Oh, no, I don't. I never went to college."

"She was murdered in March near the abandoned quarry southwest of Patagonia."

No reaction from Roger.

"Um, I'm sorry."

"There's one thing that Shelley didn't tell you," Matt said. "We didn't start this investigation because of A-Line. We started the investigation because we were investigating Emma Perez's murder. She'd been looking into wildlife death in the area, and birds that drank water contaminated with arsenic and lead—both toxic poisons found in copper slag. That's how we learned about A-Line."

"Oh."

"Did you or David talk to Joe Molina about A-Line or the FBI investigation?"

"Who? John's son?" Roger shook his head. "Not me. I don't think David did either. I mean, he wouldn't. We didn't even know about the investigation until Friday, I swear to God."

Matt believed him. Roger, at least, believed everything that he had said.

"Why did you and Tanya run Sunday night?"

"Why would we stay? Tanya said you thought I'd killed my brother-in-law! I loved David, I would never hurt him. And he loved my sister. And I knew I didn't kill him, and Tanya was really scared about Shelley and what she might do to us. I, um, knew about all this property that one of our companies owned, because we had to sign some contracts and stuff, so I thought that would be a good place to hang for a couple of days until we figured out what to do. And then Tanya said you knew all this stuff about our companies, things she didn't even know, and then I started thinking that maybe I should have paid more attention, but it seemed to be a smart plan. Mr. Duncan, our lawyer in Vegas, said I totally got it, that I was a natural."

The money laundering was a completely different situation, but one that Zack would be well versed to analyze and understand—and he'd know exactly what questions to ask. It was clear that whatever Shelley Brown and Robert Duncan were up to was illegal. When Roger and David decided to use the system the lawyers had created, they had no idea they were creating a huge problem for the illegal money laundering scheme.

"One of my colleagues, Agent Heller, is going to talk to you later this afternoon and ask more questions about the paperwork and any of your other understandings about how this system worked. If you cooperate with him, and agree to testify for us, I'll see what I can do about making a deal on the illegal dumping. But you need to know, you're going to have to come clean about everything, and I mean *everything*."

"I will. We will. Just—I don't want anything to happen to Tanya. She didn't know anything. I mean, she knew about A-Line, we just thought that would be icing on the cake, you know? Our little part of the bigger pie. But she didn't know about the financial stuff. We all just signed where the lawyer told us to sign."

It sounded like Roger didn't understand any of "the financial stuff," either, but Matt didn't say anything. Roger could be playing dumb to gain sympathy. But Matt doubted it.

"Thank you for your time."

Matt stepped out with the prosecutor.

"Why can't they all be easy like that?" she said to him.

"It may not be what it seems. I'm still missing my cop and just found out that my informant at Southwest Copper talked."

"Joe Molina? Could it have been someone else?"

"No. Molina is the only person who knew about my investigation outside of my team—and he didn't know the extent. He didn't know I had undercover agents in town. He told Brown about *my* investigation—why? And when?"

Matt immediately called Ryder and told him what he learned from Kline, then said, "I think Joe told Shelley about our investigation on Thursday or Friday. He pushed me Friday morning about when it would all be wrapping up, said we needed to just bring David in and question him. I didn't think much about it at the time—I should have been suspicious."

A minute later, Wyatt Coleman got on the phone. "Costa?"

"Yes."

"I had a heart-to-heart with Garrett DeYoung as soon as he was stabilized. And I think your boss—

Greer?—he might have raised hell with DeYoung's boss, so DeYoung was a bit more willing to talk. He finally gave me a list of the places that the Lopez brothers might be. DeYoung knew they were going after Kara. He thought he could get there and warn her off. He missed her at the bar, didn't know she walked home, and drove to her house. She didn't answer the door, so he went around back—saw them breaking in through the back door—and lost the fight."

"How did DeYoung know they were going after her?"

"His informant. According to DeYoung, the college kids had already dropped off the drugs at the quarry warehouse before going to the Wrangler— they took guns to Mexico, brought back drugs. Then went to the Wrangler. Rapport specifically made the stop to report to DeYoung. When he called Dominick Lopez to report that they'd fulfilled their job, he overheard someone in the background say they were going to hold on to Joe's girlfriend. It was brief, and Rapport didn't know that the girlfriend was the bartender from the Wrangler, but DeYoung did."

"And he didn't warn her? Rapport was killed Monday night. Kara wasn't grabbed until tonight." *Last night*, he realized, since it was three in the morning.

"I only had ten minutes with him, Matt. You can talk to him when he gets out of surgery."

"When he talked to me, he said he was tracking

the Lopez brothers hoping they'd bring him to the guy in charge. Who is it?"

"He didn't say, but I have the addresses of every place the Lopez brothers have been since they arrived in town, and my deputies are already checking them out."

"Let me know if you find anything. I'm leaving Tucson and on my way back there now. But do not engage without talking to me. We need a plan and a team."

"Understood."

"Can you put Ryder back on?"

A second later, Ryder said, "Sir?"

"Get the list from Wyatt that his deputies are checking. Map it. Analyze it. Tell me where you think they'd keep Kara."

Silence.

"What?" he snapped.

"What if I'm wrong?"

"You won't be."

Matt couldn't have Ryder doubting himself, but in a situation like this, he understood the pressure he was under.

"I will be there in less than an hour," Matt said, "but call me if you have anything before then."

CHAPTER 39

———

Early Wednesday morning
Outside Tucson, Arizona

Joe couldn't believe this was happening.

"We have to go to the authorities," he told Shelley. "Wyatt is a good guy, he'll know what to do, how to get us protection."

Joe had thought they were going to Shelley's house in Tucson, but instead she took him to a Mc-Mansion on a golf course out of town that a client of hers owned.

Joe began to wonder just who his cousin worked for.

She laughed, but there was no humor in it. He realized he didn't know this woman he'd practically grown up with, not anymore. "And tell the authorities what? That I set up a fucking *brilliant* money-laundering operation for a major drug cartel? That a stupid, irresponsible dumbass named David Hargrove fucked up the entire operation *on accident*? That now I have to dissolve everything and give them their money and the ledger of all they are owed? Money I don't have because I can't liquidate all the assets in twenty-four hours?"

She laughed, and Joe thought she was crazy. Literally crazy.

"What are you doing?" Joe said.

"The ledger is in my safe-deposit box. It has all the numbers and accounts and companies, and I'll take it to them and explain how it'll take some time to extract all that money."

"You don't have their money?"

"You think I have millions in cash just sitting around? You're not that stupid, Joe."

"They're going to kill us all, Shelley. They have Kara! Uncle Barry and Aunt Helen."

"We can disappear. I have two million dollars in cash, Joe. We can go anywhere."

He stared at her, his mouth open. "I can't believe you just said that."

"Jeez, I'm not serious."

He didn't believe her.

"Of course we can't leave," she said. "I'll work this out. Barry and Helen aren't going to say anything."

"Why would they keep quiet? They're being held against their will. Did you see Kara? They hurt her for no reason!"

"She fought back. I told them not to hurt anyone, but they still had to get her."

"I can't believe you can justify this. For years you've been working for a drug cartel and you think this is *okay*?"

"Someone had to do something!" she said. She opened the liquor cabinet in the living room and poured herself a double scotch. It was a hundred-dollar bottle of Glenlivet, and she didn't seem to care. She poured one for Joe, too, and slammed it down on the counter. "You need this. Because you need to understand something, Cousin Joe. Southwest Copper would have been gone without me. Uncle John won't fire anyone. The rules and regulations are expensive. When John stepped aside after Aunt Clare got sick, Barry saw how bad it was. He came to me because he didn't know what to do. I came up with the plan. Uncle Barry *saved* the company."

"Did you launder money through Southwest Copper?"

"No! I started that side project three years ago when I realized I would *never* make enough money as a public defender to pay off my student loans. This was different. I *saved* your dad's business. Southwest was on the verge of bankruptcy. *I* fixed it. *I* made sure our family survived. Finagled a few things, cut expenses, and we made it."

"You let a drug cartel use our land."

"They paid us well for it. Easy money. You should be grateful, not bitching at me."

"This isn't just drugs and guns. They're traffickers! In human lives? Children, even...."

"Get off your high horse, Joe. If we didn't allow them to use the land, they'd do it anyway and *not* pay."

"They talked directly with my dad when he saw them out there. Lied to him, said they were with that new mine trying to get approved."

"Smart, eh? I told them if anyone caught them on Southwest land, they should use that story. It worked."

"They could have killed him."

"They could have, but they didn't," Shelley said.

The realization that whatever plan Shelley had in mind was not going to work gradually sunk in. His dad was going to lose everything anyway, and he'd know Joe was partly responsible. All he ever wanted was to be a good son. That's why he came here to help with the company when his mother got so sick. He gave up his job and lifestyle in Phoenix to live back in Patagonia, where he swore he'd never return.

"Look," Shelley continued, "Dominick is not an idiot. He didn't want to draw suspicion to their activities, and if he killed Uncle John, it would have. He's high profile around here. Plus, they know my family is off-limits. I have the ledger, I have the account information. They *need* me."

Joe wanted to hit her. "You are insane."

Shelley scowled at him, like an angry dog. "Look, I've kept this family afloat for *two fucking years*, whether you realized it or not. So now you have to convince your girlfriend to keep her mouth shut, or yeah, she'll get whacked. You thought Barry didn't know? He did. He chose to look the other way, took the money I gave him and used it to keep *your* dad's business afloat. I was doing *just fine* until you let the fucking FBI into our town *and didn't tell me*! And you know what? Uncle Barry has always felt inferior to the high-and-mighty John Molina. Your father, the noble war hero who everyone loved. Everything he touched turned to gold. Or copper, as the case may be." She giggled, now under the influence after drinking multiple shots. Joe finally picked up the glass she'd poured for him and drained it in one long, burning swig.

But Shelley wasn't done with her rant. "Barry couldn't keep a job until your father took pity on him. He would do *anything* to prove he was worthy, even if that meant accepting dirty money. How the *fuck* do you think your father could afford your mother's extensive cancer treatments? You think insurance covered *everything*? You're a bigger fool than all of them."

Joe didn't want to listen to any of this, but there was a ring of truth in his cousin's words. Had he failed his family because he didn't want to be in the business? Had he turned his back because he couldn't stand living in a town with fewer than a thousand people and not even a one-screen movie theater?

"Kara…"

"She'll keep her mouth shut if she knows what's good for her. She doesn't know the extent of my involvement, and you can explain that you didn't know…which is mostly true."

"It *is* true!" Joe said.

"You brought the fucking *FBI* to Patagonia! You

were *helping* them! If anything, this mess is as much *your* fault as David's."

"I didn't bring them. A college student was murdered while investigating a flock of dead birds two months ago—of course the FBI is going to get involved. What was I supposed to do when they came to me?"

"You should have told me at the very beginning! I could have wrapped David up in a pretty fucking bow for the cops, and they would never have been here."

"You're delusional, Shelley. And all I did was give them access to some of our records so that they could track the A-Line trucks. I didn't know about all the rest of this until you told me Thursday night. How was I supposed to know you were…were…"

A *criminal* he wanted to say, but he was scared. For Shelley and what she'd been doing for the last two years. For his dad and the fact that he was probably going to lose his business, or more. For Kara. Dear God, Kara. He got Kara into this just because he liked her. The first girl he'd really, really liked in years, and now she was in danger and he didn't know how to get out of this.

Joe should never have told Shelley about the FBI investigation. The only reason he did was because he had been reading about liability issues on a legal aid website and wasn't certain that Agent Costa would live up to his end of the deal. He realized he should have hired an attorney to go over the paperwork with him. What if he missed something? So he'd stupidly asked her for legal advice.

Shelley had always looked over contracts for the family and the business, and he gave her the proverbial dollar just to keep the conversation between them. He told Shelley everything about Matt Costa and how the FBI had figured out that David had contracted with A-Line, a new waste hauling company, and they had very likely been illegally dumping the slag from the refinery—and possibly worse. All Joe did was ask his cousin if the FBI was honest in telling him that his dad wouldn't be liable. Joe wanted her opinion about whether there was something he could do or say to move this thing along, because he was sincerely beginning to worry that his dad would find out. If his father had known what David Hargrove was doing, he would have fired him. Then Joe was afraid his dad might be held liable—and knowing his dad, he would absolutely take responsibility. He would take the blame, sell the family house to clean it up. And that shouldn't be on him.

After he told Shelley about Agent Costa, she literally threw a book at him. Told him that together they had to end this investigation immediately because she was working for a drug cartel and letting them use Southwest Copper land to move their product.

Joe had been shocked—nothing could have surprised him more. So when she then told him that she'd been laundering money for the cartels for years, he just stared.

Well, yes, one thing did surprise him more. When she said, "We have to kill that asshole Hargrove. He should never have fucked with me. It's the only way to get the FBI out of town."

Shelley had had a million questions for Joe last Friday night. Hard for him to imagine now that less than a week had passed since he learned the truth. He was in way over his head with this thing. Who was this FBI agent, who else was working the case, who else was in town?

Joe had told her no one, just Matt Costa, and he was based in Tucson, though he came down and stayed in town occasionally. Costa had people working for him, but they were off-site, digging into the financials of A-Line and trying to figure out ownership and if anyone inside Southwest was helping David.

Shelley wasn't sold on this information, but Joe didn't know what else to tell her. It was everything he knew.

"There's this Asian guy who's been staying in town for the last few weeks. I saw Costa with him a couple of times. He doesn't look like a federal agent, but he could be. And he's been working closely with Wyatt."

Joe never imagined Shelley would kill David Hargrove. She told him the FBI needed to know he was dead, and that they would hopefully wrap up the investigation quickly. That's why she told Joe where to find David's body.

If the people we work for find out the FBI is in Patagonia, we're dead. Do you understand?

We? You, Shelley. Not me. Not dad. It's you, all you.

It's all of us. Uncle Barry knows. And now you do. And I swear to God, if you blow this, we're all dead. They'll spare no one, not even your sick mother.

Joe couldn't believe how quickly this spiraled out of control. He should never have brought Kara into this by taking her with him Saturday morning. But Shelley insisted that he keep his plans with Kara.

When they find out that David was illegally dumping, you'll be a suspect, Joe. Especially if you're the one to find the body! He'll be dead between eight and nine Saturday morning. Make sure you have an airtight alibi.

She was right. And so he went along with it. He played the part. Tried to forget, tried to enjoy Kara—and he did, for a while, and almost forgot what he was supposed to do, until they were in the abandoned church and he knew that the next stop was finding David's body.

Joe was falling in love with Kara. Had from the minute he met her. There was something so special about her…he didn't know how else to explain it. He was happy every time he saw her. When he first laid eyes on her three weeks ago, at the Wrangler, he knew she was the one.

Maybe because he hadn't been with anyone since he split with his Phoenix girlfriend. Who could he date in Patagonia? There was no one, and then there was Kara. She was both really cute and sexy. He could watch her all day and just be happy. She had a sharpness that he admired. And heart. She was everything that he wanted in a woman.

And now she was in danger. Because of Shelley.

Don't lie to yourself, Joe. It's because of you. You brought her into this. If anything happens to Kara, it's your fault.

Shelley was right. They had no choice.

"What's the plan?" he asked her.

"Bank opens at nine. It'll take five minutes to go in, get the ledger, then we head to Nogales, be there by ten thirty, tops. Trade the money and ledger for Barry, Helen and Kara."

Against his better judgment—which was in short supply lately, anyway—Joe said, "Fine, I'll do it your way, but I want a gun."

Shelley stared at him for a long minute. "I'll get you one. But as long as your girlfriend keeps her mouth shut, no one will be hurt."

Joe didn't believe her.

The rain had completely stopped by the time Matt was on the road back to Patagonia, which was good because he was driving near ninety miles an hour, which would be impossible in a storm.

Matt was frustrated that no one had found either Joe Molina or Shelley Brown. Not their vehicles, not them. A pair of agents were sitting outside Shelley's Tucson house, a pair of Wyatt's deputies sitting outside Joe Molina's house, but Matt wondered if they were already on the run.

The only bit of real good news he got as he was leaving Tucson for Patagonia was from his boss, Tony.

"Matt, I went directly to the DOJ and knocked heads together, waking up everyone of import, and finally ATF spilled the beans. DeYoung has been building a case against Hector Lopez for the last two years."

"Lopez. Like the brothers."

"Yes. Hector is their cousin, older, the head of a major cartel that primarily arms factions in Mexico that protect his crops and supply line. The network runs guns down to Mexico, then brings drugs and people back to the US to keep the income stream flowing. The brothers hire the Sangre gang to bring the merchandise from the border to safe houses all over the southwest, in Arizona and California primarily. The big reveal here is that the ATF knew that they had an American lawyer helping them launder their money, hints here and there, but nothing concrete. Now they know who. Robert Duncan and Shelley Brown. That's a major win for us because we're handing those two over on a silver platter."

Matt didn't want to think of the win. He wanted to find Kara.

"And where is Hector Lopez now?" Matt asked.

"DeYoung's last report indicated that Hector himself was coming to the States because of a major screwup in the supply chain. DeYoung didn't know what specifically, but I think you do."

"My investigation into the murder of Emma Perez."

"Exactly. That created a domino effect, put you on the trail of David Hargrove and A-Line, connected A-Line to a dozen shell corporations, which Zack uncovered to be a money-laundering pyramid. Oh—and I wanted you to know, agents in Las Vegas are about to serve a warrant on Robert Duncan. It's nice and early in the morning. They're going to have fun with this."

"I'm on my way back to Patagonia. Can you send me everything you have on Hector Lopez? Photo? Anything?"

"Already done."

Matt's phone beeped. "It's Ryder, I have to go." He switched calls.

"I found it," Ryder said. "It's the most logical place for the Lopez brothers to keep hostages, based on the list that DeYoung gave us. They went to several places in Nógales, but there's a house two point five miles northeast of the city that's remote, no nearby neighbors, and there is a large outbuilding adjacent. On maps it appears to be an oversize barn."

"Send me the coordinates."

"I will, but Michael and Marshal Coleman are already on their way. They're going to recon the property while SWAT stages a half mile from the site. By the time you get there, they should have firm intelligence."

"I knew you could do it, Ryder."

"I hope I'm right."

"You are."

Matt had to believe it. Because the longer it took to find Kara, the less chance she would be alive.

CHAPTER 40

Early Wednesday morning
Outside Nogales, Arizona

Michael partnered with Deputy Tom Porter, who Wyatt said was his best tactical officer. Michael liked him; Tom had military experience, and they had the same approach to recon.

They reached the main fire station in Nogales, which was a mile from the house where Ryder suspected Kara and the Nelsons were being held hostage. There was no way to reach the property by vehicle without alerting someone inside—it was one of only a few houses off North River Road, plus they didn't know whether the Lopez brothers had their gangbangers patrolling the area.

Michael hoped DeYoung would be fired from

ATF. When Wyatt came back from interviewing him, the seasoned cop was visibly angry. DeYoung had witnessed the Lopez gang loading twenty migrants, all girls between twelve and twenty, into vans. And he did nothing. Nothing to help them, to report them, to rescue the girls. How could any cop sit back and allow such horrific human rights abuses to occur? They may never find those girls now; they may never be able to save them. And he put that on DeYoung's shoulders.

Michael wondered if Kara had to turn her back on crimes when she worked undercover in the LAPD. He couldn't imagine her doing such a thing…yet she was hard to know. Just when he thought he understood her, he got a sense that he saw only exactly what she wanted him to see. It was a bit unnerving.

Michael hoped that Matt never asked him to go undercover again. He couldn't be forced to, but he didn't want to seem incapable of doing a job that was needed. Michael liked being up-front. He valued honesty, honor, integrity. He needed it. His childhood had been so fucked up with gang violence and trying to keep his small family together. *Failing* to keep his small family together. It's why he needed the military. The structure. The sacrifice. The honor that went with serving something greater than himself. And in that sacrifice, he found pride for the first time. That he could overcome his background and not succumb to the lowest expectations society had for a poor Black kid from Chicago.

When someone like Garrett DeYoung tarnished the badge, it made Michael see red.

And DeYoung's excuse? That there were worse crimes he needed to stop.

Worse crimes than twenty innocent children being sentenced to a fate worse than death?

Michael pushed the dark thoughts out of his head. He would get Kara back. Maybe she had some insight, some way to get him out of this mindset. But first, he needed to confirm she was in the house.

Michael wished he had a drone to fly in and look for the car, but that was off the table. Instead, he and Tom agreed the only safe way to get eyes on the place was to walk in.

The rain had stopped as fast as it started, two hours of torrential downpour and then clear skies. It made the ground muddy and slick, as the dry earth couldn't absorb the water quick enough.

The fire chief gave them a detailed map of the immediate area and told them to avoid everything south of the road. "We can get mud-or rockslides after the rain we just had, as well as flash flooding, but we should be clear up here. In the dark, though, you won't be able to see drop-offs, and there's a few steep places you'll need to watch for. But if you stay here, on the right side of the road, walk in to—" he traced his finger up the road "—here, then walk up this hill. Again, it'll be steep, but you only need to go about fifty yards up. Then turn north and walk about a hundred, hundred twenty yards. You'll see the house. The property itself is not fenced. There's a retaining wall in the back, about four feet high. They'll have good visibility all around if they're watching, except for the north side of the house, where there is an outbuilding."

"Why don't we approach from the north, then?" Michael asked.

"I wouldn't suggest that because the mountain on the north side is much steeper. In the dark it would be virtually impossible to scale."

Michael was certain he could do it, but he would need better equipment and night-vision goggles, which he didn't have. "Okay, we'll come up from the south."

Michael and Tom coordinated their signals, checked their gear and started out.

Fifteen minutes later, they saw the small one-story house. It was lit up—lights in every room. They could use that to their advantage, because if one of the suspects looked out, they would see only dark. There were no streetlights and only a back and front porch light illuminated the exterior. The barn was wrapped in darkness on the north side of the house, towering over the smaller structure.

There were no nearby houses. A dark sedan was parked in the drive, but Michael couldn't make out the details from this distance. If it was the same make and model as they knew the Lopez brothers were driving, he would confirm with Wyatt. All the SWAT team was waiting for was intel.

He said quietly to Tom, "I'm going around the retaining wall to get confirmation on the vehicle.

I'll mic you once if it's the Nissan, twice if it's not. Stay low."

Tom concurred and lay flat on the ground, his rifle trained on the rear door of the house.

Michael ran low along the retaining wall, on the mountain side of the property. So far, so good. The car was parked between the house and the barn. He wished he had full gear, because night-vision goggles would come in handy right now.

He needed to get closer. He walked around the outbuilding, which was surprisingly modern compared to the post–World War II house. He stayed close to the side of the building as he approached the vehicle from the far side.

Bingo.

He clicked his mic once. Tom acknowledged.

They had the right car; now Michael hoped that Kara was inside the house. He wanted to check, but all the blinds were closed.

Michael was about to return to where he'd left Tom when he heard a vehicle on the road. He expected it to pass—when he looked at the map with the fire chief, there were another half dozen properties up this road. But instead, it slowed. It wasn't just a car; it was a car followed by a moving truck. Michael pushed himself up against the barn and froze. The car turned up the drive; its lights flashed against the cactus and mountainside immediately in front of Michael, but thankfully missed him.

The car parked next to the Nissan. The truck passed the driveway, then backed up, all the way to the barn doors, the *beep beep beep* of the backup warning system echoing against the mountainside.

Michael was only two feet from the corner. He slowly moved to the right, still pressed up against the barn, then stopped as soon as he rounded the corner. He couldn't return to Tom without being seen by the new arrivals. He was stuck.

He pushed gently against the side of the barn, looking for any vulnerabilities. It was well made, but several of the wood planks were worn and some splintered. He found a hole near the bottom and cautiously shined his light in, to see if he could determine whether the newcomers were bringing something in, or taking something out.

Wooden crates filled the barn.

The same type of crates used to transport weapons.

Kara was trying to listen to Dominick and Rondo in the other room. They were still watching television. The soccer game ended – their team had lost – and now they were viewing a sitcom on a comedy station that played shows at all hours of the night and, apparently, the wee hours of the morning. Dominick was on and off the phone, but she couldn't make out much of anything because of the distraction of the television, and Rondo's sporadic laughter.

But she did pick up key information over the last couple of hours: they were waiting for someone who scared them.

It was subtle, something she'd picked up primarily from Dominick's tone more than what he said.

Helen had fallen asleep on the couch.

Kara had long ago stopped trying to convince Barry to help her get out of the zip ties—she could do it herself, but she'd make too much noise. But Barry said if he let her go, they'd hurt Helen.

She wanted to say, *You should have thought of that before you got into bed with those bastards*, but she didn't. She didn't want them to hurt Helen either. It wasn't her fault that her husband made a deal with the devil, or that her niece was a bitch.

The more she thought on it, the more she realized that the devil was actually Shelley Brown— not the Lopez brothers. She mentally restructured bits and pieces of information that she'd heard from Barry, the brothers and the conversation outside. Shelley seemed to be the one who knew everyone, and apparently had leverage with the brothers.

She willingly brought her aunt and uncle here. She let her family be held hostage by two violent traffickers. For what? What did she have that was so valuable that Dominick didn't just kill them all outright?

And why did Shelley think that she would survive this? What did she know...what did she have... *that protected her?*

Because the only way Shelley survived was if her death created more problems for whoever Dominick and Rondo worked for.

Shelley was a defense attorney. Okay...did she have specific knowledge or evidence that she'd withheld? Something that she was using as leverage? It was one thing to represent scumbags—while Kara didn't like it because, in her experience, criminals got more rights than cops and victims, she dealt with it. It was the process, the system, and she had to work within the system. So while, sure, she had a problem with defense lawyers, for the most part they were just doing their job and weren't actual criminals themselves.

Shelley might just be the exception to that.

"Barry," Kara finally said when she knew that Helen was asleep, her light snore almost cute if they weren't in such a harrowing situation.

"Hmm?"

He looked at her, bags under his eyes, a deep sadness etched on his weathered face. She almost felt sorry for him.

Almost being the operative word.

"You know they're going to kill me. I don't understand what's going on, but I heard too much and I'm pretty sure they don't care about me. They don't think I'm not going to go to the police."

"I'll vouch for you."

"They're not going to believe you. They have no reason to. I'm new here. You all are family, I'm not. I'm just a bartender. No one will miss me."

"Don't say that. You've been a blessing for Joe. He really loves you."

Loves? *Loves* her? Joe Molina didn't know what love meant. They'd known each other for less than a month and went out a couple of times and he thought he *loved* her? She wanted to laugh out loud.

Like she would fall in love with someone like Joe. At first she thought he was a good guy, noble, doing the right thing helping the FBI when it was hard to do because he had to keep secrets from his family.

You thought he was too good for you.

And then she had some doubts. A few chinks in his armor. His jealousy of his brother who "escaped" Patagonia. Lying to her about what he and Shelley had been discussing at Sunday dinner. His possessive streak...

And then tonight. He was weak, a liar, a manipulator. Shelley may have forced Joe into this situation, but he had options. He could have called Matt, told him what was going on as soon as he learned about it. He could have called Matt and said that his bartender girlfriend had been kidnapped. Told him exactly where they were.

Maybe he did. Maybe he did do the right thing.

She didn't think so. There was something about the earlier conversation that made her think he was more involved than he wanted to be but not willing to defy his cousin.

Maybe he would prove her wrong.

"Everything's going to be okay," Barry said. "Shelley will make sure of it."

"Are they clients of hers or something? Does she have something on them so they won't hurt us? I just don't know *what* to think."

She wanted information—needed it if she was going to figure a way out of this mess.

Barry glanced at sleeping Helen, then turned back to Kara. "Two years ago the company was in dire straits. I was always the day-to-day manager, but when John stepped back because of Clare, I took over the books. Shelley said she was working with her own clients, outside of her public defender's job, and that she'd set up multiple companies that could loan us the money. It wasn't really a loan."

It was money laundering, Kara realized.

"And Shelley said that one of the drug cartels was using our land to transport drugs. I put my foot down—but she said they'd do it with or without our permission. And getting paid for it was…well, the money was needed to keep Southwest running. I didn't want to fail while John was caring for Clare. We'll be okay. We just have to get through this hurdle and things will go back to normal."

He believed it. Or maybe he was saying it out loud because he wanted to believe it. Because he sure didn't know the half of it. He talked drugs; he wasn't talking human trafficking. Either he didn't want to know, or Shelley never told him.

She heard a car in the driveway, then a truck backing up, the sharp sound of the warning beep making her head hurt even more.

Dominick and Rondo came from the back room and, ignoring the three of them, went out front. By the sound of the friendly greeting, Kara realized this was who they were waiting for. A few minutes later, the brothers came back inside with two other men, all smiles, and Kara heard more guys talking outside.

Well, shit. With two she had a fighting chance. More than four? Hell no.

CHAPTER 41

Early Wednesday morning
Outside Nogales, Arizona

Matt arrived at the fire station at four-thirty that morning. Still dark, but the sun would be coming up in a couple of hours, and daylight was not their friend, not now.

Wyatt was talking to the head of SWAT, a seasoned cop named Alvarez. Matt approached them and introduced himself to Alvarez.

"Agent Costa, I hear you have an agent being held. Our recon team was unable to confirm whether the hostages are in the house, but there are six to seven hostiles on the property—four in the house, two or three patrolling the grounds. They arrived later, with a moving truck that is backed up to the barn, but they haven't loaded or unloaded anything yet. The marshal and I were working on coming up with a plan to breach, but we need more information before we can safely do that."

"The undercover cop is LAPD detective Kara Quinn, who has been assigned to my squad. She posed as a bartender for the last month during my investigation into the murder of Emma Perez and how it connected to illegal waste disposal. I now have those answers."

Then he gave them a brief summary of what he learned about Shelley Brown's involvement.

"I have some evidence that the Lopez brothers are responsible for six murders—and likely a whole lot more. At a minimum, we can nail them for felony kidnapping while we build our case. You need to tell your team that they are armed and dangerous. The men with them could be Sangre gang members, which my sources tell me has spread from southern California into Arizona. The gang is suspected of human trafficking, including young children. They have shown that they are violent and merciless, and we have to go into this operation knowing that they do not want to be taken alive. I would like one of them alive, but I will not lose a cop just to get them to talk. We protect each other, we protect the hostages, and we do everything we can to bring every suspect in alive. In that order."

He hated to say it—but it was what they were all trained for. In hostage rescue, save as many hostages as possible, but recognize that some could be lost.

"Finally," Matt said, "if our source is right, the new arrival may be a major gunrunner out of Mexico who is smuggling US weapons across the border to protect his drug-smuggling network. That means they could have serious firepower. Plan accordingly. Chief," he said to Alvarez, "do we know exactly where the recon team is?"

"Yes, sir," Alvarez said. He had a map of the immediate area on the board behind him. "Deputy Porter is positioned here—on the mountain, southeast side of the property, approximately thirty yards from the retaining wall. He has cover and eyes on the rear of the house. He can't see the front from his location. Agent Harris is here—on the north side of the barn. He's in a more vulnerable position and, because of the lighting and activity around the house, cannot move from his position to rejoin Deputy Porter. However, Agent Harris confirmed that there are dozens of boxes of what he suspects are military-grade weapons in the barn. They have not started loading them into the truck, but that appears imminent. The best course of action is to wait until the boxes are loaded and the truck leaves—we will set up a roadblock here." He marked the map right where the road meets the highway. "Surround them. We cannot let those weapons leave the country.

"Once the truck leaves," Alvarez continued, "we breach the house. We have to assume that the driver will be able to communicate with the residents of the house, and as soon as we stop them, the hostages will be at risk. Our goal is to enact these two strikes simultaneously, so everyone needs to be in place. I need someone here with me to relay information to both teams. Marshal, Agent—where would you like to be?"

"I'll go to the house," Matt said. "It's my cop inside."

"Okay. Marshal? You good with taking my command?"

"Yes, sir."

"Then let's do this. Get into position and wait for my signal."

Kara listened to the men on the porch. Dominick and Rondo Lopez were extremely...devout? Was that the right word? Maybe awestruck over the man they were speaking with. Awestruck, deferential, scared. His name was Hector, and he was clearly important—and likely the head of whatever operation they had going right now.

She picked up on several facts. First, the two brothers had delivered something this guy wanted. It was in the barn. The truck may not be big enough to transport everything, but most of it. That pleased Hector.

The other key fact was that Hector didn't like loose ends and wasn't pleased with the agreement the Lopez brothers made with "the lawyer." He said they were fools to think she'd bring them money; she was bringing them books, and what could he do with paper? Or something to that effect. Though Dominick and Rondo spoke English, they now talked in Spanish with Hector, very fast, so she caught maybe every third word.

Every time Kara shifted, to make sure she kept her circulation moving in her ankles and wrists, she was dizzy. The damn concussion was making her sleepy, and she knew going to sleep was bad.

The men moved away from the porch and she couldn't hear anything else until the sliding rear door of the truck slid open and the sound of laboring men filtered in.

"Barry," she said. She cleared her throat. "Barry!"

"I'm awake," he said sleepily.

How could he sleep when his life was on the line?

"You really need to help me get out of these zip ties."

"I can't."

"You don't need to do anything but find me something to cut them with. Okay?"

"I don't have anything."

"Helen's purse. It's right there."

"What if they see me?"

"Tell them she needs her medicine and you're looking for it."

He stared at her, scared. At least he *was* scared.

"I didn't want any of this."

"I know you didn't. But I understand Spanish, and they plan to kill us." They didn't explicitly say it, but Kara could read between the fucking lines. "We do not have any more time."

Slight exaggeration—she figured they had until Shelley and Joe returned. *If* they returned.

But she'd say anything to get Barry to help her.

Barry reached over and picked up Helen's purse from the floor. She was still sleeping. She'd slept through the arrival of the truck, the men coming in and out, the conversation on the porch. If Kara didn't see the slight rise and fall of her chest, she'd think she was dead.

"I failed her," Barry said quietly as he searched Helen's big satchel.

"You didn't fail Shelley. She brought this all on herself. You helped, but this was her deal."

"Not Shelley. Helen. My wife. I wanted to be better. To have my own business...but nothing I did worked. When John hired me, I wanted to be his equal, but I always fell short. We wanted kids... and I'm infertile. Me, not Helen. We were going to adopt, but by that time we were older, and we never got a child. I've always failed her."

"I'm sure she doesn't think of it like that," she said. She was *so* not a marriage counselor. Her life worked because she was responsible for one person: her.

But he loved her. Barry loved Helen like Joe's dad, John, loved his mother, Clare. That kind of devotion...it was rare. Special.

And the Wrangler's owners, Greg and Daphne? Are they rare and special too?

Maybe she just never wanted to see the successes, only the failures. And sure, there were plenty of failures out there...but it was like the glass-half-full, glass-half-empty comparison. You saw what you wanted to see. She'd always been a glass-half-empty girl.

"Her nail clippers?" He head them up. "Would they work?"

"Perfect. Put it in my hands."

Barry hesitated, then got up and walked slowly over to her. Just as he handed her the clippers, voices on the porch grew louder and the door opened.

"Sit!" she hissed.

He was frozen.

She held the clippers tight in her fist.

"What are you doing? Who is this?"

The voice was Hector. He was older than the brothers, but younger than Kara had thought from his voice.

"It's Nelson. The guy who gave us access to the land."

"Why is he not restrained?"

"That was part of the agreement," Dominick said.

Hector flat out slapped him. His partner.

Not partner. Subordinate.

Kara wanted to both laugh and cower.

This was not good.

"That agreement is null and void," Hector said in heavily accented English. "If that lawyer doesn't bring me *everything* she has, every dime, every ledger, if she even *attempts* to threaten me with the evidence she claims to have… I will cut off her tongue and make her swallow it." He stared at Kara. "This is the girlfriend?"

"Yes," Dominick said, his voice now rough and angry. He didn't like being shown up in front of his brother, Kara realized. He might turn on Hector...but Kara didn't have time to plot a psychological strategy.

Hector came over and touched her face, roughly pushed her chin up, turned her face right and left. "She's old, but blond hair, blue eyes." He pulled her hair so hard it hurt. "Natural. Always a plus."

Old? She was thirty.

She bit back the urge to tell him to go fuck himself. She hated being manhandled.

"Oh, she looks angry," Hector laughed. "This is the plan. This old man dies, the blonde gets fucked in front of her boyfriend so he knows who's in charge, then we kill her and go back to business as usual. The boyfriend so much as squeaks, we slit his throat. Dump their bodies in the desert for the red ants to devour."

"Not here," Dominick said quietly.

"What do you mean not here?"

"Too hot right now. We need to use the Yuma pipeline for a few months, then we can move back in."

"What are you not telling me? Dominick!"

Before Dominick could answer, a grunt stepped in. "We're loaded. There's six crates that don't fit, no matter how we stack them."

"We'll get them later. Go. Take the truck to the warehouse. We cross in the afternoon when our man is there."

Kara's ears perked up. They had someone on the payroll from border patrol. That was good to know.

If she got out of this alive.

Hector stared at her. Really stared at her, as if trying to read her mind. She looked away too late.

"Watch her," he told the two brothers. "She has no fear. I don't trust a woman who has no fear."

She had fear, but she'd been trained to conceal it. Letting the fear show was almost impossible because showing fear was a sign of weakness.

Usually, she could fake it well enough that most people bought her act.

She tried to turn her head away, trying to regain that fear in her expression, when he grabbed her face again with one hand and pinched her nipple hard with the other. Tears came unwittingly to her eyes.

"Better," he said and let her go.

She wanted to kill him.

But more, she wanted to lock him up and tell every convict that he was a pedophile.

She heard the truck start up, and that sound distracted Hector. He turned to tell something to Dominick that she couldn't hear. Fortunately, they were no longer looking at her. She almost had the zip ties cut through.

Barry, for his part, saw what she was doing but didn't say anything.

Hector turned around and stared at Barry, then turned to Dominick. "Didn't I just tell you to kill him?"

Hector pulled a gun and aimed it at Barry.

Kara had her hands free and tried to simultaneously break the ties on her ankles with a quick, sudden jerk.

One broke.

The other held firm.

Hector looked at her, startled. He narrowed his eyes and started to turn the gun on her.

She stood on one leg and kicked the other—with the chair—toward Hector's outstretched arm.

The gun went off as she connected and Helen screamed.

"Gunfire! I repeat! Gunfire in the house!" Delta Team leader announced through the radio, as if no one else could hear the echo.

Matt was too far away. He was stationed with the team leader on the south side of the house, while they also had two men in the rear and two at the front. The north side was inaccessible, but Michael Harris was already there and this was the kind of situation that Matt had recruited Michael for.

"Truck is within our sight—go, go, go!" Alvarez said.

But they were already moving, because the hostages were now at risk.

Matt ran down the hillside with his partner, but already Michael was closer than they were.

Michael announced, "FBI! Hands where I can see them!" as he approached the two men outside. One dropped his weapon and put his hands up, the other aimed his weapon at Michael but didn't get a shot off before Michael put two in his chest.

As he ran by, Michael ordered the second man to get down, and he complied. The west SWAT team secured him, then cuffed the fallen suspect—they didn't know if he was dead or alive, but they had to make sure he wasn't a potential threat.

The front door slammed shut; not a good sign. Gunfire blasted out the window, forcing Michael to the ground to protect himself. Matt and his partner halted, lying prone until the gunfire subsided.

Then there was silence.

And in that silence, Matt feared there was death.

Dear Lord, I haven't prayed in a long time, but save Kara. Dammit, don't let her die.

Hector, Dominick and Rondo all heard someone shout "FBI!" outside, and they froze for one second.

Long enough for Kara to push Barry down onto the floor to protect him, and to break the last zip tie.

Rondo shut the front door. "There's a big Black cop running up the stairs!"

Hector grabbed the AR-15 from Dominick's hands and started firing out the window. Glass sprayed everywhere. Kara kept her eyes averted and her head down until Hector ran out of bullets. As soon as the gunfire stopped, she lunged for the handgun he'd dropped when she kicked him with the chair.

Dominick noticed her movement before Hector did. He pulled a handgun from his waistband and aimed it at her. She already had the gun and fired before Dominick did. She felt a whoosh of heat skim her arm, but she wasn't hit. Dominick went down. He wasn't dead, but he clutched his side.

"Bitch!"

Rondo looked panicked.

Hector turned, surprised that she held the gun. He turned the AR-15 on her and pressed the trigger, but the magazine was empty.

"Drop it, asshole," she said.

At the same time, a SWAT team breached the house from the rear, and another breached from the front. Rondo made the mistake of aiming his gun at the well-armed, well-protected unit.

He was dead before he hit the ground, but not before he got a shot off...

...that hit his fallen brother in the back.

Hector dropped the gun and put his hands up. "I won't be in prison long," he said, looking right at Kara, "and I will come for you, you fucking bitch."

That's when Kara noticed that Matt was there. He pushed Hector roughly to the ground, cuffed him and read him his rights. Then he turned to her.

"Kara! Are you hit? Talk to me!"

She shook her head because she couldn't quite speak. "Barry." She managed to get out.

She stumbled over to where Barry had collapsed on the ground. He'd been shot in the upper right shoulder. Helen was holding the dirty rag that had once held ice on her facial wound.

"Barry, you're going to be okay," she said. "Tell me where Shelley and Joe are."

He looked at her and said, "Who are you?"

"Detective Kara Quinn. I need to know. Don't make this worse for you, or Helen."

"You're a cop." Barry winced as he shifted. "I don't know where they are now, but I know where they'll be this morning at nine."

CHAPTER 42

Wednesday, 8:58 a.m.
Tucson, Arizona

"I shouldn't have let you talk me into this," Matt mumbled as he looked at Kara.

Any other agent he would have said no. Kara had a concussion, multiple contusions, and she probably had a cracked rib, but she said she'd go to the hospital after they caught Joe and Shelley.

"I'm not letting you and Michael have all the fun," she said.

Barry had told them where Shelley had a safe-deposit box, and that the ledger of all the companies and bank accounts that held Hector Lopez's money was in there, plus cash she hadn't been able to launder yet.

The FBI has contacts at every bank and therefore were able to get inside before opening. Matt and Kara were in the safe-deposit vault. Michael and Ryder were in the bank security office watching the cameras along with two officers. Because they assumed that Shelley might recognize local cops and FBI agents, in her capacity as a public defender, they had an agent come down from the Phoenix FBI office who was acting as the assistant bank manager. She'd let Shelley into the safe-deposit room. Two undercover Phoenix PD cops would be waiting in line before nine for the bank to open; they were there to ensure no collateral damage.

"Are you sure you're okay?" Matt asked.

"Nothing a hot bubble bath followed by twelve hours of sleep won't fix."

Kara looked like death warmed over. Her jaw was bruised, her lip swollen, and she had a nasty cut on the side of her face. The paramedics had cleaned her up, applied ice, taped the cuts, but they couldn't determine if her rib was cracked or broken without an X-ray. Kara kept saying it was cracked and she should know, ha ha, but Matt was skeptical. He almost took her directly to the hospital, but he needed to brief Tony and the team in Tucson, get the appropriate warrants and prepare for this operation—in fewer than four hours. Since they didn't know where Shelley and Joe were staying—they could have already left town—they didn't want to blow this opportunity.

Barry could have been lying, though neither

Matt nor Kara thought that he was. Fortunately, the manager confirmed that Shelley Brown had both a bank account and a safe-deposit box.

Wyatt was staying with Barry and Helen in the hospital to ensure they didn't tip Shelley off—Matt didn't think they would. Helen didn't know anything that had happened over the last few years, and she had almost been in shock. She was admitted to the hospital for observation because of her fall. Barry had surgery to remove the bullet and seemed genuinely remorseful for his part in Shelley's machinations. Matt thought he'd known more than he claimed, but Kara said Barry didn't want to know. As soon as they confronted him with the truth, he accepted it. No denials.

Still, he had to be held accountable for his part in crimes that would take multiple agencies to sort out, even with Barry's cooperation. Matt suspected he wouldn't do time in prison if he came clean. But his relationship with his brother-in-law would most certainly be over.

He looked at his watch.

"Showtime."

It didn't take long before Michael gave Matt the signal that Shelley and Joe had entered the bank together.

The safe-deposit boxes were in one large room in the safe. There was a smaller adjoining room that was also secure where customers could have privacy with their boxes.

The detective posing as the assistant bank manager brought Shelley and Joe into the main room.

Matt could hear them talking through the door. He and Kara were on the hinge side of the door so that no one could see them when it was opened.

The detective opened the secondary door and said, "Let me know if I can do anything else for you, Ms. Brown."

Shelley walked in, followed by Joe who carried a long, wide safe-deposit box.

Matt cleared his throat as the door closed. "Shelley Brown, I'm Mathias Costa with the FBI. You are under arrest for criminal conspiracy, human trafficking, money laundering, kidnapping, murder and probably more—I'll let the AUSA and DA fight over the charges."

Shelley stared. She backed away. "What? What? You can't be here!" Then she narrowed her eyes as she recognized Kara.

Joe noticed Kara at the same time. He put the tray down on the table and stepped toward her. Matt put his hand up to stop him.

"She's a fucking *cop*?" Shelley said.

Joe looked confused. "What? No."

"Yes," Kara said.

"Kara, I… I'm so sorry," Joe said, either not hearing or understanding that Kara confirmed she was a cop. "I didn't want this to happen, believe me!"

"Shut up, Joe," Shelley said.

Matt quickly read them their Miranda rights, because he wanted to use every word they said against them. Even though he had plenty of evidence, it was always nice when they started talking.

"Agent Costa," Joe said, looking confused. "I don't understand…"

"You'll have time to explain everything to me, Joe. To say I'm disappointed in your decisions this week is an understatement."

He cuffed Joe, then searched him while Kara showed her badge to Shelley. "Turn around, put your hands against the wall."

"I will not."

"Resisting arrest? Please do."

Shelley clenched her fists, but she didn't throw a punch. She did exactly what Kara told her to do. Kara searched her, retrieved a gun, and then cuffed her.

"Kara, listen to me," Joe said.

"Shut. Up!" Shelley screamed.

"I didn't do any of this. I don't even really know what's going on. I told Shelley as a lawyer about Agent Costa's investigation and she just flipped!"

"I swear, Joe, I will kill you if you say one more word."

"Hey, Costa," Kara said, "can we tack on threatening to kill a witness to the charges?"

"Sure, don't see why not."

Joe still looked confused, and Matt took advantage of it. "Agent Harris, you can come in now."

When Michael Harris walked in, both Shelley and Joe looked equally stunned. "Agent Michael Harris, please escort Ms. Brown to the nice officer outside who will take her to the jail for booking. I have to mediate the discussion between the

AUSA and the DA—both of them really want to prosecute her."

"You can't intimidate me," Shelley said to Matt. "I know the law, and none of this is going to stick. I'm Joe's lawyer. You can't talk to him without me."

"You're being arrested for multiple felonies. You'll be disbarred."

"No, I won't. I will be exonerated, and you will pay the price."

"Are you threatening a federal agent?" Matt said.

"Don't fuck with me."

Kara said, "Sounds like a threat to me, Costa. Threatening a federal agent. There has got to be a major charge in there for that."

Kara turned to Joe. "Joe, is Shelley Brown your lawyer? Do you actually want her representing your interests?"

Joe looked even more confused.

"Shelley used you," Kara said. "I thought you were one of the good guys, Joe. But you're just like her."

"I didn't know anything that was going on until Thursday night. And even then, I didn't quite understand until now," Joe said.

Shelley screamed. *"Stop! Talking!"*

Matt nodded to Michael, who pulled Shelley from the room. She was kicking and screaming and threatening Joe and Matt.

"This is so unreal," he said and sat down.

Matt opened the safe-deposit box. Bundled stacks of cash were lined neatly in the tray, each wrapped with a $10,000 band. A black book was on top. He used the top of a pencil to open the cover, saw lots of numbers and dates but had no idea what it all meant. That was for the brainiacs in the FBI like Zack Heller. There was also a gun inside, wrapped in a plastic bag, and he was very interested in finding out why a gun was hidden here, and who it might have killed.

Most people didn't put a gun in a safe-deposit box unless they wanted to hide said gun.

Two members of the FBI forensics unit came in and took custody of the evidence so they could log it.

"Are you really an FBI agent?" Joe asked Kara.

"God, no," she said.

He breathed a sigh of relief.

Then she said, "I'm a detective with the LAPD. I just happen to be working with the FBI for a while. How'd you go from a good guy to a schmuck, Joe?"

Matt didn't think that the best way to get a potential witness to talk was to insult them, but it seemed to work for Kara.

"Shelley said that if the FBI was here, they'd destroy us. That to save my dad's company, she had to let the drug cartels use our land to smuggle in drugs and people, and that no one would believe that I didn't know about it. I swear I didn't, not until she told me on Thursday. And then she said that Uncle Barry knew, and I needed to make sure the FBI was gone or he'd go to jail. So I talked to you, Agent Costa, on Friday, and then when you didn't just arrest David Hargrove, I told her I couldn't make you do it, that you wanted to track the next waste shipment. She said he had to die. She killed him or she had him killed, I don't know. But she told me where to find his body and to make sure I had a witness with me, because you might think I did it because I was mad that he was scamming my dad. I'm so sorry, Kara."

"You used me, I used you."

"I didn't use you. I love you."

Matt couldn't have heard that right.

Kara leaned over. "Fuck. You."

Then she walked out.

"I am so sorry," he said, tears rolling down his face. "I haven't slept, I've barely eaten, I didn't know what to do."

"Off the record, Joe? You had many opportunities to tell me what was going on," Matt said. "When Shelley first told you Thursday night. When Shelley told you on Friday that she intended to kill David Hargrove. When Shelley *did* kill David Hargrove. But the kicker? When Kara was kidnapped, *you knew where she was*. You didn't call me and tell me that you fucked up and she was in danger. Instead, you went along with your cousin, left her and your elderly aunt with two violent gang members. Barry has already talked. His guilt has weighed on him for two years, but he didn't know half of what you did and he feels worse than you do. I don't need your information. You're going to do jail time no matter what. But if you write out a confession of everything that you know, I'm sure the prosecutor will cut you a deal. Because I want to put your cousin away for the rest of her life."

Joe sobbed, then he nodded. "I will."

"Good."

"Tell Kara...tell her I meant what I said."

"You don't even know her."

"I don't care. I don't care that she's a cop. I don't care about any of that. I can forgive her...why can't she forgive me?"

"Because you're a criminal and Kara's a hero."

Matt took Kara to the hospital mostly because if he asked anyone else to do it, she might talk them into taking her to the hotel room that Ryder had reserved for her.

And he needed to make sure she was okay.

She didn't want to talk about what Joe said, so he didn't push. He checked her in—being a cop had some benefits, because she went to the head of the line. He tracked down Ryder and asked him to keep an eye on Kara and let him know if she was being admitted or discharged, and if discharged to take her to the hotel.

Then he went to his office to begin wrapping up a case that started simple and became increasingly complex.

He would be working on paperwork and additional interviews all week, but he felt good about it. *Damn* good.

Ryder checked in on Kara. "I'm not staying," she said.

"I know. But I thought you might want to give this back to the rightful owner."

He handed her the bunny she'd taken from the abandoned church. He'd cleaned it up, and while it still looked old, it mostly looked well loved.

"I'll take you to the hotel when you're done."

Ryder walked Kara down to Angel and Bianca's room. When she stepped in, the kids were playing cards, but they both looked scared. It passed when they saw Ryder. They both smiled at him.

"Mr. Ryder!" Bianca said. "Thank you so much for the cards, and the flowers, they are so pretty, I've never seen anything so pretty since I left my farm."

"I'm glad you like them," he said. "I want you to meet a friend of mine. Her name is Kara, and she's a police detective."

Kara took the bunny from behind her back and handed it to Bianca. "I thought it was abandoned," she said. "I'm sorry I took it. Ryder cleaned it for you."

Bianca stared at it, then she took it from Kara's outstretched hand and hugged it, tears in her eyes.

Angel said, "*Nuestro padre le dio el conejito. Es todo lo que tenemos de él.*"

It took Kara a half minute to translate in her head. She asked in English, "Your dad gave it to you?"

Bianca nodded. "Thank you so very much," she said. "It's all I have of my papa."

Ryder and Kara stepped outside. "How are they?" Kara asked. "Tell me the truth, Ryder."

"Angel is clear. He had milder poisoning, though he was extremely dehydrated and malnourished.

Bianca is doing better but isn't out of the woods. They're going to monitor her for a few more days. She might need another red blood cell transfusion. But the doctor says it's a miracle she didn't die. Matt called an asylum lawyer he knows from Miami who recommended a local guy who has already worked another miracle. Angel is a witness to a felony and is at immediate risk of assassination if he returns home. Because they are orphans and have no known living relatives, they're going to expedite their application. Plus, they already have a sponsor."

"Wow, that is a miracle."

"It's Frank Block. The assistant director from AREA. He's been by a couple of times, going back and forth between here and the cleanup site. As soon as they're discharged, he's going to bring them to his house and go through the process of becoming their legal guardian. It helps to know people."

"I'm very happy for them."

"We told them this morning—Frank came by on his way back to Patagonia—and Angel cried. It was the first emotion other than anger that he's displayed. There's really hope for him. He's going to need counseling—he feels an enormous guilt and he's still very angry. But they're young, and Bianca has hope enough for both of them."

Kara squeezed Ryder's arm. "I'm just glad they have a fighting chance."

CHAPTER 43

Sunday afternoon
Tucson, Arizona

Matt brought Kara to his house on Sunday. Kara was impressed. It wasn't large or fancy, but what he had was nice. On the minimalist side, which she liked, but his excuse was that he didn't live here much. What was her excuse for her minimalist apartment in Santa Monica?

"A pool," she said. "We can go skinny-dipping."

He looked to the right and left, probably to see if his neighbors would be able to see them, and she laughed. "Tonight," she added. "When it's dark and no one can see anything they shouldn't."

"We can do whatever we want," Matt said. "No one knows we're here. I told everyone on the team

I was taking the day off and not to bother me. I deserve it."

"You do?" Kara teased.

"Yes. So do you."

"I agree. So we're being *sneaky*."

"Stop."

She stared at him. This was going to have to change. "Ground rules, Mathias Costa."

"I don't think—"

She put her hand to his lips. Held it there. "First, no macho bullshit. I'm a big girl. I've made my own decisions most of my life, and definitely since I've been eighteen. I'm a cop, that's all I want to be, and while I might not like that working for the feds is my only option at this point, it is what it is, and I'm okay with that. So when the shit hits the fan like it did the other day, we deal with it. As if I was any other person on the team."

"First," he said, mirroring her tone, "if any other one of my team members was kidnapped and injured in the line of duty, I would do the exact same thing."

She raised her eyebrow. "Oh?" She stepped forward. "You'd take Michael's hand?" She took his hand. "And touch it like *this*?" She ran her thumb lightly up and down his palm. He shivered. Damn. How did she do that to him?

"You know what I mean."

"Yes, I do. I know what you *think* you mean. But I get it. I can walk away. I don't want to. I like messing with you. And I really love us between the sheets. Or in the shower or up against a wall or wherever else we find ourselves naked." She looked over at the pool and smiled.

He wasn't smiling. Because all he could picture was Kara naked. In the shower. Up against the wall. In his hot tub.

He didn't care that it was ninety degrees outside.

"But we work together," she said. "Which isn't a problem for me, but since you're my boss, it gets kind of sticky." She grinned again. "I like getting *sticky* with you, Special Agent in Charge Mathias Costa."

Walk away, Matt.

Walk away? You brought her to your house. Your sanctuary.

"We have three days," he said. "The arraignments are all on Tuesday, then we have to be in DC Wednesday."

"Three days. That's practically forever."

"And then…we should…"

"Should what?" She stepped closer.

We shouldn't be here together. We shouldn't be together at all.

"Play it by ear," he found himself saying.

"See? You can teach an old dog new tricks."

He smiled. "Woof, woof," he said. He kissed her. She melted into him. More open and honest in her actions, as if showing him how she felt was more real than her words. Sometimes, just a kiss was enough. But with Kara…he wanted more.

He whispered, "Want to see my bedroom?"

"Absolutely."

The doorbell rang. Matt groaned. "Keep that thought."

He walked over to the door and looked out the peephole. Surprised. Opened the door. His best friend, Tim Armstrong, Tim's wife, Sarah, and little Trevor.

"Hey, Uncle Matt!" Trevor said and ran like lightning into the house.

Tim handed Matt a bottle of wine, and Sarah carried in two bags of groceries. "Since you bailed on us twice in a row since you've been back, we're bringing the party to you."

"Hi, what's your name?" Trevor said from behind them. "I'm Trevor."

"I'm Kara."

"Like Supergirl! Her name is Kara too! Do you watch that show? I love that show. I love *Flash* more. Whoosh!" He ran through the house and outside into the backyard.

Sarah smiled. "Matt, introduce us."

Matt didn't know what to say.

Kara stepped up and smiled. "Kara Quinn, detective with LAPD on loan to the feds." She shook first Sarah's hand, then Tim's hand.

"I'm Sarah Armstrong. I teach fourth grade. Tim's a detective with Tucson PD. We've known Matt for years—ten years now, right?"

"I should go," Kara said. "Let you have a reunion."

"Stay," Matt said. If he let her walk out, he had a feeling he wouldn't get her to come back. "Please."

He hoped he didn't sound desperate. He needed more time with Kara to figure all this out.

"Do you have tequila?"

"I'm sure I do somewhere."

"He does," Sarah said. "I hide the good stuff when I rent out the place. I'm sort of his Airbnb manager for the last five years. Were you involved with the situation down in Patagonia that Tim told me about?" She led Kara off into the kitchen, and they talked about what Kara had been doing.

Tim stared at him. Waiting for answers.

Waiting.

"I'm so screwed," Matt said.

"Oh?"

Now Tim was smiling.

"Keep this to yourself. It's…complicated."

"You fell hard, didn't you. For someone on your squad."

"She wasn't on my squad when I fell for her."

"Hey, I'm not going to say anything, and it's not like you live here. Or even visit much." Tim clapped him on the back. "But you're going to have to tell me everything, because Sarah's going to ask, and if I don't have answers, she'll be mad at me."

"All I can tell you, Tim? I've never met anyone like Kara Quinn. And I'm afraid I'm going to screw it up."

"You probably will."

"Thanks, buddy. I thought you were my friend."

"I just call it like I see it." They were still standing in the entry. Tim's attention was drawn to the kitchen in the back of the house, where Sarah handed Kara a bottle of tequila. As they watched, Kara rummaged and found two shot glasses and poured a shot for both of them. The women said a toast neither of them could hear, then drank.

"Well, shit," Tim said, "I guess I won't be the one drinking tonight."

"You can always Uber home. Or walk. It's only a mile."

"Good point. Let's join them."

Tim walked into the kitchen. Matt didn't know what he was doing with Kara, but he didn't want to let her go. Not now. And maybe he would screw it up. It's what he did. All his friends made sure he knew it.

But this time, he would try hard not to.

EPILOGUE

Tuesday, June 1
Tucson, Arizona

Billy Nixon walked out of the federal court in a daze. He didn't understand the system; he didn't know why no one was being charged with Emma's murder. The woman he loved was dead and no one cared. It was as if she was an afterthought.

It was already ninety-seven degrees at ten in the morning, but he didn't care. He didn't care about much anymore, because not a day went by that he didn't think about Emma and all that he'd lost. He staggered down the stairs as if he were drunk and realized that his vision was blurred because of tears.

He sat on the closest bench, an uncomfortable

stone seat under a tree, and put his face in his hands.

He felt helpless. As helpless as he'd felt carrying unconscious Emma up the hill nearly three months ago. Guilt coursed through his veins. Guilt that he hadn't been with her at the pond where someone attacked her. Guilt that he'd let her go in the first place. Anger too. Anger that justice had failed Emma. The system…did it even work anymore? Sorrow…he wanted to see Emma again. He wanted kids with her, he wanted to travel with her, he wanted to *live* his entire life with her.

And she was gone.

A man cleared his throat, and Billy looked up. Agent Costa. The man who said he would find justice for Emma, but didn't.

"May I sit down?"

Billy shrugged, wiped his face. "Free country."

Costa sat and didn't say anything. Billy let the anger take over from the grief and pain.

"You know this is all bullshit," Billy said.

"It feels that way now."

"*Feels* that way? It *is* bullshit. No one is paying for killing Emma. No one."

"It's not possible to prove right now."

"So they're going to get away with it!"

"No."

"You're lying, Agent Costa. The system sucks."

"Sometimes," Costa said. Billy was surprised he admitted it. "Today was a process. I know that doesn't help you right now, but the arraignments you witnessed are the first step of a long process where the system will work to present their case against Shelley Brown, Dominick Lopez and Hector Lopez. We have a lot of evidence against them. Money laundering. Human trafficking. We caught them with over one thousand assault rifles they planned to transport to Mexico. Red-handed. And we have them on murder—just not the murder of Emma."

"And why is that fair?"

"It's not. We rounded up the Sangre gang, based out of Yuma, that the Lopez brothers brought in. We know that the gang and the Lopez brothers used an outbuilding near the closed quarry to store guns, drugs, people—whatever they needed. And we know that Emma was killed less than a mile from there, on a route they regularly used to transport people, in order to avoid roads. I believe that one of the Sangre gang killed Emma, and I've talked to the US attorney. She's willing to take the death penalty off the table for Dominick Lopez if he testifies against the individual who killed her. He's agreed. His brother was killed in the raid, and Dominick was shot and is paralyzed, probably for life. He's not helping us with anything else, but between you and me, I think he's furious that Emma's murder was what started the investigation in the first place. He wants the gang punished."

"Why didn't you tell me before?" Billy asked.

"Because it wasn't settled last week. The deal was made today. It hasn't been inked, and anything can happen, but we will get justice for Emma. None of these people are getting out of prison."

Billy sat there, stared out at the courtyard that didn't do much to make the courthouse look less imposing. He didn't know if he believed Costa, but why would the FBI agent lie to him?

"I loved her," Billy said quietly.

"I know."

"I miss her so much."

"I understand Emma was an amazing girl," Costa said. "She cared about people, about animals, about doing the right thing, even against all odds."

"I should never have let her go alone."

"If you think that way, Billy, you'll never be whole again. Guilt…it can destroy the best of us."

"I don't know how to forget."

"You'll never forget. Don't expect that you will. But you need to forgive yourself. Emma wouldn't want you feeling guilt over something you had no control over. Emma wouldn't want you to stop living because she did."

Costa was right, but Billy didn't know how to stop feeling.

"You have one more year of college, right?"

He shrugged. "I don't know. I'm just not excited anymore."

"What's your major?"

"Business economics. It just doesn't seem important."

"Finish. One more year. Give yourself that time to heal. Reconnect with your friends. Try not to overthink everything. Time heals. I know that sounds cliché, but it's true. Well, not so much as heals, but gives you perspective."

"My dad wants to take me somewhere. In July we usually take two weeks to go to this lake in Montana, rent a cabin and fish and hunt. I was going to bring Emma this year. Now…well, I guess I don't know."

"Your dad seems like a good guy."

"He is."

"Go. Getting away for a couple of weeks might help. Let yourself grieve, let yourself get angry and find a way to work through it. My dad—well, he died when I was in high school, but he was my go-to guy. Anytime I had to work through something, I went to my dad."

Billy nodded. Yeah, his dad was the same.

"You can call or email me anytime," Costa said. "Christine Jimenez, the head of the Tucson office, will keep you informed as the process moves. It's a slow process. They may plead out to save their lives, or the cases may go to trial. Whatever happens, we will see justice done. I have to believe that, or I couldn't do my job."

Billy looked at the FBI agent. "Do you like your job?"

Costa nodded. "I wouldn't want to do anything else."

Billy watched as a group of people exited the courthouse. "That's your team?"

"Yes, part of it," Costa said. "I'll introduce you."

He waved them over. "Billy, you remember Ryder Kim, you met him when we first arrived in town."

"Yeah. Hey." Billy felt out of sorts. He'd been

crying not fifteen minutes ago and probably still looked it.

"Michael Harris," Costa said. "He was a navy SEAL, joined the FBI five years ago. And Kara Quinn. She's a detective who we're lucky enough to have on our team. They all did an amazing job against difficult odds."

"Thank you," Billy said, not sure what he was supposed to say.

"No thanks," Kara said. "It's our job, and I'm just glad those bastards are all locked up for the rest of their lives."

"You think they will be?" he asked.

"The system isn't perfect, Billy," she said. "But this time? I think it's going to work exactly the way it's supposed to."

"We have a flight to catch," Costa said. "Are you going to be okay, Billy?"

He nodded, though he didn't really know. Maybe. Someday.

"I meant what I said, call me if you need anything."

"I will."

Billy watched the four walk toward the parking structure. Friends and colleagues. They'd solved Emma's murder, even though Billy didn't know who killed her. Didn't know if they'd even find him.

He realized that Emma's senseless death was a catalyst for stopping a major human trafficking organization and rescuing two kids. He wanted her to be alive, he wanted to hold her and tell her he loved her.

But he found a small sense of peace that something positive had come out of tragedy.

He called his dad. "Hey, do you think we could go up to Montana earlier than next month?"

Getting away from all this was exactly what he needed if he was ever going to move forward.

* * * * *

ACKNOWLEDGMENTS

I have been blessed over the fifteen years I've been published to have cultivated an extensive group of experts who help me learn what I don't know. Doctors, nurses, cops, FBI agents, lawyers, firefighters, accountants, wildlife biologists, and more. I relied on so many people to help with the details of *Tell No Lies* that I sincerely hope I didn't forget anyone.

Sometimes I intentionally strain plausibility in order to serve the story—but because of the selfless help of others, I'm able to get things mostly right, which hopefully makes your reading experience that much more enjoyable. I write fiction and that means I get to make things up, but I want my readers to believe that these things *could* happen. I want them to feel like the people are real and the events plausible. Mostly, I want my readers to be entertained, and errors detract from enjoying the story. If I got anything wrong, blame me, and not these fine people who shared their time and expertise.

First and foremost, my best friend and the best brainstorming partner I could have found, Toni Causey. I had a nugget of an idea for this book but couldn't make the setup work. After a four-hour phone conversation (okay, we didn't talk about just the story!) I had the premise worked out and a list of articles to read about copper mining, human trafficking, and the history of Patagonia.

I should note that while Patagonia is a real place, I made everything else up.

In 2008, Steve Dupre was the public information officer for the Sacramento FBI. He was tasked with answering all my questions, and eventually he invited me to participate in the FBI Citizens Academy. He's since become a friend and helps me with virtually all my stories. Now retired and working as a private investigator, he still finds the time to respond to my emails, and I am forever grateful.

I don't know a lot about the nitty-gritty of environmental protection laws and rules. Now I know a tiny bit more. I. & E.—you know who you are. Thank you so much for your time and patience with my questions! Even though I went in a slightly different direction than I laid out to you in our phone conversation, your information was extremely valuable.

If I have any animals in my books other than dogs and cats, you know that I've tapped into my most valuable animal resource—my brother-in-law

Kevin Brennan. Kevin is a wildlife biologist for the California Department of Fish and Game, and he knows more about animals, regulations, hunting, endangered species, and birds in his little finger than I will ever know. He helped me with species identification, how birds migrate, and how to investigate a suspicious animal death. I wish I could have used all the stories he shared with me! One thing I learned that I didn't use in the book—I asked him why in California his department is called "Fish and Game" and in Arizona it's called "Game and Fish." Easy. "There are more fish in California."

I know that vultures eat dead things, but beyond that, not much else about vultures. Enter Google and an article I found by Dr Daniel Wescott with the Forensic Anthropology Center at Texas State University. The article was interesting but didn't answer a specific question I had about how long it would take for a vulture to locate a dead body. I emailed him and he was gracious enough to listen to my setup and give me a time frame. Plot critical? Probably not…but I used his information and I think the story is better for it.

When I first started writing, I found a group called CrimeSceneWriters, filled with experts in a variety of crime-related fields, happy to answer questions for writers. Law enforcement, FBI agents, paramedics, doctors, and more. But one of the most valuable resources I've found in this group is Judy Melinek, MD, CEO of PathologyExpert, Inc. Not only is she a professional medical examiner, she's also a writer, so she understands people like me. Her meticulous explanations of cause and manner of death and the role of the medical examiner were invaluable in *Tell No Lies*. I may have taken some literary license, but only because most people aren't as smart as Judy.

And, of course, my husband, Dan, who helped me find my way out of every hole I dug myself into as I wrote this story.

A very special thanks to my agent, Dan Conaway, who has stuck with me for more than a decade and counting. Dan keeps me sane and focused and manages my business with the utmost professionalism. Between Dan and his absolutely fantastic assistant, Lauren Carsley, I am in very good hands.

Behind every good writer is a great editor. I have been blessed that every editor I've had has been amazing. When we decided to launch this new series with a new publisher, I told my agent I really care about only one thing: an editor who edits. He found that person in Kathy Sagan, an editor who truly loves to edit and helps make my books as strong as they can be. She asks all the right questions, tells me when my scenes go on too long, are too confusing, or just right. Even better, she loves my characters as much as I do. Thank you for all your work on helping to make *Tell No Lies* a thrilling story.

While Kathy is part of a great team at MIRA Books, led by the amazing editorial director Margaret Marbury, I want to give a special shout-out to the art director, Sean Kapitain. I absolutely love this cover.

And, of course, my readers: without you, I wouldn't be able to do what I love. Thank you for following me into this new series.

A fun fact: I decided to set this book in Patagonia, Arizona, several months before we decided to move to Arizona. While we didn't settle anywhere near Patagonia, I feel a kinship with our new home and can't wait to explore further.

*Turn the page to begin reading
Allison Brennan's next Quinn & Costa novel,
The Wrong Victim,
available from MIRA April 2022*

CHAPTER 1

A killer walked among the peaceful community of Friday Harbor and retired FBI Agent Neil Devereaux couldn't do one damn thing about it because he had no evidence.

Most cops had at least one case that haunted them long after the day they turned in their badge and retired. For Neil, that obsession was a cold case that his former law enforcement colleagues believed was closed. Not only closed, but not a double homicide at all—simply a tragic accident.

Neil knew they'd got it wrong; he just couldn't prove it. He hadn't been able to prove it thirteen years ago, and he couldn't prove it now.

But he was close.

He knew that the two college boys didn't drown "by accident;" they were murdered. He had a suspect and he'd even figured out *why* the boys had been targeted.

Knowing who and why meant nothing. He needed hard evidence. Hell, he'd settle for *any* evidence. All his theory got him was the FBI file on the deaths sent by an old friend, and the ear of a detective on the mainland who would be willing to investigate if Neil found more.

"I can't open a closed death investigation without evidence, buddy."

He would have said the same thing if he was in the same position.

Confronting the suspected killer would be dangerous, even for an experienced investigator like him. This wasn't an Agatha Christie novel like his mother used to read, where he could bring the suspect and others into a room and run through the facts—only to have the killer jump up and confess.

Neil couldn't stand to think that anyone might get away with such a brazen murder spree, sparked by revenge and deep bitterness. It's why he couldn't let it go, and why he felt for the first time that he was close…close to hard evidence that would compel a new investigation.

He was tired of being placated by the people he used to work with.

He'd spent so long following dead ends that he'd lost valuable time—and with time, the detailed memories of those who might still remember something about that fateful weekend. It was only the last year that Neil had turned his attention to other students at the university and realized the most likely suspect was living here, on San Juan Island, right under his nose.

All this was on his mind when he boarded the *Water Lily*, his favorite yacht in the West End Charter fleet. He went through his safety checklist, wondering why Cal McKinnon, the deckhand assigned to this sunset cruise, wasn't already there.

If he wasn't preoccupied with murder and irritated at Cal, Neil may have noticed the small hole in the bow of the ship, right above the water line, with fishing line coming out of it, taut in the water.

"I'm sorry. It's last minute, I know," Cal said to Kyle Richards in the clubhouse of West End Charter. "But I really need to talk to Jamie right away."

"It's that serious?" asked his longtime friend Kyle.

"I cannot lose her over this. I just can't. I love her. We're getting married."

At least he hoped they were still getting married. Two months ago Jamie finally set a wedding date for the last Saturday in September—the fifth anniversary of their first date. And now this whole thing was a mess, and if Cal didn't fix it now, he'd never be able to fix it.

You already blew it. You blew it five years ago. You should have told her the truth then!

"Alright then, go," Kyle said. "I'll take the cruise. I need the extra money, anyway. But you owe me—it's Friday night. I *had* a date."

Cal clapped Kyle on the back. "I definitely owe you, I'll take your next crappy shift."

"Better, give me your next corporate party boat." Corporate parties on the largest yacht in their fleet had automatic eighteen percent tips added to the bill, which was split between a typical four-man crew in addition to salary. Plus, high-end parties often paid extra. Drunk rich people could become very generous with their pocket cash.

"You got it—it's next Saturday night, the Fourth of July—so we good?"

Kyle gave him a high five, then left for the dock.

Cal clocked out and started for home. He passed a group of sign-carrying protesters and rolled his eyes.

West End Charter: Profit Over Protection
Protect Fish Not Profits!
Hey Hey Ho Ho Ted Colfax has to go!

Jeez, when would these people just stop? West End Charter had done nearly everything they wanted over the last two years—and then some—but it was never good enough.

Fortunately, the large crowds of protesters that started after the West End accident had dwindled over the last two years from hundreds to a half dozen. Maybe because they got bored, or maybe because West End fixed the problem with their older fleet, Cal didn't know. But these few remaining were truly radical, and Cal hoped they didn't cause any problems for the company over the lucrative Fourth of July holiday weekend.

He drove around them and headed home. He had more important things to deal with than this group of misfits.

Cal lived just outside of Friday Harbor with Jamie and their daughter. It was a small house, but all his, his savings covering the down payment after he left the Coast Guard six years ago. But it was Jamie who made the two-bedroom cottage a real home. She'd made curtains for the windows; put up cheery pictures that brightened even the grayest Washington day; and most recently, she'd framed some of Hazel's colorful artwork for the kitchen nook he'd added on with Kyle's help last summer.

He'd wanted to put Jamie on the deed when she moved in with him, but she wanted to go slower than that. He wanted to marry her, but she'd had a bad breakup with her longtime boyfriend before they met and was still struggling with the mind games her ex used to play on her. If that bastard ever set foot back on the island, Cal would beat him senseless.

But the ex was far out of the picture, living down in California, and Cal loved Jamie, so he respected her wishes not to pressure her into marriage. When she found out she was pregnant, he asked her to marry him again—she said yes but wanted to wait.

"There's no rush. I love you, Cal, but I don't want to get married just because I'm pregnant."

He would move heaven and earth for Jamie and Hazel—why didn't she *know* that?

That's why when she finally settled on a date, confirmed it with invitations and an announcement in the San Juan Island newspaper, that he thought it would be smooth sailing.

And then she left.

As soon as he got home, he packed an overnight bag while trying to reach Jamie. She didn't answer her cell phone. More than likely, there was no reception. Service was sketchy on the west side of the island.

He left another message.

"Jamie, we need to talk. I'm sorry, believe me I'm sorry. I love you. I love Hazel. I just want to talk and work this out. I'm coming to see you tonight, okay? Please call me."

He was so frustrated. Not at Jamie—well, maybe a little because she'd taken off this morning for her dad's place without even telling him. Just left him a note on the bathroom mirror.

> Cal,
> I need time to think. Give me a couple days, okay? I love you, but right now I just need a little perspective.
> Jamie.

Cal didn't like the "but" part. What was there to think about? He loved her. They had a life together. Jamie and their little girl Hazel meant everything to him. They were getting *married* in three months!

He'd given her all day to think and now they needed to talk. Jamie had a bad habit of remaining silent when she was upset, thanks to that prick she'd dated before Cal. Cal much preferred her to get angry, to yell at him, to say exactly how she felt, then they could move on.

He jumped in his old pickup truck and headed west, praying he could salvage his family, the only thing he truly cared about. Failure was not an option.

That night Kyle clocked in and told the staff supervisor, Gloria, that Cal was sick, and he was taking the sunset cruise for him.

"Are you lying to me?" Gloria asked, looking over the top of her glasses at him.

"No, well, I mean, he's not *sick* sick." Dammit, Kyle had always been a piss-poor liar. "But he and Jamie had a fight, I guess, and he wants to fix it."

"Alright, I'll talk to Cal tomorrow. Don't you go lying for him."

"Don't get him in trouble, Gloria."

She sighed, took off her large glasses and cleaned them on her cotton shirt. "I like Cal as much as everyone, I'm not going to jam him up, but he should have come to me. I'll bet he gave you his slot on the Fourth, didn't he?"

Kyle grinned. Gloria had worked for West End longer than Kyle had been alive. They couldn't operate without her.

"Eight people total. A party of four and two parties of two." Gloria handed him the clipboard with the information of those who had registered for tonight's sunset cruise. "Four bottles of champagne, a case of water, and cheese and fruit trays are onboard. You have one minute."

"Thanks Gloria!" He ran down the dock to the *Water Lily*. He texted his boyfriend as he ran.

Hey, taking Cal's shift, docking at 10—want to meet up then?

He sent the message and almost ran into a group who were already standing at the docks. Two men, two women, drinks in hand from the West End Club bar, in to-go cups.

"Can we board?" the tallest of the four asked.

"Give me one minute. What group are you with?"

"Nava Software."

Kyle looked at his watch. Technically boarding started in five minutes; they'd be pushing off in twenty.

"I need to get approval from the captain." He smiled and jumped over the gate. He found Neil Devereaux on the bridge, reading weather reports.

"You're late," Neil said without looking up.

"Sorry, Skipper. Cal called in sick."

Neil looked at him. "Oh, Kyle, I didn't know it was you. I was expecting Cal."

"He called out. Everything okay?" Neil didn't look like his usual chipper self.

"I had a rough day."

Rough day? Neil was a retired federal agent and got to pick any shift he wanted. Everyone liked him. If he didn't want to work, he didn't. He had a pension and didn't even *have* to work but said once that he'd be bored if he didn't have something to do. He spent most of his free time fishing or hanging out at the Fish & Brew. Kyle thought he was pretty cool for a Boomer.

"Your kids okay?" he asked.

Neil looked surprised at the question. "Yes, of course. Why?"

"You said you had a rough day—I just remember you talking about how one of your kids was deployed or something."

He nodded with a half smile. "Good memory. Jill is doing great. She's on base in Japan, a mechanic. She loves it. And Eric is good, just works too much at the hospital. Thanks for asking."

"Four guests are waiting to board—is it okay?"

"There's always someone early, isn't there?"

"Better early than late," Kyle said, parroting something that Neil often said to the crew.

Neil laughed, and Kyle was glad he was able to take the skipper's mind off whatever was bothering him.

"Go ahead, let them on—rear deck only. Check the lines, supplies, and emergency gear, okay? No food or drink until we pass the marker."

"Got it."

Kyle slid down the ladder as his phone vibrated. It was Adam.

F&B only place open that late—meet at the club and we'll walk over, k?

He responded with a thumbs-up emoji and a heart, then smiled at the group of four. "Come aboard!"

Madelyn Jeffries sat on the toilet—not because she had to pee, but because she didn't want to go on this cruise, not even for only three hours. She didn't want to smile and play nice with Tina Marshall just because Pierce wanted to discuss business with Tina's husband Vince.

She hated Tina. That woman would do anything to make her miserable. All because Pierce had fallen in love with *her*, Madelyn Cordell, a smart girl from the wrong side of the tracks in Tacoma.

Pierce didn't understand. He tried, God bless him, but he didn't. He was from another generation. He understood sex and chivalry and generosity and respect. He was the sweetest man she'd ever met. But he didn't understand female interactions.

"I know you and Tina had somewhat of a rivalry when we met. But sweetheart, I fell in love with you. There's no reason for you to be insecure."

She wasn't insecure. She and Pierce had something special, something that no one else could understand. Even *she* didn't completely understand how she fell so head over heels for a man older than her deadbeat father. Oh, there was probably some psychologist out there who had any number of theories, but all Madelyn knew was that she and Pierce were *right*.

But Tina made her see red.

Tina, on top of this pregnancy—a pregnancy Madelyn had wanted to keep quiet, between her and Pierce, until she was showing. But somehow Pierce's kids had found out last week, and they went ballistic.

They were the reason she and Pierce decided to get away for a long weekend. Last night had been wonderful and romantic and *exactly* what she needed. Then at brunch this morning they ran into Tina and Vince who were on a "vacation" after their honeymoon.

Madelyn didn't doubt that Tina had found out she was here and planned this. There was no doubt in her mind that Tina had come to put a wedge between her and Pierce. After five years, why couldn't she just leave her alone?

Just seeing Tina brought back the fearful, insecure girl Madelyn used to be, and she didn't want that. She loved her life, she loved her husband, and above all she loved the baby inside her.

She flushed the toilet and stepped out of the stall.

Tina stood there by the sink, lips freshly coated with bloodred.

Madelyn stepped around her and washed her hands.

"Vince took me to *Paris* for our honeymoon for two glorious weeks," said Tina.

Madelyn didn't respond.

"*I* heard that you went to *Montana.*" Tina giggled a fake, frivolous laugh.

It was true. They'd spent a month in the Centennial Valley for their honeymoon, in a beautiful lodge owned by Pierce. They went horseback riding, hiking, had picnics, and she even learned how to fish—Pierce wanted to teach her, and she found that she enjoyed it. Fishing was relaxing and wholesome, something she'd never considered before. It had been the best month of her life.

But she wasn't sharing that with Madelyn. Her time with Pierce was private. It was *sacred*.

She dried her hands and said, "Excuse me."

"You think you've changed, but you haven't. You're still the little bug-eyed girl who followed me around for years. I taught you how to walk, I taught you how to attract men, I taught you how to dress and talk and act like you were *somebody*. If it wasn't for me, you would never have met Pierce Jeffries. And you took him from me."

"The boat leaves in five minutes." Madelyn desperately wanted to get away from Tina.

"Vince and Pierce are going into business together. We'll be spending *a lot* of time together, you and me. You would do well to drop the holier-than-thou act and accept the fact that I am back in your life and I'm not going anywhere."

Madelyn stared at Tina. Once she'd been in awe of the girl, a year older than she was, who always seemed to get what she wanted. Tina was bold, she was beautiful, she was driven.

But she would never be satisfied. Did she even love Vince Marshall? Or had she married him because of the money and status he could give her?

Madelyn hated that when she first met Pierce she had thought he was her ticket out of poverty and menial jobs. She hated that she had followed Tina's advice on how to seduce an older man.

Madelyn had fallen in love with Pierce, not because he was rich or powerful or for what he could give her. She loved him because he was kind and compassionate. She loved him because he saw her as she was and loved her anyway. But when he proposed to her, she'd fallen apart. She'd told him that she loved him, but she could never marry him because everything she was had been built on a lie—how she got her job at the country club, now they first met, how she had targeted him because he was wealthy and single. She would never forgive herself; how could he? His marriage proposal had been romantic and beautiful—he'd taken her to the bench where they first had a conversation, along the water of Puget Sound. But she ran away, ashamed.

He'd found her, she'd told him everything, the entire truth about who she was—a poor girl from a poor neighborhood who pretended to be worldly and sophisticated to attract men.

He said he loved her even more.

"I knew, Madelyn, from the beginning. But more, I see you, inside and out, and that's the woman I love."

Madelyn stared at her onetime friend. "Tina, *you* would do well to mind your p's and q's, because if I tell Pierce to back off, he'll back off."

She sounded a lot more confident than she felt. When it came to business, Pierce would listen to her, but he deferred to his oldest son, who worked closely with him. And Madelyn had never given him an ultimatum. She'd never told him what to do about business. She'd never have considered it, except for Tina.

Tina scowled.

Madelyn passed by her, then snipped, "By the way, nice boob job."

She left, the confrontation draining her. She didn't want to do this cruise. She didn't want to go head-to-head with Tina for the next three hours.

She didn't want to use the baby as an excuse... but desperate times and all that.

Pierce was waiting for her on the dock, talking to Vince Marshall.

"Would you excuse us for one moment, Vince?" she said politely.

"Of course, I'll catch up with Tina and meet you on the boat."

She smiled and nodded as he walked back to the harbormaster's building.

"What is it, love?" Concerned, worried, about her.

"I thought morning sickness was only in the morning. I'm sorry—I fear if I get on that boat, I'll be ill again. I don't want to embarrass you."

"Nonsense," he said. He took her hand, kissed it. "You will never embarrass me." He put their joined hands on her stomach. The warmth and affection in his eyes made her fall in love with him again. She felt like she loved Pierce a little more every day. "I can meet with Vince tomorrow. I'll go back to the house with you."

"This business meeting is important to you, isn't it?"

"It might be."

"Then go. Enjoy it. I can get home myself. Isn't that what Ubers are for?"

"A sunset is not as pretty without the woman I love holding my hand."

She wanted him home with her, but this was best. They had separate lives, at least in business; she didn't want to pressure him in any way, just because she detested Tina. "I will wait up for you."

He leaned over and kissed her. Gently. As if she would break. "Take good care of the woman I love, Bump," he said to her stomach.

She melted, kissed him again, then turned and walked back down the dock, fighting an overwhelming urge to go back and ask Pierce to come home with her.

But she wouldn't do it. It was silly and childish. Instead, she would go home, read a good book, and prepare a light meal for when Pierce came home. Then she would make love to her husband and put her past—and that hideous leech Tina Marshall—firmly out of her mind.

Jamie already regretted leaving Friday Harbor.

She listened to Cal's message twice, then deleted it and cleaned up after dinner. Hazel was watching her half hour of *PAW Patrol* before bath, books, and bed.

Her dad's remote house near Rogue Harbor was on the opposite side of the island from where they lived. Peaceful, quiet, what she thought she needed, especially since her dad wasn't here. He was an airline pilot and had a condo in Seattle that he lived in more often than not, coming up here only when he had more than two days off in a row.

She left because she was hurt. She had every

right to be hurt, dammit! But now that she was here, she wondered if she'd made a mistake.

Cal hadn't *technically* cheated on her. But he also hadn't told her that his ex-girlfriend was living on the island, not until the woman befriended her. She wouldn't have thought twice about it except for the fact that Cal had hidden it from her.

She had a bad habit of running away from any hint of approaching drama. She hated conflict and would avoid it at all costs. Her mother was drama personified. How many times had young Jamie run to her dad's house to get away from her mother's bullshit? Finally when she was fifteen she permanently moved in with her dad, changed schools, and her mother didn't say squat.

"You should have stayed and talked it out," she mumbled to herself as she dried the dishes. The only bad thing about her dad's place was that there was no dishwasher.

But Cal was coming to see her tonight. He didn't run away from conflict. She wanted to fix this but didn't know how because she was hurt. But he had to work, so she figured she had a few hours to think everything through. To *know* the right thing to do.

"Just tell him. Tell him how you feel."

Her phone buzzed and at first she thought it was an Amber Alert, because it was an odd sound.

Instead, it was an emergency alert from the San Juan Island Sheriff's Office.

19:07 SJSO ALERT! VESSEL EXPLOSION ONE MILE OUT FROM FRIDAY HARBOR, INJURIES UN-

KNOWN. ALL VESSELS AVOID FRIDAY HARBOR UNTIL FURTHER NOTICE.

Her stomach flipped and she grabbed the counter when a wave of dizziness washed over her.

She turned on the small television in the kitchen and switched to the local news. She watched in horror as the news anchor reported that a West End Charter yacht had exploded after leaving for a sunset cruise. He confirmed that it was the *Water Lily* and did not know at this time if there were survivors. Search and rescue crews were already out on the water, and authorities advised all vessels to dock immediately.

Cal had been scheduled to work the *Water Lily* tonight.

Hazel laughed at something silly on *PAW Patrol*. Jamie caught her breath, then suddenly tears fell. How could—? No. Not Cal. She loved him and even if they had problems, he loved Hazel more than anything in the world. He was the best father she could have hoped for. Hazel wasn't planned, but she was loved so much, and Cal had made it clear that he was sticking, from the very beginning. How could she forget that? How could she have forgotten that Cal had never made her feel inadequate, he'd never hurt her, he always told her she could do anything she wanted? He was always there for her...when she was bedridden with Hazel for two months. When she broke her wrist and Hazel was still nursing, he held the baby to her breast every four hours. Changed every diaper. He sang to Hazel, read her books, giggled with her in make-shift blanket forts when thunder scared her.

And now he was gone.

There could be survivors. You have to go.

She couldn't bring Hazel to the dock. The search, the sirens, the fear that filled the town. It would terrify the three-year-old.

But she couldn't stay here. Cal needed her—injured or not, he needed her and she loved him. It was as simple as that. Rena would watch Hazel so Jamie could find Cal, make sure he was okay.

"Hazel, we're going home."

"I wanna sleep at Grandpa's!"

"I forgot to feed Tabby." Tabby was a stray cat who had adopted their carport on cold or rainy nights. He wouldn't come into the house, and only on rare occasions would let Jamie pet him, but she'd started feeding him. Hazel had of course named him after a cat on her favorite show.

"Oh, Mommy! We gotta go rescue Tabby!"

And just like that, Hazel was ready.

Please, God, please please please please make Cal okay.

Ashley Dunlap didn't like lying to her sister, but Whitney couldn't keep a secret to save her life, and if Whitney said one word to their dad about Ashley's involvement with Island Protectors, she'd be grounded until she graduated—and maybe even longer.

"We're going to be late," Whitney said.

"Dad will understand," Ashley said, looking

through the long lens of her camera at the West End Charter boat leaving port. She snapped a couple pictures, though they were too far away to see anything.

She was just one of several monitors who were keeping close tabs on West End boats in the hopes that they would catch them breaking the law. West End may have been able to convince most people in town that they had cleaned up their act, and some even believed their claims that the leakage two years ago was an *accident*, but as the founder of IP Donna Bell said time and time again, companies always put profit over people. And just because they hadn't caught them breaking the law didn't mean that they *weren't* breaking the law. It was IP who documented the faulty fuel tanks two years ago that leaked their nasty fuel all over the coast. Who knows how many fish died because of their crimes? How long it would take the ecosystem to recover?

"Ash, Dad said not a *minute* past eight, and it's already seven thirty. It's going to take us thirty minutes just to dock and secure the boat."

"It's a beautiful evening," Ashley said, turning her camera away from the *Water Lily* and toward the shore. Another boat was preparing to leave, but the largest yacht in the fleet—*The Tempest*—was already out with a group of fifty whale watching west of the island in the Haro Strait. Bobby and his brother were out that way, monitoring *The Tempest*.

Ashley was frustrated. They just didn't have people who cared enough to take the time to monitor West End. There were only about eight or nine of them who were willing to spend all their free time standing up to West End, tracking their boats, making sure they were obeying the rules.

Everyone else just took West End's word for it.

Whitney sighed. "I could tell Dad the sail snagged."

"You can't lie to save your life, sis," Ashley said. "We'll just tell him the truth. It's a beautiful night and we got distracted by the beauty of the islands."

Whitney laughed, then smiled. "It is pretty, isn't it? Think those pictures are going to turn out? It's getting a little choppy."

"Some of them might," she said.

Ashley turned her camera back to the *Water Lily*. The charter was still going only five knots as they left the harbor. She snapped a few pictures, saw that Neil Devereaux was piloting today. She liked Neil—he spent a lot of time at the Fish & Brew talking to her dad and anyone else who came in. He'd only lived here for a couple years, but he seemed like a native of the small community. She'd talked to him about the pollution problem from West End, and he kept saying that West End fixed the problem with the old tanks and he'd seen nothing to suggest that they had other problems or cut corners on the repairs. He told her he would look around, and if anything was wrong, he'd bring it to the Colfax family's attention.

But could she believe him? Did he really care or was he just trying to get her to go away and leave West End alone?

Neil looked over at their sailboat, and both she and Whitney waved. He blew the horn and waved back.

A breeze rattled the sail, and Whitney grabbed the beam. "Shit!" she said.

Ashley put her camera back in its case and caught the rope dangling from the mast. "You good, Whit?"

"Yeah, it just slipped. Beautiful scenery is distracting. I got it."

Whitney bent down to secure the line, and Ashley turned back toward the *Water Lily* as it passed the one-mile marker and picked up speed.

The bow shook so hard she thought they might have hit something, then a fireball erupted, shot into the air along with wood and—oh, God, people!—bright orange, then black smoke billowed from the *Water Lily*. The stern kept moving forward, the boat in two pieces—the front destroyed, the back collapsing.

Whitney screamed and Ashley stared. She saw a body in the water among the debris. The flames went out almost immediately, but the smoke filled the area.

"We have to help them," Ashley said. "Whitney—"

Then a second explosion sent a shock wave toward their sailboat and it was all they could do to keep from going under themselves. Sirens on the shore sounded the alarm, and Ashley and Whitney headed back to the harbor as the sheriff's rescue boats went toward the disaster.

Taking a final look back, Ashley pulled out her camera and took more pictures. If West End was to blame for this, Ashley would make sure they paid. Neil was a friend, a good man, like a grandfather to her. He…he couldn't have survived. Could he?

She stared at the smoking boat, split in two.

No. She didn't see how anyone survived that.

Tears streamed down her face and as soon as she and Whitney were docked, she hugged her sister tight.

I'll get them, Neil. I promise you, I'll prove that West End cut corners and killed you and

Look for Allison Brennan's The Wrong Victim
Available April 2022

Don't miss the brand-new novel in the Quinn & Costa series from *New York Times* bestselling author

ALLISON BRENNAN

"Will scare you enough to leave all the lights on."
—Catherine Coulter, *New York Times* bestselling author

Order your copy today!

Be sure to connect with us at:
BookClubbish.com/Newsletter
Instagram.com/BookClubbish
Twitter.com/BookClubbish
Facebook.com/BookClubbish

MIRABooks.com

MAB1171Tall